PARAGON OF SOLITUDE

DAWN OF WIZARDS
BOOK TWO

JEFFREY L. KOHANEK

FALLBRANDT
PRESS

ALSO BY JEFFREY L. KOHANEK

Dawn of Wizards

The First Wizard

Paragon of Solitude

The Dark Lord's Design

Fate of Wizardoms

Eye of Obscurance

Balance of Magic

Temple of the Oracle

Objects of Power

Rise of a Wizard Queen

A Contest of Gods

* * *

Fate of Wizardoms Boxed Set: Books 1-3

Fate of Wizardoms Box Set: Books 4-6

Fall of Wizardoms

God King Rising

Legend of the Sky Sword

Curse of the Elf Queen

Shadow of a Dragon Priest

Advent of the Drow

A Sundered Realm

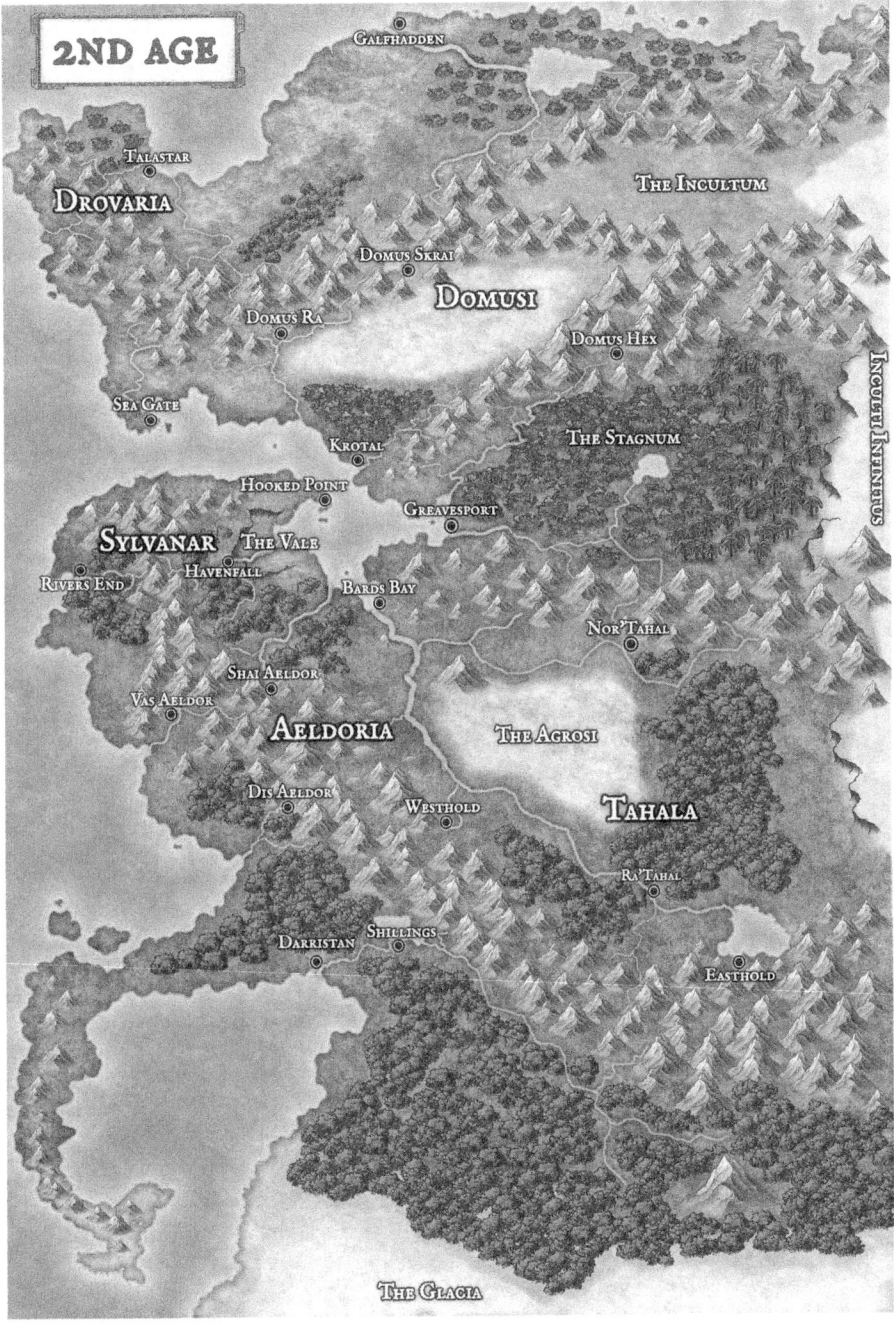

2ND AGE

GALFHADDEN

THE INCULTUM

TALASTAR

DROVARIA

DOMUS SKRAI

DOMUSI

DOMUS RA

DOMUS HEX

SEA GATE

KROTAL

THE STAGNUM

HOOKED POINT

GREAVESPORT

SYLVANAR   THE VALE

RIVERS END   HAVENFALL

BARDS BAY

NOR'TAHAL

SHAI AELDOR

VAS AELDOR

AELDORIA

THE AGROSI

DIS AELDOR

WESTHOLD

TAHALA

RA'TAHAL

DARRISTAN   SHILLINGS

EASTHOLD

THE GLACIA

INCULTI INFINITUS

JOURNAL ENTRY

Magic. It is a simple word with a complex definition and dozens of meanings. The god, Vandasal, chose to imbue the races he favored with inherent magic.

Dwarves, divided into three clans, were blessed with magic connected to earth. Most famous were those born with the ability to shape stone with their bare hands. Others exhibited the talent of influencing metals. A select few could even grace inanimate objects with a myriad of enchantments.

The Sylvan were graced with their own natural born talents. Many elves spoke to plants, able to urge and encourage plants and trees to accelerate growth or even animate as if they were sentient beings. A smaller part of the population could guide and control the weather. Other elves exhibited magic-enhanced traits such as healing, or tracking, and exceptionally rare gifts such as prophecy. In contrast, their dark elf cousins, the Drow, were born with the subtle ability to magically enhance their battle skills while those blessed with another form of magic exhibited abilities that were far more powerful. Those were called singers.

Even the wild beasts Vandasal had created were graced with his spark.

Those beings, ranging from a tiny brownie to a massive dragon, were pure magic come to life.

Humans, who were not created by Vandasal, possessed no such gifts.

The effect of this imbalance became clear during Gahagar's campaign, when he and the three dwarf clans sought to bring all cities and nations beneath one banner. That war lasted for five decades, and while it took a toll on the dwarves and the dark elves, it was the humans who suffered the most. Even in Sylvanar, which stood outside the path of Gahagar's campaign, humans born into slavery toiled at the hands of their elven masters.

I could not allow this mistreatment to continue. Humans deserved better. Until the inequity between those possessing magic and those lacking it was resolved, they would always suffer from their disadvantage.

So, I began my search for a protégé. It had to be a young human, eager and pliable yet intelligent and, most importantly, capable. That human needed to be driven by a demanding sense of curiosity. In addition, he or she had to possess an incredible sense of intuition, able to perceive the entire puzzle when only a handful of pieces lay on the table before him.

Bending fate to one's desires is a passive skill among my kind. Even with my abilities stripped to a fraction of what they once were, molding destiny toward my own ends proved possible. That was clearly demonstrated when I happened upon a young man ideally suited to become the first wizard. His name: Ian Carpenter.

I was initially uncertain if I could mold this young man into what was required, so I followed him and his companions. Doing so enabled me to monitor his actions and reactions. On three occasions, I was forced to act on my own, lest Ian perish before he could flourish as I intended. His timidity and lack of action in tense situations caused concern, yet his intuition and intelligence proved to be everything I had hoped to find. Thus, when Ian was struck down with a mortal wound, I was ready and sprung my plan into action.

Ian sat on the floor, his stomach torn open, blood pooling around him. In the daze of his blood loss, I offered him a choice. Become my protégé and live to serve my purpose or succumb to the darkness of death. He chose life. I gifted *him with the blessing of my blood, forever altering his body's chemistry. I then shared with him a spell and instructed him on how to use it.*

With the young man's wound healed, he rose from death's door and faced the Drow singer he despised so badly. Rysildar could never guess what he faced. Humans could not wield magic. Not until that moment.

Ian was victorious in thwarting the Drow singer. He then acted as the lynch pin in freeing the dwarf citadel of Ra'Tahal from the Drow usurpers, and the first wizard was born.

The story told in the following pages outlines the events following the birth of wizards. When the tale reaches its conclusion, the world will be forever changed, reshaped to my vision as I promised my brother so long ago.

SOURCE unknown

CHAPTER 1

TRAINING

Rapid footsteps carried Illian Carpenter up the mountain slope. He burst through a cluster of fir trees with his arms raised to shove aside branches covered in long, green needles. The ruckus stirred a trio of renjays into flight. The birds fluttered and banked, their red and white striped wings a shock of color against the pale blue morning sky. Ian ignored the birds and focused on the trail, having learned the hard way the folly of not watching his foot placement.

He jogged through an aspen grove, the ribbon of dirt he followed taking him past bushes covered in tiny white flowers. In the coming weeks, those flowers would turn to buds that would grow into blueberries. At lower elevations, such bushes would produce fruit sooner, but even those berries would be late this year. Winter had lingered, as had spring. Such was life on a mountain thousands of feet above the rest of the world.

The trees fell away to reveal an open glade of long grass, wildflowers, and outcroppings of gray granite. He raced across the meadow while orange and yellow butterflies flitted past. A steep rise of rock hundreds of feet tall, waited at the upper end of the glade.

When Ian reached the rock, he slowed and began scrambling up, using his hands for support while his legs did the work. Up and up, he ascended, his brow damp with sweat, his breath coming in gasps, his thighs and buttocks burning but not flagging. Not anymore.

Patches of white appeared amid the rocks. Snow lurked in recesses where the sun rarely shone. To Ian's left, the south mountain face remained thick with snow, unlikely to fully melt until well into summer. The air noticeably cooled, his breath swirling in front of him with each exhalation. The chill was a relief for his overheated body. Still, he trudged on, unwilling to submit to the weariness that threatened to slow him down. After a grueling, three-hundred-foot rise of steep rock, he reached the mountain peak, slowed to a stop, and rested his hands on his hips while savoring the view. The rasp of his panting breaths and the gentle whisper of the wind were the only sounds heard from his spectacular perch, high above the surrounding lands.

Facing east, he stared over the rolling plains of the Agrosi, five thousand feet below. Many miles away, those grass-covered hills met mountains to the north and a distant forest to the east and south. The first time Ian had crossed the Agrosi, early the previous autumn, he'd had an encounter with wild horses led by a unicorn. The experience had been both frightening and awestriking. Those emotions had tripled when a trio of werecats attacked the herd. The unicorn's magic had foiled the attack, and with the werecats disabled, the herd rode off safely. At the time, Ian had thought he had seen the best and worst the Agrosi had to offer. Such beliefs had turned out to be far from the truth. A terrifying battle with a giant rock troll later that same evening proved as much.

His next trip across the Agrosi occurred just weeks after the first visit. That experience could not have been more different. By then, something had awakened inside of Ian – a power that gave him the confidence he had previously lacked. Having his master's calm assurance at his side likely had something to do with it as well. The two of them had crossed the rolling plains without incident despite sighting numerous strange beasts along the way. That journey had brought Ian to his new home – a place of solitude, focus, and mysteries he had yet to unravel.

The experiences of the previous year left an imprint on Ian, but none as much as his dalliance with death and the consequences of his subsequent resurrection. The gift awakened inside him created new possibilities and inspired an insatiable desire for him to progress. Once lost and wandering through life without a goal or sense of self-worth, Ian was now the first human to wield magic. His new identity as a wizard created a new sense of purpose that he was determined to fulfill. He was uncertain about where his training would lead, but so long as he was promised the opportunity to increase his might, he would do whatever his master required of him.

The thought reminded him that he was expected to return soon. Climbing a mountain was merely his first task of the day.

"I suppose I had better head back." In the tranquility of his surroundings, his voice sounded like an unwanted invader. Armed with silent resolve, Ian turned back to the steep, rocky slope and began his descent.

~

THE SUN APPROACHED its apex as Ian crossed a flat shelf of gray rock and slowed to a stop. The plains of the Agrosi stretched out to the east a thousand feet below him while the mountain peak he had just visited loomed over his shoulder. The mountains to the north, the forest to the east and south, and the rolling fields of grass between them combined for a beautiful view. On a cloudless day, as this, Ian could see the distant bluff to the southeast where Ra'Tahal stood. The dwarven citadel had been his home for half a year.

With his reflection on the time spent in Ra'Tahal came a mixture of emotions. Ian and his people had suffered the hardships of forced servitude after a traumatic and terrifying abduction from his home village of Shillings. The initial fear and hatred Ian had felt toward his dwarven captors had slowly eased until a violent coup saw the dwarf leaders slaughtered. With their fates in the balance, Ian and his brother found unlikely allies in a small team of dwarves, fleeing the city and beginning a quest that led him to an entirely unexpected future. Somehow, Ian had found friendship with his former captors. When considering how it all began, he realized he now missed those dwarves. *Someday, I will return to see what has become of them.* An entire winter and much of spring had passed since Ian left the citadel for his new mountain home, and he had not interacted with anyone, be it dwarf, elf, or human, other than his master in that span.

A sigh slipped out as he realized that his time outside was over. *I suppose I should go see what he wants of me next.*

Turning from the view, he approached a granite boulder standing four times his own height. He rounded it and ducked into a dark, narrow crevice between the boulder and the rocky mountainside. The gap soon widened to reveal a hidden cavern.

Daylight seeping into the recess gave faint shape to the cave, its walls jagged and irregular. Ian advanced with his arms in front of him until he reached the back wall. His fingers ran along the cold granite as he felt for a knob of rock. When he applied pressure to the knob, it sank in, a click resounded, and a section of the wall swung open to reveal a tunnel bathed in violet light. He entered, pushed the door closed, and turned toward a bronze sconce mounted to the tunnel wall. An orb glowing with a purple aura rested on the sconce. He lifted the orb and it continued to shine, its soft light eating away at the darkness as Ian advanced deeper into the mountain.

A curved tunnel brought him to another chamber, one far larger than Ian would have thought possible until seeing it for the first time two seasons earlier.

Dozens of cylindrical columns stood in rows throughout the chamber. Each column was six feet in diameter and spaced thirty feet from its nearest neighbor. Orbs like the one in Ian's palm rested in sconces mounted to each pillar. The glow emanating from the orbs painted the chamber in soft light akin to dusk just after the sun had set on a cloudless day.

Ian descended a run of stairs carved into the mountain and began across the chamber. Platforms positioned at varying heights jutted out from the columns, reminding him of mushrooms growing out of the side of tree trunks. Ropes dangled just three feet off the floor, the other end secured to a ceiling two hundred feet above. Higher up, a network of catwalks ran between the columns, turning and branching randomly like a labyrinth.

Ian's curiosity was instantly aroused the moment he had first visited the exotic, unnatural gallery, stirring questions which his master avoided answering, as he often did. He reached the far end of the space, where a short tunnel brought him to a room with a more obvious purpose.

A hundred feet in diameter, the outer walls of the study were covered in books nestled on shelves carved into the stone. Tables, chairs, and a ten-foot-thick column made of wooden slats occupied the middle of the room. The column ran from the floor to the twenty-foot-tall ceiling and consisted of hundreds of openings, each six inches square and three feet deep. A ladder leaned against the cylindrical storage cell, its upper end connected to a metal rail. Scrolls occupied four openings in the lower portion of the column, while the rest of the compartments sat empty. Something of which Ian was all too aware.

The voice of his master echoed in Ian's head as he recalled first asking about the strange column. *One day, scrolls crafted by you will fill every slot in the column. When that occurs, you will have achieved your objective. Until then, you will study, train, and perfect your craft.* In six months, Ian had made little progress in filling the slots and none in the manner he wished. By his account, that left him with over eight hundred scrolls remaining, and at his current rate, he would be an old, wizened man by the time he finished.

At the far end of the chamber, he passed through another doorway and entered the kitchen. Just as in the other caverns, glowing orbs resting in sconces mounted to the wall illuminated the space. Cabinets, shelving, and racks covered the wall to his right while a massive brick oven waited straight ahead. To the left was a table made of oak surrounded by eight chairs. Seated at one end of the table was the only other occupant in the underground complex.

Ian placed his orb in the empty sconce near the entrance and approached the seated man. A jug of milk, two empty cups, and two sets of silverware rested on the table in front of him.

"I am back, Master Truhan, and before noon." Ian grinned expectantly.

The man lifted his gaze from the book on the table, his bright blue eyes measuring Ian as they always seemed to do. He ran his hand through his blonde hair and leaned back in his chair. As always, he was dressed in black, today wearing a shirt with twisting, gold patterns on the collar and lapel.

"Your strength and endurance have improved," Truhan said. "But the days are growing longer and to measure your progress by the sun's position would be inaccurate at best. Worse, consider how you will feel when the season turns to autumn and the days shorten." It was just like him to compliment Ian only to follow it up with another statement that completely negated any semblance of approval.

Ian frowned. "You expect me to keep scaling the mountain even when autumn arrives?"

"I expect you to train your mind, body, and magic until you are prepared for the greatest test."

"Which is?" Even as he asked, Ian knew the answer would be nebulous at best.

"The future will reveal that test one day. Your job is to be ready when that time comes."

Cryptic responses were commonplace when dealing with Truhan. While Ian had grown to expect as much, he still found it irritating and frustrating.

Knowing that the man was unlikely to concede, Ian had learned to change topics rather than dwell on the ones that would provide no satisfaction. "What would you have of me next, Master?"

"I was expecting you." He lifted the carafe off the table and poured milk into the cup sitting before him. "If you check the oven, you will find our midday meal ready. Dish us each a plate, sit, and eat. After that, you are to visit the baths, and once you are bathed and dressed, we will set off for the Hall of Divining."

Ian had expected as much. He often spent his afternoons in that chamber – another source of frustration.

He approached the oven, slipped a pair of thick leather mitts on his hands, and opened the door. A wave of heat washed over him as he reached inside and removed a metal pot occupied by a thick chunk of beef. Reaching in with the other hand, he removed a pan with two potatoes encircled by asparagus bathed in butter. After setting the pan and pot on the warming rack above the oven, he opened another door, from which wafted warm air blessed by the scent of freshly baked bread. He removed a pan with four steaming hard rolls, set it down, and lifted a knife, fork, and large spoon out of a canister on the counter behind him. With mouthwatering scents tantalizing his senses, he began cutting the pot roast. In the back of his head, he again considered the mysteries of the kitchen.

The oven was always hot, never had to be lit, and emitted no smoke. Now that he was beginning to understand magic, the enchantment that created the oven's heat had grown into a powerful curiosity that remained just beyond his comprehension. The chamber beside the kitchen, cold enough to coat things stored there with a sheen of frost, remained a bewildering conundrum as well.

He finished cutting slabs of meat, slid two onto each plate, and added a potato, greens, and two hard rolls before bringing the plates over to the table. One plate, he placed before Truhan, the other in front of the chair across from the man.

They ate in silence, as they always did. In that silence, Ian's thoughts turned to his master's expectations. He was to again visit the Hall of Divining. Anxiety twisted his stomach at the mere thought of it. His training was never easy, and although the physical aspects of it had added strength and endurance while testing his resolve, nothing challenged him so much as divining. He just hoped it would not get him killed.

CHAPTER 2
THE HALL OF DIVINING

Dressed in robes, his feet in sandals, Ian climbed a twisting staircase. Trousers, boots, a tunic, and a cloak had been required for his climb to the summit of Mount Tiadd, but such restrictive clothing was not conducive to using his abilities, as he had discovered. Loose robes allowed the energy to flow freely, so that had become his garb of choice. His footwear was less critical, but since he was in the controlled environment of his underground complex, sandals were the next best thing to bare feet.

Ian carried an armload of thick birch branches, while Truhan led the way with a glowing orb held before him. Beyond the aura emitted by the orb, shadows lingered, longing to reach out and touch Ian should the light of the globe fail. The spell that powered the orbs remained beyond Ian's understanding, so he had no idea if any of them would expire one day.

The long climb soon had Ian's thighs burning, but he endured. Two seasons ago, back when he had first made the grueling ascent, he had needed to stop and rest more than once and was convinced that the staircase had no end. Having made the ascent dozens of times by now, he knew better. The stairs were not endless, their number somewhere north of eight hundred. As the thought flitted past, Truhan crested the last stair and began down a dark tunnel. A closed door, stained as black as night, waited at the passageway's end.

Truhan approached the door and paused to look over his shoulder. "Remember what I told you about this chamber."

"I know. The enchantments protecting it are dangerous. Touch nothing." His master's serious demeanor when first giving the warning had given Ian pause. That, along with the nature of the room, had struck a chord and Ian needed no reminder. Of course, with an armful of wood, he was unlikely to try and open a door himself anyway.

With a finger held up, his renowned smirk absent, Truhan added, "And do not attempt to enter this chamber without me, at least not until your abilities are advanced far beyond what they are today."

Truhan extended his bare palm toward the door, stopping an inch away. A shimmer of light, starting at the man's hand, rippled and spread across the door. Magic. Ian was certain of it, but he could sense nothing apart from what his eyes told him. When the light reached the door frame, it began to glow. Truhan turned the knob, pulled the door open, and Ian followed him inside.

They entered a circular rotunda with doors in all directions. Like the one they had just opened, each door was stained black and marked by a symbol encircled by silvery script. No two symbols were the same. Ian now knew that each represented a different enchantment, the result ranging from freezing a person solid to causing one's skin to burst into flames. None sounded like something he wished to experience. An eight-pointed star graced the floor, each tip thrust toward one of the doors.

Truhan turned right and selected the second door from the direction they had come. Again, he held his palm out and light shimmered across the door, spreading from the symbol in the center until it reached the frame, which began to glow. The man then turned the knob, pushed the door open, and headed down another dark tunnel with Ian close behind. The corridor soon brought them to another curving staircase, where they resumed their ascent.

～

Hundreds of stairs later, the tunnel leveled and opened into a chamber that evoked fear and wonder in equal measure.

Smooth, seamless walls surrounded a circular cavern fifty feet in diameter, the walls arching toward each other until meeting at the apex of a perfect dome, twenty-five feet up. The tunnel they had just emerged from was the only way in, and although the chamber was hidden deep in a mountain, it was well illuminated.

Dangling from the center of the domed ceiling, much like an over-sized beehive, was a five-foot-tall crystal shimmering with warm light. More than that, it emanated a tremendous power that sang to Ian, the intoxicating thrum making him light-headed and feeling like he had downed five pints of ale in rapid succession.

He followed Truhan toward the middle of the chamber. Once positioned directly below the massive, shining gem, Ian stared up at the crystal and marveled at the perfect facets, cut to create the shape of a dodecahedron.

"Focus." There was a gravity to the way Truhan spoke. "Don't allow the magic of the source to distract you."

Ian lowered his eyes to meet his master's gaze. *The source.* Until his first visit to the chamber, Ian had never considered where magic came from. Yet, when he basked in the energy emanating from the crystal, he could not deny the truth. Magic, as he knew it, dominated the chamber and demanded he open himself up to it. Holding that magic at bay required more restraint than anything he had ever imagined.

"What would you have of me today, Master?"

"Drop the wood in your arms here." Truhan pointed toward the charred area on the cavern floor between them. "That should give you a clue."

"Fire again?"

Truhan nodded. "Some time has passed since you last attempted a flame spell. Perhaps today will bring success."

His own repeated failures haunted Ian. He did not need to be reminded of them. Rather than retort, he asked in an even tone, "If it does not?"

"We shall try again in a few days, be it fire or something else."

Ian had tried his best to do as his master had instructed, yet his inability to progress plagued him and ate away at his confidence. "What if..."

"No." Truhan shook his head. "You will succeed. If not today, soon. When the first comes to you, the others will be easier to attain. You have protection constructs memorized, as proven by your repeated success in conjuring shields. Moreso, you have discovered how to manipulate those shields, so you have some understanding of how constructs function.

"However, that type of spell is limited in nature while energy spells offer expansive possibilities. If you can discover how to craft one energy construct, additional variations and applications are a matter of divining and experimentation. So, we will resume divining now and see where it leads."

Pushing his doubts aside, Ian gave a firm nod. "I will try, Master."

"Do not *try*. Do it, and all will be well." Truhan handed him a chunk of white chalk. "Now, sit and relax. Slide into meditation while I light the fire."

Beneath the humming crystal, Ian settled on the chamber floor. Three feet from where he sat, Truhan built a pyramid of crossed sticks. He then produced a flint and striker while Ian closed his eyes.

Relaxed, his mind cleared of thought, Ian hummed softly to himself, his song a harmony to the aria of the crystal above him. He slid into a void, drifting away from his body as he slipped into meditation. Doing so had taken many weeks of practice, but now that he knew how to open himself to it, the act came naturally. In the ether, he floated as if buoyed by the crystal's song. He removed his mental block, and magic flooded in, his heart quickening and senses buzzing from the raw power thrumming through him.

He opened his eyes to a crackling fire a stride away, the flames licking the length of the burning sticks. Holding on to the magic, he extended his mind toward the flame while focusing on its color, shape, and heat, as he had done so many times before. Flickers of raw energy danced amid the flames like a hundred fireflies sparking to life and then fading just as quickly. As Ian stared at the sparks of energy, he caught brief glimpses of a pattern he had never seen before. *Truhan said to seek out the signature, and when I am in tune with it, something more will appear. Maybe this is it.*

Rather than concentrate on the energy within the flame, he allowed his mind to drift, and within the void, he found peace and harmony in a way he had never achieved before. The flames slowed, the sparks of light lasting longer until he saw them not as individuals, but as one. In concert with each other, the bursts of energy created a distinct pattern that tantalized Ian in a profound way.

Like the construct of protection, this one had a solid circular core, but made of a different pattern. The other core consisted of intersecting, curved lines. This one was filled with layered starbursts amid straight lines. The second and third rings were also different than those of the construct he had been taught. Strange yet intriguing runes marked the inner ring while the other was a simple wave pattern that came to point at eight locations around the loop. In his excitement, Ian slid out of meditation, the construct faded, and his surroundings crashed in.

Although the construct was no longer in his vision, Ian recalled it in his mind's eye. Still holding onto his magic and determined to retain his new discovery, he willed the construct into creation. Akin to a ghostly apparition made of pale, white light, the design hovered before his outstretched hand. Without looking down, Ian reached for the chalk beside him, held it in his fingers, and began to draw on the cavern floor without taking his eyes off the construct before him. His hand moved swiftly, recording the complex pattern, taking care to reproduce exactly the shapes, lines, and runes present within the core and both surrounding layers. Finally, he looked down and examined the construct drawn on the floor. It was a perfect match to the one wavering in the air before him.

Truhan stood over Ian. "Is this what you saw?"

"It is." The excitement filling Ian's chest crept into his reply.

"And you hold that same construct in your mind, ready for use?"

"I do."

"Use your magic, Ian," his master urged. "Test it."

Ian allowed even more energy to flow into him. Like a well filling up, magic flowed in until he thought he might burst. His skin glowed with its power.

When he directed the energy through the construct, a cone of flames burst forth, incinerating the sticks and spreading to cover half of the chamber. A wave of heat struck Ian forcing him to raise his arm to shield his face while he rolled away. Magic ceased flowing through him as he completed a second roll. The fire disappeared, and the heat receded to a hot yet bearable temperature.

Strides from the scorched rock, he lay on his stomach, overwhelmed and numb after the intoxication from his magic. Weariness seeped in, making him feel as if he had just climbed to the mountaintop again.

"Well," Truhan approached Ian and stood over him. "You certainly did not hold back, did you?"

Ian crawled to his hands and knees, still stunned. "I did not mean to..."

"When you are this close to the source, it is easy to allow a raging river of magic to flow through you, but it comes at a cost. In future, I suggest you add a mental dam to reduce the flow, especially when testing a new construct. If you blow this chamber up, you'll be dead and gone and so will the magic emanating from this crystal."

Nodding numbly in response, Ian climbed to his feet. The magic had fled him, but the chalky version of his discovery remained drawn on the floor. After dozens, if not hundreds, of failed attempts, he had discovered a new spell at last.

"I did it." Ian did not try to restrict the wonder from his voice.

"As I knew you would...eventually." Truhan clapped Ian on the back. "Now, go over there and grab a scroll. Record this construct, and we will return to our quarters. It has already been a long day, so tomorrow, I will explain how you can test versions of this construct to create different results."

Ian frowned. "But we only just got here."

The man laughed. "You stared into those flames for two hours before recording the construct."

"I did?" To Ian, it had felt as if only a few minutes had passed.

"Which is what you can expect when you truly find harmony within yourself. Now you know what is required to divine the signature of a natural element and how it affects you. Your perception of time slows, allowing you to see what others cannot, but it comes at a cost. Time passing much more rapidly than what you perceive is a small price to pay. However, I have heard of Galfhadden monks losing weeks while in a meditative trance."

While the idea of losing such track of time seemed incredible, Ian found himself struggling with a question he had asked his master on numerous occasions. "How do you know all of this?"

Lips pressed together, Truhan stared at Ian for a beat before responding. "I thought you were past asking such questions."

Not satisfied, Ian pressed him. "You claim that you cannot wield magic as I do, yet you are able to disarm the enchanted doors leading to this chamber."

"As I explained, that is not magic. It is a learned procedure."

"And the spell I used to defeat Rysildar. You were the one who showed it to me. Where did you learn it?"

Truhan frowned at Ian. "You are not conveying the respect I expect from my protégé."

"If I better understood why you are doing this, it would help me focus on my training."

The man visibly considered the request before speaking. "Fine. You may ask but know that I am limited as to what or how I may answer."

Limited by whom? Ian wanted to ask but reconsidered. He was likely to get few answers to his questions, so he chose to focus on what mattered most."

"Back in Ra'Tahal, you saved my life. Why?"

The man appeared to consider his response before speaking. "I saw potential in you and chose to take a risk."

"Why was it a risk?"

"Frankly, I was uncertain if you would survive it. As you may have noticed, my blood is different from that of others." Truhan took a deep breath. "But that was not the only risk. My actions themselves can be a risk, and should I take direct action, it will draw attention I must avoid...for now."

"Attention from whom?"

"My brother."

Somehow, Truhan's responses only created additional confusion that led to more questions, but rather than continue down that path, Ian chose another route.

"The construct you showed me last autumn, where did you learn it?"

"As you have now discovered, each spell has its own signature. You simply need to look for it. Let's just say that I was victim of a similar spell many years ago. It was the result of a different sort of magic, but the signature hidden in the energies was the same. For a great while, I dwelled on what I had learned from that experience, and I eventually arrived at a startling conclusion: If I could find the right human and alter the chemistry of his blood, I believed that human would be able to draw on the magic of this crystal and direct it into a similar construct. As it turns out, I was correct."

Ian blinked. "When you sent me after Rysildar, you didn't even know if it would work?"

"Frankly, I was surprised that you survived the alterations to your body's chemistry. Humans are not intended to have so much metal in their blood."

"Metal?"

"When you cut your hand two weeks past, did you not notice?"

Ian recalled the incident. The blood oozing from the cut sparkled like light coming through a stained-glass window. The spot where it had dripped on the cavern floor remained altered, changing from granite to crimson crystal. The idea that metal surged through his veins was as bizarre as the replies Truhan gave in response to Ian's questions. Rather than satisfying his curiosity, each answer spurred additional questions.

"Why does the metal glow?"

Truhan smiled and pointed at the crystal. "This is the source of the magic you use. The sparkling light in your blood is the metal's response to the source. It is akin to the reflection of light off a mirror. When you allow the magic in, your blood fuels your power while your mind and the constructs you weave give that magic shape." He clapped a hand on Ian's shoulder. "You are the world's first wizard, Ian. Others will follow, and when that happens, they will need guidance. Continue your training, study hard, and discover as many constructs as possible. These things are vital if you are to pass on my teachings to others."

Ian blinked. "You expect me to teach others?"

Truhan laughed. "Of course. You didn't expect me to do it, did you?" He pointed to the construct drawn on the floor. "Now, record the construct on the scroll. Take care to ensure it is exact. Any variation will alter the effect, which could create unexpected results or even cause the spell to have no effect at all. While a useless construct causes no harm, an altered effect could result in anything, including setting yourself on fire."

Jerking in alarm, Ian blinked. "It could kill me?"

"Magic is a tool and a weapon. Like other tools, it can be useful when applied properly. It can also be harmful toward enemies or even kill the user if wielded incorrectly."

Ian recalled using a wood chisel in his father's shop. The man had warned Ian not to pound the chisel along wood with his other hand nearby. The chisel had bounced and the edge bit into his thumb, drawing blood. That same chisel had helped him shape a bassinet that was later sold for two silver pieces.

He knelt and stretched the scroll out beside the chalk drawing. "I will take care to record it precisely."

"Good. When you are finished, we will return to the warren. Then I must go away for a time."

Ian looked up at Truhan. "You are leaving again?"

"I will only be away for a week or so." Truhan walked to the side of the chamber and waited in the tunnel entrance, making it clear that the conversation was finished despite the questions bouncing around Ian's head.

The man had not spent more than two weeks with Ian before leaving for a short span. He never said where he went, and Ian never saw him leave or return. After each journey, Ian would find their food stores replenished, but he never saw a wagon, a cart, or the beasts of burden one might use to haul the crates, sacks, and barrels of food that occupied the cold storage room. The entire situation was a conundrum further mystified by Truhan's lack of transparency.

With Truhan leaving soon, Ian realized that the answers he had provided would have to satisfy him for now, so he set to recording the fire construct. All the while, unasked questions occupied his thoughts, many regarding the very nature of his master. Those were among the most compelling, but they were also the ones Truhan strictly refused to answer. *Who and what are you?* Ian wondered if he would ever know.

CHAPTER 3
A MISSION

oli. A distant call echoed in the darkness, encouraging Arangoli Handshaw to stir. A warm light shone in the mist above him. Even as he swam his way up toward the light, the weight of exhaustion dragged him back down.

"Goli!"

The volume and suddenness of the shout made Arangoli flinch. His eyelids flickered open. The sun shone through an open curtain, stabbing at his eyes like a sharpened dagger. He winced and held up his arm to shield his face. His head pounded to the beat of his pulse, and his mouth felt like a werecat had used it as a privy. Peering through bleary eyes, he found a familiar face looking down at him. The male dwarf wore his black beard in a split braid that lay upon his barrel chest. The dwarf's coat was a dark red with gold trim, matching the crown resting upon his brow.

"Korrigan?" Arangoli was uncertain if he was still dreaming. He reached out with one hand, gripped the king's beard, and gave it a tug.

Korrigan slapped the hand away. "Stop that."

"Why did you wake me?" he croaked.

"It is a beautiful spring day, and I thought you might care to enjoy it." Korrigan arched a brow. "That is, unless you intend to sleep until summer."

Through strength of will, Arangoli forced himself to sit up. A low groan slipped out as he set his feet on the floor. The smooth stone felt cold beneath his bare feet. He raked a hand down his face. A terrible thirst clutched at his throat, so he reached for the tankard on his nightstand. Just as his fingers drew near it, Korrigan slapped his hand away.

Arangoli frowned. "Did you come just to torture me?"

The king's hand clamped onto his shoulder, forcing Arangoli to meet his intense gaze. "I am concerned," Korrigan said. "As winter waned, you slipped back into your old habits. When was the last time you were sober?"

"I..." Arangoli struggled to respond.

Korrigan spoke in a stern tone. "The snow has thawed in the lowlands and even the mountain passes are now open. You claimed that you were trapped here for the winter, so I allowed you and the others to drown yourself in ale while lying around and doing nothing productive. That must end. Now."

Arangoli sighed. "We are warriors, Kor. The Drow have been flushed out. Who do we fight, now?"

"I have a mission that requires strength and must be led by a name that commands respect. I need you, Goli."

"A mission?" Suddenly interested, Arangoli burst to his feet. The room teetered, and he gripped the bedpost to stabilize himself. "What mission?"

Korrigan shook his head. "I need your head cleared before I reveal what must be done. I don't want to have to explain it twice. Set the ale aside." He gestured toward a pewter pitcher and an empty glass on the table. "I brought you some water. Drink that and chase it down with more. Eat a solid meal, and, for the sake of us all, take a bath. When you are cleaned up, and the fog in your brain has cleared, come see me."

The king crossed the room and paused at the door. "Your job is to lead. Thus far, you have led the Head Thumpers into a drunken stupor. Give them a kick in the arse. Get them straightened out. You will need them at your side and the way it currently stands, they are no good to anyone." He turned, his footsteps fading as he traversed the corridor and headed downstairs.

With a sigh, Arangoli sat back down on the bed and rubbed a hand over his face. "Korrigan has the right of it."

For many weeks, a voice inside had tried to convince Arangoli to ease away from his endless drinking. But night after night, one tankard led to three, which then turned to a dozen. That's when things began to blur, his count fading into a haze of boisterous laughter and spilled ale. He was not the only one, for the ten dwarves living with him were just as guilty. Those dwarves were warriors, trained to follow the lead of their captain, so that is where the blame lay. *Your king needs you,* Arangoli thought. *It is time to make him and your people proud.*

He stood, approached the table, and lifted the pitcher to his face. Cool, refreshing water sloshed across his dry tongue and down his parched throat. Liquid trickled out of the corners of his mouth and ran down his beard. By the time he lowered the pitcher for some air, most of it had been emptied. He set it down and shuffled over to a vanity with a bowl resting upon it. The mirror on the wall reflected a dwarf with red eyes, a thick black beard, and dark purple irises. His hair was a mess, his beard matted with bits of food stuck in it. Arangoli lifted his arm and sniffed. He pinched his face and choked from the stench.

"I do stink," he admitted.

He tore off his tunic, grabbed a bar of soap, and dipped a washcloth in the bowl. Energized by the prospect of a looming mission, he began scrubbing away.

~

DRESSED IN FRESH CLOTHES, beard combed and hair straightened, Arangoli descended the main level of his home in Ra'Tahal.

The building had once belonged to Arangoli's father, Arangar, before he became king and gifted it to his son. After all, the king and queen lived in the lavish royal quarters on the upper floor of the central keep. What need would he have for a modest, two-bedroom home near the citadel's outer wall? The thought of his father stirred memories he rarely reflected upon.

When Arangoli was still a child, Arangar had departed with King Gahagar on a campaign to take over the world. For the better part of fifty years, Gahagar had waged war across the realm with Arangar at his side. Meanwhile, Arangoli had trained to become a warrior, a profession particularly suited to his personality and natural abilities. After two decades of such training, he headed off to war, with his fellow recent graduates at his side. That group of young warriors called themselves the Head Thumpers. Together, they dreamed of earning fame as heroes who tipped the balance in the dwarven army's favor, surviving wild battles and basking in the spoils of victory. Together, they joined Gahagar's army and proved themselves in battle by handing the Drow a vicious defeat. It was the beginning of a promising career, destined to lead to fame...until Gahagar died. Without the great king to bond the three dwarven tribes together, the campaign dissolved. Each dwarf clan returned to their ancestral home, leaving the young and eager warriors with no enemy to fight. That is when Arangoli's troubles began.

He reached the main level and stopped to look over the common room. It was nothing short of a disaster.

Of his eight wooden chairs, three remained whole but only one still stood upright. Splintered wood and refuse littered the kitchen floor. A lean dwarf lay sprawled out on the table, his mouth twisted to the side, cheek smashed against the tabletop. Below the table, another dwarf slept on his side, hugging a pillow while his head rested on the stone floor. Another lay across the kitchen counter with a towel over his face. The towel sank into his mouth with each inhale and bubbled up with each exhale.

The sitting area was just as bad.

Clothing and tipped over tankards covered most of the floor and furniture. A large fireplace made of stacked stone stood along the sitting room wall, the fire from the previous evening now just blackened coals. On the hearth lay a dwarf with a hand on his paunch, his face blackened, his tunic stained with soot. In one corner near the fireplace, a lean dwarf with a narrow, white beard sat with his back against the wall, head drooping, his chin and beard resting against his chest. The head of another dwarf leaned against the opposite corner while a string of drool ran down his mahogany brown beard.

Two more dwarfs were slumped in the padded lounge chairs near the fireplace, both with their heads hanging down the back of the chair, exchanging alternating snores. The tenth dwarf occupied an entire loveseat while parts of his extensive body spilled over the edge of the seats. Not only was he the largest person in the room, but he was also the loudest, his snoring causing the windows to rattle.

Three empty barrels stood beside the front door while another with a spigot still stuck in it sat on top of one of the empties. Arangoli gave the upper barrel a shove. It tipped up with relative ease, informing him that it also had been drained. The four barrels had been purchased just two days prior.

He turned from the barrels, approached the heavyset dwarf on the loveseat and nudged him with his knee. The dwarf snorted, turned his head away, and resumed snoring. With his head still pounding, Arangoli's patience rapidly waned. He bent, lifted a half-full tankard off the floor, and dumped it on the sleeping dwarf's head.

The dwarf gasped, coughed, and rolled off the sofa, forcing Arangoli to jump backward.

"Time to wake up, Gortch," Arangoli announced.

On his hands and knees, the overweight dwarf looked up. His face was wet from his heavy brow to his bearded chin. Unlike most dwarves, Gortch had no mustache and the way his dark beard framed his round face made it appear even rounder. He pushed himself to his knees and rubbed his globular nose.

"You got ale up my nose, Goli."

"I need you awake."

The big dwarf climbed to his feet. "Well, you got your wish." He waved a meaty fist in Arangoli's face. "Now, tell me why I shouldn't beat you silly."

"Korrigan was here. He has a mission of great import. I don't have the any details, but I am going to meet with him now. I need you to wake the others and have them clean this place up. Clean yourselves up as well. I don't know where we are headed, but we are leaving right after our midday meal. It may be days before we can eat hot food again."

Gortch lowered his fist. "The king has work for us?"

"Isn't that what I just said?"

"Aye, but why now?"

"How do I know?" Arangoli walked over to the door, opened it, and spoke over his shoulder. "Return these kegs to the brewery but don't bother exchanging them. We won't need others for a while."

Before Gortch could ask another question, Arangoli closed the door behind him and stood in the shade of his house. The air was cool but not cold and even less so when he stepped into the late morning sun. A pair of dwarves walked by, both nodding a greeting while saying his name. They were vaguely familiar, but their names eluded him. Such was common for Arangoli, for his prowess in battle had earned him fame even before his father became king. His fame swelled even further when he led the rebellion against the Drow who held Ra'Tahal hostage. *I never sought the adoration of my people.* Yet, that is what he had earned.

The stories that followed were often embellished until the truth became a small sliver of what everyone believed had happened.

With such tales exchanged among his people came expectations that weighed upon Arangoli. Some called him the second coming of Gahagar, but he knew better. There would never be another Gahagar the Impregnable. Despite this knowledge, Arangoli felt responsible for his clan, especially after his father's failure to protect them from the Drow incursion. His parents had paid a steep price for that mistake, as did dozens of others.

Before he dwelled too much on his own mistakes or those of his father, he slapped his own cheek. "Focus, Goli. The past is the past. Leave it be while you look forward."

With his back to the sun, he headed south, toward the citadel's center.

The narrow streets, barely wide enough to drive a wagon along, were bordered by buildings crafted with dwarven precision. Every line was true, every corner square, the seams between stone blocks nigh imperceptible. Practicality was the core of dwarven design, and that held true for the entire citadel. Even the thick, towering walls that bounded the fortress were more than expected, for those walls were thirty feet thick with doors and windows facing the interior. Shops, apartments, and warehouses occupied three quarters of that space while the outer rim was nothing but solid, impervious stone.

Clusters of dwarves roamed the streets – males, females, a handful of youths, shopkeepers, workers, and guards. All knew Arangoli by sight. Some stared wide-eyed, as if his silhouette was alight with magic. Others called out to him. A few even fell to one knee in a sign of fealty, something that caused Arangoli to cringe and hurry along. He did not want such burdens. It was why he had shunned the crown in the first place.

He came to an open square and crossed it, heading toward the central keep – the largest building in the citadel. The keep stood twelve stories tall and was as wide as a city block. It housed the city guards, bureaucrats, and most of the notable members of the Tahal clan in addition to a host of servants. Arangoli entered the keep and made straight for an open stairwell, where he began a long ascent.

His hangover still lingered and his headache returned by the time he reached the top floor. There, he paused for a breath, wiped his damp brow, and headed along a corridor lined by tapestries which opened into a square chamber occupied by four armored dwarves bracketing a pair of ornate doors stained black. The guards all stood tall, or at least as tall as a dwarf might stand, and thumped fists against their breastplates.

One stepped forward. A soldier Arangoli knew well. A dwarf with braided beard, a bald head, and a scar on his cheek. "Welcome, Captain," Vargan said.

"How are things with the new recruits, Vargan?"

"Oh, not too bad. Many still have dents and dings I must hammer out, but most have taken shape quite nicely. Give me another season with them, and they will be well honed weapons ready for brandishing."

"Until the fight begins," Arangoli noted. "You never know how one might react until weapons clash, blood is spilled, and their lives balance on the edge of the blade."

"True," Vargan nodded. "Still, we dwarves take pride in our resilience. Few are likely to fold when fear comes for them."

"I pray it is so."

"Kor... The king is inside, waiting for you."

"Thanks, Vargan."

Arangoli walked past the guards, entered the dining hall, and paused halfway between the doorway and the long table in the heart of the room. Indirect sunlight coming through large windows along the far wall illuminated the spacious chamber.

Korrigan stood over the far end of the table, his attention fixed on a map spread out before him. A leather pouch rested on one corner of the map, holding it in place despite the breeze coming through the open window.

Without lifting his gaze, Korrigan said. "It took you long enough."

"As you suggested, a bath and a change of clothing were warranted."

"More than warranted." The king stood upright. "You might want to burn those clothes. I fear they are beyond saving."

Crossing the room, Arangoli shook his head. "You always had a flair for overdramatizing things."

The comment drew a smile. "It amuses me, which is a rare feeling of late."

"You are finding the throne uncomfortable?"

"Try sitting on it, and you will find the same."

"No thank you." Arangoli looked down at the map. It depicted the realms of Drovaria and Domusi, two adjacent nations to the distant north. The first was ruled by the Drow, the latter by Clan Argent, the dwarven cousins to Clan Tahal. "What's with the map?"

Korrigan looked down at it and sighed. "Nothing good, I fear."

"Is this why you wanted to meet with me?"

"Yes." Leaning over the table, Korrigan pointed toward a seaside city nestled in a bay along the continent's north shore. "This is Talastar."

"I am aware."

"Last year, your father made a bargain with the Drow. Rysildar."

Arangoli's face darkened upon hearing the name. He resisted the urge to spit and instead replied, "He was the singer who killed my parents and the council before holding Ra'Tahal hostage."

"The very same. While one element of that bargain placed Rysildar here in the citadel, another side of the bargain had your father send an envoy to Talastar, along with several stone shapers. Since the Drow broke this agreement by their sinister actions, I sent a missive to Queen Liloth, demanding the return of our people."

"I would have done the same."

"Well, winter struck soon after my messenger departed. Severe weather, along with a myriad of other issues, slowed the journey. The worst of it came when he was caught in a winter storm that closed Van Nor pass for weeks."

"Why not take a ship to Talastar? It would be faster and far easier."

"True, if not for the pirates who control the west coast. Ships don't dare sail anywhere between Sea Gate and Talastar. As a result, trade with Galfhadden has been all but eliminated."

"Alright. So, this messenger took an inland route. What happened after this blizzard?"

"When the pass finally opened, he continued north and eventually reached Talastar only to find the city abandoned."

"Abandoned?"

"Completely. In fact, Black Gate stood open, so he wandered inside and conducted a search of the city but found nobody. No dark elves, no dwarves. Nothing. The shops had been stripped bare, the homes empty apart from dust-covered furniture. It is as if the entire populace vanished. However, there was one strange and concerning thing he reported."

"What was that?"

"Castle Umbria, home of Queen Liloth herself, was destroyed. All that remained was a pile of rubble."

Arangoli scratched his bearded chin. "Strange to be sure, but what does that have to do with me?"

"Spring has passed and summer is here. Even the snow clogging the mountain passes must yield to the sun's might. I need you and the Head Thumpers to travel to Drovaria, find our people, and bring them home."

"You want us to escort some stone masons halfway across the world? We are warriors, Kor. Can't you find someone else for such a mundane task?"

Korrigan grimaced. "Did you not hear a word I said?"

"I heard, but..."

"Something is wrong, Goli. Talastar is the Drow capital and Castle Umbria home to the queen. For one to be abandoned and the other destroyed, something dire must have occurred. Even Gahagar's campaign stalled when facing Talastar's fortifications. Yes, he would have eventually captured the city if not for his death, but this news is still alarming. What if it is only the first city of many to suffer such a fate?"

"I hadn't considered that." Arangoli admitted. "Do you think it'll be dangerous?"

"Traveling such a distance is certain to be rife with risk. What you find on the other end may require every bit of skill and bravery your crew can muster."

"Hmm. It does sound more interesting when you put it that way." He nodded firmly. "We will do it."

"As I expected, which is why I have the staff gathering provisions. Go and brief your squad. When they are cleaned up and presentable, return here for a meal with me. After you have eaten your fill, you will retrieve your belongings and embark on your journey."

"Are you certain we cannot just take a ship to Talastar? We are not afraid of pirates."

"These are not just pirates. We are talking about a fleet of ships sailed by merciless killers. These pirates fall under the banner of someone called The Dreadnought."

"So, getting there by ship is unlikely?"

"Apparently, it is impossible to find a sailor willing to risk sailing west of Sea Gate. Unless you own a ship..."

Arangoli sighed. "No."

"Then, from Sea Gate, you will travel inland, but do not fear." Korrigan lifted the pouch off the table and set it in Arangoli's palm. The contents jingled and felt solid. "This is enough gold to buy passage to Sea Gate and purchase a few horses when you land. From there, you will ride north. You must reach Talastar as soon as possible. When you get there, search for clues as to where the Drow went and why they fled the city. Hunt them down, find our people, and bring them home."

"After six years, we are returning to Talastar."

"Aye." Korrigan clapped him on the shoulder. "The scene of Gahagar's death is where your quest begins."

CHAPTER 4
TRIAL AND ERROR

The towering columns of the training chamber surrounded Ian like sentinels watching to ensure no stranger entered the warrens hidden beneath Mount Tiadd. Considering that the entrance to the complex was a thousand feet above the Agrosi, a dangerous land that few ever crossed, it was unlikely anyone would ever venture into those halls, even if the tunnel opening was not hidden.

Standing in the middle of the chamber, Ian studied the scroll spread on the floor at his feet. On the scroll was a complex drawing of concentric circles. At the core was the distinct pattern of an energy construct. His master had alluded to a broad range of spells that might result from that core – the type of energy and the spell's behavior dictated by the two outer rings.

For this particular spell, the second ring of intertwined runes and twisting lines denoted fire. The third and final ring was what gave the fire shape. Wavy lines ran through that circle, in a simple, flowing pattern. As Ian knew after testing the construct numerous times, those lines resulted in a cone of flames. Now, he was to experiment and determine other uses for the spell.

Anticipation thrummed through his veins and caused his stomach to squirm. His heart thumped like a drum, his armpits damp as he prepared to experiment. With Truhan away, he was all alone, so nobody else would get hurt if the spell went poorly. Of course, that also meant that there was nobody to help Ian should things take a bad turn. He quelled the thought, wrestled with it for control, and banished it to a corner of his mind. Fear would not rule his actions. Not any longer.

Ian opened himself to the source. Magic flowed in, filling him with tingling energy, his head dizzy with it. He extended his hand and willed the construct depicted on the scroll to appear. Semitransparent lines of white light materialized, the lines shimmering as they connected to one another, the construct forming from the core outwards until it was complete. Although the process took no more than two seconds, in his state of concentration, Ian watched it all unfold in slow motion.

With the construct complete, Ian prepared to test it. Again. A controlled burst of energy flowed from his body, accompanied by a flick of his hand. The pulse of his magic passed through the construct, and a cone of flames burst forth, the fire creating a wave of heat before fizzling away.

"Alright, Ian," he said to himself. "Let's try something different."

Holding the construct in place, he willed the outer ring to change, the waving lines curling into themselves, turning into a series of interconnected swirls. Bracing himself, he released a pulse of magic through the construct. Fire burst forth and split into a dozen tornados, each four feet tall and three feet in diameter at the top. The blazing cyclones spun outward, spreading as they twirled. One crashed into a column in a slash of flames, splattering and disintegrating while scorching the stone. In rapid succession, four more struck pillars with a similar result while the remaining cyclones meandered across the floor. The flaming twisters turned and began to head back toward

Ian. Three more crashed into columns in a spray of sparks, leaving four firestorms, two of which were coming straight for Ian. Alarm turned to panic. He spun around and ran as the tornados chased him.

Ian raced across the floor, the columns speeding past him. He glanced over his shoulder as a firestorm struck a column and snuffed out in a puff of black smoke. Three others spun toward him, snaking as they closed the gap. When he realized he could not outrun them, Ian's panic tripled. He turned, angling between two columns before turning again. The cyclones all followed, two of them striking columns and splattering flames in all directions. Still, the last remaining firestorm pursued him, now only strides away.

At the next column, Ian made a desperate leap to the side. Blazing bits of stone skittered past him when the tornado crashed into the pillar. He landed on his hands and rolled sideways three full revolutions before coming to a stop. There, he lay, panting from both exertion and tension. A pain in his leg had him look over his shoulder and find his robes on fire. He cried out and started rolling to snuff out the flames. After rolling back and forth a half-dozen times, he lay on his back, panting from exertion.

Laughter echoed through the still chamber as he lay there and reflected on his brush with death. His laughter quelled, he sat up and examined his robes as the last wisps of smoke rose from them. The burn still stung, but the fire was gone.

He rose to his feet and frowned at the hole in his robes. "I guess it is time for new clothing."

Crossing the floor, Ian retraced his steps and came to the spot in the chamber's center, where he had cast the spell. He squatted and picked up a tiny, charred piece of parchment with a sigh. The scroll depicting the cone of fire spell was destroyed.

"I had better go draw a new one before I forget the first."

As he turned to head back to his study, he made a promise to himself to draw an extra copy of every construct before a new one was attempted. A smile then bloomed on his face as he realized what he had accomplished.

"I did it. I discovered a new version of a fire construct."

More importantly, the effect resulting from his alterations had given him unexpected insight. He now had an indication of how the outer ring of the spell worked and what might be possible if he altered it in a different way.

Feeling satisfied and proud of himself, Ian's pace quickened. He looked forward to experimenting again but would take more care to ensure his safety when doing so.

~

IAN SAT at a desk in a chamber surrounded by books. The globe in the sconce mounted to the column beside the desk provided sufficient light as he recorded his latest finding on a sheet of parchment. When his quill ran dry, he dipped it in the inkwell and refilled it. As always, he traced the construct with care, ensuring that every line, curve, and symbol within was exact. The process took Ian over an hour, after which he began recording notes along the bottom of the scroll, describing the resulting spell and its effects. As he finished, approaching footsteps drew his attention toward the door.

Truhan walked into the study, appearing the same as always, his golden hair combed, his chiseled face smooth, his aqua blue eyes sparkling. "Greetings, Ian. How has my protégé fared while I was away?"

Straining to contain his excitement, Ian gestured toward the column in the chamber's center, Twelve of the compartments now occupied by scrolls. "I have identified seven alternative fire constructs to add to the cone of flames. Each has a different effect, ranging from a single flame to a huge conflagration, from something suitable for igniting a candle to others that are only suited for battle."

Truhan walked past Ian and approached the column. Of the slots that now stood full, eight were in a single, vertical row. He pulled a scroll out, unrolled it, and stared at it with his brow furrowed. "Fireball?"

It was the construct Ian was most excited to discuss, so he stood and approached the man. "This one can be used in numerous ways. Each fireball seems to have weight – a source of gravity in its center. The fire spins around that point and can be manipulated. I was able to use it in conjunction with the shield construct to hold it in place while applying additional fire, which caused the fireball to increase in size. With a thrust of the shield, I launched the fireball across the room."

"Is that what happened to the scaffold in the testing chamber?"

The image of the scaffold burning replayed in Ian's head. The flames had swiftly consumed the wooden structure, burning through the three-inch diameter poles and the ropes holding them together. In mere minutes, fire danced along the entirety of the towering frame. Not long afterward, the structure had collapsed in a heap of twisted, burning poles.

"As you instructed, I was experimenting with variations of the original construct." Ian shrugged and flashed a sheepish grin. "The scaffold catching fire was unintentional."

Truhan laughed. "That, I did." He arched a brow. "The fact that you dislike climbing the scaffold must just be coincidence."

Ian gave him a sheepish shrug.

The man rolled the scroll back up and returned it to the slot. "It was clever of you to combine the use of two constructs to control the result."

"Well, I must admit that my research did not occur as smoothly as it might seem."

"How so?"

"I destroyed two sets of robes and suffered more than one burn, but none were serious." Ian rubbed a tender spot on his forearm. Similar to the burn on his shin, the injury was red, sore and lacked hair.

"I warned you to proceed with care," Truhan scolded. "Dying during training would defeat the purpose, and I would be forced to start over with someone else."

The comment was like a flaming arrow to Ian's pride, striking at the heart of it and setting it ablaze. "Someone else?"

Truhan patted Ian's back. "Do not worry. I do not intend to replace you, not after I've invested so much."

The words did nothing to mend Ian's emotional wound. The turn of conversation had confirmed something Ian had privately wondered about since leaving Ra'Tahal. *He does not genuinely care about me, only about what I can do for him.*

"Now," Truhan said, "I am curious to know if you have attempted to make alterations to the spell's second layer."

"Second layer?" Ian shook his head. "I only altered the outer ring."

"And when you did so, which was the least dangerous version?"

"The one that creates a tiny, candle-like flame."

"Test out that construct while altering the energy signature of the second ring. You have displayed an impressive intuition. Let's see if you can produce something unexpected." The man walked off, leaving Ian alone.

His gaze fell to the construct gracing the scroll on the desk. He had not considered what might result if he altered the fire aspect of the spell. Curiosity tempered by concern had him weighing his options. It only took a few moments before he found himself longing to experiment.

～

SEATED on a rock a thousand feet up, Ian stared out over the Agrosi. The wind blowing across the expansive fields caused the long grass to bend and waver, creating a scene not unlike swells flowing across the open sea. That wind powered ships, taking the vessels from port to port. It left him wondering what else might be possible if he could harness the wind. With that in mind, he crossed his legs, closed his eyes, and slid into meditation. In a blanket of peace and serenity, he hovered in the void. Then, he opened himself to magic, allowing a trickle to flow in. In his mind's eye, the magic gently twisted and flowed, creating mesmerizing designs made of misty light.

He opened his eyes and stared down at the plains. Sparks of light flitted across the grass, slowing until the scene froze solid. There in that gap where time had stopped, a construct materialized.

The core was identical to those used in the fire spells he had learned. The outer ring was akin to that of the spell that yielded a cone of fire. The ring in between reminded him of those he conjured when wielding a shield spell. It was that ring on which he focused, memorizing its design from the layered lines to the twisting runes that defined it. How long he examined the construct, he was uncertain, but when he relaxed and slipped out of meditation, he found the sun kissing the western horizon.

Climbing down from the rock, Ian turned toward the copse of pine trees on the slope beside him. He extended his hand, crafted the construct, and powered it with his magic. A blast of wind shot out. The pine boughs waved furiously while the upper portion of the trees bent against the might of the gale. When Ian relaxed the spell, the trees whipped back upright. Pleased with himself, Ian was not done, for he was inspired by what he had discovered and his intuition screamed of a connection.

He altered the outer ring until it was identical to what he used when crafting a spell of protection. With the core and inner ring remaining as they were during the previous spell, he sent magic through it. A ghostly disk of air appeared before him. Curious, he tentatively stepped on it. The air supported him, but it felt squishy to the step with a fluttering pressure against his feet. It made him imagine a powerful wind constrained to the shape of the platform. That wind blew up, against him, keeping him elevated but not blowing beyond the disk's upper surface. He expanded the disk, took a few strides, and soon found himself three feet above the ground, supported by air that had been hardened and formed in a way he did not realize was possible. In that moment of surprise and satisfaction, he lost concentration.

Ian fell. His feet struck the slope first, but the angle caused him to lose balance. He tumbled backward, rolled, and crashed right into a bush. With effort, the shrub seemingly unwilling to let him go, rose to his feet and climbed back toward the tunnel entrance. His strides quickened as he rounded the boulder and ducked into the dark tunnel. He could not wait to show Truhan his latest discovery.

CHAPTER 5
CHALLENGE

The charred remains of the scaffold were no longer of use, so Ian was forced to find another means to ascend to the upper reaches of the testing chamber. Determined, he approached a rope dangling from the high ceiling, gripped it, and jumped. He wrapped his legs around the rope, pinching it between his knees and ankles while pulling with his arms. Up and up, he went, his steady pace a reflection of his determination. Two seasons ago, climbing the rope would have been beyond him, but a hearty diet along with weekly training sessions had changed that for the better.

Hand over hand, he ascended, the rope swaying to the rhythm of his movements. Twenty, forty, sixty, eighty feet up, he continued until he was above the nearest platform. He pulled a hand free, opened himself to his magic, and conjured a construct. His magic poured through it and a platform of hardened air appeared. He stepped onto it and hopped to a ring of stone jutting out from a column a hundred and twenty feet above the floor.

"Good." Truhan's voice echoed off walls of smoothly carved rock. He stood at the far end of the chamber, three hundred feet away. "Now, let's see how fast you can reach my location. Remember, you cannot touch down until you pass the line I have drawn at my feet." Although the stripe of white chalk was too distant for Ian to see, he knew it well. The elusive goal had haunted his dreams.

"I know." Ian's voice echoed across the distance.

Ian had attempted the trial dozens of times without success. *Today will be different.* The tricks he had added should provide him with the advantage he had been seeking – an advantage made possible only by his magic.

With a plan firmly etched in his head, Ian prepared a construct around each hand. He would not fall, since that would likely kill him, nor would he fail.

He called out, "Tell me when!"

Truhan lifted the massive brass hourglass from the pedestal beside him and turned it over. "Now!"

Ian burst into a run and leapt. He rapidly conjured a platform of air, landed on it, took two strides, and leapt again while casting another disk of hardened air. A quick step and leap later, he plunged toward the floor with his arms stretched out. His hands latched onto a rope, his body flinging around that fulcrum point while his momentum sent the rope swinging forward. At the top of the arc, he let go and sailed fifteen feet to land on a catwalk. He rolled with the fall and hurried back to his feet, only to step on the hem of his robes and fall face-first, straight toward the catwalk edge. Panic clutched at his throat, causing it to tighten. He urgently slapped his hands on the catwalk and stopped his momentum with the upper third of his body dangling over a deadly drop.

He pulled himself backward, climbed to his feet, and took off at a run, his heart racing from the exertion and anxiety of the near fall. At the end of the hundred-foot-long catwalk, he leapt and grabbed ahold of a rope. The rope swung out and back like a pendulum while Ian lowered himself. He kicked with both legs, adding his own weight to the rope's momentum as it swung forward again. At the top of the arc, he let go and fell while drifting forward. His feet found a platform, and he rolled with the fall, and rolled into the column running through the middle of it. Pain shot through his hip, the collision certain to leave a bruise, but he ignored it, scrambled to his feet, and set his eyes on the goal below him.

Ian embraced his magic as he jumped. He cast a disk of solid air, landed on it, and sent it plummeting downward. When it appeared he would strike the floor with too much speed, he raised his hand and the disk beneath him slowed to a stop. He hopped off, over the line Truhan had drawn across the floor, and shot the man a grin.

"Well done." His mentor nodded. "Your confidence and skill have both improved greatly."

A warmth of pride swelled in Ian's chest.

"However," Truhan picked up the hourglass. "You have failed."

To Ian's surprise, the sand had already collected at the bottom. "But, but, but..." he stuttered, "How could I travel the length of the chamber any faster?"

"That is for you to figure out. Your mind is your greatest weapon, so use it. You will find things are much easier if you think them through first."

Think them through? Ian had been practicing and planning how he would beat the challenge for twelve weeks. Although the magic he used was a recent discovery, days of training with it had given him confidence that was now shattered. *How can I think on it more than that?*

Truhan gestured across the room. "Now, go visit the baths. We have other business to deal with when you are finished."

When his master turned and walked away, Ian's chin dropped to his chest. His head and shoulders slumped in defeat as he shuffled toward the adjoining tunnel.

~

Steam surrounded Ian. He stood in the hot end of the pool, the water's surface just above his shoulders. Beads of sweat gathered on his head while his body soaked up the water from the hot spring that fed the pool. It smelled of sulfur, but that was a small price to pay for the heat that soothed his sore muscles.

Eventually, the heat became too much and chased Ian away. He waded across the pool, where cooler water greeted him, its flow gently tugging at his legs. Two springs flowed into the baths, one hot, and one cold, both mixing with one another before flowing out of the chamber. Where the water went afterward, Ian was uncertain. He assumed it was somewhere underground since there was no sign of the spring on the hillside below the tunnel entrance.

A flat, submerged rock allowed him to step out and stand on the rock shelf beside the pool. With careful steps, not wishing to slip and fall, he eased along the shelf until it widened. A towel waited for him on a rock near the exit, which he used to dry himself before wrapping it around his waist and heading down a tunnel illuminated by a single orb at its midpoint. Just past the light, a curtain covered a doorway in the side of the corridor. Ian lifted the orb off the sconce with one hand and used the other to pull the curtain aside. Pale light sent shadows skittering to the corners of the small chamber. A bed was positioned against one wall while a wardrobe stood opposite from it. Between the two stood a table with an empty cup resting on it. The quarters were simple and no bigger than a ship's cabin. There were moments when Ian felt the walls closing in and tons of rock threatening to crush him, but those moments had come early in his stay. In time, he had grown to think of the room as his own. The rest of the complex belonged to his master.

Ian opened the wardrobe doors. Inside, robes of assorted colors dangled from hooks. Breeches, tunics, and smallclothes lay folded in neat piles on a shelf above the robes. He dropped the towel, grabbed his small clothes, and pulled them on. Next, he chose robes made of a dark blue fabric that gave him a funny feeling when rubbing it between his thumb and fingers. The sensation often gave Ian a chill, causing him to shiver, and not because of the cold. He slid his arms into the robes and wrapped them around himself. From a hook with a dozen narrow strips of fabric, each of a different color, he chose a silver sash and tied it around his waist. He liked how it contrasted with the dark blue robes.

Briefly, he longed for a mirror, so he could gaze upon himself to see how he looked, but such was not to be. There were no mirrors in the complex, and Truhan refused to indulge Ian's desire for one. So, he slid his feet into a fresh pair of sandals and padded out into the corridor with the globe of light in his palm.

When reaching a split in the tunnel, Ian chose the right path, the rock walls forming a gentle curve. A few dozen strides later, a light appeared from ahead. Ian approached it and emerged in the study, where he found Truhan standing beside a table upon which rested half a dozen thick books. A glance toward the bookshelves revealed no notable gaps.

His brow furrowing as he approached the table, Ian asked, "I am bathed and dressed. What would you have of me, Master?"

The man rested his hand on the top book. "I hope these will offer clues."

Ian looked down at the books on the table, all more than three fingers thick. "Clues to what?"

"Honestly, I don't know…yet." As usual, there was a hint of amusement reflected in Truhan's eyes. "While your training and development are critical, it will not be enough. What we must accomplish is monumental and additional advantages are required."

"Accomplish? Advantages?"

"The future is unwritten, Ian, but as it draws closer, the possible outcomes become more limited. Something dark approaches, but in that darkness, another possibility lurks. When it arrives, we must be prepared."

The cryptic declaration only left Ian more confused. "What are you talking about?"

"I just told you. The future."

Ian threw his hands in the air. "Why do I even bother? You never give a straight answer."

Truhan scowled. "I will remind you that I am the master in this relationship."

"I know. I just..." Ian stammered, searching for the right words.

"Listen," Truhan sighed. "Forget the future and focus on the now. Can you do that?"

"I...Yes."

"You are to read through these books and look for something of interest, something that sparks your curiosity. Rely on your intuition. It will serve you well."

"Why me?"

"Because, I have other things to which I must attend."

"You are leaving again?"

"In a few days. In the meantime, you are to hone your physical abilities in the morning, your magic in the mid-day, and this research in the evening." Truhan clapped a hand on Ian's shoulder and stared him in the eyes. That stare held a gravity Ian had rarely seen from his master. "I fear we have little time. As I said, something is coming. If we fail, it will consume our world."

CHAPTER 6
NEGATIVE ENERGY

Thump. Thump. Thump. Ian's pulse hammered in his ears while anxiety twisted his stomach. Alone, he stood in the testing chamber. Despite his determination, what he was about to attempt held an undeniable danger. His still healing burns and ruined robes had proven as much.

He opened himself to the source. Power flowed into him and the world thrummed with light, color, and scents that eluded him when not holding his magic. Extending a hand before him, he willed a spell into existence – a disk of white light surrounded by a pair of concentric rings. The energy construct was one used to craft a single, tiny flame. As instructed by his master, he altered the inner ring while the core and outer ring remained intact. The intersecting lines twisted into a different pattern resembling an inverse of the fire spell. He examined it closely to ensure it was even and balanced. Satisfied, he set his jaw and channeled a thread of magic through it while bracing for what unknown effect might take place.

A burst of frozen mist burst forth, swirled in the air, and dissipated.

A wave of cold washed over Ian, as if he had opened a door to a snow-covered yard and then hurriedly closed it.

"It worked," he said to himself, his tone mixed with awe and pride.

But he was not done.

He focused and altered the outer ring, changing it to the one that resulted in a cone of flames when used with the inner ring denoting fire. Again, he channeled his magic through the construct. A cone of icy darts burst out and shot across the room. The shards shattered off columns, twinkling chimes echoing throughout the chamber as the remains fell to the stone floor. The sound reminded Ian of shattered glass.

Again, pride and a sense of accomplishment filled his chest.

But he was still not finished.

Struck by intuition, Ian changed the disk in the center. The energy core folded inward, the starbursts inverting, the lines around them bending in the opposite direction. When done it appeared like an inverse version of the energy construct core he had come to know. Again, he channeled a thread of magic through it. The result was quite unexpected.

A murky void appeared in the air before Ian. It was unlike anything he had ever seen. Rather than being black in color, it was more akin to an absence of light. In fact, it seemed to consume surrounding light as glowing streaks darted toward it and disappeared.

An invisible force tugged at Ian, causing him to stumble toward the twisting blob of darkness. He firmly planted his feet and leaned back, bracing himself against its draw. The orbs on nearby columns began to quake. Suddenly, an orb rolled off its sconce, flew across the room, and was swallowed by the darkness. Another shot toward the void with Ian in the way. He urgently ducked, the globe narrowly missing him before it plunged into the abyss.

The burnt remains of the scaffold shook and folded toward the void.

A charred pole broke off, shot across the room, and was swallowed by the murk. Others followed in rapid succession.

The pull increased in strength, causing Ian to fall forward. He landed on his stomach and began to slide across the floor. Panic gripped him for a beat before he recalled his magic. He projected a construct, channeled energy through it, and formed a shield. The draw on Ian relented but the force pulled on the shield itself. At first, Ian tried to resist, but he knew it would only delay the inevitable. Desperate, he altered the shape of the shield while feeding it to expand it until it was thirty feet in diameter. He then folded the shield around the void, pulling the sides together until they met to form a sphere. The shield rippled, quaked, and then collapsed in on itself.

An explosion shook the chamber. A blast of air thrust Ian across the floor and hurled him into a column. Pain shot through his side, and his ears rang. His breath came in gasps, each draw like a knife to his ribs. Groaning, he rolled over, sat up, and looked across the room.

The void, his shield, a quarter of the scaffold remains, and half a dozen globes were all gone.

Motion from the entrance drew Ian's attention as Truhan rushed in. The man slowed as he approached Ian. His lips moved, but Ian heard nothing above the ringing in his ears.

"What?" He said in a loud voice.

Truhan drew closer. "What happened?" The words sounded distant although he was standing just strides away.

Ian climbed to his feet, groaning and then gasping from the pain in his side. He held a hand to his sore midriff and eased into an upright position. "I was experimenting, as you instructed."

Doubt apparent, Truhan said, "And?"

"I inverted the heat aspect of the candle spell and it resulted in icy cold air."

The man furrowed his brow. "So other versions of the spell would result in ice rather than fire?"

"It appears so."

"Then, what was the explosion?"

"I..." Ian hesitated but realized there was no avoiding the truth. "Since I had success inverting the middle ring of the spell, I thought I would try doing the same with the core."

The man's voice climbed an octave. "You inverted the core of an energy construct?"

Ian shrugged. "I was curious."

"You created a negative energy spell, you dolt! You could have killed yourself and destroyed this entire complex. If unchecked, the mountain would have collapsed in on itself!"

Ian blinked in shock. "I didn't know."

"Ignorance is no excuse for recklessness."

"But the idea was so compelling, I really wanted to see what would happen."

"You *really* wanted to?" Truhan threw his hands in the air and turned away. "Really wanted to?" The man walked off. "He really wanted to test it. If he really wanted it, then I am certain the laws of physics would understand. It's not as if he could have destroyed himself and everything in miles, not if he *really* wanted to try the spell."

The man continued talking to himself as he faded through the doorway.

~

BENEATH THE LIGHT of a glowing globe, Ian read through a tome heavy enough to knock someone unconscious if struck over the head with it. The book was written in Dwarvish and detailed the early campaigns of Gahagar the Impregnable, the great dwarf king who had nearly conquered the world.

The author included unnecessary and often menial details ranging from the counts of sacks of produce and livestock required to feed

Gahagar's army to the number of arrows and crossbow bolts spent in battle. The story's tone and pace were as much of a slog as the details. The result had Ian nodding off repeatedly before he gave in and closed the book, deciding he was ready for bed.

He rose to his feet and padded across the library. His gaze went to the dim light seeping beneath the door to the neighboring chamber, and he stopped to stare at that slice of light with longing. As the only physical door in the complex, other than the enchanted doors on the path to the Hall of Divining, this turned the room beyond the door into something of great interest. More than once, Ian had come close to testing it although Truhan had warned him against doing so. The door led to his master's private chambers. During times when Truhan entered or exited, Ian had caught glimpses of a dimly lit room occupied by pedestals and shelving upon which rested mysterious objects made of metals, wood, and stone. His curiosity insisted he investigate, but his master's warning lingered. *Your skills are mighty, but you are not prepared for the wards that protect the dangerous secrets this chamber contains. Any attempt to enter without my assistance will be a dance with death.*

The door suddenly opened, causing Ian to jerk with a start, his heart hammering in his chest.

As Truhan walked out, Ian caught another peek into the shadowy interior. A warm glow pulsed at the chamber's far end, its source blocked by a pedestal in the middle of the room. His curiosity raged as the man pulled the door closed.

"Are you finished for this evening?" Truhan asked.

Uncertain if the man would scold him for giving up, Ian attempted to defend his choice. "The book has a plodding pace and little plot. Oftentimes it feels more like a ledger than anything else."

"But it is from Gahagar's reign, is it not?"

"It is, though I am well into the book and have found nothing interesting. In fact, I can barely remain awake when I read it."

Truhan rubbed his jaw before nodding to himself. "Mark your page with a ribbon and set that book aside. Tomorrow, begin with another book. If you reach the quarter point and it does not hold your interest, move on to another."

Ian frowned. "Most of those books are thick and the writing is difficult to read. It could take me days to reach the quarter point."

"And I will be away for a while, so that, along with your physical training and magic experiments should keep you busy while I am away."

"How long this time?"

"A week, I suspect."

"When do you leave?"

"I will be gone before you wake." Truhan walked off, heading down a shadowy tunnel, his footsteps fading into silence.

"Alone again," Ian sighed and headed down another tunnel.

When he reached his room, he removed his robes, washed his face in the bowl of water on his vanity, and dried off. He then draped the towel over the globe on the wall, blotting out the light. In the dark, he shuffled a few feet, found the bed, and crawled beneath the covers.

In the solitary silence of his cell beneath a mountain of rock, Ian fought off his loneliness. Often, he was too busy or exhausted to dwell on his confinement, but there were times when he thought his heart might break. While the days often blurred together, today was Beltane, the first day of summer and a holiday he had looked toward with eagerness every year. But this year was different. This year, he was alone, and that stung him to the core.

His longing began with his mother and father. This was his eighteenth Beltane, a full year beyond his passing into adulthood, but during the celebration the prior year, his entire family had been together, healthy, happy, and ignorant of the trouble plaguing other parts of the world. A few days later came the dwarf attack during which an explosion killed his father. Many had died that day, and those who did not were caught and shackled. Ian, his mother, and brother were all taken as slaves, along with most of the village. Time, fortune, and heroic deeds had earned their freedom, but in the end, it also left them separated.

Ian missed his mother's hugs, her delicious cooking, and the care she had provided whenever he was ill. He missed his father's support, guidance, and quiet strength. Lastly, he missed his brother's cama-raderie.

Where are you, Vic? It was a question Ian had pondered often. At some point, he intended on tracking down his brother. During winter, with snow and freezing weather on the mountain as natural impedi-ments, it had been easy to dismiss the idea of venturing out to find Vic. Now, with the snow melted and weather turned, his longing to leave the mountain railed against his determination to see his training completed.

The last time Ian had seen his brother was just before leaving Ra'Ta-hal. The parting had been difficult, but Ian had been eager to begin his training at the time, and he knew Vic had found someone special in Revita, so his brother would not be alone either. Then, just before Ian left, Winnie kissed him. That kiss replayed in his mind for the thou-sandth time, the warmth and softness of her lips on his, tingling and causing his body to react. Until that moment, he hadn't viewed Winnie in a romantic light. For as long as he could recall, another girl had held fast to his heart.

Where are you, Rina? He sent the thought out into the ether. No answer came. None had since her disappearance just weeks before the Drow betrayal that led to Ian's own flight from Ra'Tahal.

He longed to see Rina's smile, to hear her laughter, and to inhale the flowery scent of her golden hair. He missed their conversations and those moments when she would touch his arm or brush against him.

Lacking her companionship, a constant for most of his life, was perhaps the most difficult aspect of his new life as a recluse.

Memories of Rina danced through his mind as he slowly drifted off to sleep.

CHAPTER 7
HAIR OF GOLD

Safrina Miller sat on a shaded terrace, staring into space while softly repeating memorized words to herself. The terrace had become a place of solace and learning for Rina, the latter taking place every morning after breaking her fast.

The silky material of her dress kept her cool despite the summer heat. The color of the fabric matched her bright blue eyes and nicely complemented her long, golden hair. While she had often longed to be more like the curvaceous human women when back in her home village of Shillings, her lean, willowy build fit in perfectly in elven society. Now, Rina was determined to learn how she might further adapt to life among the Sylvan, if not for herself, for the person who occupied her dreams both day and night.

Bright sunlight shone down on a view she would not have believed existed a year ago. A city of spires, arches, and domes amid golden-leafed trees stretched out before her. It was a city of hope and beauty, inspired by the graceful and sophisticated elves who lived there, despite the human slaves working for them. Rina tried to convince herself that the slaves were simply part of Sylvan culture. A small voice inside railed against the notion. She had been a slave herself, torn away from her home, her family, and the only life she had ever known. Since the day the dwarves invaded Shillings, her life had been under the control of others. Even now, without the chains of slavery binding her, she felt like a leaf caught in a swift flowing stream. Worse, she feared a waterfall looming.

A soft touch on her arm stirred Rina from her trance. She looked up at the female elf standing over her. "Yes?"

Isra-Shi tilted her head and gave Rina a stern glare. She had high eyebrows and wore her brown hair in a tight bun, which gave her gaunt face a severe expression even when she was pleased. As far as Rina could tell, Isra-Shi was never happy. "You did not respond."

Abashed, Rina blinked and shook her head. "I am sorry. I didn't hear you."

"I asked you to repeat the phrase you first learned this morning." Her tone made it clear that she was losing patience. With Isra-Shi, it did not take long for her coldness to turn bitter.

Rina, still attempting to master Elvish, recalled the sentence, mostly consisting of words which were already familiar to her. "Welcome to the palace. The king and queen are currently indisposed, but it would be my pleasure to spank you."

"Not *spank*." Isra-Shi pressed her lips together. "The word is *serve*."

"Serve," Rina repeated in Elvish. Similar to many other words spoken in the flowing, elegant language, the word felt strange to her tongue. "The two words sound very similar." Listening to others and understanding their conversation had turned out to be much easier than speaking the language. There were subtleties that eluded her unless she made a concerted effort with her pronunciation.

"Trust me. There is a significant difference. Now, let us continue the conversation. You will proceed as if I were a guest." The elf woman stuck out her chin in a haughty expression. "Thank you kindly. I will take some tea."

Rina replied in the same language. "As you wish. Pardon me while I get that for you."

After a barely perceptible nod, Isra-Shi said. "That was better. Your accent is atrocious, but at least you no longer sound like a toddler. Continue to practice. I will meet you here again tomorrow, right after breakfast."

Before Rina could reply, Isra-Shi walked off, her slippered feet barely making a noise as she crossed the tiled terrace, passed beneath an arch, and faded from view.

Rina turned back toward the railing and sighed. "Alone again."

Since Princess Shria-Li's disappearance, Rina spent most of her time alone. It was not by choice, but she was a stranger to this city and its people. The other humans might be slaves, but even they had active roles in Sylvan society. With no family, no friends, and nothing to occupy her days other than attempting to learn a complex language, eat, and sleep, Rina found herself longing for something, anything to happen to her.

A familiar male voice behind her spoke in Elvish, "I have found you."

Her heart leapt and a smile spread across her face before she even turned toward him. "Your Majesty."

Fastellan lifted a finger and furrowed a brow. "As you might recall, you are to refrain from such titles while we are alone."

With platinum hair, chiseled facial features, and eyes as bright as the sunlight glinting off the golden leaves above her, Fastellan was as handsome as anyone Rina had ever met. She lost herself in his golden eyes while kneading her hands in a struggle to contain herself. Four weeks had passed since she had last seen him. Thrice that span had passed since he had last held her in his powerful arms. The heat of their kiss still warmed her dreams.

"I have missed you," she said softly.

"And I, you, my flower. Each time I see you, somehow, your petals are more entrancing, your bouquet more bewitching. These things haunt my dreams and consume my waking thoughts."

A flutter stirred in her chest, and she had to restrain herself from plunging into his arms. To stave off such urges, she sought to alter the conversation. "Where have you been?"

"I have just returned from Shai Aeldor. While there, I made a bargain with Kobblebon to secure additional dwarven engineers and masons, including two more stone shapers. In fact, my retinue and I journeyed north with these new workers for three days before we parted. They continued toward Shadowmar while I turned east for Havenfall. Winter just relented its grip on the mountains, so with improved weather and additional craftsmen, the construction will advance at a faster pace than ever."

Shadowmar. He had mentioned the castle in the mountains before, along with the promise that he would take her there one day. "What of me?"

"You must abide living in Havenfall a while longer. Tell me, how do you fare with your studies?"

Rina sighed. "I am learning your language the best I can, but I believe Isra-Shi is frustrated. Elvish is so...foreign. The sentences are backward and many words sound similar while having vastly different meanings." *If only I had a skill with language as Ian does.*

The thought caused her to wonder what had become of her dear friend, a thought that frequently arose when she was alone. Over half a year had passed since she last saw Ian. She worried for him and missed him greatly. *I hope I see him again, someday. The spirits willing, it will happen soon.*

Fastellan reached out and took her hand. "Doing your best is all anyone can ask. We all have skills, and your strengths lie in other areas."

Inside, Rina wanted to ask what areas. Instead, she smiled. "You are too kind."

His free hand touched her cheek while his golden eyes locked onto hers. "And you are too beautiful."

Her heart thumped like a drum. "I am here anytime you wish to see me."

"I wish it could happen more often, but I am bound by duty. Soon, that will change. Soon, you and I will be together."

Despite wishing for nothing more, guilt twisted her stomach. "What will that do to Tora-Li?"

"She need not know. Our marriage has been one of convenience from the start. She extends no love toward me and expects none in return. I suspect she will fulfill her needs discreetly, and I will not press her on the issue. So long as you and I take care to do the same, all will be well." He dropped his hand and let go of hers. "Remain steadfast. Continue learning what you can. I will do my best to shield you, at least until we find Shria-Li."

"The search continues?"

"It will not end until I find her. I am certain that she is not in Haven-fall, and I have trackers placed throughout the realm. Should any find signs of her, I will know. Sooner or later, this mystery will be solved and my daughter will be returned to me." He backed away. "I must again leave Havenfall at daybreak, and there is still much to do before I depart."

Disappointment sank in and darkened Rina's hope like spilled ink staining a clean white dress. "So soon? Where do you go, now?"

"I head to Shadowmar to monitor the castle's progress and to ensure proper execution, which is more critical than ever after the concessions I made to Kobblebon. I will return shortly. Until then, continue as you are and do your best to stay away from Tora-Li. Your presence reminds her of Shria-Li, which stirs sorrow and anger in equal measure. She wishes you gone since our daughter is not here for you to attend. So long as the queen is otherwise occupied and you remain out of her sight, she is unlikely to press the issue."

Rina nodded. "I understand."

He turned and walked off, leaving Rina alone. Again.

~

After waiting a proper amount of time to ensure nobody connected her with Fastellan, Rina left the terrace and headed down a long corridor. She turned the corner and the corridor opened on one side with a series of arches standing over the Garden of Life. Lining the corridor across from each arch were massive pots covered in a mosaic of tiny, colored tiles. Palms with broad fronds grew in each planter, the tops of them nearly reaching the ceiling some twenty feet above. Each pot occupied an alcove only slightly wider than the bulging midriff of the pottery. Three arches down, she paused and stared up at the massive, golden tree in the garden's center. Visiting the garden had become a frequent pastime. The tree's presence was unlike anything Rina had ever experienced, emanating a sense of peace and contentment that helped ease her loneliness, if even just for a bit. Voices carried from the heart of the palace, causing Rina to turn in that direction.

At the corridor's far end, Tora-Li stood with her back to Rina while issuing orders to a pair of servants. The queen had likely not yet seen Rina. Fastellan's suggestion replayed in Rina's head. *Do your best to stay away from Tora-Li.*

She spun around but realized that the end of the corridor was too distant for her to flee without the queen spotting her. The arches were two stories above the garden, so jumping down was likely to result in injury and might also cause a ruckus. Without any better idea as to how to avoid the queen, Rina hurried across the corridor, slipped into the alcove behind a massive pot, and stood still. She reached down, gathered a fist full of cloth with each hand, and pulled her skirts tight. To her own ears, her breaths were as noisy as a blustery wind, her pulse like a drum thumping in her ear. Above that noise, she heard someone approaching. Another set of footsteps joined the first but came from the other direction. As the two people drew near, Rina's breathing calmed and quieted.

A male voice spoke in Elvish. "Good day, My Queen."

"Evarian," Tora-li replied. "What brings you to the palace?"

"I hear that Fastellan has returned, and I seek an audience." The last sounded like a demand.

"My husband is occupied, and he leaves for Shadowmar first thing tomorrow."

"This is unacceptable." The male elf did not try to hide his anger. "The barrier is failing, and the attacks grow worse. A roc killed two Valeguard just last week and the creature made it beyond the palace before it was taken from the sky. The apothecary was all but destroyed when it crashed down. Cultivators and their plants both died because of this negligence. Something must be done and soon."

"I am queen here, Evarian." Tora-Li said in a stern tone. "I am aware of what occurs in my realm."

Rina carefully peered around the pot. The male elf wore blue armor, had brown hair, and bright green eyes. He stood tall and proud with an exotic spear in his grip. Over his shoulder, he wore a golden longbow.

Evarian spoke with his lips tight. "Our people suffer and things will only grow worse if the situation is not addressed. Instead, your husband is distracted by the construction of a pointless fortress high up in the mountains."

When the male elf glanced toward the pot, Rina hurriedly pulled back and prayed he had not seen her.

"You are not king, Evarian," Tora-Li said. "You do not understand the weight of the crown or the complexities that come with the position. My husband has never done anything if not for the good of the Sylvan."

"I am the greatest warrior of our people. Use me, my queen. Allow me to lead an expedition into the Vale."

"You wish me to turn against my husband...your king?"

"If he is not here to govern, his voice cannot be heard, nor does he hear the cries of his own people. Be bold, Your Majesty. Take action."

A long moment of silence passed before the queen replied.

"The king has ordered you and the other Blue Spears to remain in Havenfall and protect our fair city if attacked. I support that decision and you will obey it until your orders change."

Evarian huffed, thumped the butt of his staff on the floor, and stomped off, passing through Rina's narrow view between the vase and the wall. Soon after, Tora-Li headed in the same direction. When the corridor fell silent, Rina emerged from her hiding place to find herself alone and the queen beyond view. At a hurried pace, she headed in the opposite direction considering what she had overheard.

A part of her felt sorry for Tora-Li. The queen remained loyal to Fastellan although she was trapped in a loveless marriage. Such sacrifice for her people was honorable, and it stung Rina to think that she might come between them. Yet, she could not stop thinking about Fastellan – his golden eyes, his sculpted figure, his lips brushing against hers. The mere idea that she might spend the rest of her nights in his arms caused her heart to swell and her head to swoon. The highlight of her brief conversation with him replayed in her head. *Soon, you and I will be together.* While Rina remained concerned about how her being with Fastellan would affect Tora-Li, he was all she dreamed of, day and night.

CHAPTER 8
WELLSPRING RIVER

Rested and ready for something, anything other than spending another minute in bed, Arangoli opened the door to the cabin he shared with Gortch, and Rax. The others were still sleeping, and with no reason to rouse them, Arangoli quietly eased outside and closed the door behind him. A cool breeze grabbed his beard and tousled his hair, the sky above blanketed in clouds. He wrapped his cloak around his shoulders and followed the narrow deck that ran between the cabins and the river barge's outer railing.

The foredeck, an open area twenty feet wide and just as long, came into view. An island of benches, each facing a different direction, stood in the middle of the deck. Netting covered the pile of crates nestled in between the benches and bound them together. Dwarven crew members stood at the rectangular barge's front corners, each holding a pole three times as long as their own height. Of the Head Thumpers, only one stood on deck, leaning against the front rail while peering downriver.

Arangoli approached the rail and stood beside him. "Did you rest well, Paz?"

The breeze bent the lean dwarf's braided beard around his neck, making it appear as if he wore a scarf made of white hair.

Pazacar turned toward him. "Well enough, but one can sleep only so long."

"Aye. This may be an effortless way to travel, but it is dull."

"It did allow me to read the book I brought, but with that finished, there is little to challenge the mind."

"We could spar," Arangoli offered.

"Against you? With real weapons? I think not."

"I promise not to hurt you."

"You said that last time. As you recall, you broke my leg."

"Well, you should have blocked that blow."

"I did, but my quarterstaff snapped."

"Your new staff is reinforced by dwarven steel," Arangoli noted.

"I'll admit that this staff is unlikely to break, but my bones remain wary and they prefer to stay intact."

Arangoli sighed. "Fine."

The sun peered through a break in the clouds and shone down on the barge, giving its passengers a brief bit of warmth as the barge rounded a bend in the river. The two long time companions stood quiet, staring out over the railing.

Trees with freshly sprouted leaves lined the riverbank while reeds thrust up from the water near the shoreline. The river's surface appeared relatively calm, but its current was sufficient to keep the barge moving at a pace thrice as fast as walking. For that alone, it was preferable to traveling on foot, as they had during the first leg of their journey.

After departing from Ra'Tahal, a half day of walking brought them to Castor's Landing, some fifteen miles downriver. The next morning, they boarded a barge loaded with goods bound for Bard's Bay. Their passage had been arranged by Korrigan, including meals and three cabins while the ship's crew occupied the fourth. Yet, two restful nights sandwiched between restless days trapped aboard the small craft had

Arangoli longing to reach Bard's Bay. Although the river's current carried them forward, the craft headed into the wind and made it seem as if the elements themselves were battling against them.

Squinting at the wind, Pazacar asked, "What do you think happened in Talastar?"

"Hmm." Arangoli scratched his cheek. "I hadn't given it too much thought." Dwelling on puzzles was not in his nature. Pazacar, on the other hand, was drawn to such conundrums.

"I have," Pazacar said.

"And?"

"If the story told by the messenger is true, Something chased the Drow from the city."

"What makes you say that?"

"The shops were stripped of wares, yet there were no bodies. If they had died there, where are the corpses?"

"What of the destroyed castle?"

The lean dwarf shrugged. "My guess is that either the enemy that drove the Drow out demolished the castle, or the Drow did it themselves."

"Why would they do that?"

"Maybe so the enemy could not take it for themselves. Maybe as a way to trick the enemy into believing that something had happened to the Drow. Or, maybe, it was a trap set to kill anyone who entered. Who knows what lies beneath all that rubble?"

"Good point."

"Two questions remain unanswered."

"What questions?" Arangoli knew that Pazacar was going to share whether he asked or not, but he thought it good manners to ask first.

"What or who posed a great enough threat for the Drow to abandon their sacred city?"

"And the other?"

"Where did they go?"

68

Where. That was the question Arangoli needed answering. "Wherever that is, we should find our people."

"And until we reach Talastar, we are unlikely to uncover any clues that might answer either question."

The barge eased around another point, the view expanded as the river met the bay, and the first signs of humanity appeared.

Rows of docks thrust out from the east bank where the river met the seawater. Warehouses and shops stood over the shoreline. The rooftops of a seaside city covered the gentle hillside beyond the waterfront. A gravel road ran parallel to the shoreline. Uphill streets intersected with that road. In the distance, a portion of the harbor was visible around the bend. Much of the harbor was obscured by a two-story-tall wall of stone that began across from a point jutting out into the water just beyond the last riverside dock.

"Bard's Bay." Although they had a great distance yet to travel, Arangoli was thankful to reach their first destination.

Pazacar pointed toward an island rising from the center of the bay. "Look at what happened to the Carcera."

A blocky tower surrounded by ramparts stood upon the island. A single dock and stairs carved into a steep hillside were visible from Arangoli's vantage point. The gate at the top of the stairs stood open, and much of the tower had turned black.

Arangoli realized the cause of the charred stone. "There was a fire."

"The gate is broken off, and the place appears abandoned."

"You sound sad. I thought you hated that place."

"Oh, my stay at the Carcera was one I'd not like to repeat. However, the prison held many criminals. Some were imprisoned unfairly, as we Head Thumpers were. Most, however, were the worst of human, elf, and dwarf societies. There were hundreds of them. If the prison is vacant, where did they go?"

Arangoli grunted. "I don't know, nor do I care. We have a mission and must not get distracted this time."

Pazacar arched a brow. "Do you truly believe we can avoid all distractions?"

"No, but if we do not try, they will soon consume our attention, and we will forget what we are about."

The barge angled toward the nearest dock. Made of wooden boards, the dock stuck eighty feet out into the river and was ideally suited for the barge.

When they drew near shore, the crew thrust their poles down into the water and used them to guide the nose of the craft. With one hand on the tiller and the other pointing, the captain shouted orders from the small cockpit above the cabins. Mere moments passed before the barge bumped against the dock and the crew began to secure the lines.

Arangoli stepped back from the rail. "It's time to stir the others. I'll stop by the starboard cabin. You poke your head into the port side cabins. Tell everyone to gather their things and meet on shore."

"Aye, Goli."

While Pazacar headed down one side of the craft, Arangoli took the other. As he reached the door to his cabin, Captain Darrigar, a bald dwarf with a bushy brown beard, came around the corner.

"Captain Arangoli! I was hoping I might see you before you are off." Darrigar extended his hand.

Arangoli clasped the other dwarf's forearm. "Thank you for providing passage to Bard's Bay. We would have drinks with you tonight if not for the orders from King Korrigan."

"I understand. Whatever your quest, I wish you luck. I suspect that anyone who gets in your way will need it threefold."

"Ha!" Arangoli clapped the man on the back. "Well said."

A cluster of ten men came down the dock. All were armed, some with swords, others with cudgels. Two more stood on shore holding loaded crossbows. The men wore mismatched armor and clothing, as if they had scrounged up anything available regardless of its color or fit. A strip of red cloth was tied to the upper arm of each one of them.

"Excuse me," Darrigar said. "I need to see what this is about."

Turning to the door, Arangoli opened it and was greeted by a rumbling snore. He stopped between the two sets of bunks, spread his arms wide, and slapped his palms together. The clap amid the quiet was akin to thunder in the dead of night. Both Gortch and Rax sat up in a lurch, the latter striking his head on the low ceiling above his bunk.

"Ouch!" Rax held a hand to his forehead.

Gortch blinked and groaned. "What'd you do that fer?"

"We landed in Bard's Bay. Unless you prefer to help Captain Darrigar row this thing upriver to Castor's Landing, I need you up and on shore in two minutes. So, gather your things and get moving."

The big dwarf turned and lowered his feet to the floor before rubbing his eyes. "One of these days, Goli, I am going to make you sorry. It's unwise to mess with a fat dwarf's sleep."

"As my father once said, I wouldn't know wisdom if it was pounded into me."

Arangoli bent and snatched the weapon harness from beneath his bunk before sliding it over his head and shoulder. With his war hammer on his back, he retrieved his pack, slung it over one shoulder, and headed out the door.

Darrigar and two crew members stood on the dock, in discussion with one of the men. Nine toughs wearing red armbands stood further down the dock, those with cudgels holding them ready. The conversation appeared heated, which caused Arangoli to frown.

He walked along the rail, stepped through the opening, and onto the dock. "What is this?"

Darrigar turned toward Arangoli. "These men claim to own the riverside docks. They demand five gold pieces in order for us to sell our wares in the city."

"Five? That is robbery."

The man standing beside Darrigar said, "The price is the price. Deal with it or leave." He stood more than a head taller than Arangoli, who was tall for his kind. The man's head and face were covered in stubble. A nasty purple scar ran across his thick, exposed bicep. He wore a longsword on one hip, tan trousers tucked into his boots, and a brown, leather jerkin that left his arms exposed.

"And who are you?" Arangoli asked.

"They call me Scourge. I am captain of the Southside Blades and the right hand of Lokix."

"Who the blazes is Lokix?"

Scourge sneered. "Someone you don't want to meet."

"What does any of this have to do with us selling wares in your city? Clan Tahal has been doing business in Bard's Bay since it was no more than a tiny seaside village."

"Things have changed in Bard's Bay." He pointed toward the island. "The Carcera is no more, nor is the corrupted man who controlled the city. The Blades rule the riverfront and the docks. If you wish to unload your wares, you will pay. Should you try anything, you will die."

Anyone close to Arangoli knew that he could not back down from a challenge. He reached over his shoulder, pulled his war hammer from its harness, and held it across his body. "My name is Arangoli. This is my weapon, Tremor. Have you heard of me?"

The man snorted. "No. Why?"

"That is only because no man, elf, dwarf or monster I have faced in battle is alive to repeat it."

Scourge laughed. "Is that supposed to scare me?" He gestured. "You are vastly outnumbered. Try anything, and you will be the one no longer around to repeat names."

"Is that so?" A deep breath later, Arangoli shouted. "Head Thumpers!"

Dwarves began to emerge from the barge cabins. In moments, ten armed dwarven warriors stood on the barge's deck.

"Who is outnumbered now?" Arangoli grinned.

The man turned, cupped his hands to his mouth, and bellowed, "Southside Blades to arms!"

Men, each appearing rougher than the last, poured out from a warehouse. Like the other toughs, a red band was tied to their upper arms. In moments, a full two dozen armed men stood on the shore, in addition to the eight lined up on the dock.

Scourge turned to Arangoli. "Who is outnumbered now?"

Arangoli shook his head. "I think your math is wrong."

"What? We exceed thirty men. You have no more than a dozen."

"That might be, but each of my warriors is worth three of yours, and that doesn't even include me."

"I am through arguing, you blazing, smart mouthed runt." Scourge grimaced, stepped up to Arangoli, and thrust a finger into his chest. "Leave..."

The man's eyes bulged in pain when Arangoli grabbed his finger and snapped it backward with a sickening crack. Arangoli then drove his hammer into the man's stomach. A cry of pain escaped just before the hammer struck. A thump resounded when the enchanted weapon released its spell, launching the man backward and into his crew. Gang members stumbled into one another, knocking two of them off the dock and into the water. Chaos erupted.

CHAPTER 9
UNNECESSARY RISK

Immediately after delivering the blow to Scourge's stomach, Arangoli dropped to one knee and ducked his head. Two crossbow bolts sailed past, one of them striking a barge crewmember in the arm.

The Head Thumpers responded. Eight of the dwarves leapt over the railing to land onto the dock while Rax, with his short bow ready, raised it and loosed. The arrow plunged into the chest of a man holding a crossbow. The dwarven warriors charged down the dock, toward the enemy's main force.

Arangoli, still on the dock with Scourge and his men between him and shore, burst forward with a roar. His hammer came around and struck a man attempting to draw his sword. The hammer thumped, shattering bones as it collided with an upper arm. The force of the blow drove the man sideways into his companions. Several Southside Blades stumbled and two more fell into the water.

A sword thrust out from the group, forcing Arangoli to twist to avoid being skewered. The next thrust, he blocked with his hammer. The sword careened off the hammer shaft, its path redirected into the arm of a man swinging a cudgel. Arangoli drove his heel into the knee of the nearest swordsman, sending him into the path of a gauntlet-covered, meaty fist thrown by someone other than Arangoli. The punch struck the man in the temple, snapping his head to the side. He lost balance and fell into the water.

Arangoli backed from the enemies and spied Gortch at his side. "Thanks."

Gortch pulled his spiked mace from the loop on his hip and held it ready. "I wasn't about you let you have all of the fun."

Scourge climbed to his feet while his four remaining companions held their weapons ready. "Now you die, you bearded runt."

"Come and get me," Arangoli growled.

The man glanced from side to side. "Jordy, Newt, Cash, Torv, ready yourselves. We are five against their two. If we strike at the same time, they cannot stop us."

Beneath his breath, Arangoli whispered, "Don't move."

Before Gortch could reply, he darted forward with his hammer raised high. As expected, the human enemies stepped backward while Tremor crashed down. A thump released from the weapon caused the entire dock to quake. The board struck by the hammer folded in a spray of splinters, leaving a one-foot gap across the width of the dock.

"Attack!" Scrouge came forward with his sword before him.

Anticipating as much, Arangoli backed away and held his hammer ready.

With Scourge in the lead, the five swordsmen advanced, stepped over the gap, and attacked.

Arangoli leapt backward, out of the reach of their sword thrusts, striking the tips of three swords with his hammer. Clangs resounded and two of the men dropped their weapons. Continuing the momentum of his swing, Arangoli ducked low and swept his foot out as he came around. The two disarmed men both stepped backward, right into the gap. Cries of surprise and pain rang out as they fell. Arangoli's boot caught Scourge by the heel, hooking it and sending him off balance. The man landed on his back with an "Oof."

Gortch bellowed and charged, his spiked mace coming around as he met the last two standing enemies. The men attempted to block the attack, but the mace and the power of the dwarf wielding it crashed through the swords, knocking one aside and sending the other spinning off into the water. The big dwarf continued his charge and bowled the two men over. One stepped into the gap and fell, the force of the motion breaking the leg stuck through the dock. The other went flying into the water after his fallen sword.

Scrouge rolled and rose to his feet with a scowl. Ready to be done with the fight, Arangoli attacked. His hammer smashed into the man's face with enough force to launch him a dozen feet down the dock. He landed, rolled once, and lay still, his nose smashed flat and his face bloodied.

On the shore, the battle raged with eight Head Thumpers in a cluster, fighting off a force twice as large. The dwarves used swords, axes, and shields to block the tentative strikes while Pazacar's quarterstaff twirled with fury, daring any enemy to come too close. Downed men lay on the ground nearby, more than one with arrows sticking out from their bodies.

Rax, out of arrows, slid his bow over his shoulder, climbed onto the barge rail, and hopped onto the dock. Two injured toughs lay on the dock, both choosing to roll off and into the river upon seeing Arangoli and Gortch coming toward them.

"Ready with that rapier?" Arangoli asked as he approached Rax.

The lean dwarf drew his weapon, waved it with a rapid slash, and bowed. "At your service, Captain."

"Ha! Right then." When Arangoli reached him, Rax fell in line and began walking to his right side.

To the left, Gortch tapped his mace into the thick, leather gauntlet on his other hand. "Let's end this."

They stepped off the dock and burst into a charge, coming in behind the enemies surrounding the other Head Thumpers. The blindside onslaught was brutally effective.

The hammer crushed the spine of one enemy. The mace cracked the skull of another. A rapier thrust skewered a gang member. Other humans spun toward the new threat, which was a fatal mistake. The dwarves in the center, no longer surrounded, attacked. Blades of all sorts sliced through the enemy gang members, joined by the strikes of a quarterstaff. Cries rang out. Blood sprayed through the air. Corpses soon littered the ground. And just like that, the fight was over.

Turning slowly, Arangoli sought out another enemy. None remained standing. Of those on the ground, a few moaned in pain but most lay still. Those in the water swam toward a neighboring dock, all save one, who headed toward shore. Arangoli slid his war hammer back into the harness on his back and set off in that direction. The man crawled onto land, his clothes dripping, his head sagging as he gasped for air.

Arangoli grabbed a handful of the man's soaking wet tunic, lifted his upper body off the ground, and dragged him a few strides.

"Let me go!" The man exclaimed.

With a forward push, Arangoli did just that. The man flew another few feet before landing on his hands and stomach. Setting the toe of his boot to the man's midriff, Arangoli flipped him over. He appeared no older than mid-twenties. His breeches were torn at the shin, the white of bone sticking through them. The area was stained with crimson.

"Please, don't kill me," The man pleaded, his face twisted in agony.

"What's your name?"

"Jordy."

"Ah. My name is Arangoli. Perhaps you have heard of me."

"No." Jordy winced. "Should I have?"

"I suppose not." While Arangoli preferred to avoid the adoration of his own people, he also felt slighted that his name was not more widely known. He didn't care that it didn't make sense. It was just how he felt. "Why did Scourge try to squeeze us for gold?"

"Those are the rules."

"Who makes the rules?"

"Our boss. Lokix. He runs the Southside Blades."

"I see." Arangoli looked around. "Where are the city guards?"

"There are no more guards."

"What about Commander Kaden."

"Dead."

The news caused Arangoli's brows to rise. "Who rules the city, then?"

"We do."

"The Southside Blades?'

"Yes, along with two other crews."

"I see." Arangoli rubbed his jaw. "Does this have to do with what happened to the Carcera?"

"We killed the prison guards and set the building ablaze. I'll never go back."

The gears turned and clicked into place. "I see." He glanced toward Pazacar, who stood a few strides away. "We did this to the city, didn't we?" As the smartest in their crew, Arangoli frequently asked such things of Pazacar.

"It appears so."

"As I feared." He looked down at the sopping wet man. "What of the harbor?

"My leg. It hurts," the man moaned.

"Yeah. It looks bad. I wonder how it would feel if I stomped on it a bit."

"No!" Jordy thrust his palms up toward Arangoli. "Please. Don't." The last came out as a whimper.

"I won't, so long as you answer my questions."

"Fine. You asked about the harbor?"

"Will we run into more of your gang there?"

"No. Creskin's Crew controls the harbor. They dress in black."

"And they demand gold in order to use the port?"

"Yes."

"So, Kaden is dead. There are no city guards. And criminals now run the city?"

Jordy sighed in exasperation. "Isn't that what I just told you?"

"Huh." Arangoli grunted and turned toward his crew. "Our plans have changed. Sorry, but a hot meal will have to wait. Gather your things. We are heading straight for the harbor to find a ship bound for Sea Gate." He then remembered another thing Korrigan suggested. "Let's also try to avoid any unnecessary fights, per King Korrigan's command."

Gortch arched his heavy brow. "Like the one we just finished?"

"Yeah."

"You were the one who started the fight," Gortch noted.

"I realize that."

"Good." The big dwarf grinned. "I just wanted to be sure you knew who to blame when this gets back to Korrigan."

"Why would it get back to Korrigan?"

Gortch pointed toward the river. The barge was already a hundred feet out into the water with the crew rowing hard, heading upstream.

Arangoli stomped onto and along the dock. He cupped his hands to his mouth and shouted. "Darrigar! Where are you going? We dealt with the gang! You won't have to pay!"

The captain yelled back, "Best of luck to you, Goli. We are finished here."

Without a doubt, Darrigar would report what happened upon his return to Castor's Landing. Word would soon reach Ra'Tahal, and the truth would be twisted and embellished until the entire clan was reciting how Arangoli the Fierce slayed fifty armed men all by himself.

Shoulders slumping, Arangoli sighed and walked back toward shore to join his crew. They needed to find a ship and get out of Bard's Bay before any more trouble found them.

Once Arangoli was in the lead, the other ten dwarves followed him along the waterfront road. They passed the ferry station, which sat empty, and just afterward, came to where the city's outer wall began. Across from the wall was a point jutting a few hundred feet into the bay, creating a natural break between the bay and the river.

Pazacar, walking alongside of Arangoli said, "I can't blame Darrigar."

Still bothered by the turn of events, Arangoli argued, "But we fought Scourge and his gang so he wouldn't have to pay the gold."

"Let's be honest, Goli. You took Scourge on because you don't like bullies."

It was a well-known fact among Arangoli's team. "Fair enough."

"However, if you were listening, those men were part of a larger gang. What do you think would happen to Darrigar if he remained here when word reached this Lokix character?"

Arangoli frowned. "I hadn't considered that." He reflected on the question briefly before coming to an obvious conclusion. "If I were Lokix, I would send more men to secure the waterfront and would make an example of whoever crossed me."

"And if we had departed Bard's Bay while Darrigar and his barge remained to find a buyer for his goods?"

Realizing the truth, Arangoli sighed. "Then the barge captain and his crew would be the targets."

"That was my thought as well."

"Well, it's too late now."

The road turned east as it continued to run parallel to the wall. The harbor came into view. Four ships were in port, two moored along each of the two piers. Dockworkers busily unloaded the crafts, stacking crates, barrels, and sacks into wagons. Clusters of men in black monitored the activity. A dozen warehouses of varying sizes waited across from the piers, outside the city wall.

"The man I interrogated mentioned men in black," Arangoli noted.

"Yes. They report to Creskin," Pazacar said in agreement. "He is a nasty bloke and one I would think twice before crossing."

"You know him?"

"He ran a gang inside the Carcera. I never met the man, but I have seen him. He stands close to seven feet tall and cuts an imposing figure. Worse, he is a ruthless dog who reportedly enjoys violence as much as he loves gold."

"Sounds like the type who needs a good whooping to set his mind straight."

"Goli..."

"Don't worry." Arangoli waved him off. "I'll only fight if we are attacked first. Right now, I just want out of this place." He angled down toward the nearest pier. "Let's find a ship."

A gentle downslope brought them to the foot of the pier, where a group of four toughs stood, watching their approach. Two were men, one a woman, and the fourth a male Drow. All were armed and wearing scowls. Arangoli gave them a nod and continued past. He marched along the pier while surveying the two ships. Both had three masts, but one was nearly twice the width of the other. The wide one had a quarterdeck in the back and a forecastle rising at the front while the lean one had a flat bow. Between them, he preferred the smaller craft, judging it to be the faster of the two. The name Sunstreak was painted on the ship's stern, eliciting the impression that reinforced his assumption. When he spied a dwarf in a red coat standing on the quarterdeck, his decision was made.

A man carrying a crate emerged from the ship's hold, crossed the plank to the pier, and slid the crate into the wagon bed. As the man turned back toward the plank, Arangoli shouted for his attention.

"Ho!"

The man turned toward him. He stood six feet tall with an athletic build. The man lifted a wide-brimmed hat from his head, wiped the sweat from his brow, and replied. "Yes?"

"Greetings. I am seeking someone. "Can you tell me who captains this ship?"

"A dwarf named Kasgan. Do you know him?"

"Kasgan! He is my cousin," Arangoli lied. "Will he be disembarking soon?"

"Sorry. Like the others, he intends to leave the moment his hull is emptied."

"The others?"

The man frowned and glanced toward the Head Thumpers. "Are you new here?"

"We only just arrived." That much was true.

"Ah. Makes sense, otherwise you'd know that nobody stays in port anymore. As it stands, it is difficult to get ships to deliver goods here in the first place."

"Is that because of the gangs?"

The man cast a nervous glance toward the cluster of men in black, standing just a dozen strides away. He whispered, "This city is being held hostage. If I were you, I would leave and never come back."

"I may just do that." He approached the man and clapped a hand on his back. "Thanks for the information. If you don't mind, my companions and I will help you load your wagon."

"I can't afford to pay you."

"No payment needed. Consider it a friendly gesture in times when friends are needed."

The man grinned. "In that case, my name is Dennard."

"Nice to meet you, Dennard. You can call me Goli."

"There are thirty crates in all. With this many hands, it should go quickly."

As the man crossed the plank, Arangoli waved to his crew. "Come along. Let's get this ship unloaded."

He marched across the plank and into the shadowy hull, where he was met by a pair of sailors, one stout and bald with a goatee on his round face, the other tall and lean with long, greasy hair tied in a tail. The short one frowned and grabbed Dennard by the shoulder, stopping him.

"Who is this?"

"These dwarves agreed to help me unload. The faster I finish, the sooner you can push off."

"Huh," the sailor grunted. "That sounds alright, I guess. Just keep to the goods we agreed upon."

"Right." Dennard turned and pointed to a stack of crates along the port side of the cargo hold. "These are the crates we are to unload."

Arangoli directed the Head Thumpers toward the crates. The dwarves followed Dennard, each lifting a crate before heading back out the door. Gortch stopped beside Arangoli, who watched as if he were the job foreman.

"What are you doing?" Gortch asked.

Arangoli whispered, "Distract the sailors while I head above deck."

"Alright."

"Tell the others to come back on board, even after they are finished unloading the crates. Don't let the sailors stop you."

Gortch clenched his gauntlet-covered fist and grinned. "Got it."

The two sailors intently monitored the crates. Considering them distracted, Arangoli stepped back into the shadows and headed toward a ladder at the rear of the hold. The trapdoor at the top stood open with sunlight coming through. He climbed up and stepped on deck, where three sailors stood in a cluster, having a quiet conversation. None were looking in his direction, so he made straight for the quarterdeck where the dwarf in the red coat stood, reading a scroll. When Arangoli climbed the quarterdeck stairs, the dwarf looked up from his reading. His auburn beard was tied in a single, long braid while a wide brimmed black hat shadowed his face.

The dwarf scrutinized Arangoli from head to toe. "Who are you?"

"My name is Arangoli."

"Arangoli Handshaw?" the dwarf asked with arched brows.

The mention of his last name drew a smile. "That's me. Are you Captain Kasgan?"

"I am."

"I assume you are from Clan Argent?"

"Just as you are from Clan Tahal."

"Aye."

Kasgan glanced toward the cluster of men in black on the dock below. "The real question is, what are you doing on my ship?"

"My crew and I require passage to Sea Gate."

"I am bound for Hooked Point."

"Your plans could change. I have coin and could make it worth the effort."

The dwarf narrowed his eyes. "Sea Gate is all the way across the Inner Sea, and the area is dangerous. I will pass."

"Name your price."

Kasgan shook his head. "I told you..."

Arangoli pulled his war hammer over his shoulder. "In that case, I am commandeering your ship."

"What?"

"You have heard my name before."

"I said as much, didn't I?"

"And my reputation?"

"You are a warrior."

"As are my ten companions."

"The Head Thumpers."

Across the deck, dwarves began to climb out of the trapdoor.

"Here they come, now."

Kasgan crossed his arms over his thick chest. "Are you threatening me?"

"Only if you don't agree to take us to Sea Gate."

"This is coercion."

Arangoli shrugged. "Call it what you like, but my mission is important and I will not be denied."

The captain glared at him. "Fine, but I want to be paid."

"But you said..."

"I know what I said," Kasgan snapped.

"Very well. How much?"

The ship captain narrowed his eyes. "Two gold pieces."

"And you'll feed us?"

"You said there are eleven of you?"

"One eats like two dwarves, so you may as well assume twelve."

"I can make that work."

Arangoli held out a hand. "Done."

Kasgan reached out and they shook, but he did not appear happy.

"What's wrong?" Arangoli asked.

"You agreed too easily." Kasgan grimaced. "I should have asked for more."

"Ha!" Arangoli laughed. "Perhaps you'll get the chance to earn more before we are done."

"Now, if you will excuse me, I need to address my crew and set sail."

Kasgan descended and crossed the deck, approaching his crew members, who appeared confused by the presence of the dwarves gathered on the ship.

Satisfied that he had secured passage across the Inner Sea, Arangoli leaned back against the rail and smiled. The ship captain may not have cared for his methods, but there would be plenty of chances to win him over by the time they reached Sea Gate. The next part of his plan relied on it.

CHAPTER 10
COURTING TROUBLE

Masked by darkness, Revita Shalaan gripped a stone jutting up from the wall above her, found another for the toe of her boot, and climbed up. The process continued as she passed a second story window, reached the eave, and pulled herself up onto a moonlit rooftop. Moving at a crouch, she scurried across the roof and slowed as she came to the opposite edge, where she peered down.

A courtyard waited below, illuminated by eight torches along the perimeter. Across the courtyard, a heavy wooden door filled an archway large enough for a wagon. The three wagons parked in the courtyard were empty and horseless. At the hub of the circle the wagons formed was a bubbling fountain. Six stable doors, all closed, the interior of each thick with shadow, stood along the far side of the courtyard. The low hum of chatter and warm, flickering light came from an open doorway across from the stables. The balcony above the doorway stood empty, the pair of doors leading to it closed with only darkness visible through the glass panes.

Revita crept along the roof, rounded a corner, and stopped above the balcony. With practiced ease, she slid over the edge of the roof while gripping the eave. Arms stretched above her, she dangled over the balcony, swung a foot onto the marble railing, and let go. Silently, she climbed from the rail to the balcony and approached the door. A gentle turn of the handle later, she eased the door open and peered inside.

A room twenty feet long and just as wide was dimly illuminated by the moonlight and torches in the courtyard. Snores and the gentle wheeze of the men sleeping in the room greeted her. She counted four beds, all occupied.

Silent footsteps carried her across the room, where she opened another door. Amber torchlight bled in while she quietly slid out and pulled the door closed. The corridor stood empty, illuminated by a torch near its center. The murmurs of quiet conversation came from her right. Preferring to avoid the inhabitants who were awake, she crept in the other direction and stopped outside another closed door. A gentle turn of the knob proved it to be unlocked. The door swung open, and she peered into a dark room. Like the last, she counted four beds, all occupied.

Following the hallway, she rounded a corner and came upon more rooms with their doors closed. She tried them all in turn and found most rooms occupied, with only a handful of beds empty. When she reached the corridor's far end, she descended a staircase that brought her to a kitchen illuminated by a single candelabra. The room was a mess with sacks and crates of food stacked along one wall while pans, pots, bowls, and utensils lay strewn across the countertops. The oven was dark and cold. She crossed the room and opened a door to peer into a dining room illuminated by moonbeams streaming through a series of narrow windows. The room consisted only of a dozen empty chairs surrounding a long table made of dark wood. Another closed door waited on the far end of the room. She reached the door and eased it open. Beyond was a moonlit parlor with a wall of barren shelves to one side. On the other side, among four chairs, sat a round table, with two empty bottles and a dozen cups on it. A corridor waited at the far end of the room.

Revita entered the dark hallway and came to a door, where she paused to listen with her ear against it. When she heard nothing, she opened the door a crack. Inside was a single, four poster bed, occupied by a large person. Immediately, she knew who slept in that bed. Lokix. Her hand went to the blade on her hip, her fingers caressing it while she weighed her options. The man deserved a slit throat, and while the act might create a stir amid his crew for a brief time, someone else would inevitably replace him, and nothing would change apart from the one who leads them. A voice inside her head whispered *you promised Vic that you would not court trouble*. Stifling a sigh, she pulled the door closed and continued down the corridor.

When she rounded the corner, she found light coming from ahead. Hushed male voices came to her as murmurs. She advanced, opened two more doorways, and found additional beds, some occupied by sleeping men. When she reached the last doorway, this one standing open, she took care to remain in the shadows. Beyond was a sitting room illuminated by a chandelier with two dozen candles burning. Six men sat around a table below the chandelier, playing cards. A pile of silver and copper coins rested in the middle of the table.

"Your coin is mine again," said one man as he laid his cards on the table.

"Blasted!" Another man slammed his cards down.

A third one snorted. "You are a lucky arse, Ulvar."

The others dropped their cards on the table and swore in frustration. The winner swept the coins toward himself.

A tall man with a lean build rose to his feet. "I've lost enough for tonight. Come on, Bohan. It's time to make our rounds." The man patted the rapier on his hip as he said the last bit.

"Aw, alright," groaned a man with heavy shoulders, thick arms, and a sizable paunch. When the man stood, he matched the lean one in height but carried twice the weight.

"Get up, Jessel." The lean man poked one of the seated men.

"Why me?"

"Since you're out of coin, you can let us out the gate. Just don't fall asleep on us. If we can't get back in, I swear I'll pour syrup in your smallclothes and dump a colony of fire ants down them."

The comment stirred a hearty round of laughter.

The three men came straight toward Revita, who backed through a doorway into a dark bedroom. She stood rock still as the men walked by, strolled out the open courtyard door, and faded into the night.

That was close. In truth, she had experienced many near discovery moments in her profession, some coming far closer to disaster. Yet, she now had the information she came seeking. What to do with it, she had yet to determine.

She snuck across the corridor and ducked into the staircase leading to the second floor.

～

VICTUS CARPENTER STOOD IN A DOORWAY, huddled in darkness. The moon painted the building across the street in pale light while shadows covered the narrow drive and lurked in every recess. Somewhere nearby, a dog barked. Relentlessly. He strained to listen beyond the steady yapping. *Come on, Vita*, he urged silently. The waiting left his mind too much time to wander, to worry, and to conjure up unsavory reasons for her delay.

Footsteps briefly proceeded a pair of silhouettes heading in his direction. One had a bulky frame, the other was tall and lean. Both were too big to be female. To avoid notice, Vic backed a step. The metal head of the mattock on his back clanged against the window in the door. He froze. So did the two shadowy strangers. A long, tense beat of silence followed.

Light flared as the lean stranger unshuttered a lantern. The light, aimed right at Vic, forced him to squint.

"Whaz going on here?" A deep voice intoned.

"Looks like a thief. I bet he intended to rob us," another male voice replied.

"No," Vic shook his head. "I was just waiting for someone."

"Strange place to wait for someone, here in a dark alley."

The first voice added, "And right across from our hideout." The man released an "Oof. What'd you do that fer?"

"It's a hideout, you dolt," the other chided harshly. "It's supposed to be a secret."

"Oh. Yeah."

A sigh followed. "Now, we have to make sure this thief doesn't tell anyone."

"Wait," Vic said. "I am no thief. I won't tell anyone. I don't even know who you are." In truth, with the light in his eyes, he could not even see the men's faces. As for not being a thief...that was not entirely true.

The burly man pulled out a club and took a step closer. He wound back, preparing for a devastating blow.

Vic, with his arm already raised to shield his eyes, reached over his shoulder, gripped the mattock jutting above it, and pulled the weapon free in one motion. The mattock handle came down hard, – striking the big man's hand, and sending the club clattering to the street.

"Argh!" The man bellowed as he gripped his wrist.

Without pause, Vic flipped the mattock and thrust the weapon's head into the man's significant gut, eliciting a heavy grunt. The attacker stumbled backward, tripped, and fell to the ground.

"We were only going to beat you silly." The man holding the lantern growled. "Now, you die."

With his free hand, the thin man drew a rapier and held it before him. Focused on the deadly blade, Vic stood ready. The man thrust. Vic twisted. The rapier tip slid past him and tore through his cloak. The attacker drew back and slashed, forcing Vic to urgently raise his mattock. The blade clanged off the pick head.

If the fight continued with Vic only defending himself, he was certain to be skewered, so he attacked.

With a backhand swing, Vic forced the man to jump backward. He followed with a kick aimed for the man's sword hand, but the man was too quick jerking his arm and blade back. The motion left his other side open and Vic swung. The pick end of the mattock shot into the open shutter of the lantern, tearing the lantern from the enemy's grip and launching it down the street. The light died out and gloom rushed in.

With his eyes not yet able to adjust after being blinded by the lantern light, Vic could not see the enemy blade, so he dove to one side. The rapier clanged off the wall right where Vic had last stood. Rolling to one knee, Vic launched a wide, sweeping strike as his attacker did the same. The mattock point bit into the enemy's calf as the rapier swept over Vic's head, close enough to cut through his hair. Electricity crackled from the mattock, arcing up and down the enemy's leg. The attacker cried out, dropped his blade, and collapsed.

A meaty fist flashed in the moonlight, giving Vic just enough notice to tilt his head. The blow glanced off his cheek and sent him falling on his side.

The burly enemy stood over him and raised a foot, prepared to stomp Vic's brains all over the street. Before the heavy boot could fall, a knife flashed and buried in the man's neck. He staggered back with one hand around his throat, his eyes wide in shock. The man fell against the moonlit wall, slid down it, and fell still.

A lithe, shapely silhouette strode toward Vic and stood over him. "I thought you were going to wait quietly and not court trouble."

"Vita," Vic sighed. "You took long enough."

"I would say I finished at just the right time. Any later and your face would be far flatter and far less pretty," she quipped while helping him to his feet.

Vic dusted himself off. "I prefer my face to remain as is."

Revita patted his cheek. "So do I."

He bent, gripped his mattock handle, and yanked it free from the downed man's leg. The sparks winked out, and the alleyway plunged into shadow. He looked at the burly body lying against the moonlit wall. "You didn't have to kill him."

"He was going to kill you. Why treat him any differently?"

While true, it still bothered him. "I just…"

The man with the hole in his calf groaned, and Revita squatted beside him. A grunt and a jab later, she sheathed her dagger. Vic did not have to ask what she had done.

When she stood, she held a bolt of red cloth in her hand.

"Why do you have that?"

"This arm band marks them as members of the blades. Grab the other one. We may find them useful at some point."

Rather than argue, he approached the large, dead man, untied the red band from his arm, and shoved it in his coat pocket as he stood.

"Let's go before anyone comes looking for these two," Revita said. "Discovering them dead right outside of their headquarters is bound to make Lokix and his men angry, so it is best if they don't catch us here."

"Agreed."

She led him down the narrow alley, turned at the torchlit corner, and took stairs down to the street below. Together, they crossed the city of Bard's Bay, weapons held ready and eyes furtively searching the darkness for threats. Come morning, the two dead men would be taken to the harbor square and burned along with any others who died that night. Vic had little doubt that there were others. Since early winter, he could not recall a single morning with fewer than four bodies stacked in the pyre.

~

AFTER AN UNEVENTFUL JOURNEY across the city, Vic followed Revita to a building with a broken window and missing door. She paused briefly, looked up and down the vacant street, and ducked inside with him a step behind. They navigated the dark confines, passed a staircase bathed in moonlight coming through a second story window, and stopped outside a door leading beneath the stairs. She opened the door, knelt, and fumbled in the dark. A click resounded, followed by creaking. An even darker opening appeared as a trap door revealed a hole in the floor. Revita slid in and descended a steep staircase.

Vic cast one last glance back toward the open shop door. The street remained empty, for which he was thankful. When he turned back toward the closet, Revita was out of sight, so he followed, pausing to close the trap door on the way down. As he reached the bottom and his boots touched down on the dirt floor, light bloomed.

He turned to find Revita standing beside a lantern, illuminating their simple underground hideout. She removed her black leather coat, exposing a lean yet distinctly female figure wearing a dark blue tunic and brown breeches that hugged her thighs and hips. She pulled a dark blue ribbon from her ponytail and shook her head, causing her raven hair to spill over her shoulders. With coppery skin and large, brown eyes, she looked nothing like anyone from Vic's hometown of Shillings.

"You are so beautiful," he muttered without realizing it.

She smiled, her white teeth a stark contrast to her coppery complexion, somehow doubling her beauty. A single brow arched. "Are you attempting to lure me into your bed?"

"We have shared the same bed since autumn."

Her hips swayed overtly as she approached him to place a hand on his chest. "You say that as if you have not enjoyed our time together."

He gripped her wrist and slid his other hand to the small of her back. "Nothing could be further from the truth."

Her lips met his – warm, soft, and impossible to deny. His heart thumped, his blood heating, but he could not allow her to distract him. Not yet.

With reluctance, Vic pulled away.

"What's wrong?" She asked while staring into his eyes.

"We need to talk first."

She bit her lip and gripped his tunic. "I find it more interesting to talk afterward."

"Revita. This is serious." He rarely used her full first name, choosing to do so when he required her attention. In this case, it worked.

Releasing a sigh, she stepped back and put a hand on one hip. "Fine. Talk."

"Those two men tonight..."

"Deserved what they got. Like the others, they are the dregs of society. Had we left them alive, they would have killed the next person who crossed them."

"Dregs of society? Interesting perspective from a thief."

"I steal for the challenge and target those who can afford it." Revita sneered. "Those bastards pray on the weak and those who struggle to survive." Her tone took on a sharp edge as her anger flared. "They kill without care or cause. I am nothing like them."

"I am sorry. I did not mean..."

She held a palm toward him. "I know. Do not worry. I am angry with them, not you."

He released a deep breath. "That is good to know. There is much to do yet, and your anger has many targets."

"You do realize we could get killed doing this, as it nearly happened tonight."

Despite the truth of her statement, his resolve held firm. "What happened to this city is our fault, Vita. Until we rectify it, I cannot leave. My conscience and honor will not allow it."

When she crossed her arms, he feared she might escalate the argument. Instead, she shook her head. "I can't believe I have saddled myself with someone who would risk his life for honor and expect no payment in return."

He closed the distance and slid a hand onto her hip. "Perhaps it is my sense of honor that drew you to me in the first place."

"Oh, the first draw was your handsome face, followed by your tight little arse." She reached around and pinched him.

"Ouch."

She smiled. "Admit it. You enjoy my advances."

His own smile demanded to be revealed, an urge he could not deny. "I'll admit I enjoy just about everything about you."

"Just about?"

"Well, there is the matter of your knives..."

"My knives saved your arse tonight."

"And I am thankful."

"Perhaps you would care to demonstrate your thanks?"

"Oh, I will." He again had to squash his own urges and hold out just a while longer. "However, let's finish our discussion first."

"What discussion?"

"We were talking about the Southside Blades. What did you find out?"

Revita shrugged. "As we thought, the manor is their headquarters."

"I surmised that when the two toughs attacked me."

"Well, there are two ways in, both barred from the inside, so picking locks is not an option. One is through the manor's front door, the other a drive leading to an interior courtyard."

"How many were inside?"

"I counted twenty-seven sleeping and another sixteen empty beds."

"Was anyone awake?"

"Six of them were playing cards on the main level, including the two who found you in the alley. I snuck out right after they left to patrol the grounds."

Vic did not need to be reminded of those two. "Even after the incident down at the riverfront, their numbers are too high for us to take on directly." Just the previous day, the Southside Blades had come across someone who had refused to bend to their demands. The Blades lost over twenty men in the process. Whoever it was they had crossed, Vic wished he could find and thank them. Rumor said it was a squad of dwarves who left on a ship that very same day.

Revita suggested, "We can wait until they break into small groups and then confront them, as we did with the two tonight."

He frowned. "They confronted me. I was just defending myself. What you suggest is akin to extermination."

"You are the one who demanded we deal with the vermin who run this city."

"I know," Vic sighed. "It would be easier if we did not have to do this alone."

"We could hire help, but that would require gold we don't have." She gave him a naughty smile. "I could steal some gold for us, you know."

He shook his head. "No. Mercenaries are not trustworthy. If all they care about is coin, what prevents them from turning on us if someone else offers more or if our coin runs out."

"So, then what?"

"We cannot be the only people here who wish law and order ruled the streets rather than gangs with clubs, bows, and blades."

"Law and order? This place was a cesspool even when Commander Kaden ran the city."

"That's because Kaden was corrupt and corruption breeds contempt for law."

"Well, that contempt has reached new heights. This city is now too dangerous even for my liking."

Frustration about the situation had Vic clenching his jaw. *Kaden and his guards may have been corrupt, but the criminals now ruling Bard's Bay are far worse.* He then tried another approach. "Perhaps we could leave and recruit help."

"From where?"

"Korrigan said that he owed us for our part in freeing Ra'Tahal..."

She held her forearm up, reminding him of the bracer she wore. "This was our payment, remember. Do you think he still owes us?"

"I suppose not. Maybe a few of his warriors would join us for another reason."

"You would pay the dwarves?"

"I'd rather inspire them. If they fight for a cause they believe in, they will fight harder and loyalty to the cause will hold them fast."

She smirked and shook her head while wrapping her arms around his neck. "You and your ideals. I'd roll my eyes and laugh if I didn't think you were serious."

"I am serious. About this and about you."

"Despite my transgressions?"

"I knew you were a thief the day we met. You steal, cheat, and kill without it tainting your conscience. Yet, I cannot resist your charms."

"We make a fine pair," she purred.

His tone matched hers when he replied, "That, we do."

Their lips met, and this time, Vic allowed the rising heat within him to burn. He held her close, began to kiss her neck, and worked on removing her tunic. Her moans and his heavy breaths joined the thumping of their hearts.

～

REVITA LAY naked with a blanket draped over her body and her head on Vic's bare chest. A candle on the shelf across the room provided the only light in their underground hideout – a single room cellar that had become her latest home. Although she had only just reached her twenty-fifth Beltane, the places she had called home numbered in the dozens with only her previous abode in Greavesport having lasted for more than a year. Her current home was small, windowless, and had a dirt floor, yet she had never been happier.

She was honest enough with herself to admit that Vic's companionship made all the difference, but the independent, survivalist aspect of her railed against the idea of needing someone...anyone else. At the same time, she found herself trying to be the person he perceived her to be, rather than the self-centered, arrogant, and greedy thief persona she had spent a decade developing.

His chest rose and fell to a rhythm that reminded her of a ship on the sea. The thought stirred the memory of her fleeing Greavesport to join Vic, his younger brother, and a trio of dwarves on their way to Bard's Bay. That journey had led to her breaking into an infamous prison to free a larger group of dwarves who called themselves the Head Thumpers. In the process, Revita had decided to release other prisoners with the hope that she and those in her party might escape amid the chaos. She never considered the possible consequences for that decision. *It is my fault that this city is now run by criminals.* Vic was too kind to place the blame on her, but she knew better. Thus, she could not argue when he demanded they remain in the city rather than continue on to Hooked Point as they had originally planned. They needed to see how the Bard's Bay fared in the aftermath of a rather violent coup. The change had been gradual, but as winter turned to spring and spring to summer, the situation had only grown worse.

Three gangs now ruled the city, each claiming a different district. Honest businesses were forced to pay for protection or risk losing everything. Citizens only dared to go out during the day and even then, their pace was rushed and their presence fleeting. Each day, the situation seemed to worsen as the gangs gained new members and added strength. Revita doubted there was a single independent thief, tough, or smuggler remaining in Bard's Bay other than herself. *There are only two of us, and the gangs range from dozens to hundreds of members in each. What can we do against those odds?* That same question troubled her every night. *If only the gangs would fight each other, this would be easier.*

She gasped aloud and raised her head as the idea took hold.

Vic blinked and looked down at her. "What's wrong?"

"What if the Southside Blades picked a fight with Creskin's Crew?"

He snorted. "The Blades are down a third of their members and not even half the size of Creskin's Crew now. To do so would be suicide. Besides, they seem content on controlling the riverfront and the surrounding district."

"That is likely what Creskin believes as well, for now. But what if Lokix tried to expand his control to include the harbor?"

"Creskin would never allow it. Even with reduced traffic, the harbor is the most valuable district in the city."

"Exactly."

He arched a brow. "I sense a scheme. Explain."

She pushed herself up to her knees and grinned. "You and I will take actions that hurt Creskin and we will do it in a way that places blame on Lokix and the Southside Blades. When pushed far enough, Creskin will have to act and will take out Lokix and his men. It will solve one problem while likely reducing his own force in the process."

Vic smiled. "That'll do. What about Torrigan's Toughs?"

"Once Lokix is out of the way, we can do something similar to Torrigan."

"And that would leave us only with whatever remains of Creskin's Crew."

Revita shrugged. "We will figure that out when the time comes."

Longing lit Vic's eyes. "I never realized how sexy a shrug could be until now."

She looked down at her naked body then met his gaze. "Are you ready for another go?"

He grabbed her hands and pulled her toward him. "More than ready."

Their lips met, and they fell into each other's arms.

CHAPTER II

THE SHADOW REALM

Ian turned the page, compelled to keep reading despite the weariness tugging at him. He ignored it. After weeks of pouring through books, seeking anything of interest, he had finally found something that demanded his attention, and he was reluctant to stop until he finished reading. Transfixed on the words before him, the study and the rest of his surroundings may have been a thousand miles away. When a hand clapped on his shoulder, he jerked backward with a yelp, and tipped his chair over. He toppled to the floor and looked up to find Truhan standing over him.

"Have you been reading all night?" The man asked.

"What?" Ian's pulse thumped in his ears like a smith shaping stubborn iron. "Where did you come from?"

Truhan smirked. "That is a question even I cannot answer."

Ian sat up and rubbed his eyes. "What time is it?"

"The sun was rising when I reached the tunnel entrance."

"Oh. No wonder I am so tired." With a groan, Ian climbed to his feet and dusted his robes off.

"So, you were up all night. I suspect you found something notable."

The excitement of sharing his discovery washed away Ian's weariness. He picked up a book off the table and tapped it with his finger.

"After pouring through four books and finding little of interest, I came across a passage in this one. Would you care to hear it?"

Truhan grinned. "I fear you might explode if I said no, so read on."

Leaning in, Ian ran his finger along the text and found the paragraph he thought best to begin. He cleared his throat and began to read aloud.

"In the eighth year of Gahagar's reign, a ball of fire lit up the night sky. The sight drew all of Ra'Tahal's residents outside to gape in awe. The flaming object steadily drew closer until it seemed that it might strike the citadel itself. The massive, roaring fireball hurtled just above the central keep and continued westward before crashing to the ground miles beyond the outer walls of the lower hold. That very night, Gahagar led a squad of his warriors out to investigate.

"They arrived to find burning trees surrounding a crater a hundred feet deep and three times as wide. In the heart of the crater was an object three feet in diameter and glowing like it had just emerged from a forge. They returned the next day to find the object cooled, the surface reflecting the afternoon sun like polished armor. Yet, when they drew near the object, it reacted, heated up, and the glow returned. Day after day, Gahagar and his crew returned to the crash site only to find that time did not alter the behavior of the strange, metal object. Obsessed with this metallic rock that fell from the sky, Gahagar devised a plan to capture it and make it his own.

"His engineers designed an elaborate machine with claws made of metal, attached to winches, chains, and pulleys. They rolled the contraption out to the crash site and used the claws to lift and hold the object while towing it back to the citadel. The king then bade his most gifted metal wrights to melt down the meteor and craft a sword unlike any other the world had ever seen.

"The forging of the sword consumed three long years and claimed the lives of numerous metal wrights. The sword was named the Caelum Edge – the Sky Sword. In Gahagar's eyes, it would be the greatest weapon ever created.

"When the blade was finished, Gahagar attempted to claim it, but his hand was burned when he touched the hilt, for the sword turned to flame. Anyone nearby was forced to back away from its heat. The sword of ages proved impossible to wield, but King Gahagar was nothing if not stubborn.

"Resolute, he used the Paragon to craft armor unlike anything the world had before seen, for the armor was forged of Gahagar's own flesh, making the dwarf king impervious to weapons and resistant to heat. As the only person able to wield the Caelum Edge, Gahagar would one day rule the world."

"Stop," Truhan held up a palm. "I have heard this story before. Everyone knows Gahagar's campaign lasted fifty years before he died mysteriously outside the walls of Talastar."

"But what is the Paragon and how did it turn the king's flesh to armor?"

"I...don't know."

"Well, there is more."

Truhan arched a brow. "Go on."

"With flesh of armor, Gahagar's aging ceased, and with the added longevity came great patience. Before he would even begin his campaign, the great king sought to understand the surrounding lands, cities, and fortresses, so he might know where to focus his efforts. He sent out four teams of explorers to record in a journal what terrain and obstacles they might discover, in addition to the nations, cities, and people who lived there. I was reading the fourth and final of these journals when you startled me."

"I see." Truhan rubbed his jaw. "What did you learn from the journals?"

"Much more exists of the world than I had guessed. While the nations, cities, and castles outlined in the journal are extensive, I have yet to glean anything that strikes alarm."

"In that case, it is time for you to visit the baths. After that, we will eat and then return to the Hall of Divining. It is time to try something new."

~

ONE THOUSAND, seven hundred, and twelve. It was the total number of stairs Ian counted as he, again, followed his master to the Hall of Divining. The two of them ascended in silence until nearing the chamber, when Ian's head began to buzz from the thrum of energy emanating from ahead. The awe Ian had previously felt toward the source of magic had turned into trepidation and anxiety. Although the last visit had opened new possibilities for his magic, the wild, overpowering result of the spell he had tested so close to the source had been nearly disastrous. He was honest enough with himself to acknowledge his fear of what might happen should he use a spell in that chamber again. At the same time, he refused to voice his reluctance to his master, so he repeated an earlier argument with a slightly different approach, as a last, desperate tactic.

"I still don't understand why we must do this. I've barely explored what can be accomplished with energy constructs. There are so many possibilities..."

Truhan stopped just outside the chamber, his silhouette bathed in the glow emanating from the source. To Ian's shock, the man's eyes grew wide with fury. "Stop!" He spoke in a firm tone, his voice deep, commanding, and loud enough to cause Ian to jerk backward. "You are the pupil. I am the master. You will do as I say."

Ian wilted. His gaze dropped to the tunnel floor, and he kneaded one hand with the other. "I...I...am sorry."

When his eyes flicked up to meet Truhan's, the man's expression softened. Truhan closed the gap between them and laid a palm on Ian's shoulder. "Listen, Ian. I have encouraged you to be inquisitive, confident, and independent. All are necessary traits to build upon if you are to be effective outside of these halls. I am unaccustomed to others arguing with me, which is why I reacted as I did." He paused a beat to stare into Ian's eyes. "We do not visit the Hall of Divining on a lark. I only bring you here out of necessity. If I did not, your progress would advance at a far slower pace. A darkness lurks out there, and it will soon touch your world. You must be prepared, or the result could be catastrophic."

"A darkness?"

"You will soon understand." Truhan turned and headed down the tunnel and into the illuminated chamber.

Ian followed, his gaze immediately going to the glowing crystal from the domed cavern. He briefly wondered what would happen if he touched it. *Would the magic overwhelm me, or would it consume me?* One or the other seemed inevitable. The thought caused him to cringe.

Truhan stopped beneath the crystal, reached into his coat pocket, and pulled out a peculiar item. It appeared like a pyramid-shaped chunk of glass.

"What is that?" Ian asked.

"This is quartz."

The comment brought a frown to Ian's face. "But it is so clear."

"It is pure and flawless, cut, and polished, all for a purpose."

"Which is?"

Truhan's smirk returned. "You shall see in short order. Now, sit and prepare your mind."

With legs crossed, Ian sat on the chamber floor. Above him, the crystal pulsed with energy. Its hum whispered and tantalized him with what he might accomplish should he find a way to harness the breadth of its power. The thought sent a shiver down Ian's spine.

Truhan squatted and set the prism down on the chamber floor, directly beneath the crystal, a mere stride away from where Ian sat. The light from the source refracted through the prism and sent ribbons of rainbow-like light in three directions. The man turned the object until one of the multi-colored rays pointed at Ian.

"Stare into the prism, Ian. Allow your mind to drift, to see what might be. Open yourself to the possibilities."

Relaxed, his mind cleared of thought, Ian hummed to himself and slid into a void. In the ether, he floated in the buoyancy of the crystal's song. When he opened himself to the magic, it flooded in, his heart quickening and senses buzzing.

His eyes opened to the prism and the beam of colored light. He relaxed his focus, the image blurring to nothing but colors and light. There, he hovered in a peaceful bubble while magic railed around him like a ship in a storm. The colors began to shift, to churn, to twist. The light swirled, stretched, and expanded, spreading over Ian and wrapping behind him until it blotted out his surroundings. It then began to swirl around him until he sat still in the eye of a tempest. Wind arose from the storm, ruffling Ian's hair and robes, buffeting him until he feared what would happen should he move.

Then, the wind was gone. So was the cavern, the crystal, and Truhan.

Ian found himself in a city made of dark stone. He spun in a slow circle, his gaze sweeping his surroundings as he attempted to get his bearings. The streets were barren, the sky blanketed in gray. The air held the chill of late autumn, forcing Ian to hug himself for warmth.

"Where am I?" he muttered.

The gentle whistle of the wind provided the only reply.

With a lingering sense of disorientation, Ian crossed the square and entered a narrow street. Doors stood open and swung in the breeze. Beyond diamond-shaped windowpanes and open doorways, empty, shadow-filled rooms lurked. A chill climbed up Ian's spine and triggered a shudder. It felt as if he were being watched although he saw no signs of life. Ian's pace quickened, his head turning left and right, his eyes flicking about as his anxiety heightened. The street followed a gentle curve. As he rounded the bend, he spied open space ahead and made straight for it.

A sprawling plaza waited at the end of the street. The square was empty apart from a single, towering statue of a warrior gripping a spear-like weapon. Across the plaza stood an imposing castle. Ian surveyed the area, his gaze lingering on each street that bordered the plaza. Nothing moved. The city appeared abandoned.

He crossed the plaza and approached the statue for further examination.

The sculpture loomed above him. The surface was blackened with a green sheen, making him believe it was once bronze that had succumbed to the elements over the course of centuries. At first, he thought it in the likeness of a man, but the large, pointed ears and lean frame made it clear that it was not human. A blade the length of the warrior's forearm jutted out from one end of the weapon. It was a design he had seen before, wielded by dark elves.

"Drow," he muttered.

Just saying the word stirred memories of Rysildar and his betrayal against the dwarves of Ra'Tahal. Ian had almost died that day and came even closer to death when he next met Rysildar. Yet, in the end, it was the Drow singer who had died instead of Ian.

Dismissing the memory, he continued toward the open castle gate, passed through it, and paused.

The castle, its wall the same dark, dreary stone as the rest of the city, loomed over him. Its charcoal towers and crenulations appeared like shadowy arms reaching toward the gray sky.

Ian gasped when he saw something flicker in the window of the tallest tower. He stared at the window, watching and waiting for another sign of movement but only saw darkness within. Finally deciding that it had just been his imagination, he shifted his attention to the door of the main keep. It stood open, as if to invite him inside. An inner voice screamed to turn and leave, but Ian ignored it, for his curiosity demanded that he advance. Still, he did so with caution. The building's shadowy interior was even creepier than the streets. He stopped inside the doorway and listened while his eyes adjusted to the dim lighting.

An entrance hall stretched out before him, the far end thick with shadow. Stairwells, doorways, and corridors branched off from the hall while tattered, worn tapestries adorned the walls in between each opening. With timid steps, he began across the hall while peering into each open doorway. Darkness lurked from within each chamber. *What is this place? What happened to the people who lived here?*

"Who are you?" A voice rasped from behind.

Ian' heart leapt into his throat. With a lurch, he spun around, extended his hand, and opened himself up to allow his magic to flow through him. Nothing happened. He then realized why the city had felt so empty and dreary. It wasn't just the lack of life. He felt no magic.

A hooded figure in black robes emerged from the shadows of a stairwell. The robe hem ruffled as the being soundlessly glided across the floor. Terrified and lacking his magic to protect himself, Ian backed away. The robed figure stopped, as did Ian, the gap between them roughly five strides.

"I ask again," the ragged voice said. "Who are you?"

After swallowing the lump in his throat, Ian found his voice. "I am Ian."

"You are human." It was not a question.

"Um...Yes."

"How did you get here?" The creature rasped.

"I am not sure. I don't even know where I am." He glanced at his surroundings. "What is this city?"

"This is no city. It is the mere shadow of a once great citadel." The figure tilted its head. "Throughout history, few have had the ability to enter the shadow realm. To my knowledge, which is considerable, none have been human."

Ian's brow furrowed. "The shadow realm?"

A moment of silence followed before the figure replied. "You truly do not know, do you?"

A shake of his head was Ian's only reply.

"I see." The figure turned back toward the stairwell. "Follow me if you seek answers but be warned, you may not like what you learn."

The stranger faded into the stairwell, leaving Ian alone and torn between his desire to learn more and his concern that the invitation might be a trap. His curiosity, spurred by his preference to avoid being alone in the desolate citadel, won out.

He hurried into the stairwell and began ascending. A turn at the first landing revealed dim light seeping through a doorway on the floor above. When he reached that level, he turned again just as the stranger rounded another landing. Soon, no more than a half dozen treads separated them, but the climb was nowhere near over. Up and up, Ian continued. Six flights up, the doorways he passed were replaced by narrow, arched windows as the only source of light. A dozen additional flights later, the staircase ended before a closed door of black-stained wood.

The robed figure opened the door. The hinges groaned, the sound causing Ian's hair to stand on end. The stranger faded from view while Ian held still, fearing he had made the wrong decision. *I should not be here.* In the marrow of his bones, he knew it was true, for everything about the place felt wrong. Still, he could not turn back. Not when answers were so near.

He climbed the last few stairs, passed through the doorway, and entered a circular chamber filled with oddities. Bizarre contraptions dangled from the vaulted, cone-shaped ceiling. Tables covered in vials, shards of crystal, and thick tomes, most of them lying open, occupied the middle of the room. Cabinets and shelves holding trinkets, tools, and books stood along the walls. Light from the gray skies seeped through windows in four directions. Ian approached the nearest window, peered outside, and realized where he stood.

"We are in the tallest tower."

"Welcome to my parlor."

He turned to face the other person. "I gave you my name. Would you share yours?"

"You may call me Eidolon."

Ian frowned. "That is an Elvish word."

"You speak Elvish?"

"I do."

"And this word means what?"

"It refers to a sort of phantom or the specter of a person."

"So, it does." Eidolon turned and approached a tapestry depicting stars, diagrams, and runes. Lines connected some of the stars to form a pattern Ian had never seen before. "What do you know of prophecy, Ian?"

Having read numerous works referring to prophecy, Ian was familiar enough with the subject to know what it was. At the same time, the mystical nature and inexact references found in the prophecies he had studied left him doubting their validity.

"Prophecy involves predictions of the future. The passages I have read seem to be intentionally vague, so one can mold them to fit events after they occur."

"Ah. A skeptic. Yet, you walk the shadow realm."

"You mentioned the shadow realm before. What is it?"

Eidolon stood at a window and gazed out into the gray. "There are many worlds. Some are distant, others closer than one might ever guess. The shadow realm lies between the waking world and that of dreams."

"I don't understand."

"When you peer into a mirror, what do you see?"

"My own image."

"Is the person in the mirror real?"

"No. It is only a reflection. Everyone knows that."

"The shadow realm is akin to a reflection as well, a reflection of the world of the living but lacking life."

Ian considered the statement before replying. "Is that why this city feels so empty?"

"Yes...and no."

"Now, you are just speaking in riddles." The behavior reminded Ian of Truhan.

"Life is but a series of riddles one must solve." A gaunt, ghostly white hand emerged from Eidolon's robes, turning in a gesture. "Drow inhabited this citadel for millennia, but a darkness recently descended upon the city, forcing the dark elves to flee. Thus, the city feels much the same in the waking world as it does here, the shadow realm."

"A darkness? What darkness?"

"I speak of the same darkness that will soon consume your world."

"What? Is there nothing that can be done?"

"The future has yet to be determined, but the time nears where no alternate fate remains viable."

The ominous statement caused the hair on Ian's arms to stand on end. "Is that why I am here?"

A gnarled, white finger pointed at Ian. "Perhaps. Yet, you say you do not believe in prophecy."

Ian frowned. "What does prophecy have to do with anything?"

"Those who have the gift wander the shadow realm seeking answers. This is where they discover what might be, but knowing how prophecy functions is not necessary. Most often, a foretelling over-whelms those with the ability, leaving them unaware of having touched my realm."

"If I have this ability, I know nothing about it, nor do I know how to use it."

"That is where I can help." Eidolon held up a single finger. "I warn you, should I unlock your ability to see what might be, I cannot reverse the process."

The warning caused Ian to hesitate, but then Eidolon's ominous statement rang in his head. *I speak of the same darkness that will soon consume your world.*

"Do it," Ian said in a voice far firmer than his resolve.

Eidolon glided forward. Even up close, Ian could not see the face hidden in the shadows of his hood. A white, boney hand was lifted and placed against Ian's forehead. The icy cold touch caused Ian to stiffen and gasp. His vision went white, and he staggered backward.

Ian's breath came in gasps. The room spun, causing him to stumble. He reached for the wall and missed. The floor came at him. He landed hard with his forearm stopping his face from striking the stone tiles. There, he lay for a few breaths while his vision returned and pulse settled. When Ian looked up, he and Eidolon were not alone.

Ghostly figures of Drow moved about the chamber only to flicker and fade. Others appeared and slipped away just as rapidly.

Confused, Ian staggered to his feet and gripped the windowsill. When he glanced outside, he saw people in the city – riders on horse-back, warriors gripping weapons, males, females, and children going about their day. All were Drow. Like those in the tower chamber, the people flickered and faded before reappearing in other locations.

"What is happening?" Ian voiced.

"You now see the reflection of possible futures for this city."

"This is prophecy?"

Eidolon laughed. It was an uncomfortable sound. "Not in the least. Prophecy requires focus, which opens the door to possibilities. If you have the gift, your own intuition will guide you and provide the instruction required to avoid an unwanted outcome."

"Unwanted outcome?"

"Yes, such as the end of all life in your world."

Ian could think of nothing worse. "What do I do?"

"I suggest you begin with a specific individual – someone you know well. Picture that person in your mind and fill in the details, their hair, eyes, smile, personality, the way he or she smells...anything that reminds you of that person."

"That sounds easy enough. Then what?"

"Then, you shall see." Eidolon turned and walked to the door.

"Where are you going?"

The mysterious figure paused in the doorway but did not turn as he spoke. "Follow your intuition, Ian. Let it be your guide."

Eidolon glided down the stairs, his black cloak swirling behind him until he was gone.

For a time, Ian stared at the doorway while considering the bizarre encounter. The stranger's last words rang in his head. *Follow your intuition, Ian. Let it be your guide.* With that in mind, he turned away, his gaze sweeping the room. It was quiet and lonely, an eerie echo of the city outside. A longing tugged at Ian, a desire for companionship. Somehow, the dreary solitude of this place was even worse than when he was left alone in his underground home.

"I miss Rina," he muttered.

His mind conjured her image as it often did. Like an artist blindly painting a memorized scene, his imagination filled in the details he had appreciated time and again.

The sun illuminated her golden hair, a dress of green clung to her lean frame, the blue of her eyes sparkled like jewels, and most important of all, there was her smile. Even his memory of her smile lifted his spirits and made his heart sing. Then, something happened.

The world around Ian shifted. The shadowy, dull study turned to vapor, and when the steam cleared, Ian stood in a glorious, sunlit garden. In the garden's center stood a tree unlike any Ian had ever seen. The trunk was as broad as a house and hundreds of feet tall. High above him, an umbrella of golden leaves spread out to blot out the sky. The afternoon sun shone in at an angle and glinted off the leaves, making them appear as if they were made of metal. A serene pool of water surrounded the tree. Shrubs and a rainbow of flowers encircled the pool. Beyond the garden stood a palace of unmatched grace, the structure consisting of columns, arches, and narrow spires stretching toward the heavens.

Stunned, Ian slowly turned while drinking it all in. As he completed his turn, he spied movement amid the arches – a female figure in a blue dress, her blonde hair in a braid draped over one shoulder. Although her dress was unfamiliar and he had never seen her hair in a braid before, Ian recognized her immediately.

His heart leapt.

The urgent need to see her, speak with her, and hug her coiled inside Ian's chest and spurred him into motion. He raced along a curved, uphill path bordered by flowering shrubs and emerged below the arched terrace.

Slowing to a stop, he waved and called out. "Rina!

She did not react. Instead, she rested her elbow on a railing, supporting her chin with the back of her hand while her blue eyes stared into the garden. There was sadness in those eyes.

From the corridor leading to the terrace came another figure – tall, lean, his pale hair tied back by a crown of golden, twisted branches. He was perhaps the most handsome male Ian had ever seen. Notably, he had seen this particular elf before. *King Fastellan.*

The king approached Rina and stood at her side. She turned to him, her hand going to the king's chest while his slid around her back. She gazed up into his eyes while he touched her chin. *What is this?* Ian was stunned, for adoration filled the eyes of Fastellan and Rina alike.

His surroundings again turned to vapor, fading until all was white. A new scene took shape.

Rather than standing in a garden, he now stood amid columns and statues occupying a tiled courtyard. At one end of the area was a closed gate made of black metal. A castle stood at the other end of the yard. A craggy, narrow peak of gray stone loomed above the castle.

A tower door opened, and Rina walked out onto the castle yard's outer wall. She wore a gray cloak, the wind whipping it wildly as she attempted to hug it to herself.

Again, Ian called her name. Again, she failed to react and, instead, stared out into the distance.

Ian rushed across the courtyard and up a staircase beside the wall. When he reached the top, the view opened, and he realized that the castle was positioned on a column of rock that had split off from a snow-capped mountain. A thousand-foot-deep chasm separated the fortress from the mountain itself. Taking care to avoid the side with the steep drop, he walked along the wall, toward where Rina stood.

She suddenly turned, her gaze sweeping past Ian and settling on something behind him. He looked over his shoulder as the gate opened and a horse rode through. Upon the horse was Fastellan. The king stopped his steed and dismounted in the middle of the yard, his gaze on Rina the entire time. As the king strolled across the yard, toward the staircase, Ian made his way toward her.

"Rina?" Ian asked as he drew near.

Rather than reply, she approached Ian with a smile that lifted his spirits. As he opened his arms to greet her, she froze. Her eyes widened, her expression turning from delight to horror. When a shadow fell over Ian, he realized she was reacting to something behind him.

Ian spun around to find a towering, muscular creature standing over him. The beast stood ten feet tall. It wore a shredded tunic over a smooth, hairless torso, muscular arms bulging through the tears. Although it appeared to be human, its brown, fur-covered legs and head were that of a bull. Fireside tales of heroes and monsters had inspired Ian's imagination as a child. Among those tales was one of a monster whose description matched what stood before him.

A minotaur. The thought passed through his head just before the creature reached for him.

Rather than gripping his throat, as Ian had feared, the monster's hand passed through him and latched onto Rina instead. With one hand and little effort, the beast lifted Rina up and turned to dangle her over the edge of the terrifying drop. She kicked and squirmed, but to no avail. The minotaur shook its head in fury and tossed her body as if it weighed nothing.

"No!" Ian cried out as Rina plummeted into the chasm.

He leaned over the wall as his throat constricted in horror. Before she struck the ground, his surroundings vaporized and turned white.

CHAPTER 12
VISIONS

Ghostly shapes flitted through a fog of pale light. The blurred images and soft edges then began to form into something more solid. When the mist faded, Ian found himself standing on a second-floor balcony beneath a darkening sky. The balcony overlooked a city square. A harbor waited beyond the square, its docks lined by boats and ships moored for the evening. People of all races – human, dwarf, elf, and dark elf – occupied the square. The buzz of chatter and occasional sprinkles of laughter filled the air.

Ian leaned against the railing and surveyed the crowd for a familiar face, but he found none. The seaside city was unknown to him, as was the reason for his visit. While confused, he was thankful that the scene was peaceful after his prior, horrific vision.

As the sky darkened further, torches bloomed to illuminate the square. Then, screams arose.

A horde of dark, humanoid figures raced in and tore through the crowd. The hairless monsters stood the size of a human but with green skin so dark, it was nearly black. The creatures moved with frightening quickness, slashing at throats, faces, and torsos in a tempest of blood and terror. Ian watched in frozen shock, helpless and horrified.

Armed guards rushed in to confront the monsters, but they were rapidly overwhelmed. People tried to flee down connecting streets, but the attacking horde was too fast and cut them down from behind. More and more monsters poured into the square and flooded down connecting streets. A trio of young women huddled against the wall below Ian as monsters came at them. In reaction, he attempted to draw on his magic and cast a spell. Nothing happened.

The monsters converged on the women. Talons flashed. Screams rang out. Blood splatter coated the wall, forcing Ian to turn away in revulsion. *Why is this happening?* As the question flitted through his brain, the scene shifted.

～

HE STOOD UPON A TOWER. Stars dotted the night sky, and the moon hovered above the horizon. Confused and filled with trepidation, Ian approached the low wall bordering the tower rooftop. The view expanded, and he gasped.

A citadel huddled below the tower, nestled against a rocky cliffside. Torches illuminated the central keep, its surrounding towers and the citadel's outer wall. Upon the wall stood the squat, burly forms of dwarf warriors. Hundreds of them. On the ground, thousands more huddled in the narrow streets. While this was all of interest, what caused Ian's reaction awaited outside the citadel.

In the moonlight, tens of thousands of dark, humanoid shapes spilled across the open fields and rocky slopes. It was akin to watching a deadly disease spread across its host. In the span of a few breaths, the horde reached the citadel and a fierce battle erupted.

War machines mounted atop the wall and tower rooftops burst into action. Boulders the size of a wagon bed sailed into the sky and fell among the attacking mob. Trebuchets with buckets attached to them flicked gallons of dark liquid out over the attackers. Flaming arrows followed, and when they struck, explosions and flames flashed in the night, illuminating the host. Again, Ian gasped. Attacking the citadel were the same, strange monsters from the prior vision, but this time, he better grasped their numbers, far beyond counting.

The monsters began to swarm over the wall. The battle was frantic, but the dwarven defenders were soon overwhelmed.

~

THE SCENE CHANGED AGAIN and again, but each outcome was the same. Like a swarm of locusts consuming vast fields of crops and leaving nothing behind, the infestation of monsters slaughtered without hesitation and left nothing living behind. Barren cities and lifeless wasteland were sorrowful memories of what once was.

A hopeless sensation overcame Ian, for he had foreseen the end of all things and in that end, there was nothing but oblivion. He fell to his knees, covered his eyes, and wept.

When he lowered his hands, someone stood before him. In shock, Ian jerked and fell to his backside, for the person standing over him was instantly recognizable, yet impossible to be real.

"This...this cannot be real," Ian stammered. "I must be dreaming."

"Despair," the other version of himself said. "Do not allow it to overwhelm you, for only upon the wings of hope can you be lifted above this horrific ending."

The way the other Ian spoke sounded wise and confident. "Who are you?"

"I am you, or what you will become in time."

As Ian stood, he realized that the other version of himself appeared older, his beard grown in, wisdom reflected in his eyes. "How is this possible?"

The other Ian turned and gazed into the distance. "This possibility is both the most likely and the most disturbing. I cannot blame you for your reaction, but you must know that your fate and that of the world have not yet been settled. The actions and decisions of those involved can alter destiny and deliver another outcome."

The visions Ian had witnessed clung to him like a parasite that left him in a fevered fog. He sorted through what he had experienced, the horde of monsters, the screams of their victims, and then he returned to his first vision - the image of Rina standing on a castle wall, a monster from legend, and her plummet to a sudden and violent death.

"Rina. I must save Rina."

The other Ian turned toward him. "Should you ignore the fate of the world, saving her will only bring her to the same ending as the others."

His mind conjured the image of dark-skinned monsters coming after Rina. Just before their deadly talons bit into her terrified flesh, he banished the thought. "What are those creatures?"

"They are called orcs. They come from another place, an underworld of gloom, hatred, and death."

"There must be something we can do to stop them."

The elder Ian nodded. "Now, you have hit upon the subject on which you must focus."

"What can I do?"

"The rules of prophecy are strict and to break them might result in an outcome even worse than what you see before you."

"What is worse than this?"

"I cannot guess, but I also cannot chance it. The best I can do is offer guidance."

While Ian could not comprehend why the older Ian could not provide a direct answer, he was desperate. "What can I do?"

"Seek out the Paragon."

"What is the Paragon?"

The elder Ian turned transparent and gradually faded.

"Wait!" Ian shouted. "What is the Paragon?"

Everything around Ian turned to white vapor.

～

SOMETHING SHOOK IAN. The pale mist around him shifted, parted, and turned to a rainbow of color. The colored light dimmed to reveal his surroundings.

He was back in the Hall of Divining. Truhan stood over him with his hand on Ian's shoulder. When Ian realized he was screaming, he stopped and silence fell over the chamber. Ian panted as if he had run for miles. His exhaustion made his limbs and eyelids heavy.

"Are you well, Ian?" his master asked.

"I...don't know." The hopeless sensation of his vision lingered. Ian shook his head and staggered to his feet.

"You screamed and shouted strange things." Truhan turned Ian to him and intently peered into his eyes. "What did you see?"

"I saw..." Ian swallowed hard. "Monsters. Death. Destruction. It was the end of everyone, of everything."

"Monsters?"

"Orcs."

"How do you know of orcs?"

"You have heard of them?"

"They are an abomination, banished to the underworld before time began."

The statement was odd in more ways than one.

"In my vision, these creatures swept over the land and cities alike, destroying all living things."

"If orcs have found a way to our world, it could be disastrous. Legend claims them to be extremely quick, able to climb just about any surface, and a mere scratch from their poisonous talons can kill in seconds. Worse, their numbers swell unlike any natural creature, for they multiply by feasting on the carcasses of their prey."

Ian had never heard of a monster such as this. "That sounds awful."

"Yes," Truhan nodded gravely. "We must find a means to prevent such a dire fate."

Ian's own voice echoed in his head. *Seek out the Paragon.* "I saw myself."

"What?"

"In my vision, I spoke with myself, but an older version of me."

"That is...odd." The man frowned. "I have never heard of such a vision."

"My elder self said that I must seek out the Paragon."

Truhan's frown deepened. "The Paragon mentioned in the histories surrounding Gahagar?"

"I suppose so."

The man cocked his head. "But you don't even know what the Paragon is or where to find it."

Ian's gaze dropped to the floor. "I know, but the vision was so powerful, so compelling..."

When a hand gripped Ian's shoulder, he lifted his gaze to meet his master's.

Truhan stared at him with a steel intensity. "Prophecy cannot be ignored, Ian, especially one of such gravity. You must find the Paragon."

Ian shook his head. "But I have read all of the histories regarding Gahagar and have found nothing to indicate what the Paragon might be or where to find it."

"There might be another way."

"How?"

"You must ask Gahagar himself."

"But King Gahagar is dead."

"Exactly." Truhan spun and strode toward the chamber exit.

Ian scrambled after him. "What does that mean?"

"The answer will soon reveal itself."

~

THUD. Another thick tome landed on the table, bounced, and settled, joining the dozen already lying there. Ian stood in the study, a stride from the table, confused about what his master was doing and irritated that the man refused to explain his actions.

Truhan stood on a ladder that leaned against the bookshelf. Repeatedly, the man would remove a book from the top shelf, peruse through it, mutter to himself, and then drop it to the table.

Curious, Ian flipped open one of the books and peered inside it. Elegant, flowing script covered the page. "Elvish?" he said aloud. "I didn't know you had any books written in Elvish."

"This shelf contains my only Elvish works. Each is quite old and exceedingly rare." The man sighed, closed the book in his hands, and dropped it.

The book struck the table right in front of Ian, causing him to flinch. "If these books are so rare, why are you treating them so badly?"

Frustration tainted Truhan's response. "Because none of those books are the one I am seeking." He snatched another thick book from the shelf and paged through it. Moments later, he hoisted the book over his head. "Aha!"

As the man scurried down the ladder, Ian rounded the table to meet him. "What is it?"

"This is a book of prophecy. Elvish prophecy." Truhan set it on the table, opened the book to a page near the end, and tapped it with his finger. "This prophecy is over a thousand years old. Few know of it, even among the Sylvan."

"What does it say?"

"You are the translator." Truhan turned the book toward Ian. "Translate."

Ian looked down at the curled, flowing text, read it, and began to speak it out loud in his own language. "...the great dwarven king shall pass into history, leaving his people in turmoil. While the Sylvan avoided being drawn into the conflict that reshaped the land, the peace and prosperity that enabled Sylvanar to flourish cannot last forever.

"Within a child of the Sylvan there lurks a dark ability, one marking the end of the second age, the end of Sylvanar, and the downfall of her people. When the death speaker is revealed, mark it well and take heed. The natural world is one of balance, and this dark ability, able to bridge the worlds of life and death, mirrors a twisted wound in the land itself. This wound, this scourge, filled with shadow and hatred, festers and spreads like an infection intent on extinguishing life itself. In this darkness, the Sylvan cannot remain untouched.

"The Sylvan king brings disgrace and with that crime, a curse upon him and his race. The Sylvan fade from the world as a new age replaces the old. Will it be an age of darkness or new life? Seek out the dead, for the answer passed with them long ago."

Ian reread the passage in silence. When finished, he shook his head. "I have trouble understanding what this has to do with me or my vision."

"Don't you see it, Ian?"

"Well...it says something about seeking out the dead."

"Yes! What else?"

Again, he read over the text. "The prophecy mentions a dark ability and something called a death speaker."

A smile stretched across Truhan's face. "Very good. I knew you were a bright lad."

"But what does it mean?"

Truhan lifted the book from Ian's hands and gently eased it closed. "It means that you must go to Sylvanar and seek out this death speaker. You must then convince him or her to assist you on your quest."

"My quest to find the Paragon?"

"Of course."

"How can a death speaker help?"

"By asking Gahagar himself about this mysterious prize."

Suddenly, Ian understood, which left him incredulous. "You want me and this death speaker to get answers from a dwarf king who has been dead for years?" The idea of having a conversation with a rotting corpse seemed simultaneously ludicrous and bone chilling.

"It is the only way." Truhan set the book down on the table and gave Ian a hard stare. "Should you fail, consider your vision."

Ian blinked as a disturbing image flashed in his head, a scene involving hundreds of thousands of demented monsters swarming over cities and killing everyone in sight. A dark, twisted, desolate land and rotting corpses were all that would be left in their wake.

CHAPTER 13
A TWISTED PLOT

Rina leaned against a tower balcony rail, hugging herself against the chill of night. The balcony stood outside the chambers she had shared with Shria-Li until the elf princess vanished. Despite it being two hours after nightfall, the golden aura emanating from the Tree of Life provided soft light, illuminating the palace and the garden surrounding the tree.

As she stood there, Rina reflected on the morning when she woke to discover the princess missing. At first, there was no cause for alarm. Shria-Li often woke before Rina and would visit the garden or go for a walk through the palace grounds. As she typically did, Rina had stepped out onto the balcony to greet the morning sun. Finding a rope tied to the balcony rail had been the first indication that something was amiss.

A frantic search of the palace followed, joined by a pair of Sylvan officers interrogating Rina. They were rude and accusatory toward her, leaving her in tears. That is when Fastellan walked in to save her. He berated her interrogators, sent them away, and approached Rina with words of comfort. When he was certain she knew nothing of his daughter's disappearance, he departed to lead the search.

More than a full season had passed since that day, and Rina had still not heard from Shria-Li nor did she have a clue as to where she might be. Despite not being involved in the disappearance of the princess, Rina felt responsible. She had been in the neighboring room at the time and was the last person to see her. *I pray she did not leave because of me.*

Male voices in the garden drew her attention. She leaned over the rail and spied two armored elves standing on a narrow path bordered by lush shrubbery. One wore blue armor, the other's had the warm tint of dwarven steel. Rina recognized the first as Evarian, head of the Blue Spears. The other was undoubtedly a palace guard. They appeared to be in a heated discussion.

Unable to sleep despite the hour and driven by an undeniable curiosity, Rina rushed inside, cinched her robes tight, and headed for the chamber door. She hurried down the stairs, her slippered feet barely making a sound. At the bottom, she made straight for the exterior door, opened it, and slipped outside. She tip-toed down the stairs leading to the garden floor. A curved path bordered by flowering foliage waited at the bottom of the stairs. The shrubs stood too tall to see beyond, so Rina eased forward while listening. She did not have to creep far down before she was able to hear the conversation.

"...will never condone such action. He believes that the creatures in the Vale are a critical part of our world." The voice belonged to Chavell, captain of the palace guard.

"At what cost?" Evarian hissed. "We have an opportunity to act. Should the barrier fail completely, how many innocents will die? Our births were already uncommon and have become exceedingly rare over recent years. Should the Sylvan suffer significant loss, our people may never recover."

"It is not that I disagree, Evarian. I have a duty to honor the commands of my king."

"You also have a duty to your people, Chavell."

"What would you have of me?"

"If the king will not condone what must be done, perhaps we can remove him."

"You speak of treason." Chavell bit off the last word as if he could not stand the taste of it.

"Fastellan is not true royalty and was never meant to be king," Evarian hissed. "He stepped in because Tora-Li was weak, inexperienced, and lacking the confidence to rule on her own. Even now, she remains passive and too meek for the throne, but if Fastellan were out of the way, she would have no reason to back his decree."

"I will *not* murder my own king."

Silence loomed after Chavell spoke, that quiet stretching long enough where Rina wondered if they had walked off until Evarian finally replied.

"It need not be the king. I may have another way."

"What do you mean?"

Evarian said, "Since the king is away, I will use this time to prepare. Contact me when he returns. By then, I will be prepared to reveal my plan."

"Very well. Now, I must go and complete my rounds before the guards begin to wonder if something is wrong."

When footsteps came toward her, Rina gasped in alarm. She scurried back toward the palace but realized she would be easily spotted if she tried to climb the staircase. So, when she reached the stairs, she eased between the wall and a flowering hibiscus. There, she stood still and held her breath praying that the shadows would mask her from notice.

Chavell's footsteps drew near and the guard came into view as he climbed the stairs. His expression appeared troubled in the glimpse she was able to catch when he walked by. Rina waited stock-still until he ascended and the door at the top of the stairs opened then clicked shut. Only then did she exhale.

CHAPTER 14

SUBTERFUGE

A grunt rumbled in Vic's throat as he lifted two sacks of flour. Beneath that significant weight, he crossed the ship's hold, passed through the open hold door, and began across the plank. Ahead of him was another man hefting a sack of flour. The man's tan tunic was darkened by sweat. He wore a brimmed hat that matched the tunic while a pair of suspenders held up his chestnut brown trousers, their bottoms tucked into his black leather boots.

Upon reaching the pier, Vic passed a quartet of men in black, none appearing to pay him much attention. All four men were armed, two with swords, two with loaded crossbows. There were a dozen other men like them arranged in clusters of four and spaced along the length of the pier. The black outfits denoted them as members of Creskin's Crew, the scars and sour expressions marked them as dangerous thugs. Vic privately wondered how many among them were part of the prison break and how many had joined up after Creskin had taken charge of the harbor district.

Vic reached a waiting wagon, dumped the two sacks into a wagon bed, dusted off his hands, and wiped the sweat from his brow. "That's the last of it, boss."

Dennard clapped Vic on the back. "Another solid day of work, Vinny. I need to pay the captain. I'll be right back." The man, whose height was similar to Vic's but with a bit less muscle, walked up the plank and disappeared into the ship's hold.

Vic stared at the ship for a moment and then glanced toward the shore on the western side of the bay. Clouds scattered across the sky glowed orange and pink, the sun already hidden below the horizon. Two ships floated out in the bay, one with its sails down as it prepared to anchor for the night while the other sailed toward open waters. Night was fast approaching – a night likely to result in far more deaths than usual. He just hoped that neither he nor Revita were among the corpses added to the pyre the following morning.

He dismissed those dark thoughts, turned toward the wagon, lifted the tailgate, and began to secure it while staring toward shore. One wagon was still being loaded on his pier while dockworkers unloaded a pair of ships on the other pier. All the while, men in black monitored the area, all part of Creskin's Crew. The gang members were armed with weapons and scowls that turned to harsh glares should anyone stare too long, as Vic had discovered numerous times over the prior two days. As the second tailgate pin was set in place, Dennard strolled out of the hold.

The man spoke as he crossed the plank. "If you had told me a year ago that I'd be paying this much for flour, I'd have thought you daft."

"The city needs food," Vic said.

"True, but too many ships now avoid Bard's Bay. Those that do come don't even disembark. A third of the city's inns have closed down and the others struggle to survive."

A sailor appeared in the hold doorway, lifted the plank, and pulled it in. The sailor cast one furtive glance toward the men in black standing near Vic, then pulled the hold door closed.

"See. Even Captain Javonne intends to push off and spend the night in the bay rather than in a slip."

Vic had nothing to say. He knew the situation and was determined to change it.

"I'll secure our escort, so we can deliver this to the warehouse," Dennard walked over to the nearest group of men in black. A quiet conversation ensued.

Vic again glanced toward the darkening sky, attempting to measure when dusk would turn to nightfall. His stomach churned with a mixture of anxiety and anticipation.

A hand clapping Vic on the shoulder caused him to lurch from his musings.

"Hess and his men are escorting us," Dennard said. "Let's go."

The man rounded the wagon on one side while Vic took the opposite side. They both climbed into the seat with Dennard taking the reins. Their escort split up with two of Creskin's men shifting to each side of the wagon. The driver snapped the reins, the horses whinnied, and the wagon lurched into motion. At a leisurely walk to match the deliberate pace of their escort, the team pulled the full wagon toward shore.

With his anxiety rising, Vic kneaded his hands. Graced with a gregarious nature, handsome looks, and natural athleticism, he rarely dwelled on thoughts of failure. This was one of the rare occasions where concerns about things going wrong continued to invade his thoughts.

"You are a quiet one, Vinny." Dennard spoke in a loud voice, above the clopping of hooves and rumbling wagon wheels.

Vic shrugged. "I don't have much to say right now."

"You have been working for me for two days. In that time, we've had less than an hour of conversation between us."

"I have just been focused on the work."

"I'll say. You loaded twice as much freight as I did in the same amount of time. I swear, I've never met anyone who works harder than you."

"My father always told me to take pride in my work, whether it's creating a piece of furniture or moving sacks of flour."

"Furniture?" Dennard arched a brow. "Are you a carpenter?"

A man with a torch in hand strolled toward the wagon and paused to light a lantern mounted to a post rising from the pier. Lanterns along the shoreline were globes of amber amid the failing daylight. Torches along the city wall beyond the harbor flickered in the sea breeze.

"My pa was." Memories of Vic visiting his father's shop brought a sense of loss. I miss you, Father. The fact that he hadn't thought of his father in weeks filled him with guilt.

With a sidelong glance, Dennard asked, "Was?"

Vic looked away. He had done his best to avoid personal subjects, hoping to keep from getting close to Dennard, but the man had a straightforward way about him that made it difficult to avoid getting pulled in. Realizing he had to say something, he explained, "He died last summer."

Dennard patted Vic's back. "I am sorry to hear that. Just hold tight to the memories, and he'll always be with you."

Desperate for another topic, Vic asked in a voice too quiet for their escort to hear, "How do you like working under Creskin?"

The man sighed. "It's not as if I have a choice. This wagon, these horses, and my warehouse are my business. Without them, I'd have no way to earn the coin I need to live. The fees Creskin charges are many times what I was paying in taxes when Kaden ran the city, but I can still feed my family." As the wagon rolled off the pier and up the gravel harbor road, he gave Vic a sidelong glance. "Cities like this change hands over the years. Some are like sunshine, some are cloudy days, and some are downright hurricanes. All I can do is endure the current storm and pray for sunshine. For the sake of my wife and my son, I hope the weather changes soon."

The man has a wife and a child. The realization had Vic regretting what was coming. That regret was offset by the hope that his actions would end the storm besetting Dennard and the other honest citizens of Bard's Bay.

The wagon passed numerous warehouses and turned down an alley too narrow for the escort to run astride the wagon. The men in black fell in behind the wagon while the horses took them toward a gravel courtyard. As the wagon rolled into the courtyard, Dennard stopped his team, climbed down, and approached the warehouse door opposite from the alley mouth. He pulled a cord over his head. Dangling from the necklace was a key he used to open the lock. The man then pulled the chain and slid the door open, the wheels on the metal track above the door squeaking noisily. Darkness, thick and impossible to penetrate, dominated the building's interior. When the man turned around, a shadowy form emerged from the darkness behind him.

"Look out," Vic shouted.

Dennard spun toward the open doorway as someone rushed toward him. The person wore a dark cloak, the hood up and covering his or her face. A cudgel came around, the arm swinging it encircled by a red band. The cudgel struck Dennard in the head with a thud. The man collapsed in a heap.

"Get him!" A man shouted from behind Vic.

The armed escort split with two men in black rushing past the wagon on one side, two on the other. Dennard's attacker spun and raced into the dark building.

～

REVITA SAT ON A CRATE. Waiting. In one hand, she held a cudgel. From the palm of her other hand, a glowing disk illuminated a small area around her. Darkness lurked just beyond the light disk's aura. The cluster of barrels, crates, and sacks beside her were her only companions.

As an experienced thief, waiting in silence was nothing new to Revita. She did so with patience honed from years of capers that relied on stealth and timing. This particular scheme might be different in other ways, but stealth and timing remained paramount.

A rising noise came from outside as a horse drawn wagon drew near. The noise stopped, replaced by muffled voices, spurring Revita to pocket her light disk. The crunch of footsteps preceded the lock and chain on the door clinking as Revita ducked behind a barrel. The door rolled open. The dim light of dusk seeped in through the entrance. A man stood in the doorway. Beyond him was a horse drawn wagon and Vic, who had his own role to play in their charade. Masked in shadow, Revita eased from her hiding spot and crept toward the door. As the man in the doorway turned away, Revita closed in.

"Look out!" Vic shouted.

Knowing the man was about to turn toward her, Revita rapidly closed the gap, wound back, and swung a backhand blow. The cudgel struck the back of the man's head. He toppled over like a felled tree.

Shouts came from beyond the wagon. Men in black raced toward the warehouse with weapons drawn. Revita spun and bolted into the darkness, relying on her memorization of the building's interior. She rounded the cluster of barrels and ducked between them and the interior wall.

The men reached the doorway and stopped. Two held swords. Two gripped crossbows. All were larger than Revita and even taller than Vic.

"I can't see anything," one man muttered.

"Hush, Gracen," another man growled.

"Sorry, Hess."

"We know you are in here," Hess called out into the dark warehouse. "This building, its contents, and the man you attacked are under Creskin's protection, which you have violated. You are trapped with no way out. Give yourself up, and we will let you live."

Cupping her hand to her mouth while turning her head, Revita called out in a weak voice. "Help!"

"He has a woman in there," a man exclaimed.

"Shut up," Hess snapped. He then raised his voice. "A hostage won't help you. Come out now or die."

Revita stepped out from behind the barrel and strode toward the men with her hands spread before her. Just to the right of where Hess stood, the wagon driver remained unmoving apart from the rise and fall of his chest.

"Stop right there," Hess demanded when she was fifteen feet away. "Where is the woman?"

Revita pulled her hood down to reveal a smirk. "*I* am the woman."

Hess snorted. "Don't think we will have mercy on you. Creskin demands everyone in his district follow his rules. Crossing him requires an example be made."

The four men focused on her, two of them with crossbows leveled in her direction. They did not see the cloaked figure approaching from behind. *I need to distract them for just another moment.*

Revita argued, "You said you would not kill me."

"True. However, by the time we are finished, you might wish you were dead." He thrust a finger in her direction. "Arrest her."

The other three men in black strode toward Revita. She made a fist with her right hand while bringing that hand toward her opposite shoulder. Her finger touched a button on her palm. When pressed, the metal plates along the bracer on her forearm popped up to form a jagged crest of razor-sharp spikes.

"Look out!" One of the men shouted.

Too late.

She opened her fist while flinging her arm toward them, launching the spikes just before she dove to the side. In rapid succession, the spikes struck the three men. Thwap, thwap – the two crossbows fired bolts, one of them tearing through her cloak, the other passing through the space where she had just been standing.

Revita landed on her hands, rolled, and came up to her feet with her dagger in hand. One of the men was on the ground with a spike jutting from a bloody eye socket. Two others were wounded, one with a spike in his arm and the other with a pierced shoulder. Her last three spikes had missed completely. *Oh, crap.*

Hess shouted, "Help! We are under attack!"

Suddenly, the plan had gone from bad to worse.

CHAPTER 15

FRAMED

Vic waited until Hess and his men positioned themselves before the open warehouse door. He then climbed off the wagon and hurried toward the pile of refuse at the side of the courtyard. There, he tipped up a crate to reveal a black cloak, a red armband, and his mattock. While Hess issued demands of surrender to Dennard's attacker, Vic secured the band to his left arm and slid the cloak on. He then lifted his weapon and began across the courtyard, with careful, quiet steps.

As Hess commanded his men to arrest Revita, Vic dropped to a crouch. He advanced on the gang leader while staying low, as Revita had instructed.

She attacked the men advancing on her, launching a spray of spikes, one of which missed the enemies and sailed right over Vic's head.

When Hess spun around and called for help, Vic froze. The gang leader's eyes widened upon sighting Vic crouching two strides away. In reaction, Hess thrust with his sword.

Vic urgently rolled sideways, dodging the attack. He came to his feet as Hess swung a wide slash. Raising his mattock, Vic blocked the attack, the sword blade clanging off his weapon's shaft. He then followed with a punch, striking Hess in the jaw. The man staggered. With the opening, Vic made an overhead chop. The pick end of the mattock plunged into the base of his attacker's neck. Sparks of electricity sizzled up the left side of the man's face. Hess fell to his knees and toppled to his side. He twitched and convulsed before falling still.

⌇

Revita spun away from a sword thrust and came around with her dagger extended. The tip sliced across the arm of her attacker, causing the man to drop his blade with a cry. As one attacker staggered back, she turned toward the other, who had tossed his crossbow aside and drawn a dagger.

"Come on, wench. I'll make you bleed." He shifted his balance from side to side with the dagger before him.

She snorted. "Not likely."

He put his foot on the sword hilt and slid it backward, toward the man she had just disarmed. "Pick it up, Gracen. Let's finish her."

The man with the sliced bicep and a spike in the opposite shoulder squatted and lifted the blade with both hands, his face twisted in a mixture of pain and anger. The two slowly advanced on Revita, who bent her right elbow to hold her bracer between them and her. Beyond them, Vic finished Hess, who collapsed to the ground.

"Vic!" She shouted. "Get down!"

He spun toward her and dropped to the ground. The moment he was down, she pressed her fingers to the two gems on the inside of her bracer. The spikes buried in her attacker's arm, shoulder and eye sped toward her, as did the three that had missed with her initial attack. The spell that connected the spikes to the bracer was incredibly powerful, and the recall of the projectiles could not be denied.

One spike shot through an attacker's chest and another plunged through the stomach of the other. In rapid succession, all six spikes reconnected to the bracer then lay flat. Her attackers stumbled and collapsed.

~

Vic climbed to his feet, dusted himself off, and glanced toward Hess. The man stared into nothing, his neck and shoulder slick with blood.

Shouts came from the far end of the alley. Alarms rang in Vic's head. *Reinforcements are coming.*

"Vita! Let's go!" He spun and ran back to the wagon.

Once in the seat, he gripped the reins and snapped them while pulling hard to the right.

Revita raced in and hopped on beside him as the wagon looped through the courtyard. A squad of Creskin's men charged in from the far end of the alley, armed with swords and crossbows. With a snap of the reins and a shout, Vic urged the horses to go faster. The soldiers came to an abrupt stop.

"Run!" The man in the lead bellowed as he spun around.

A collision occurred among Creskin's men, two falling down while two others accidentally loosed crossbow bolts. One bolt shattered off a neighboring wall. The other sailed over Vic's shoulder, just missing his head. The guards scrambled out of the alley with the horses chasing close behind. Upon reaching the alley entrance, the guards turned right, as expected. As planned, Vic pulled on the reins and turned his team left.

The horses, the loaded wagon, and the two passengers sped down the torchlit gravel road running between the docks and the waterfront warehouses. Creskin's men gave chase. Even with the loaded wagon, the horses outpaced the men and the distance between them steadily increased. Those with crossbows stopped and loosed. Two bolts struck the wagon and a third sailed past.

Another cluster of men in black came rushing in from the west pier. The horses towing the wagon raced ahead while the guards took an angle to cut them off. Vic turned the team before reaching the guards, steering the wagon toward a warehouse. Again, he tugged on the reins, turning the team just before colliding with a building. The wagon's back end slid across the gravel, and the back wheel bounced off the wall, sending a shudder across the wagon. The two lead men closed in and leapt. One landed head-first in the wagon bed. The other grabbed the side rail, his boots skittering across the gravel road as he tried to pull himself up and avoid the wheel behind him.

"Take the reins," Vic handed them to Revita before she could reply.

He grabbed his mattock off the seat, spun, and climbed up as the man in the wagon bed stood and drew his sword.

"You die now, thief," the man growled.

The man swung left and right while stumbling from one foot to another. Stacks of flour lay between his spread legs and to each side of his feet. The other man flipped up, rolled over the rail, and fell inside the wagon bed, but Vic ignored him while focused on the enemy blade swinging back and forth. He had to strike before the second enemy drew his weapon. Just as the sword swung past, he leapt and kicked his feet up. The wagon's forward momentum added to his motion. His feet struck the swordsman in the chest and launched him backward. The enemy tumbled over the tailgate and was gone. Vic landed on his back, rolled away from the other enemy, and found footing among sacks of flour.

The other gang member rose to a stance and thrust with his sword. Vic chopped sideways, his mattock knocking the strike aside. He immediately drove the head of the mattock into the man's gut. The man bent with a grunt and made the mistake of taking a step backward. Over the rail he went, his feet flipping up in the air as he cried out. He landed in a puff of dust as the wagon sped away.

Vic slid his weapon into the harness on his back, climbed back onto the seat, and took the reins from Revita. The wagon drew near the riverfront, rounded the bend where the city wall ended, and the pursuers faded into the night.

As planned, Vic turned onto a curved, hillside road and drove the wagon toward the manor the Southside Blades used as their headquarters. The wagon reached the top of the hill, rounded the manor, and slowed before turning down the adjacent alley. Another hard pull of the reins caused the wagon to stop right where he had been discovered by two guards just two nights prior. Without a word, he and Revita climbed off the seat and ran down the alley. Just before emerging, they each tore off their armbands and pocketed them. Vic headed down the road, eager to be far from the scene as soon as possible but stopped when Revita grabbed his arm.

"Give me a moment."

With her hood still over her face, she approached the arched opening leading to the manor's interior courtyard. She pulled a folded note from her inside pocket, bent, and drew a small knife from her boot. With a firm stab, she drove the knife through the paper and into the wooden door, pinning it in place.

Revita walked back toward Vic and gave him a nod. "Now, we can go."

Although he wanted to ask about the note, Vic stifled the question and led her away from the manor. They kept to the shadowy side of the street until reaching a staircase, where they descended a flight and stopped at the edge of another quiet street.

"That was close," Vic said.

"I told you before. Timing is everything when executing stunts like this."

"What was with the note?"

"I added it to ensure the wagon and flour are found inside their compound."

"What did it say?"

"It said that the wagon and flour were gifts from Torrigan as an overture for the two gangs to unite against Creskin."

Vic laughed. "That is only going to worsen the situation when Creskin comes after Lokix and the Blades."

"That was the point. The ploy cost me a throwing blade, but they are easily replaced."

Vic glanced down the street. It was empty. He suspected that honest citizens were bolted inside their homes. Since the criminal gangs had taken control, few others dared to brave the streets at night. However, the darkness may have masked things too well. "Do you think they saw the armbands?"

"I suspect so. If not, your story should set the blame squarely on Lokix, at least enough to convince Creskin to investigate."

"My story. I almost forgot." Vic handed his mattock to Revita. "Take my things back with you." He pulled the cloak off and shoved it into her arms before removing the armband. "I had better run back right now and check on Dennard. I just hope you didn't hit him too hard."

"I know how to knock a man out without killing him. He will be fine. Just remember your story."

Vic recalled the plan. "I am to tell him that I ran to get help."

"And that you saw it was the Blades who attacked and stole the wagon."

"I just hope Creskin and his men buy the story."

"We will know in a few days." She squeezed his hand. "Now, go."

Vic ran off, cutting across the city as he made his way toward the harbor gate.

CHAPTER 16

A SOLO VENTURE

Ian emerged from his underground home and stood on a rock shelf to peer into the distance. High above him, stars twinkled in the pale blue of dawn, as if attempting to garner attention before daylight completely hid them from view. Below him, the Agrosi stretched out in all directions around Mount Tiadd. To call the vast plains surrounding the lonely mountain dangerous would be an understatement. The thought of crossing the Agrosi alone caused Ian's stomach to churn.

He turned toward Truhan, who peered into the distance as if searching for something. "Master?"

"Yes, Ian."

"I would appreciate your company for a while longer. Perhaps you could join me for a day or two?"

Truhan turned toward him. "We have been through this three times over."

A sigh slipped out. "I know. You claim that you cannot be involved, that it would attract too much attention. From whom or what, I still don't understand. Yet, whatever attention you wish to avoid surely cannot happen out here in the wilds, right?"

"There is much you do not yet comprehend, and there are some things I am loath to explain. Suffice it to say that only within the tunnels behind me am I fully able to escape notice."

"Still, you crossed these plains with me last autumn. Could you not do it again?"

"The world is changing, Ian. Your abilities are a significant aspect of that change. I suspect that your use of magic is already affecting the balance of power in the world. The moment that balance tilts too much in your direction, it will attract attention I must avoid...for now."

This was another one of the times when Truhan spoke of things in a bewildering manner. His statements and reasoning hinted at something significant, a secret Ian longed to decipher, but every time the hints offered began to paint a picture, the pieces disintegrated and slipped through his fingers like tendrils of smoke.

A small sack dangling in front of his face pulled Ian out from his brief reverie.

"Take this." Truhan set the sack in Ian's palm, causing its contents to jingle.

"You are giving me coin?"

"Two gold pieces and twenty silver marks. It will aid you on your journey. While your magic is mighty, you cannot conjure food nor can you sail across the sea with a spell alone."

"Thank you."

"The provisions in your pack should suffice until you reach Bard's Bay."

The reality that he would be traveling alone weighed upon Ian like a mountain of stone, threatening to crush him. "What if I get lost?"

"As I explained, you are to maintain a westward heading until you reach the Wellspring River. From there, the river will take you north to Bard's Bay. Once you reach the city, seek a ship bound for Hooked Point.

The gold is for you to bribe the captain to drop you off near the Vale. If the gold does not convince him, you must find other means."

"Another means?"

The man rolled his eyes. "Magic. I refer to magic."

"Oh. Yeah."

"Once you reach the Vale, seek the river that flows through the valley. It will lead you to a towering set of waterfalls. Your destination, Havenfall, resides between the falls. Seek an audience with King Fastellan and explain the gravity of your quest. The elves are a haughty and self-important lot, but they would never ignore a prophecy, especially one with such dire consequences."

"I will...try."

"You are no longer a boy, Ian. You are a man, and while I demand you defer to my guidance while you are here, out there, nobody is your master. You must project strength if you expect to command respect."

Despite his master's reassurance, confidence eluded Ian. Rather than voice his doubts, he replied with a numb nod.

Truhan gripped his shoulder. "You are Barsequa, the first wizard. Your legacy begins now. Go and make me proud."

At that moment, Ian realized that Truhan had become a father figure to him, filling a critical role after the loss of his own father just a year earlier. Hearing those words stirred a need within Ian, who suddenly wanted nothing more than to fulfill Truhan's vision and enact the role of a hero intent on saving the world. *Someday, others will tell tales of my bravery and might. My name will become legend.* Ian could think of nothing more rewarding.

"I will not fail you, Master," Ian said with renewed confidence.

His master's smile filled Ian with pride, as did the words, "I know."

With that, Ian hefted his pack and began down the meandering mountainside path.

From behind, Truhan called out, "And don't forget to continue training. You must master your abilities and do so with a sense of urgency."

Ian turned and shouted. "I will train every day."

"Be well, Ian. We shall meet again, soon."

Inspired, with his spirits boosted by the morning sun shining through the surrounding aspens, Ian strolled along the path with feet feeling as if they were lighter than air. The next time he glanced backward, the rocky outcropping stood empty with no sign of Truhan. Alone and into his journey, Ian considered what lay ahead.

Earlier that morning, while loading his pack, Ian had studied a map of the region. In addition to the five miles required to reach the bottom of the mountain, he would need to cover another twenty-some miles across the Agrosi to reach the river. It would take him the entire day to travel such a distance under good circumstances. Should anything go wrong along the way...

Suddenly worried about being stuck on the dangerous grasslands at night, he broke into a run.

～

IT WAS mid-morning when Ian emerged from the tree-covered slopes of Mount Tiadd and paused to survey the area.

Open swaths of chest-high, green grass covered the rolling hills before him. The grass shoots bent and wavered with the wind, making the land itself seem as if it were stirring. Although he sighted no immediate threats, danger might be lurking over any hilltop or hidden in the long grass itself.

The mid-morning sun shone down with a warmth that forced him to remove his cloak and shove it into his pack. He then put the sun at his back and headed west while keeping the mountain slope to his right. The long grass required him to forge his own path, and in mere moments, he found himself wishing he had a staff or a scythe. He considered the use of magic, but no spell he knew was appropriate, his options ranging from impractical to outright terrifying. An image flashed in his mind – him using a cone of fire to burn a trail across the plain and the wind-fed fire spreading until it became an inferno that set the entire Agrosi ablaze. *Don't even think about it*, he chastised himself. As he crested a hilltop, he gasped and came to a hard stop.

No more than fifty strides away stood a massive animal covered in white fur. The beast faced away from Ian as it munched on grass. A daunting rack of silver-tinted antlers jutted out from its head. Ian knew of only one creature matching its description – a great elk. From what he had read, the animals were rarely sighted, which resulted in most scholars considering them to be a mere myth. Ian now knew that they were no myth. The beast raised its head and looked to the side, giving Ian a true sense of its size.

The elk towered above the grass, its back some eight feet off the ground. The silvery rack on its head spread out four feet from each side of its head. When it moved, sunlight glinted off the antlers, making them appear as if they were made of metal. The elk then shifted, lifting its thick hooves as it turned. The curved shadows of muscle rippled beneath its shimmery white coat. Mesmerized by the majesty of the giant creature, Ian stared in wonder rather than reacting as he should.

The elk spotted him and froze. Nothing moved other than the flaring of its nostrils as it breathed, seemingly in time with the gentle swaying of the surrounding grass. Beneath the scrutinizing glare of the elk, Ian held his breath and remained still. A long, tense moment followed before the elk reacted.

An angry snort came from the beast, causing Ian to jerk back a step. The elk dug at the ground with one massive hoof, and then it charged.

Like an avalanche rumbling down a mountainside, the behemoth raced toward Ian with surprising speed, far too fast for him to outrun. It drew near, lowered its head, and prepared to gore Ian with the sharp points of its silver antlers. At the last moment, Ian reacted.

In the span of a heartbeat, he conjured a construct, the first construct he had ever learned. A shield enveloped Ian, forming a bubble only he could see. The beast crashed into the shield while lifting its head, scooping Ian off the ground and launching him like a catapult.

The sky and the ground spun again and again until Ian suddenly crashed down. The bubble spell held fast, but the shock of the impact rattled Ian's brain. He lost concentration, and the spell crumbled. The bubble popped and he tumbled through the long grass until coming to a stop some eighty feet from the elk. There, he lay still, panting while squeezing his eyes shut against the thumping in his head. With effort, he opened his eyes and found himself on his back, facing the sky. His vision was blurred and surrounded by ghostly shadows. The shadows crept in. His eyes drifted closed as he slipped into darkness.

∾

Boom. Thunder rumbled. Ian's eyes flickered open. A raindrop struck him right between the eyes. He rubbed the water away and peered up through the long grass. Gray clouds blanketed the sky. *Where am I?* The swaying grass reminded him of the Agrosi, and he suddenly recalled the encounter with the elk. The sun had been shining at the time. Clouds now covered the sky and daylight was waning. *I missed most of the day,* he realized. Worse, a storm was imminent, which meant he had missed ideal weather for travel.

Lightning flashed. Another raindrop struck his forehead. The next landed on his chin. Then it began to pour.

Ian sat up and found his pack lying an arm's length away, his cloak sticking out from it. He grabbed the cloak and slipped it over his shoulders, pulling the hood over his head. With his feet beneath him, he stood slowly while turning to survey his surroundings. The mountain loomed above him just to the north. Open grasslands spread out to the east, west, and south. There was no sign of the elk or anything else.

With a sigh, Ian wrapped his cloak around himself and resumed his journey, heading southwest. Rain pummeled him while the ground turned to mud that stuck to his boots. He prayed for the rain to end and hoped to locate shelter before it was too dark to see.

~

THE STORM LASTED ONLY AN HOUR, for which Ian was thankful. By the time the clouds cleared from the western sky, the sun had set but daylight still illuminated the horizon. With this meager light as a guide, informing him of his direction as well as giving shape to the shadowy landscape, Ian trudged through mud until he crested a hilltop and spied an island of black. He altered his path, heading toward the oddity until he drew near and realized what it was. Rock.

He climbed up the outcropping, slipping and nearly falling from the slickness of the mud on his boots. In the middle of the rock was a recess roughly six feet in diameter. There, he sat down and hugged his damp cloak around himself, happy to be out of the wind and the mud. His teeth chattered, for the temperature had dropped after the rain passed. *I need to warm myself.* Without any other ideas, he drew upon his magic.

The rush filled him, causing his heart to race and head to spin. From memory, he cast an energy spell, channeled magic through it, and a cone of fire burst forth. Bright waves of amber bloomed in the night as the blaze raged and enveloped the boulder across from Ian. The heat emanating from the inferno blanketed his front side. It felt good at first but soon it became too intense, forcing Ian to look away and shield his face. He maintained the blaze until the heat overwhelmed him. When he withdrew his magic, the flames doused. Ian lowered the arm shielding his face and found the boulder across from him aglow with an amber hue. He held his hands toward it. Waves of warmth licked his palms.

Ian settled in and gnawed on a chunk of dry bread while watching the clouds creep across the sky. Darkness graced by twinkling stars had claimed the heavens by the time Ian drifted off to sleep.

~

BENEATH THE TWILIGHT OF PREDAWN, Ian resumed his journey south. By the time the sun crested the ridgeline in the distant east, the trees along the southern border of the Agrosi were within view. An hour later, he reached the tree line, where the ground began to slope downward. Through gaps in the trees, he spotted a ribbon of water meandering along the bottom of a ravine. Rocky cliffs, dark pines, and pale leaf trees covered the far side of the river valley.

Descending the steep slope, Ian wove between trees and through underbrush consisting of ferns, bramble, and berry bushes. Thrice, he almost tumbled down the hillside, each time catching a branch or stump just in time to avoid disaster. All the while, the rush of water beckoned from below. An hour into his descent, the trees parted and the river came into full view.

Dark blue water flowed past while white foam swirled around rocks jutting above the surface. A quarter mile to the northwest, the river flowed out of view as it rounded a bend. Upstream in the other direction, a stream joined the river, creating a split with both directions obscured by forest. Trees and shrubs covered the steep banks as far as Ian could see...until he noticed a small beach near the downriver bend. There was something familiar about the beach. Ian then noticed the stern of a rowboat amid the long grass bordering the sand. *It's the same boat we took from Bard's Bay last Autumn.* Inspired and hopeful, he began making his way along the riverbank.

After rounding a few hundred trees and enduring a trying encounter with a bramble bush that left a tear in his cloak, Ian climbed onto a boulder to stand five feet above the river's surface. The pale beach waited across the river. Nestled in the long grass on the inland side of the beach was the rowboat, exactly how he remembered it. He gazed downriver, knowing that Bard's Bay awaited where the river met the sea. A full night and day of constant rowing had taken Ian and his companions that distance. Going downstream would be easier and a far preferable option to walking.

"But how to cross the river?" That was the question he had to answer.

Unwilling to swim in the snowmelt-fed water, certain to be frigid and leave him shivering in his boots, he considered other options. Unable to come up with a natural solution that provided comfort or confidence, he decided to try using his abilities, which posed another dilemma.

"Can I make it that far?" he said aloud, knowing nobody would answer.

The beach stood three hundred feet away, three times farther than his best prior attempt at levitation. Yet, he saw no trail on this side of the river, and he loathed the idea of forging a path all the way to Bard's Bay. Determined, he adjusted his pack, focused on the boat, and took a deep breath. After a calm, silent beat, he drew upon his magic, allowing it to flow in and gather until he thought he might explode. Light, sounds, and all sensation took on a sharp edge, threatening to cut through him should he allow the pressure to continue to build.

Arms stretched at a downward angle, Ian formed two similar constructs. He channeled magic through one construct, forming a platform of air beneath his feet, lifting him off the rock. Straining to maintain his spell while extending it, he continued until he hovered fifty feet above the river. With his other hand extended behind him, he released a powerful blast of air, propelling himself forward.

Ian launched across the water, the far bank racing toward him. Quickly, he swung his back hand around until it faced forward. Again, he channeled magic, this time forming an invisible ramp of air stretching from the beach toward him, ending twenty feet above the river. With a desperate thrust of the last bit of magic he could manage, Ian slowed himself just before reaching the ramp. He landed on his belly, driving the wind from his lungs before sliding and rolling down the ramp. His momentum carried him onto the beach and across it while sand swirled around him. His shoulder struck the boat with a thud, and he finally came to a stop. A gasp followed as sweet air filled his lungs. There, he lay for a time, panting until his breathing calmed. Finally, he sat up with a groan. His shoulder was sore and his robes were covered in sand, yet he was intact and nothing was broken. He peered across the water and realized the ludicrous nature of what he had just attempted. Silently, he thanked the good spirits that he had not died.

As he rose to his feet, Ian groaned from soreness. He dusted himself off, scooped up his pack, and set it in the boat. With the boat's stern firmly in his grip, he pulled. It moved only a few inches. Determined, he kept pulling, slowly easing the boat to the water's edge. When the stern reached the water, he moved to the bow and began to push. Soon, the back half of the boat was afloat. Another push and the boat slid into the river. Ian tried to leap onto the boat, slipped off, and his feet fell into the shallows. He pushed off the bottom and tipped over the edge, into the boat. His boots and the hem of his robes were wet, but he had made it.

Ian pulled the two oars from the bottom of the boat, set each oar pin in place, and began to row. When he drew near the middle of the river, the current quickened, sweeping him downstream. He set the oars inside the boat, lay back and gazed up at the singular, puffy white cloud in the pale morning sky. How long it would take to reach the city, he was uncertain, but an easy, uneventful day lay ahead of him. Considering the tense ordeals he had endured in the first leg of his journey, a lazy ride downstream sounded like a pleasant break.

CHAPTER 17

RECRUITMENT

Flames flickered in the breeze, clinging to the remaining husk of what was once the home of a wealthy merchant. That home had become the headquarters of a criminal gang for half a year. Now, it was a blackened skeleton of charred stone and broken beams. Bodies littered the courtyard as well as the street and alley outside. There was no telling how many other corpses had been consumed in the blaze. The glow of the fire caused the smoke over the riverfront district to glow with an angry red aura. Beyond the smoke, a blanket of darkness covered the cloudy night sky.

Revita stepped over a man in black, his torso sliced open from hip to hip, his entrails spilled out beside him. A stride away, a man with a red band on his arm lay face down with a bloody splotch in the middle of his back. It was a grim scene without a living person in sight.

Vic's voice came from behind her. "This is worse than I anticipated."

"At least our plan worked."

"But at what cost?" Despite the ruthless treatment the citizens of Bard's Bay had endured the prior two seasons, the sight of the dead gang members brought a notable sorrow in his voice.

153

She turned toward him. "There is no way to rid this city of vermin other than extermination. Think of the citizens you are helping, not of the price paid for their liberation."

He sighed. "I know. I just...feel bad for the innocents caught up in this."

"Is this about Dennard's wagon again?"

"His wagon, his horses, the flour he paid for but was unable to sell, the people going hungry from the lack of food..."

She gripped his hand. "Lokix and his crew are finished. At least a dozen of Creskin's men lie dead here as well, and that doesn't include the six we eliminated while stealing the wagon."

"That still leaves two gangs, one of which likely numbers over a hundred ruthless criminals."

"Remaining in Bard's Bay to deal with this was your idea."

"How many times are you going to remind me?"

She smirked. "That depends on how often you lament about the actions we are forced to take to address the issue."

He nodded. "Fair enough. We have an objective, and I need to remain focused." He glanced around. "I just wish there was a less violent solution."

A whinny came from the darkness.

Vic turned toward the sound. "Did you hear that?"

"Yes."

When he headed down the road, she hurried to catch up to him. They moved beyond the glow of the fire and followed the pale ribbon of the downhill, gravel road. The trees along the road appeared like a wall of darkness against the sky, which had just begun to glow with predawn light. Another whinny resounded, followed by a snort. Vic angled toward the sound and stopped.

A pair of horses stood in the long grass between the road and the trees. A wagon was attached to the team, the wagon bed tilted at a steep angle.

"It's Dennard's wagon and team." Wonder replaced the haunted regret that had tainted Vic's words moments earlier. "They survived the fire."

Revita rounded the wagon and found the reason behind the odd angle. "This wheel is broken off the axle."

"Repairing a broken wheel costs far less than replacing a wagon and two horses."

"True," she admitted. "Are you going to go tell Dennard that you found it?"

"No. We are going to pay to get it repaired first."

Their coin was running low. "Vic..."

He spun to face her. "This is going to happen, Vita."

Rather than retort, she smiled. "I guess I'll just have to steal some more coin."

"If you do, don't tell me about it. I don't want to know." He looked up. "Daybreak is upon us. Let's go get some breakfast and find a wain-wright. I want to make sure nobody else happens upon the horses before we get back."

～

THE MIDDAY SUN peeked through a gap in the clouds, warming Vic and forcing him to squint. He sat alone on a wagon seat with the reins in both hands, driving the team down the same harbor road he and Revita had used just two days prior when stealing the wagon. The irony was not lost on him.

The wagon rolled past the west pier, where a pair of ships were docked. Workers busily unloaded cargo into wagons, as he had expected. Men in black stood in clusters, monitoring the situation, also as expected. However, the quartets of guards had dwindled to trios. He wondered if the change was only for the day, considering the nighttime battle against Lokix, or if Creskin's crew had been diluted enough for the change to be permanent. He then spied a cart rolling from the eastern pier, the man behind the cart immediately familiar. Visibly straining as he pushed the cart uphill, Dennard leaned into his work. The ground leveled as he reached the harbor road, where he paused to wipe his brow. As Vic and the wagon drew near, the man turned toward the wagon, his eyes widening.

"Whoa!" Vic called out while pulling on the reins.

The horses slowed and the wagon came to a stop just strides from Dennard.

"You found my team!" the man exclaimed.

"And your wagon."

"Where? How?"

"I suspect you heard about what happened last night."

The man's expression darkened. "It's all anyone on the docks can talk about. Creskin's men were sure to point it out as an example of what would happen to anyone who dares to cross their boss."

"Well, Lokix may have paid a steep price, but his loss is your gain. I found the wagon near his manor. The team must have escaped, but they didn't make it far with a broken wheel."

Dennard rounded the wagon and frowned. "Where did you get the new wheel?"

"I found a wainwright and had it repaired."

"You didn't need to do that."

"I owed you..." Vic stopped when he realized he could not say more.

"Nonsense. The theft wasn't your fault."

Hurriedly, Vic found a plausible excuse. "I should have found a way to stop them."

"Hess and his men attempted the same and died for it. Better that you ran for help than risk your life for nothing. You dying would have done neither of us any good."

"I suppose you have a point."

"Of course, I do." Dennard gestured toward the cart. "Now, I can stop using this old thing and move goods the way they were meant to be moved." He grinned. "With horses doing the work."

"I am glad to have helped."

"Now that I have a wagon again, would you like to come back and work for me?"

"I..." Vic froze before another word could be uttered.

A familiar figure stepped off the east pier and headed toward the city gate. He wore a black cloak over gray robes. His face was bearded, his hair a bit longer than Vic remembered, but his build, profile, and manner were unmistakable.

"Ian?" Vic said just loud enough.

Ian turned and gaped. "Vic?"

Dennard frowned. "Vic? I have been calling you Vinny for over a week."

Vic didn't even hear the man. Instead, he jumped down from the wagon and took off at a deliberate walk. Ian began toward him and then suddenly burst into a run. Arms wide, Vic welcomed his brother with a big hug, lifting and spinning him a full turn before setting him down.

Ian grinned. "I am so glad to see you. What are you doing here?"

"I was going to ask you the same thing."

With a snort and a gesture toward the pier, Ian said, "I was trying to buy passage on a ship, but I can barely even get anyone to talk to me."

"Passage? To where?"

Ian's gaze flicked to Dennard. "I...will tell you later."

"Who is this, Vinny?" Dennard asked. "Or should I call you Vic?"

Trapped without a plausible story to avoid the topic, Vic chose to delay his answer, instead seeking a more secluded setting. "How about we help you unload this cart to your wagon and then follow you to the warehouse?"

"Very well. Then what?"

"Then, I will provide some answers to both of you."

Ian said, "Something tells me you are in trouble."

"Not just me. The entire city. But no more about that until we are in private."

Without another word, Vic grabbed a crate from the cart, hefted it, and lumbered over to the wagon.

～

REVITA STROLLED through a busy square occupied by carts, wagons, and people purchasing goods from farmers and vendors selling their wares. She entered a street connected to the square and paused outside a shop full of various oddities ranging from rugs and kitchenware to weapons. The shop reminded her of the Trade and Barter in Greavesport but on a smaller scale. A man with a sword on his hip stood just inside the door. He was tall with broad shoulders and a narrow waist. A hood cast his face in shadow, but he undoubtedly watched the patrons passing in and out of the shop.

The guard would make the shop more difficult to rob during the day, but Revita preferred to work at night anyway, choosing stealth and expert burglary skills over something more brazen and bound to attract attention. Still, she needed coin, and this shop seemed as good a target as any, perhaps better than most if the owner could afford to pay for a guard.

Passing the guard, she stepped inside and casually began to browse. Of course, shopping was the furthest thing from her mind. Her true intentions were far less honorable. Yet, she remained aware of the cloaked guard near the door. Hoping to avoid suspicion, she lifted a gray cloak from a hook and held it before her as if to examine it, using the ruse to see if the guard was looking in her direction. The man's eyes met hers and she gasped in recognition.

"Essex?"

The man frowned and turned to look outside.

She set the cloak back on the hook, approached him, and spoke in a quiet tone. "I thought you died with Kaden."

He did not look at her. "You must be mistaken. My name is Sampson."

Any good thief trained themselves in keen observation and memorization. That included people as much, if not more, than anything else. "I know those eyes. I know it is you."

He looked back at her. "And how do you know this?"

"Last Autumn, you made the mistake of delivering me to the Carcera."

A brief pause followed before he responded. "Ah. I now recall you from the misguided attempt to rob Kaden. Let me guess...you getting caught was intentional."

She smirked. "You aren't as stupid as you look."

He glanced from side to side. "Which is why I remain alive. Now, please leave before you draw the wrong person's attention."

Revita's plan to steal from the shop was rapidly discarded in favor of another idea. "Where can we talk?"

He took a deep breath, set his jaw, and then sighed. "Meet me at Jolly Jasper's Inn at dusk. Come alone. If anyone else is with you, I am out. Betray me, and you'll wish you had just walked away."

She strolled past him and stopped while staring up the street. Over her shoulder, she said, "I will see you then."

❦

"...which is why we stole your wagon." Vic avoided looking into Dennard's eyes while sharing his story. Shame already left him wanting to flee. He did not wish to see the sting of betrayal in the man's eyes. "We drove it to the manor where Lokix and his men lived, put a note on the door telling him that the wagon, the team, and the load of flour were gifts from Torrigan, and left."

A long and uncomfortable moment of silence had Vic shifting his gaze from Dennard to Ian and back.

"So," Dennard rubbed his chin. "You intended to put the blame on Lokix, so Creskin would go after him?"

"Yes."

"You lied to me about your name and everything else."

Not everything, Vic thought. He opened his hands in supplication. "If there had been another way, I would have taken it, but..."

The man flashed a palm, stopping Vic in mid-sentence. "The lump on my head is still sore, but that was the least of the pain I experienced in this ordeal. I won't pretend that your stealing from me does not hurt, nor am I happy about wasting so much coin on a wagon full of flour that I won't recover. However, your intentions were on the side of good. Your plan worked, and there are certainly fewer criminals for the citizens of Bard's Bay to contend with, but Creskin remains in power and until that changes, we remain under the thumb of oppressors driven by greed and corruption."

During the entire conversation, Vic's brother had remained silent. Until now.

Ian furrowed his brow. "These criminals who rule the city...I assume they disposed of Commander Kaden."

"Yes. Last Autumn."

"As I thought," Ian said. "This happened after we released them from the Carcera."

"What?" Dennard exclaimed.

Guilt further darkened Vic's face. "It was not our intention to have this happen."

"Why would you free the likes of Creskin?"

Ian explained. "We broke into the prison to rescue some friends. Freeing a few other prisoners was meant to be a distraction, so we could escape. We never suspected that they would overwhelm the guards and free all the remaining prisoners. Even then, who would have guessed that they would capture Bard's Bay and hold her citizens hostage?"

Dennard crossed his arms over his chest, pressed his lips together, and frowned. His displeasure was obvious, and he had a right to be upset. The prison break had all but destroyed his city.

Although guilt and shame warred inside him, Vic spoke to fill the silence. "We cannot change the past. Freeing our companions from the Carcera was necessary, and I would do it again. Now, I am just trying to clean up the mess I helped create."

"Speaking of creating a mess," Ian asked, "Where is Revita?"

"She is in Bard's Bay with me and committed to our cause." Vic frowned. "Brady and Henrick left shortly after we arrived."

"They came here with you?"

"Yes, after Korrigan became king and freed our people. Some remained with the dwarves, some returned to Shillings, and some chose to go elsewhere. Brady and Henrick left with us, but when Revita and I decided to remain in Bard's Bay to deal with the gang problem, those two moved on, seeking a more stable situation. Last I heard, they were heading toward Hooked Point."

"Like them, I also need to leave soon." Ian looked Vic in the eyes. "I'd rather not travel alone. Perhaps you and Revita could join me?"

Vic frowned. "You are my brother, and I would love to come with you, but I cannot leave Bard's Bay until we deal with Creskin and his men."

"If I help you here, then what?"

The memory of Ian repulsing dozens of Drow with his magic flashed in Vic's head. "Your...abilities would certainly be welcome, but the three of us won't be enough against over a hundred criminals armed and ready to kill anyone who dares to cross them."

Dennard uncrossed his arms. "Abilities?" He looked Ian up and down. "He looks a bit small to be much of a warrior."

"You don't understand," Vic said.

"Say it clear, and maybe I will know what you are talking about."

Vic looked at Ian, who nodded. "Ian can do magic."

"You mean like the beggars who try and hide a nut beneath a trio of cups and make you guess which one?"

"No. Real magic."

Laughter from Dennard echoed throughout the warehouse.

Ian said, "He is telling the truth."

When neither Vic nor Ian gave in, Dennard's laughter quelled. "Very well. Let's see it."

Arching a brow, Vic stared at Ian, waiting.

"If I must." Ian strolled past Dennard and stopped just inside the warehouse doorway.

Hands extended, he stared at the wagon outside, still loaded with crates of potatoes. For a long beat, nothing happened. Then, the wagon rose up off the ground, not stopping until it was five feet up with the harness connecting it to the two horses drawn so tight, it appeared it might snap.

Jaw and eyes gaping, Dennard moved closer to the wagon, bent over, and peered beneath it. "How?"

The wagon slowly lowered back down. When the wheels touched the gravel, Ian dropped his hands and sighed.

"I told you," Vic said. "He can do magic."

Turning from the wagon, Dennard asked, "What else can you do?"

Ian shrugged. "Lots of things, ranging from launching fireballs to creating shields that can stop any weapon."

"Fireballs?" Vic didn't know Ian had access to such dangerous spells.

"I have been training, Vic. You will be surprised by what I can do now."

"That's it," Dennard said.

"What" Vic asked.

"I am in."

"You wish to help us?"

"I don't know anything about swords or bows, but I can drive a wagon and swing a sledgehammer. If you can come up with a plan to wipe out Creskin and his crew, I will be happy to do my part. Better yet, I know at least ten other honest businessmen who would risk everything for a chance to rid themselves of the affliction that plagues our city."

Vic glanced from Dennard to Ian as he fully grasped the new situation and the opportunity it offered. For the first time in over half a year, he and Revita were not in the fight against tyranny by themselves.

He flashed an honest smile, spurred by the well of hope bubbling within. "How soon can you get started?"

"I need to finish this load, and I have one more shipment lined up. Once that wagon load is in the warehouse, I am free."

"Perfect. We've about four hours of daylight remaining. You go on about your business. Ian and I will go find Revita and let her know what is afoot. We will then come with you."

"Come with me?"

"The three of us are going to visit your friends and see how many are willing to join the rebellion."

THE LAST MOMENTS of daylight clung to the sky as Revita ducked into a narrow alley, navigated past refuse, and rounded a crate, all the while watching for any signs of movement. Her hand remained near her dagger hilt, ready to react should anyone attempt to give her an unfriendly greeting. The dark alley led to a small gravel yard. Keeping near the wall, she approached the building's back door, opened it, and stepped inside, pausing to survey the room.

Lanterns mounted to wooden posts provided warm, dim light to the inn's dining room. Fewer than half the tables were occupied despite it being prime dining time. The occupants were all male, two of them dwarves, the other seven humans. In the far corner, draped in shadow, sat Essex.

She crossed the room, careful to take a path out of reach of any patrons, intent on avoiding any chance of one of the men making unwanted advances. Her typical response to such actions involved blades, which would draw unwanted attention. When she reached the table, she settled in across from Essex, who was huddled over a bowl of stew.

"Were you followed?" Essex asked without looking up.

"I grew up on the streets. I know how to get around without notice."

"Good." He scooped a spoon of beef and potatoes into his mouth.

"You probably want to know why I am here."

He glanced up with a brow arched. "Hopefully, you are looking for a tumble."

The man was not unattractive. A year earlier she might have taken him up on the offer. "Sorry. This is about business."

"What business?"

"Bard's Bay itself."

"What about it?"

She leaned in and spoke softly. "You cannot like the way of things as they stand."

A cloud passed over his face. His mouth twisted in a deep frown before he looked back down at his bowl and scooped a spoonful of stew. "What of it?" He slid the spoon into his mouth and chewed.

Revita glanced over her shoulder to ensure nobody was within hearing distance. "Lokix and his crew are finished."

"I heard."

"That was my doing."

He paused with the spoon in front of his lips. "The way I hear it, Creskin stomped him out for a misstep."

"The misstep was what I meant. It was done to place blame on Lokix. Creskin's Crew did the rest."

"Well, thank you for removing a few dozen of the leeches who have been sucking the life out of Bard's Bay. Too bad over a hundred of them remain."

"That's why I am here. I want you to help squash the rest of the buggers."

"What can I do?"

"You can lead. You can fight."

"Lead an army of two?"

"Surely there are others in the city who will follow you."

Essex sat back and stared at her before replying. "There might be a few, some of whom followed my orders before the city was flipped on its back."

"That's a start."

"There are still too many in Creskin's Crew."

"We will reduce their numbers."

"Who is we?"

"I have not been working alone. In fact, my partner is recruiting others as we speak."

He narrowed his eyes. "What of weapons?"

"You have a sword."

"Aye. Most of my men do as well, but we need to outnumber Creskin if we hope to retake the castle."

She smiled. "I cannot reveal the details but suffice it to know that the castle walls won't hinder our plans. If I can get you safely inside, will you lead the assault to oust Creskin?"

"Oust him? I want that murderer to hang for what he's done."

Revita shrugged. "I honestly don't care how you deal with him. I just want to see the excessive protection fees gone and put an end to the praying upon innocents and the blatant corruption."

"Why do you care?"

"Does it matter? I am giving you a chance to get back at him...unless you would prefer to just waste your days away as a guard at Orgal's Barter Shop."

"And then what?"

She leaned back and draped an elbow over the chair beside her. "Then, I will leave this armpit and move on. Hopefully, whoever replaces Creskin is somewhat better than Kaden was."

"Kaden had his faults. He and I did not always agree, but at least he had enough honor not to pray on the weak and enough sense not to squeeze every last ounce of blood from his subjects."

"In truth, I don't care what Kaden did or did not do. I just want to fix the current mess and be on my way."

Essex pushed the bowl away, wiped stew from his beard, and gave a firm nod. "I will do it."

She grinned. "As I suspected. How about I buy you an ale and we can talk about what comes next."

~

IAN STOOD IN AN ABANDONED BUILDING. Broken furniture, dust, and debris lay strewn across the floor. Strides away, Vic knelt in the closet beneath the stairs, fumbled in the darkness, and raised a trap door. The situation had Ian curious, but he resisted asking questions after Vic's warning that he was to remain quiet and watch for anyone passing by. There was no need to be concerned with the latter. The street outside was vacant with nary a sound coming through the broken front door. While crossing the city, Ian and Vic had come across only one other pair of men, both dressed in black and giving threatening glares as they walked past. At just an hour after nightfall, the city seemed like a shell empty of life. It felt odd and wrong.

"Come down." Vic whispered from below. "Watch your step. It is steep."

Ian shuffled into the closet, squatted, and felt around until he found the lip of the opening. He sat, lowered his leg, and caught a stair with his heel. With care, he turned and began to climb down. His foot slipped, and he dropped into the hole. Fear of injury had him desperately swinging his arms as he tried to grab ahold of something...anything.

"Oof," he grunted as arms wrapped about him and stopped his fall.

Vic chuckled in his ear. "Wizard or not, you are still the same little brother I remember."

Ian found footing on a dirt floor as Vic held him up. "Thanks."

"Stay here. I need to close the trap door."

Appearing as a shadowy silhouette, Vic climbed the steep stairs, toward the pale outline of the opening above. He pulled the trapdoor closed, and the opening disappeared. The darkness became so thick, Ian could not see his hand when waved before his face.

"Can I make us some light, now?" Ian asked.

Chuckling as he descended, Vic said, "Yes."

Ian cast a spell that created a tiny flame burning in the air midway between his palms.

"That is handy." Vic reached for a lantern, opened it and pointed. "Can you light this?"

Applying a bit of will along with a gesture, Ian moved the flame so it slid into the opening. The lantern bloomed to life to reveal a cellar. The shelving along the walls lay mostly empty and a single bed sat against the cellar's far end. The remaining furniture consisted of only a table, two chairs, and a storage chest that sat at the foot of the bed.

"It's not much," Vic said, "But this is home. For now."

Ian nodded. "This is certainly not much. I do find it ironic that we both have been living underground, especially after you spent an entire summer in the mines below Ra'Tahal."

Vic's smile melted. "That was a challenging time. While this place is a dingy hole in the ground, it has proven safe. And Revita has been here with me."

Ian noticed the look in Vic's eyes when he said her name. "You really like her, don't you."

"She makes me happy." Vic crossed the room, pulled out a chair, and sat. "Come and sit." He reached for a pitcher on the shelf beside the table, grabbed a pair of metal cups, and began to pour.

As Ian sat across from his brother, Vic pushed a cup toward him. "What is this?'

"Water." Vic took a swig. "I figured you'd be thirsty after today."

"My waterskin has been empty for hours." Ian tipped the cup up and downed its contents in one long swig. "Ahh," he sighed in satisfaction.

"So," Vic began. "What have you been doing the past two seasons?"

"Training."

"You look good. Healthy, even."

"When I, um, gained my abilities, something else in my body changed. My stomach problems have been less of an issue. In addition, Truhan does not just have me practicing magic. He has made me work my body. He says that my magic will do no good if my body fails me."

Vic nodded. "That makes sense."

"It was hard at first. In fact, I hated it. But the stronger I grew, the better I felt. Now, I can run up the mountainside without needing to stop and rest."

Reaching across the table, Vic grabbed Ian's shoulder and gave a friendly shake. "Just watch, soon you'll be bigger and stronger than me."

Ian grinned. "I doubt it." Vic stood four inches taller than Ian and outweighed him by a fair margin, all of it muscle.

Vic took another swig of his water and sat back. "Are you hungry? We have some bread left from yesterday."

"No. The meal we ate with Dennard and his friends was more than sufficient."

"Feeding them wiped out the last of my coin, but it was worth it if they join us as they promised."

"True."

A quiet settled in, the silence tainted by discomfort. Even though they were brothers, Vic was three years older than Ian, which had kept them at different stages of maturity while growing up. Had they been the same age, their interests had still rarely aligned. Both issues often created an awkwardness between them that Ian struggled to get beyond.

The quiet became too much, so Ian filled the void with another question. "Have you seen mother?"

"No. Vita and I came straight here after leaving Ra'Tahal."

Ian had expected as much. "I hope she is safe."

"Why would she not be safe? She is in a dwarven stronghold."

Memories of his vision roused Ian's anxiety, causing his stomach to churn. He again saw hordes of dark-skinned creatures swarming over the land and slaughtering anyone who came in their path. *How do I tell Vic?*

As if reading Ian's mind, Vic said, "You mentioned the need to travel by ship. Where do you go and why?"

"I must go to Havenfall."

Furrowing his brow, Vic asked, "Isn't that an elven city?"

"It is."

"Why?"

Uncertain of how to share the details, Ian began with a vague reply. "I seek someone there, someone who can provide answers."

"Answers to what?"

How do I tell him about my vision? Ian barely believed it himself. If his master had not convinced him to react, he likely would have found a way to dismiss it. "Something bad is coming, Vic."

His brother frowned. "Like a storm?"

"Worse. Much worse."

"What does that have to do with you traveling to this elven city?"

"I am seeking someone who can get me answers."

"Answers to what?"

"What is the Paragon, and where can I find it?"

"The Paragon?"

"Yes."

"Hmm." Vic cocked his head and pressed forward. "This thing you search for, you make it sound important."

"Right now, it is the most important thing in the world."

His brother followed with a firm nod. "In that case, if you can help us resolve the trouble here in Bard's Bay, I'll come with you, assuming I can get Revita to agree to it as well."

"Do you think she'll do it?"

"I'd love to say yes, but that woman is often unpredictable. Still, I'll do my best to convince her."

Ian was relieved. He needed help from someone he could trust. While he remained uncertain about Revita, Vic would never betray him or let him down.

CHAPTER 18

COMMITMENT

Ian strolled along the streets of Bard's Bay after leaving Vic and Revita alone in their small underground apartment. He knew Vic intended to broach the idea that he and Revita join Ian on his quest to find the Paragon, yet he tried not to dwell on how his brother intended to convince her. Having spent the evening on the floor of the cellar with them in the bed just strides away, he was thankful that he had not seen or heard anything embarrassing – something that had occurred once before.

With it being late afternoon and nothing for him to do until sunset, Ian decided to make the best of his time rather than waste the opportunity. He headed northeast, away from the city's center as he sought solitude. Soon, the gaps between buildings grew more pronounced, trees filling those spaces until the trees far outnumbered the buildings.

He reached the outer edge of the city, where the road curved toward the sea. Far across the water, dark, angry clouds blanketed the distant horizon. Rain would fall when the cloud reached land, but the storm was at least an hour away, allowing him the time he needed.

A split in the road left him with a decision, and he chose to take an uphill route bordered by foliage and rocks. The road ran along a ridge, curving with the hillside up to a sharp bend. He rounded it and continued up, slowly rising above the seaside city. It wasn't until he reached another bend and a large, stone building came into view that he realized where he was.

A switchback away, beyond a thin veil of trees, a castle loomed at the top of a bluff. Guards dressed in black stood on the walls and in clusters before the castle gate, made of black iron bars with spiked tips thrust into the ground. Three towers loomed above the wall and the rest of the castle.

The portcullis began to open, the clanking of chains echoing inside the gate tower. When the gate was halfway open, the men before the gate shifted to the side and the thunder of hooves arose. A quartet of guards rode through the gate, turned, and came down the road. Ian's heart leapt into his throat.

Urgency demanded he hide, but his body and mind were not in sync. He spun in a hurried search for shelter and stumbled over his own feet. He caught himself, scraping his palms on the road, and quickly stood. The hillside above was too sparsely populated while the one below consisted of shrubs, trees, and shadows. He took two steps and leapt out into the air while drawing on his magic. He wrapped a shield around himself while simultaneously compressing the air below him, creating a furious upward draft. The wind slowed his fall. He landed hands-first and rolled while expanding the shield. It struck a tree trunk, stopping him.

The horses slowed and came to a stop on the road above him.

"Look at those trees," one man said. "The breeze is light today, yet the branches are swaying like a tornado is overhead."

"Maybe a dragon or a roc flew overhead."

A deep voice, thick with a Dwarvish accent snorted. "Ye had best hope we don't face a monster such as those."

The first voice said, "Could a monster like that stand against a hundred twenty of us?"

"Ye don't wanna find out. Let's go and collect today's fees, so we can get back and open that new barrel of Aeldor ale."

The thunder of hooves arose again as the horses trotted off, rounded the corner, and headed along the next switchback. Ian waited until the riders passed by below him before rising to his feet. A brief inspection revealed a tear in the hem of his robes and a scrape on his elbow in addition to his sore palms. He climbed down the hillside, rejoined the road, and continued down until the ground leveled. There, he followed another gravel path running parallel to the shoreline east of the city.

The road bordered a steep bluff dropping toward the sea. A mile from shore, the white of sails shone brightly in rays of sunlight shining through a gap in the clouds, creating a stark contrast against the approaching storm. The ship angled toward the harbor, likely delivering goods that would be sold for two to three times the price offered in other ports. Such had become life in Bard's Bay. In less than a day, Ian had come to realize why his brother was so adamant in rectifying the situation they had inadvertently created.

He rounded a point and spied a sheltered cove filled with dark rocks. Ian decided the cove was ideal, so he broke from the road and followed a dirt trail along the hillside, above the shoreline. When the path ended, he climbed down to a large rock shelf jutting out toward the water. Waves crashed into the rocks at the cove's mouth while gulls circled overhead. There, Ian settled cross legged on the flat shelf of rock, pressed his palms together, and closed his eyes. In mere moments, he sank into meditation, allowing his mind to wander while his body rested.

The voice of his master echoed in his head. *Don't forget to continue training. You must master your abilities and do so with a sense of urgency.*

Ian had used his magic several times since leaving his mountain home, but those uses had been in reaction to something, rather than being intentionally planned. If he was to truly advance, he would need to do so with intention, and that included learning knew spells. As proven by his misguided attempt at a negative energy spell, experimentation came with risks to him and anyone else around. To avoid any victims should a spell go awry, he had sought refuge from others.

His mind drifted on the lullaby of crashing waves. *The waves,* he thought. *They contain energy. Can I read that energy and harness it in the form of a spell?* Determined to find out, he allowed magic to flow into him, its song firm and steady in contrast to the periodic rhythm of the waves. Opening his eyes, he stared into space, waiting for a wave to crash against the rock in the hope of catching sight of the energy signature. All the while, magic hummed through him, filling him with its energy and daring him to unleash it.

A wave struck the rocks in the cove and sent a fanning spray of white high into the air. The drops rained down as the wave rolled forward and sloshed against the rocky shore just strides away. Yet, Ian caught nothing of the signature he had hoped to discover. Unwilling to give up, he held onto his magic while keeping his mind disconnected from his body. Repeatedly, waves crashed against the rocks, each seeming more violent than the last as the storm marched toward him, stirring the sea into a frenzy.

A fork of lightning crashed down, its light flickering across the cloudbank. The white of the flash left an afterimage unlike any Ian had ever experienced. Adrenaline brought on by a rising excitement pulled him out of his meditation, but the image, burned into his eyes by its brightness, hovered before him.

The construct's core was identical to the other energy spells, but the symbols and intersecting lines surrounding it were unique. Ian dug through the pack at his side, located a chunk of chalk, and began to sketch on the water-smoothed surface of the rock. Moving with quick, confident strokes, he recreated the construct's inner and outer rings, finishing the latter just as the image in his eyes faded.

Ian pocketed the chalk and stood. His magic demanded release, and his curiosity required him to bend to that wish. With a hand extended before him, he crafted the construct, giving it an energy core while surrounding it with two rings exactly matching his sketch. With a thrust and willpower, he channeled magic through the construct.

A bolt of lightning shot outward, splintered, and then arced down into the sea half a mile away. A flash of energy shimmered across the water and then went dark.

Excited to try his new spell again, Ian turned to stare at the rocky hillside across the cove. He thrust his hand toward the cliff, over two hundred feet away, and allowed his magic to flow out. A bolt of lightning shot across the gap and struck the wall of rock. Shards blasted from the strike, which left an indentation a foot deep and three feet wide. The cavity and area around it were black as coal.

Ian turned his palms toward himself and grinned. He had learned a new spell, one that might turn out useful. He stepped back and stared down at his sketch. Lightning flashed in the corner of his eye. Thunder boomed five seconds later. The storm was drawing near, but Ian would not leave until he had memorized every detail of his new discovery.

⁓

TWO DOZEN MEN and dwarves stood amid the crates and barrels in Dennard's warehouse. Ian visually weighed the odd collection of males. Some were only a few years older than Ian while the oldest two both had gray hair. Those dockworkers, traders, and shopkeepers, all contacts of Dennard, had come to join the fight and, while most seemed fit enough, none appeared to have military experience. They stood in small clusters, engaged in conversation while Ian, Vic, Revita, and Dennard looked on. Waiting.

Nervous that Dennard's men might lose patience or courage and leave, Ian leaned close to Revita. "Where is he?"

"He will be here," she said with conviction.

"What if he changed his mind?"

"While that is possible, there was a fire in his eyes when he agreed to help us. I am skilled at reading people, and Essex is not one to shy from his commitments."

A knock came from the door. Thump, thump, thump. Pause. Thump, thump, thump.

Dennard unhooked the latch and slid the door open to reveal a puddle outside and shadowy figures standing in the night.

A tall, athletic man strolled in, his head covered by the hood of his cloak. He wore a sword on his hip, and his firm, confident movements informed Ian that he knew how to use it. A string of eleven others followed him in, two of them dwarves, one an elf, the others all male humans. The man in the lead stopped a stride from Revita and lowered his hood. His black hair was cropped short, his beard graced by gray streaks along his jaw and chin. He looked over the room with a steely gaze in his brown eyes. Ian recognized him immediately.

"Took you long enough, Essex," Revita said.

"You wanted recruits, but today's storm slowed my efforts. It took me until tonight to locate these two dwarves." Essex gestured toward the stout pair, one with a braided black beard, the other with a brown one dangling to his belt. "By then, it was already dark and I had to go and fetch the others from the Jasper's before coming here."

Vic shifted position to stand beside Revita and gave Essex a firm nod. "Now that you are here, we can get started."

Essex stared at the crowd across the room. "They don't look like warriors."

"Have you ever been hit by a hammer?" Dennard asked.

"Actually, yes. Hurts like hell."

"Even cobblers know how to swing a hammer. Half of them work hard labor every day, so they are strong enough. We also have access to a blacksmith, a tanner, a fletcher, a baker, a carpenter, a mason, two dockworkers, and three traders. Each of the traders owns a wagon and a team to pull it."

Essex rubbed his jaw. "In truth, some of those skills might be useful." He then looked at Ian. "Ah. I know you."

Ian nodded. "You arrested me last autumn."

The man looked Ian over and snorted. "I hope you know how to use a weapon better than what I witnessed during that ridiculous robbery attempt."

"I don't intend to use a weapon."

"In that case, stay out of the way, so you don't get yourself or someone else killed."

When Ian's nostrils flared, his brother gripped his wrist.

"Just let it go," Vic said in a soft voice. "Essex is not the enemy."

A year ago, Ian would have wilted in the face of a warrior like Essex. Now, he stood resolute and met the man's intense glare. His magic gave him the confidence he had lacked before. His reaction and willingness to fight the man surprised even him. *You are known for having a cool head, Ian. Don't lose it now.*

"Very well," he said in an even tone.

"You convinced us to come here," Essex said. "Now, please share exactly what you intend."

Revita furrowed her brow. "You already agreed to help plan and lead the assault."

He shook his head. "Impossible. I thought you had more people than this. Thirty people cannot take a castle held by over a hundred men. Worse, only a third of us are battle trained."

"We have a secret weapon," Vic said.

"What would that be?"

Does he mean me? Ian wondered until Vic clapped him on the shoulder.

"We have a wizard," his brother said with a smile.

The man frowned at Ian. "What in the blazes is a wizard?"

"Ian. Show the man."

With a nod, Ian stepped away. He approached a lone barrel standing in the center of the warehouse. At Ian's request, the empty barrel had been placed there, anticipating that a demonstration would be needed to convince the others. Although a display of power was required, it needed to be one that came without the risk of injuring anyone in the warehouse. Using the empty barrel as his target would do just that but only after he first removed the spigot plug.

His jaw set in determination, Ian held a hand toward the barrel and formed an energy spell. He then made a fist, and drove all of the air from the barrel, out of the spigot hole. The barrel shot across the room. Without air or anything else inside the barrel, the air pressure outside it caused the wooden slats to implode. A deep thump shook the building, the noise causing many to jerk with a start. Mutters came from the wide-eyed onlookers. A furrowed brow was Essex' only reaction.

Ian turned from the pile of splintered wood and strolled back toward Essex while dusting his hands off. "Try to stay out of my way, so you don't get yourself killed."

Revita laughed. "He turned your own wisecrack back on you, Essex."

The former captain of Kaden's guard stared at Ian. "How did you do that?"

Shrugging, Ian said, "Magic."

"Real magic?"

"You saw it for yourself. How else would you explain it?"

"What else can you do?"

Ian crossed his arms and arched a brow. "A lot."

"Can you get us inside a castle?"

"Yeah. I know I can."

"And once inside, you can open the castle gate?"

"If that is what is required."

"Hmm." Essex stared into space, seemingly considering the situation. He then nodded. "Maybe there is a chance."

"A chance is all we need," Vic said. "That, and a plan. The five of us..." He gestured toward Revita, Ian, Dennard, Essex, and himself. "Will talk to each of our recruits. When we have a clear grasp of what each can offer to our cause, we will form a plan."

CHAPTER 19
WARNING

Rina repeated a series of words in Elvish, following each word by its translation spoken in her native tongue. Her studies had shifted from mundane conversations to rarely used terms. While she was still not completely confident when speaking Elvish, her grasp of the language had expanded to the point where it invaded her dreams. When she completed the task, her tutor glanced toward the sky. The sunbeams filtering through the golden tree leaves above came down at a steep angle, informing her that noon was fast approaching.

"We are finished for today," Isra-Shi announced. "You have made commendable progress over recent weeks. You no longer sound like a toddler fresh off the teat." It was as close to a compliment as Rina had heard from the stern elf.

"Thank you, Mistress Isra-Shi."

"For your next phase of learning, I wish you spent some time in the city."

"Spend time in the city?"

"I wish you to find reasons to engage in conversations with my people. Your confidence and comfort with our language will improve with regular use. Refrain from leaning on your native tongue. It is a crutch you no longer require."

"Yes, Mistress."

"Be well, Safrina. I will see you tomorrow morning." Isra-Shi crossed the terrace, her soft footsteps fading as she entered the corridor.

Rina held tight to her tutor's mild compliment as a prize to cherish. She was improving. That alone gave her added confidence in speaking the complex language. Still, the idea of venturing into the city filled her with anxiety that caused her stomach to growl. *I will eat something and then visit the city.* Immediately, she chose her first destination. It was a shop she had visited before, which offered some semblance of comfort.

∼

A CREAM shawl covered Rina's shoulders. Beneath it was a blue dress with skirts that ruffled in the midday breeze. She approached the wall of arches that bordered the half of the garden not contained by the palace. Beyond the wall, the view opened to the glass domes, layered terraces, and narrow spires of Havenfall. Sunlight glinted off the golden-leafed trees scattered throughout the city.

A short staircase brought her to a circular plaza paved with white stone tiles. A ring of pillars surrounded a fountain in the heart of the plaza. Water gushed from a column above the fountain, spilled over troughs mounted to the top of each of the eight pillars, and rained down into a pool at ground level. A series of arches stretched in eight directions, allowing the aqueducts to send water to districts throughout the city. She crossed the plaza, followed the path between two trees, and continued down a hillside path beneath one of the aqueducts.

The trees parted to reveal another paved square, this one surrounded by buildings. Citizens dressed in pastel fabrics crisscrossed the open space, some carrying baskets, some carrying sacks. Elves worked beneath the shade of awnings sticking out from the buildings along the plaza exterior. Humans, all dressed in white to denote them as slaves, carried goods across the space. At the plaza's far end, Rina stopped and gaped at what had become of the apothecary.

What had once been a place of peace, beauty, and the perfect marriage of civilization and nature was now a pile of rubble – the roof collapsed, the walls crumbled, the area littered with debris. In her head, she recalled overhearing Evarian's conversation with Tora-Li. *A roc killed two Valeguard just last week and made it beyond the palace before it was taken from the sky. The apothecary was destroyed when it crashed down.* Fear of being discovered at the time had caused Rina to pay little attention to the details. Whether she had dismissed his statement or doubted its validity, she had not considered its impact until now. *It is true.*

With sorrow in her heart, she approached the building, or what remained of it. The pleasant scents of flowers and herbs had greeted her during her previous visit. This time, the destroyed building smelled only of rock and dust. She ran her hand along an alabaster pillar lying amid the debris while recalling the beauty and grace it used to represent.

A female voice speaking Elvish came from behind her. "Have you come to mourn the dead as I do?"

She turned to find a familiar face standing a stride away. "Miral." She was the female cultivator Shria-Li had introduced Rina to during the last visit, half a year earlier. "I did not hear your approach." Rina glanced toward the rubble. "This is horrible. I did not realize the extent of the damage until now."

"It fills my heart with sorrow." Although no tears were visible, Miral's voice was thick with them. "I visit every day, but the wound in my soul festers."

"What happened to the plants you kept here?"

"They are now trapped in a prison made of dust and debris."

"And the other cultivators who worked here?"

With heartbreak in her eyes, Miral stared into the rubble. "I am the only one who remains."

"Oh, my." Rina could not imagine being inside the building when it collapsed. "That must have been awful." She glanced around to ensure there were no prying ears. "I have heard rumors. What truly happened here?"

"A roc broke past the barrier. The Valeguard chased the creature inland, but not before it scooped up a male elf – one of our rain dancers. The creature lifted the captive elf toward the sky, and the Valeguard attacked. A ballista bolt pierced the bird's eye. The roc, a bird the size of a house, crashed down upon the apothecary."

"Oh, my. Where were you?"

"I was returning to work after running an errand." She pointed across the plaza. "I was standing there when the creature crashed down." A tear ran down her face. "Dust swirled, blocking my view for a time before it cleared. Screams came from inside the building, but my feet refused to move. I was overcome by the suffering coming through the connection with the plants I cared for. It held me in shock for some time before my legs responded and I approached the building. I was able to rescue a handful of plants, but most remained buried beneath this rubble." Miral stared into space. "They die slowly, wilting from lack of sunlight, water, or care, but I can do nothing to help them. Where are the workers? Someone needs to remove the rubble before it is too late."

Rina thought it was odd for Miral to focus on the plants rather than the elves who were lost in the accident, yet she was still learning about Sylvan peculiarities. *Perhaps cultivators feel more for plants than they do for people.* The notion would have been unthinkable just a year prior, but Rina had seen enough to understand that elven culture differed as much from her own in many ways.

"Please. Excuse me. I prefer to be alone right now." Miral walked off, strode into the ruins and sat on a broken bench. She placed her face in her hands and wept.

The sight broke Rina's heart, yet what could she do?

Shouts drew her attention. She turned and searched for the cause of the disturbance. Elves emerged from buildings along the far side of the plaza. All stared down a connecting street, toward what, Rina was uncertain until the clopping of horses arose. The steeds trotted out from the street, riding in pairs. At the fore was a standard bearer, the wavering flag above him marked with the image of a golden tree in a circle of green and black. A field of blue surrounded the circle.

A regal figure draped in gold and green armor rode beside the flag bearer. A crown of golden leaves rested upon the king's head, holding his pale hair from his proud, gorgeous face. A green and gold helm rested in one arm, the other gripping the reins. Four pairs of mounted guards rode behind him.

The standard bearer announced in a deep voice, "Out of the way. King Fastellan returns."

"He has returned." The mere sight of him lifted Rina's spirits.

The retinue crossed the plaza and faded down another street at the far end, on their way back to the palace.

Before Rina even knew what was happening, her feet were taking her back toward the palace. She imagined him holding her, caressing her, kissing her, and promising that he would never leave her again. Of course, such thoughts were pure fantasy, but they were all she had for now. She still did not understand how she and Fastellan could be together without it affecting Tora-Li, but he had repeatedly assured her that all would be well. Left between the choice of dwelling on guilt for her feeling as she did and believing him, she chose the latter.

Then, another thought came to her.

"Evarian." She needed to warn Fastellan. Some plan was to take shape, and she feared he was the target.

~

THE PALACE WAS busy with guards and servants crisscrossing the entrance hall. Rina paused to survey the area in search of Fastellan. When she did not see him, she approached the throne room door. Four elven guards, one of whom was female, stood before the closed doors.

"Pardon," Rina said in Elvish. "I am seeking King Fastellan. Is he in?"

"The queen currently holds court and is meeting with Captain Chavell. The king is not present."

Chavell? He was the one conspiring with Evarian. "But the king has returned?"

"Yes. Word of his arrival just reached us, but we have not seen his majesty."

Rina glanced down the adjacent corridor while considering where she might find Fastellan. Since he had come in on horseback, she strode off toward the stables.

Minutes later, she emerged to find the horse master and three humans rubbing down a team of horses with their heads in a water filled trough. A pair of guards stood just a few strides away from the horses, but there was no sign of Fastellan.

Rather than linger, Rina stepped back inside and made for the nearest staircase, where she ascended to the top floor. The moment she spied guards outside the door to the royal suite, she knew she had found him. Her stomach quivered in anticipation. With a calming breath, she smoothed her dress and headed down the corridor. Among the guards was a face he recognized, a youthful elf with long brown hair held back by a leather band. He stood tall with a hooked nose and gray eyes. In his hand was a spear made of dark wood and warm-tinted metal.

When Rina drew near, she addressed him. "Good afternoon, Askan."

The squad leader turned toward her, his eyes lighting in recognition. "Greetings, Safrina."

"I need to speak with Fastellan."

"The king just returned from a long journey and gave us orders to ensure he remains undisturbed."

She bit her lip. "I am afraid that the reason for my visit is urgent."

"Give me your message, and I will share it with him."

Can I trust him? If Chavell was in on the conspiracy, any other guard might be as well. "I cannot do that." She opted to try to appeal to him in another way. Her hand slid onto his chest. She batted her eyelashes. "I desperately need to speak with the king. He told me that I am to come to him any time I need his support. There has never been a greater need than now."

Askan frowned and glanced toward the door. "Not enough time has passed for him to fall asleep, so I am willing to risk his wrath. Just so you know, I am going to tell him that you insisted."

She nodded. "I will happily assume blame."

The elf squad leader knocked, the wrap of his knuckles echoing in the quiet corridor.

Fastellan's voice came from within. "I said I was not to be disturbed."

"Pardon, your majesty, but she says it is urgent." Askan replied in a loud voice.

The door flew open to reveal Fastellan with only a towel around his waist. Lithe muscles rippled beneath his smooth, tawny skin. His lips were drawn back in a sneer, his hair disheveled. He appeared like he was prepared to dress Askan down until he saw who stood among the guards.

"Safrina." The anger slid away from Fastellan's face. "What are you doing here?"

Rina gaped at his lean, muscular torso. Her heart began to race. Through force of will, she closed her gaping jaw and replied, "I must speak with you," She glanced toward the guards. "In private."

"I only just arrived after a long journey."

She replied in a quiet but intense tone. "It is urgent."

After a beat of consideration, Fastellan nodded and stepped back. "Come in."

Rina stepped into the royal suite and found it to be even more impressive than she anticipated.

The chamber was expansive and open with two terrace levels above where she stood. The far wall was all glass and curved out to create a half circle. A short run of stairs led down from the elevated entrance area where she stood. At the bottom of the stairs was an indoor garden surrounding a fountain. A tree with golden leaves stood in the center of the fountain. It appeared identical to the Tree of Life but on a much smaller scale, the tree's upper reaches falling just shy of the ceiling, thirty-some feet above. Open doorways waited at both ends of the chamber, not only on the lower floor. but both upper levels as well, giving her an impression as to just how expansive the royal quarters truly were.

"What is it?" Fastellan asked.

Rina turned her attention to him, her eyes drawn to his naked torso before climbing to his face. Her thoughts became jumbled by the thumping of her heart "I...um...weren't you wearing armor earlier?"

"I removed my armor at the stables and handed it to a servant for cleaning."

"Oh." She had a tough time concentrating.

"Listen, Safrina." Fastellan spoke softly. "This is an inconvenient time. We cannot be seen together, not like this. I fear rumors already swirl."

Rumors. The words sliced through the murk in Rina's head. "I fear a plot against you."

He blinked. "A plot? By whom?"

"This elf named Evarian."

He pressed his lips tightly together. "I see. And why do you believe he is plotting against me?"

"I overheard him talking to one of your guards in the gardens."

"Which guard?"

"Captain Chavell."

Fastellan frowned. "I have known Chavell my entire life. He is among my best friends. He would never betray me."

"And he told Evarian as much."

"What then?"

"I...don't know. Evarian claimed to have another idea, but he needed more time."

The king rubbed his jaw with his free hand, his other fist still holding his towel up. "Can you tell me anything more?"

"I..." She shook her head. "Not that I can recall."

"Well, thank you for bringing this to me. I will be more vigilant, both in watching for signs of trouble and concerning my own safety. I may also speak to Chavell, but I must consider how best to approach the subject." He gestured toward the door. "You should go before..."

The door opened. Tora-Li stepped in and stopped dead to glare at Rina, who stood a stride from her nearly naked husband. "What is this?" There was a sharp edge to the question.

"Close the door, my sweet," Fastellan said.

"Why?" She hissed. "Do you fear the guards learning the truth?"

He moved past her and pushed the door closed. In a soft voice, he said, "Calm down. This is not what you think."

The queen put a hand on one hip. "Are you now trying to tell me what to think?"

"Not at all."

"Then, why do I find you alone with our daughter's attendant? Unless she has found Shria-Li, I cannot think of a good reason for her to be in *our* apartment."

He moved closer and put a hand on her arm. "Safrina sought to warn me about a plot."

The queen's hard expression softened. "A plot?"

"Yes. It seems that Evarian tires of pressing me for approval to advance his agenda."

"You don't think..."

"I don't know what to think. As of now, I intend to be careful while quietly investigating the issue."

Tora-Li glanced toward Rina. "I still want her gone."

"She has done nothing wrong."

"Our daughter is missing!" Tora-Li insisted, "Why would her attendant remain at the palace?"

"I am looking for Shria-Li..."

"She has been gone for two seasons. Still, this...human occupies her chambers as if she were some...replacement."

He rubbed her arm. "Nobody could replace our daughter. Shria-Li is of our blood, the sapling we have raised since birth. She will be found."

The queen pressed her lips together. "I still want her gone."

"And she is leaving now." Fastellan nodded toward Rina. "Thank you, Safrina. You are dismissed."

Rina dipped a curtsy, walked to the door, and stepped out. The guards stared at her, judging her. She suddenly felt self-conscious and had to stifle the urge to run. Hugging herself, she walked off while a tear tracked down her cheek.

CHAPTER 20

SEA GATE

"All fives!"

Arangoli groaned. "You've the dark lord's luck, Kasgan."

The ship's captain swept the coins from the middle of the table. They joined the sizable pile he had collected. "Lady luck rules the seas, Goli. A sailor must show her proper respect at all times. Tis' wise to give her thanks when blessed with a sunny day and a strong tail wind and to beg for forgiveness when storms damage yer hulls. Like any lady, she'll treat you well if you do the same."

Kasgan had invited Arangoli and two other dwarves to roll dice in his cabin. The game had consumed much of the afternoon and helped to pass the time, a welcome respite after five days aboard the ship.

Gortch leaned back in his chair, crossed his arms over his paunch, and grimaced. "Well, she appears mighty cross with me. I am out of coin."

The captain laughed. "So long as you're not cross with me, Gortch. I'd hate to wake up with you sitting on my chest."

Rax snorted. "Sounds like a crushing defeat to me."

Gortch reached for Rax, who jumped to his feet and spun away. "When I get my hands on you..."

"I know," Rax grinned. "You're gonna eat me."

The chair beneath Gortch tipped backward and fell to the cabin floor when he stood. "Wrong. I'm gonna *feed* you." He waved his meaty fist. "How about a mouth full of knuckles?"

"Yikes!" Rax threw the cabin door open and raced outside with Gortch stomping after him.

When the door swung closed, Kasgan shook his head. "I wouldn't want to be Rax right now."

Arangoli waved the comment off. "Oh, those two are like brothers. It's why they go at it all the time."

"It seems the dice game is through." Kasgan did not hide the disappointment from his voice.

"Yeah. You swindled us out of enough coin for today."

The ship captain scooped his winnings into a pouch. "This will be our last game. We should reach Sea Gate in just an hour or two."

"Yes, then, we will have to advance on foot." Arangoli arched a brow. "It's just too bad you won't sail to Talastar." He had not given up despite Kasgan's insistence that it was too dangerous.

"Years ago, I would have been happy to do so. As it stands, nobody with any sense attempts it."

Time to hit him where it hurts. "I am surprised a proud dwarf like you is afraid of pirates."

Kasgan bristled as he stood. "I am not afraid. I am just looking out for my ship and crew."

Arangoli, not willing to give in, tried another approach. "I think I heard somewhere that certain goods only come from Galfhadden."

"That's right. Silks from there are especially valuable."

"And how is the price with no ships sailing around the northern peninsula?"

"Oh, last I heard, silk was running somewhere north of eight silvers a yard in any of the free cities."

Arangoli whistled. He had no reference for the normal price of the rare fabric, but Kasgan seemed properly impressed, and that was enough for him. "Can you imagine the profit from just a single run to Galfhadden and back?"

The ship captain stared into space, his eyes filled with longing. "I certainly can." He shook his head as if to clear it. "But that is mere wishful thinking. The Dreadnought rules the western shore. Rumor says that he has gathered more than a dozen ships, each filled with a crew of bloodthirsty pirates. The risk is not worth a handful of extra gold pieces." He walked to the door. "No, it's just not worth it."

The door opened, the captain stepped out, and Arangoli was alone.

~

STANDING at the ship's bow, the wind grappled at Arangoli's beard as if attempting to remove it. The late day sun forced him to squint, even if the wind in his face had not. Through those narrow slits, he surveyed the approaching land and the city along the shoreline with interest and curiosity. It was his first visit to Sea Gate, the westernmost of the Free Cities, positioned where the Inner Sea met the Endless Ocean.

Sunstreak slid past a rocky point and into the bay, the breeze lessening, the waves smoothing. As the ship drew closer to the city, the hills overlooking the bay blocked out the sun. The wind fell away and a quiet calm embraced the ship and her passengers. In that calm, Arangoli drank in the view.

The shoreline was shaped like a crescent moon which began at a point to the southeast, curved west, and continued until the shoreline ran a northeast heading. Steep hillsides covered in green foliage bound the city, leaving a relatively flat, narrow strip of land between the slopes and the bay. The result was a peaceful, protected harbor of pure beauty.

Like most seaside cities, Sea Gate was walled off from potential naval attacks. The wall ran from north to south with a thick tower rising from each end. Docks lined the northern half of the shoreline, many of them occupied by fishing boats. Two piers, each hosting a single ship, thrust out from the harbor's midpoint, directly across from the only visible gate, above which stood a third tower. Dark rocks and steep cliffs dominated the southern half of the waterfront, making it all but impossible to land watercraft without severe damage. Unlike other ports Arangoli had visited, no buildings stood outside the city walls. He then noticed the catapults – one at the top of each tower and five others stationed on flat, rocky shelves along the peninsula at the south end of the bay. Vigilant guards stood beside each of the war machines while others marched along the top of the wall.

"It is like a fortress," Arangoli said.

"Aye," Pazacar replied from his side. "Not only is it a natural bay, the protected backside and rocky point to the south make defense simple. Any ship coming too close is subject to projectiles launched by the catapults. If an enemy makes land, the wall will slow them enough for archers to pick them off. The wall's curvature ensures that there are no blind points and without any buildings outside the wall, there is nowhere to hide."

Rax, who stood to Arangoli's other side, added, "Impressive."

From beside Rax, Gortch grunted. "You are impressed by anything bigger than you, which is pretty much everything."

"In that case, I must be doubly impressed by your wide arse." The moment the last word came out, Rax dodged, causing Gortch to miss when he tried to snatch his arm.

"Come here, you smart mouthed runt."

Rax backed from the rail. "You could try to catch me."

"Bah," Gortch waved it off. "I'd rather save my energy for the ale waiting for us."

The mere mention of ale had Arangoli longing for a deep pull from a foamy mug.

As the ship neared the south pier, Captain Kasgan shouted out orders. The crew responded, the men in the rigging scrambling to furl the sails while those on deck reeling in and tying off lines. The ship gradually slowed as it drifted into position. Lines were thrown to posts rising above the pier and pulled taut, straining before the ship relented and settled into place.

Arangoli turned to his team. "Hold tight for a minute before you go and gather your packs. I need to speak with Kasgan."

He headed across the deck, pausing briefly to avoid colliding with a sailor carrying a massive coil of rope. When he reached the ship's stern, he climbed the quarterdeck.

The captain turned toward him. "Ah. Goli. I assume you stopped by to pay me."

"Here's your gold." The coins clinked together as he dropped them into Kasgan's palm. "I have more if you are willing to take us to Talastar."

Kasgan frowned. "We've been through this."

"I know. I promise I won't tell others that you are a coward for not braving the voyage."

The captain's mouth tightened. "You had better not."

"It's just a shame is all."

"Why do you say that?"

Arangoli reminded him, "It would be an opportunity for you to be the only ship running trade from the inner sea to Galfhadden…"

Sighing, Kasgan said, "Don't remind me."

"In addition, this is the one time you'll have the best fighting force in the world on board your ship. Even if trouble did find you, now you would be equipped to meet those pirates with force."

With his last seed planted, Arangoli turned and descended to the main deck. He only made it a few strides before Kasgan called out.

"How much?"

Arangoli looked over his shoulder. "How much what?"

"Gold. How much gold would you pay to reach Talastar?"

Feigning contemplation, Arangoli tapped his lips before responding. "I'd be willing to pay another eight gold pieces."

"Eight?" Greed filled Kasgan's eyes. "Make it ten, and you have a deal."

Ten was the number Arangoli expected all along. "Done."

"However," Kasgan held up a finger. "We need to stay the night. If I don't allow my crew the chance to unwind with some drink and a hot meal, I risk a mutiny."

Arangoli grinned. "I risk the same with my crew, so I agree."

"Wonderful. That will give me a chance to sell the goods I have on board while I procure something that will yield the best profit in Galfhadden."

"What do you intend to buy?"

"Wine." Kasgan flashed an eager grin. Every barrel I can find."

"In that case, I wish you luck. What time do we depart?"

"I will get my ship loaded tonight and will be ready to sail an hour after sunup."

"We will be here." Satisfied, Arangoli whistled as he crossed the ship's deck to inform his crew of the new plan.

~

FRIENDLY RIBBING and laughter surrounded Arangoli as he and the Head Thumpers approached the city gate. Just before reaching the opening, a quartet of guards stepped out. Two crossed halberds, blocking the way while the other two stood to both sides of them, each with a hand on the pommel of their sheathed sword. A fifth guard circled in front of the others and stood with his feet spread apart. With his arms crossed, he eyed the dwarves. Beyond the gate, a dozen armed guards huddled near a bubbling fountain, some of them staring at Arangoli.

"Hold!" The guard in front demanded. "I am Sergeant Saxon, and I am responsible for the safety of our fair city."

"Greetings, sergeant." Arangoli bowed with an exaggerated flourish.

The friendly sentiment was met with a scowl. Saxon said, "You are far from home. We don't see many dwarves here."

"Aye. We have traveled far, but we still have far to go."

The sergeant narrowed his eyes in suspicion. "What is your business in Sea Gate?"

"My companions and I are here for only a brief stay. We intend to eat our fill and wash it down with drink before retiring for the night. Come daybreak, we will be on a ship and away."

Saxon's gaze slowly swept over the dwarves. "You are armed."

"You are observant."

"The use of weapons is forbidden within these walls."

Pazacar stepped forward while leaning on his staff. "My companions have no intention of using their weapons, I assure you."

"What of your staff?"

"Oh, this is no weapon. I use it to walk since a wagon ran over my leg." Pazacar shook his head. "It was mangled terribly. Would you like to see the scars?"

"That is not necessary." Saxon turned to Arangoli. "If the rest of you intend to enter the city, we must put bands on your weapons first."

"Bands?"

"They are sealed. Break the band before you leave, and you break the law."

Arangoli shrugged. "Very well."

Saxon whistled and the guards standing at the fountain approached the gate. The men held orange cords, each less than a foot long. They split up with one approaching each dwarf other than Pazacar.

"Take off your harness," said the guard who stopped before Arangoli.

"As you wish." After lifting the harness over his head, he held it before him.

The guard wrapped the orange cord around the harness and over the hammer head. Another guard came along with a crucible held between two mitts. He poured out some of the contents, which turned out to be melted wax.

The sergeant pressed a ring into the wax, right where the two strip ends met. "There. You'll have to break the seal to use the weapon, which I suggest you avoid until you are away from Sea Gate."

"If I break the seal?"

"You break the law and end up in jail. Kill someone, and it's the gibbet for you." The sergeant moved on to Gortch and pressed his ring into the seal around his belt and mace.

Arangoli glanced at Pazacar and grunted. "This place is strict."

"So, it seems."

When finished, the guards returned to their post.

"You are free to enter the city," Saxon said. "Stay out of trouble."

"I avoid trouble whenever possible." Arangoli strode through the gate, ignoring the snorts of disbelief from his companions.

They crossed the square inside the gate and randomly chose one of the five streets connecting to it. Citizens on foot and shopkeepers standing in open doorways stared as the team of dwarves walked past. The buildings stood two stories tall, some with external stairwells. Often, the lower floor was occupied by a cobbler, artisan, a bakery, or a half dozen other businesses.

They came to an intersection and paused. Laughter came from the building at the opposite corner. It stood two stories tall and three times the width of the other shops. A door stood open at the front, bordered by a line of windows. Above the door, the sign depicted a chubby pig leaning back in a chair with one hoof on its belly. The pig wore a broad smile while holding up a bare chicken leg with the other hoof. The words above the image said The Happy Hog. To coincide with the name, the tantalizing scent of roasted pork filled the air.

"It appears we found an inn," Pazacar said.

"I hope it makes us as happy as that pig." The pleasant aroma caused Arangoli's stomach to rumble.

"The way it smells is already making me happy," Gortch noted.

"And in an hour," Rax smirked. "It will be impossible to tell you apart from the pig on the sign."

Gortch grunted. "Well, nobody can tell the difference between you and that scrawny chicken leg the pig is holding."

Rax chuckled and put his arm around Gortch's shoulder. "Let's go get a drink."

The two of them led the way into the tavern.

With the dinner hour imminent, the inn was already quite busy with over half of the tables occupied. There was not a dwarf among the patrons, most of whom were male. A pair of Drow seated in a dark corner were the only two who were not human.

The dwarves headed straight for the bar at the rear, where a tall man with a hunched back stood washing mugs over a tub of soapy water. The man noticed them, set the clean mugs down on a towel, and sauntered over.

"Dwarves," the barkeep said.

"Human," Rax replied.

"Sorry. We don't see much of your folk around here."

Arangoli said, "We are only in Sea Gate for the night. Do you have any rooms available?"

The barkeep looked them over. "Not enough for the lot of you."

Rax waved it off. "No need to worry about rooms for now. I need a drink."

"You've coin?"

Arangoli set a handful of silvers on the bar. "Give us a round and ten servings of whatever you have cooking. It smells wonderful."

The barkeep grinned, swept the coins into his hand, and gave a nod. "Drinks on the way."

While the man was away, Arangoli leaned with his back to the bar. It felt good to be on solid land after four days of the swishing and swaying he experienced onboard Sunstreak. He then thought about the cord around his weapon. Curious, he examined the crowd but did not see a weapon among them. The mere idea was foreign. As a warrior, he had carried a weapon for half his young life, even before he was gifted his enchanted hammer. Even within the walls of Ra'Tahal, warriors like him wore weapons on a regular basis.

"Nobody is armed," Pazacar noted, as if reading his mind.

"I noticed the same thing," Arangoli admitted.

"This city must be safe."

"For now. Imagine if an enemy force stormed in."

Gortch snorted. "Did you see the fortifications?"

"Yes, but even the most impressive defenses can be bypassed. We proved that last Autumn." He did not need to mention them infiltrating Ra'Tahal for them to know what he meant.

A voice came from behind him. "Here you are. Four drinks with more on the way." The barkeep rushed off as Arangoli turned around.

Rax snatched a mug, brought it to his lips, and took a big swig. He pulled the mug away, coughing and choking. He wiped red away from his lips while his eyes watered. "This is not ale!"

Arangoli lifted his mug and peered inside. It was filled with red liquid.

"It is wine." The barkeep spoke over his shoulder from across the bar. "We rarely have ale in these parts."

"Why not?" Arangoli asked.

"This land is unsuitable for growing grain. However, there are two valleys just north of here that produce the best grapes in the world."

The man finished filling four more mugs and brought them over. "Do not worry, you will get used to it." He set the mugs on the bar and raised a finger. "Just beware, ale is weak in comparison. Too many mugs and..."

The dwarves laughed with Arangoli replying. "We are dwarves. We are hearty, not like you soft humans." He took a long drink. The wine was fruity with a bitter aftertaste. "You are right about one thing."

"What's that?" The man asked.

"I can get used to this." Tipping his mug up, Arangoli proceeded to pour the remaining contents down his throat.

CHAPTER 21
INCARCERATED

A distant rumble echoed in the darkness. Where it came from, Arangoli was unsure. Another rumble followed, this one sounding closer. His eyes blinked open to a dimly lit cell. He was sitting with his back against a stone wall, his head leaning to the side and supported by the adjacent wall. Across from him was a wall of iron bars. Beyond the bars, moonlight illuminated a room with a shallow puddle in the middle. Drops of water fell from the ceiling, into the pool. Plop. Plop. Plop.

He sat forward, winced, and rubbed his neck. It was sore, and his head pounded like a hammer against an anvil. His mouth was dry, his throat parched.

A rumble came from the shadows, and he realized that Gortch lay on the floor beside him. A third dwarf also slept in the cell, one who was much smaller and curled on his side. Arangoli reached out and grabbed the leg of the smaller dwarf.

"What?" Rax jerked awake. He sat up and rubbed his eyes. "Where are we?"

"Jail, it would seem."

Gortch snorted, stirred, and rolled to his side. "Quiet," he mumbled. "Tired."

Arangoli shoved the big dwarf. "Get up, Gortch."

"Hey!" Gortch opened his eyes and pushed himself to a sitting position. "It's still dark. Why'd you wake me?"

"We are in jail."

"I know," Gortch yawned.

"You remember?"

"Yeah."

"What happened?"

"You started a fight. Lots of furniture and a few windows were broken."

Arangoli could not recall much through the haze in his brain. "Did we win?"

"We always win."

It was true. "How did we end up here?"

"After the fight, we resumed drinking and even emptied a second wine barrel. That's when the city watch stormed the taproom. Everyone but the two of us had passed out by that point, and when you tried to explain to the guards, you toppled over. Rather than try to fight them alone, I thought it best to comply."

Rax rubbed his head. "I feel like sheep dung. I never want to drink wine again."

Gortch grunted, "I don't blame you, but what about ale?"

"I am not cross with ale."

All three dwarves chuckled.

A familiar voice came from nearby. "What are you laughing about?"

Arangoli stood, crossed the small cell, and stuck his face against a gap in the bars. Through them, he spied Pazacar in the cell beside his.

"Hey, Paz. Who is in there with you?"

"Orvatz and Fesgar."

Another familiar face appeared at the next cell down. "We've three of us in this one," Brannigan announced.

From the last cell, Artgan called out, "We need to get out of here."

"Hold tight," Arangoli turned from the bars. "Rax. Please tell me you can beat this lock."

The lean dwarf climbed to his feet. "After our stay in the Carcera, I always keep my beard knotted." He pulled a small pick from one of the knots. "Just so I have a place to hide these." Another appeared from the knot below. "This should only take a moment."

Rax approached the bars, reached his arms through, and began working at the lock in the door. Moments later, the lock clicked and the door swung open. He stepped out with a grin. "Easy as our friend, Gortch, downing a mug of ale."

"Aye," Gortch nodded.

"Great." Arangoli followed. "Now, free the others while Gortch and I watch the stairs."

Arangoli circled the puddle and stopped at the foot of the stairs. Warm light was visible at the top of the staircase.

When Gortch reached him, Arangoli whispered, "Where are our weapons?"

Gortch pointed up. "In a storage room beside the barracks."

Arangoli glanced back as the door to the second cell swung open. "When we get to the top, you and I will lead the way. If anyone sees us, we will need to silence them immediately."

Balling a fist, Gortch nodded. "I'll be ready."

Dwarves gathered behind them as each cell was opened. Once everyone was freed, Arangoli crept up the stairs. At the top, he stuck his head out and looked in both directions.

The light came from an open room to the right. Voices carried from that direction. To the left was a short corridor with two closed doors. He stepped out and peeked around the corner, into the open room. There, a pair of guards sat at a table, neither facing in his direction. Two closed doors waited at the far end of the chamber while the exit stood at the side of the room. The light came from a lantern on the table.

Pulling back, Arangoli tapped Gortch on the shoulder, flashed two fingers, and pointed toward the room. The big dwarf nodded and followed when Arangoli snuck out. They tip toed across the room, holding close to the wall while the two guards continued their discussion. As Arangoli drew even with the table, one of the guards looked in his direction. The man's eyes widened, his mouth opening as he prepared to cry out. Before any sound came out, Arangoli's fist struck the man square in the nose, snapping his head back. Gortch came at the other guard from behind and threw a hard punch, striking the man's temple and knocking him out instantly.

The first guard appeared dazed, yet he remained seated and conscious, so Arangoli grabbed him by the hair and slammed his head on the table. The man's eyes rolled, his head flopped, and he fell over, forcing Arangoli to scramble. He caught the chair as it tipped over and gently set it down.

"That was close," Arangoli whispered. "Where are our weapons?"

"In here." Gortch approached the left door, tested the handle, and opened it to a dark room.

Arangoli glanced toward the staircase, where Pazacar peered around the corner. He gestured for the others to follow as he snatched the lantern off the table and joined Gortch in the storage room.

It took only seconds to locate their weapons, which they began to pass out to the others. When armed, they stepped back out.

The door to the neighboring room opened, the man in the doorway freezing. His mouth opened, and a cry rang out. "Wake up! The prisoners escaped!"

Arangoli charged toward the man and bowled into him. The impact sent the man flying backward and sliding across the floor, between two bunks even as men sat up in the beds. There were twenty bunks in total, all occupied by stirring guards.

Urgently, Arangoli grabbed the door and pulled it closed. He then backed from the door while drawing his hammer from the harness, breaking the seal on the cord in the process. With a hard downward strike, the hammer snapped the doorknob off. Cries of alarm came from inside the room as the other half of the doorknob followed.

He turned toward his companions. "Out. Now!"

They raced outside to a sky graced by the light of early dawn. The building they had just vacated stood below the city wall, near the south end of Sea Gate.

"To the harbor!" Arangoli burst into a run, leading his team down the quiet, narrow streets of the sleeping city.

When they reached the end of the street, it opened to a plaza with a fountain in the center. To the right, the city gate – a pair of heavy wooden doors – stood closed. Four guards posted at the top of the wall stared out toward the harbor while another six guards stood just inside the barred gate.

Arangoli turned toward his companions. "We need to rush in, take them out quickly, and reach the pier before more guards show up."

"What about the guards on the wall?" Rax asked.

"While we deal with the guards on the ground and get the door opened, you, Paz, Orvatz, and Fesgar make straight for the tower door. When you get to the top of the wall, neutralize the guards."

"Got it."

"Try not to kill anyone. So far, only a fight and a jail break are counting against us, and both can be soon forgotten. Murder is another thing. Is everyone ready?" Arangoli's gaze briefly met the stare of each of his ten companions. All had faith in him as a leader, and he knew he could count on every one of them in times of crisis. "Alright. Let's go."

They burst into a run across the plaza. The guards at the gate turned, their eyes widening as they reached for their weapons. The ring of swords emerging from scabbards echoed in the quiet morning. The dwarves struck.

Arangoli held his hammer with a hand at each end of the handle while raising his arms high. As he reached the nearest guard, he slammed the hammer handle across the man's helmet with a mighty clang. The impact lifted the guard from his feet. The man was unconscious before he hit the ground.

Turning, Arangoli found three other guards already on the ground while the two remaining men used their swords to keep Brannigan and Gortch at bay. Coming in from behind, Arangoli launched a low swing of his hammer, clipping through the legs of both guards and sending them crashing to the ground with a clatter. Dwarves came in from all directions, silencing the men in seconds.

An arrow struck the ground between Gortch and Arangoli, splintering as it bounced off the cobblestones. Another plunged into Brannigan's shoulder. He staggered to one knee and clenched his teeth in pain.

"Beneath the wall! Now!" Arangoli slid his free arm beneath Brannigan's uninjured one. He helped Brannigan to his feet and rushed over to the door, the arch over it blocking the guards above them from view.

With their backs to the doors, they waited while the sound of fighting came from above. Cries of pain preceded silence.

"Alright." Arangoli slid his hammer into the harness on his back. "Gortch, help me with the bar."

One dwarf stood at each end of the thick slab of wood holding the gate closed. Gripping the beam with both hands, Arangoli and Gortch lifted it away, carried it to the side of the gate, and dropped it. The beam bounced and rolled before settling.

"There may be guards outside, so be ready," Arangoli warned.

He pulled one side of the gate open and darted his head out to ensure the area was clear. The tower door opened, and the four dwarves he had sent to the top of the wall emerged.

"To the ship!" Following Arangoli's shout, the eleven dwarves burst out through the gate and raced toward the pier.

"Stop!" The cry came from a cluster of guards on patrol outside the wall, a few hundred feet to the north.

The guards broke into a run and shouted alarm as Arangoli raced onto the pier. He made straight for Sunstreak, the ship moored as they had left it the prior evening. No planks were out, so Arangoli leapt when he reached the nearest line. He caught the rope with both hands, his body swinging wildly from the momentum. Lifting his legs, he hooked his feet over the rope and began to shimmy up. When he reached the rail, he pulled himself up, over, and landed on the deck. His head still pounded from the wine while everything in his body begged him to lay still and rest, but the city guards were gathering and time was short, so he rolled over, climbed to his feet, and ran toward the stern.

He reached the door beneath the quarterdeck and tore it open. Early morning light seeping through the open door pierced the dark interior.

Kasgan sat up from his bed and blinked at the light. "Goli? What are you doing here so early?"

"We need to set sail," he replied between gasps.

"I had planned to..."

"Now! The city guards are after us. Set sail, or you won't get your gold."

The threat of losing out on his windfall had the ship's captain scrambling to slide his boots on. He then ran out the door and began shouting to wake his crew even as dozens of guards poured out of the city gate.

Arangoli found the plank and slid it out. It tipped down and bounded on the pier. The Head Thumpers hurried up the plank with Brannigan coming last. Sweat beaded his brow and his leather vest was matted with blood.

Captain Kasgan emerged from the stairwell and paused when he saw the guards running toward the pier. He shouted urgently, "Hurry. To your stations!"

The sailors, some of them only half dressed, rushed out of the stairwell and scattered. Some climbed the rigging while others began untying the lines that secured the ship to the pier.

Kasgan raced past Arangoli, hurried up the quarterdeck stairs, and stood at the helm.

The ship began to drift from the pier even as the guards ran along it.

From the rail, Arangoli cupped his hand over his mouth and shouted. "Sorry to leave in such a rush. We've an appointment to keep."

Sergeant Saxon stood in the front of the guards, his face red with fury. "Come back to Sea Gate, and I will see you hanged."

"For starting a fight and leaving jail early?"

"You brandished your weapons and attacked my guards." The man waved a fist. "You made me look a fool!"

Arangoli shook his head. "Don't give me credit for that. You look a fool all on your own." He turned to his team. Most panted from the run, Gortch with his hands on his knees and his face red. Among them only one was wounded, and although not seriously so, dealing with it was the first order of business.

"Alright, Brannigan," Arangoli said. "Let's see about removing that arrow and sewing you up. Something tells me that we will need you in fighting shape soon."

CHAPTER 22
HIDDEN IN PLAIN SIGHT

Trees lining the hillside cast long shadows across the gravel road. The sun, a ball of amber light hovering over the western horizon, came into view when the wagon rode past a gap in the trees. Just as abruptly, another grove of trees blocked the sun from view. The wagon came to a sharp turn, rounded the bend, and renewed its uphill climb.

Vic sat in the seat beside Dennard, the wagon driver whose mood appeared resolute. The ride had been quiet, neither man making the effort to spark conversation. What needed to be said had already been said. All that remained was the need to act. Despite Vic's desire to find a less violent solution, Essex pushed for a ruthless assault of the castle with no quarter offered. Even the shopkeepers and dockworkers agreed that it was the only way. With the knowledge that people were about to die while hoping he, Revita, Ian, and his companions would be spared, Vic did not wish to talk.

For the third time during the drive from the harbor, Vic slid his hand in the gap between the seat and wagon bed to ensure his mattock was still there. When his fingers located the leather-wrapped handle, he had to resist the desire to draw the weapon. The castle came into view as he pulled his hand back. Standing at the top of the rise, the three-story-tall walls surrounding the keep were bathed in the orange light of the setting sun.

Over his shoulder, Vic spoke to the barrels in the wagon bed. "We are almost there."

No reply was given nor was any expected. Barrels rarely spoke.

The wagon climbed the last stretch, the ground leveled, and it rolled toward the gate. The guards posted outside the gate parted with four moving to each side of the wagon as it came to a stop. Men in black looked down from the top of the wall. Whether their hard glares or the crossbows they held were more daunting, Vic was uncertain.

The guards took position to each side of the wagon and stood with their feet a shoulder width apart. One gripped a halberd while two others held axes ready. The rest wore swords on their hips, many of whom rested a palm on the hilt. Diverse types of leather armor, be it coats, pads, bracers, or jerkins covered much of their upper bodies. While no two guards wore the same exact garb, all were dressed in black.

"What is your business?" A man asked in a gruff tone. He appeared to be in his thirties, his thick shoulders straining against his black leather jerkin. The man's heavy brow was furrowed and a scar ran from his eye to his jawbone, the lower portion leaving a hairless streak through his brown beard.

Vic glanced at Dennard, and when their eyes met, he gave a brief nod.

"What is your name, friend?" Dennard asked.

"My name is Rubens. I am one of Creskin's lieutenants, but I am not your friend."

The man's gruff tone did not appear to bother Dennard. "My name is Dennard. I'm a trader with a warehouse on the docks. I have six barrels of ale and was told to deliver them here." The reply had been rehearsed as had other responses he was to give depending on where the conversation led.

Rubens appeared unsatisfied. "Wedlund handles all of the castle deliveries."

"Yes. I know."

"Where is he?" the man pressed.

"I suspect he is in his warehouse swearing in frustration about now." Dennard went on to explain, "You see, the axle on his wagon broke this afternoon."

The timing of the axle breaking was the result of carefully planned sabotage.

Dennard continued, "He paid me to make the delivery rather than forcing you to wait another day. I suspect he was worried about what might happen if the ale did not arrive as planned."

In truth, Wedlund nearly wet himself at the thought and thanked Dennard and Vic profusely when they agreed to make the delivery. Being nearby to react when Wedlund ran into trouble was no coincidence.

One of the men snorted. "We tapped our last barrel yesterday and it was gone before sundown. Another night without ale would have upset a few of us for certain."

Rubens glared at the man who spoke. He then turned his attention toward Vic. "And who is this?"

"Vinny. I pay him to help me at the docks." Dennard said, "You don't expect me to unload these barrels by myself, do you?"

When the guard grimaced, another man spoke up. "I think we can trust them, boss. Just a few days ago, when working a shift on the docks, I saw these two unloading a ship. In fact, I think it was this guy who had his wagon stolen by Lokix."

"That's right," Dennard nodded. "Luckily, the horses fled the fire and Vinny found it near the waterfront with a broken wheel. I'd like to thank you all for dealing with Lokix. No way could I have paid for another wagon and..."

"Stop!" Rubens sighed. "I've heard enough."

Dennard shrugged. "Where do you want us to unload?"

"Drive in, turn right, and round the castle. The cellar door is in the back. When the barrels are down there safely, come back to the gate straight away. Try anything, and it'll end badly for you."

The guards stepped back from the wagon.

The leader pointed toward the sky and shouted. "Open the gate!"

Chains clanked as the portcullis began to rise. When it was halfway up, Dennard flicked the reins and his team advanced at a walk. The wagon rolled through the gate and into the gravel castle yard. As bidden, Dennard turned right while Vic stared up at the castle.

Although the blocky central keep was made of pale stone, it emanated a darkness, as if tainted by the vermin who occupied it. Towers rising three stories above the four-story main structure stood at the keep's four corners. That building housed over a hundred of the most ruthless criminals in Bard's Bay. Those men had slaughtered Kaden for sentencing them to prison. They then claimed his residence and established control over half of the city. Whether they had done so simply for revenge or simply driven by a thirst for power, Vic did not care. He was determined to see Creskin and his crew eradicated, regardless of the cost.

The wagon rounded the corner and the stables came into view, tucked near the cliff wall at the rear of the keep. They rolled past the rear tower and turned again. A tongue of low, stone walls jutting out from the rear of the keep. It became immediately clear that the pair of closed doors at the end of the peninsula led to the cellar. As the wagon settled strides from the cellar entrance, two men emerged from the central keep's rear door. The men approached the wagon, causing concern to roil in Vic's stomach.

"Ho!" One of the men called out, "Is that our ale?"

"It is." Dennard climbed down from the wagon seat.

"It's about time," the other man said as the pair drew near.

Patting the nearest barrel, Dennard said, "Well, your ale made it here safely, despite a few challenges. We are to load it into the cellar. Are you here to help?"

"If drinking the ale is helping, the answer is yes." The man chuckled at his own joke.

The other man replied, "No need to bring them all to the cellar. We will take one off your hands right now." He rounded to the rear of the wagon and began to pull the tailgate pins loose.

Vic gulped as panic set in. "There is no need. We can do it."

The man pulled the second pin and pulled the tailgate free. "No. You can take the rest down to the cellar."

When the man reached for the first barrel, Vic glanced toward Dennard, whose eyes had grown wide with fear. *What would Revita do in this situation?* He tried to imagine himself as her, calm and collected. The answer came to him as the two men in black lifted the barrel from the wagon.

"I wouldn't open that barrel quite yet," Vic shook his head in warning.

"Why not?"

"That's the one that fell off the wagon when the horses got spooked. It happened before we had the tailgate in place. I'm surprised it didn't explode."

The two men looked at each other, one arching a brow, the other frowning.

"Sounds like it'll be a foamy mess," one man noted.

Dennard added, "Actually, both rear barrels got shaken up. Hold on while Vinnie and I get a better barrel out for you."

Vic hopped into the wagon, grabbed the upper ring of the next barrel in the wagon, and rolled it on its edge, moving it to the rear. He then jumped back down and stood beside Dennard. "Hand us that barrel, and you two take the good one."

The two men passed the barrel to Vic and Dennard. It was heavy and full of sloshing liquid. With the new barrel held between them, Creskin's men walked off toward the rear castle door.

Only when they were gone did Vic release his breath. "That was close."

"I nearly loaded my drawers," Dennard said.

"I am glad you didn't. What if they had grabbed the other rear barrel?"

"Then, my drawers would have been done for."

"We all would have been done for." Vic nodded toward the wagon. "Let's set this down until we get the cellar doors open."

"Good idea."

They set the barrel down, and Vic worked his fingers. The barrel's weight had driven the metal lip on the bottom into his flesh. Carrying the barrels down would not be fun.

While Dennard walked over to the cellar door, Vic leaned close to the other rear barrel and spoke in a faint voice. "We are going to take the first barrel down. Hold tight. We will be right back for you."

The barrel did not respond.

With the doors open, Dennard returned to the wagon, where he and Vic lifted the first barrel yet again. They headed to the open door with Vic in the lead. He backed down a stone staircase that grew darker with each step. The air was dank and smelled of must. By the time they reached the dirt cellar floor at the bottom, they were surrounded by darkness.

Vic continued backing up while looking over his shoulder. Through the gloom, he spotted shelving a few feet away and stopped. "This is good."

"Agreed."

They set the barrel on the floor, dusted off their hands, and ascended toward the failing daylight at the top of the staircase.

The next barrel was noticeably lighter than the first. In contrast to the lessened weight, Vic released a dramatic groan. "Oh. This one is so heavy."

Dennard snickered as they entered the cellar doorway.

Revita's muffled voice came from inside the barrel. "Careful, Vic. I have knives and I know where you sleep. You might wake to find a prized appendage missing."

This time, Dennard laughed aloud.

Vic grinned. "I was just making sure you hadn't passed out from lack of air."

Her voice came from the barrel. "That's why we removed the cork."

He continued down the staircase, taking care not to drop the barrel. "And you are certain you can get out?"

"If Ian can't do it, I will find a way myself."

They reached the bottom, crossed the dirt floor, and set the barrel with Revita inside next to the first barrel. Vic patted the barrel while leaning close to it. "Just be sure to wait until all is quiet."

"You just be sure not to bar the cellar door."

While Vic knew as much, her reminder was welcome. Trapping her and Ian down there would be a quick way to disrupt the plan.

He said, "We have three more barrels to carry down, so do try to be patient."

"That is easy for you to say. You don't have your knees in your face and your arse falling asleep."

Vic and Dennard chuckled as they climbed the staircase. The next two barrels were as heavy as the first, even if the contents were not all the same. They carried them down and set them near the others without pause or comment. Then came the last barrel, which felt just as light as Revita's.

As they descended, Vic asked, "Are you well, Ian?"

A beat later, Ian's voice came from inside. "I am well enough."

"It'll be dark in about twenty minutes. Most of Creskin's men should be in the castle by then."

"Alright."

They set the barrel with the others. "Be well, Ian."

"You, too, Vic."

Without another word, Vic followed Dennard up the staircase. Shadows moving at the top had them both pause. Two men stood in the doorway. After shooting Vic a look over his shoulder, Dennard resumed his ascent.

"Are the barrels all down there?" A man asked in a gruff tone.

Vic recognized the voice as Rubens, the squad leader from the castle gate.

Dennard emerged from the staircase. "Yes. All but the barrel two of your men carried off for them to tap."

Rubens looked toward the castle. "Those buggers didn't wait for us."

The other guard said, "Can you blame them?"

"No. Suppose not." Rubens pointed toward the wagon. "You two ride to the castle gate and wait for us. We will inspect the barrels and then meet you there."

Vic peered into the dark cellar and wondered if Ian and Revita had heard what was said. If either of them made a noise while the guards were in the cellar, they would be discovered and their plan would be in ruins. He could not risk it.

"This is bullocks!" Vic shouted, hoping Ian and Revita heard him.

Rubens spun toward him. "What is your problem?"

In a loud voice, Vic said, "I am to meet a girl for dinner, and now we have to wait for you to inspect the five barrels you just saw us ride in with? If she leaves before I show..."

The guard stepped close to Vic with his chest puffed out. He glared while his hand rested on the pommel of his sword. "You'll do what?"

Wishing to avoid a fight, Vic stepped back. "I'll have to chase her down again, I guess."

The other guard asked, "Is she pretty?"

"Pretty enough. Better yet, she has an edge to her and is eager."

"Nice." The guard grinned.

Rubens elbowed his companion. "What are you going on about?"

"Ouch." The man rubbed his ribs. "Give the kid a break. Wouldn't you be upset if you had plans with an eager lass?

The man grunted. "I suppose." He waved. "Go on. We will be quick about it, and you'll be on your way."

With the hope that his shouting had given Ian and Revita warning to remain still and quiet, Vic climbed into the wagon, joining Dennard. The driver snapped the reins, turned his team, and drove the wagon around the castle. Vic's gaze remained on the cellar entrance until the corner tower obscured the view. He lifted his gaze to the darkening sky. Dusk would soon give way to nightfall, and a battle would take place. People would die, that much was certain. He just prayed that he and those close to him were not among the corpses come sunrise.

CHAPTER 23

PATIENCE

Eyes closed, Ian floated in the still void of meditation. A soothing blanket of serenity enveloped him, allowing him to disconnect from the discomfort his body endured in the tight confines of the barrel. In his mind, he hovered above a cluster of barrels in the dark cellar.

Male voices came from the stairwell, joined by the approach of footsteps. One man held a lantern that shed light on the barrels and nearby shelving. The two men stood over the barrels while in quiet conversation. A man tipped a barrel on edge and dropped it back down, causing it to rock briefly as the contents sloshed from side to side. The pair turned and climbed the stairwell, the light fading with their footsteps. The door was closed and the cellar fell silent.

Ian drifted in the void, where time meant little, so he had no idea when it occurred, but a voice called to him.

"Ian."

It was a woman's voice.

"Ian."

I know her.

"Ian!" Revita shouted.

Opening his eyes, Ian returned to his body. "I am here."

"I know you are here, you dolt." She sounded close to him, yet her words were muffled by the barriers between them. "Get me the blazes out of this thing."

"Right." The ache of his squeezed physical position suddenly became oppressive. "Give me a moment."

He held a palm up, drew in raw magic, and cast a spell. A circular disk of white light appeared, consisting of two rings surrounding a circular core. Magic flowed through the disk and formed a cylinder of air, three inches in diameter and stretching from the bottom of the barrel to the top. When he channeled additional magic into it, the cylinder expanded. The wooden barrel groaned and the top suddenly popped off. The metal ring clanged off the cellar ceiling before it and the lid careened off a shelf and fell to the floor. The wooden slats surrounding Ian unfolded like a flower blooming. All this, he felt and heard, but could not see. Blackness, thick and impenetrable, surrounded him.

While gripping a pair of slats sticking out at an angle away from him, Ian stood. He stretched, worked his sore muscles, and groaned.

Revita's voice came from his right. "Do you have to be so loud?"

"Sorry." He cast another spell, a tiny flame appeared, and his immediate surroundings became visible. He stood amid four barrels. "Can you knock, so I know which is yours?"

A finger jutted out from one of the barrels and wiggled. "Will this do?"

"Yeah. Sorry. I forgot about the spigot hole." While maintaining the flame, he cast another spell, targeting the rim of her barrel. "Hold still."

The spell's pressure, applied to the inner surface of the rim, caused it to creak and then snap open. It fell to the floor and the barrel slats, like his own, popped open. The lid, with nothing to hold it in place, fell into the barrel and landed on Revita's head.

"Ouch." She grabbed the lid, tossed it aside, and rose to her feet. "Oh, it feels good to stand."

"I know what you mean."

Revita produced a glowing disk and looked around. "These barrel parts should burn well if we stack them up."

The two of them pulled slats from the broken barrels and made a pyramid of wood in the center of the intact barrels, making sure to rest a few slats at an angle, bridging the base of the pyramid to the neighboring barrels.

"Perfect." She headed toward the stairs. "Before you do anything else, let's make certain we can get out of here."

He maintained his flame and joined her. They climbed the stairs and stopped near the top, which was blocked by the cellar doors.

She pushed on a door, testing it before sighing. "Locked."

"Can you unlock it?"

Revita reached into her coat and pulled out a small object. "I can unlock anything."

The lock clicked open a moment later. She opened the door, and moonlight shone in. The light in her hand faded as she pocketed both lock and pick before creeping outside.

"Come on," she said.

He doused his flame but held on to his magic.

The rear castle yard was vacant. A narrow gravel path appeared as a pale stripe leading to the rear door. Amber light flickered in half a dozen windows along the rear of the castle.

"It is dinner hour," she whispered. "Most of Creskin' men should be inside. Now is the time to strike."

Ian had anticipated and dreaded this moment since the plan was first conceived. *Vic is counting on you. The people of Bard's Bay deserve better. This is for them.* Those thoughts pushed him beyond his trepidation.

Ducking back through the open cellar door, Ian descended into darkness. When he reached the bottom, he cast another spell, this time forming a narrow cone of flames that flooded the space in amber light. Ian lowered the cone until the fire enveloped the pyramid of wooden slats. A moment later, he withdrew the spell but the slats continued to burn. The fire crackled as it licked the wood and spread to the slats leaning against the intact barrels.

Ian spun and rushed up the stairs while surrounded by flickering firelight. He reached the top and raced past Revita. "Run!"

They sped off toward the stables. Just before reaching an open stable bay, the two barrels of naphtha among the load delivered by Vic and Dennard ignited. The thump of an explosion hammered in Ian's ears and echoed in his chest as his body was propelled forward. He landed a dozen feet away and tumbled into the empty stall. Darkness crashed in.

~

THE DARK of night surrounded Vic and Dennard as they rode along the drive leading back to Bard's Castle. Moonlight shone between the trees along the road, and stars dotted the evening sky. It was a peaceful scene soon to turn ugly. Anxiety left Vic's armpits damp. Again, he reached behind the wagon seat to ensure his weapon remained where he had placed it. He then glanced backward, the contents of the wagon bed covered by white tarps. Two more wagons rode behind theirs, forming a train that wound its way around a switchback before rolling toward the castle gate.

Torches mounted to the top of the wall wavered in the breeze while a pair of large lanterns burned just outside the closed gate. As before, eight men in black stood outside the portcullis while a few others loitered inside the castle yard.

With a call and a hard pull on the reins, Dennard stopped his team thirty feet shy of the gate, where the wagon was softly bathed by the light from the lanterns.

The guards, led by Rubens, split apart and approached the wagon just as before. "What are you doing back?" Rubens asked.

Dennard explained, "When I reached my warehouse, Wedlund was waiting for me with another delivery. In fact, this delivery was enough to fill three wagons, two of which were already loaded."

Vic found himself impressed by how easily Dennard delivered the lie.

Rubens looked at the odd shape beneath the tarp in the wagon bed. "What is it?"

"A gift from Magistrate Hargrave."

The man frowned. "The man who runs Greavesport?"

"That's him. As I understand, he is sending an envoy due to arrive in a day or two. This is a goodwill offering to ensure that Creskin trusts him and will listen to the offer he is about to make."

"So, what is it?'

Dennard looked from side to side, leaned close, and whispered. "Treasure."

"Three wagons full?"

Vic said, "Don't you think we should get it inside, where it is safe?" He looked over his shoulder. "We were being followed…"

As he said it, six men on horseback rode into view. The riders rounded the bend and stopped beyond the firelight and short of the rear wagon. There, they sat in silence. Watching.

"Who are they?" Rubens asked.

"Torrigan's men," Vic growled. "They followed us."

"They would dare to risk our wrath?'

"They must have gotten wind of the treasure in the wagons." Vic hoped the distraction would continue to buy them time.

"Wait a minute," one of the men said. "Why would you deliver treasure we didn't even know was coming? Wouldn't you just keep it for yourself?"

The questions had been expected to arise, and the response Vic had prepared was weak at best. *Come on, Ian,* Vic urged before replying. "And risk angering Creskin?"

Rubens drew his sword, the blade singing as it left its scabbard. "Lift the tarp."

Vic blanched. "But Torrigan's men..."

"We outnumber them and they appear content to watch for now anyway." He leveled the blade at Vic's chest. "The tarp. Now."

Raising his hands to ensure that the man did not suspect any resistance, Vic climbed down and stood alongside the wagon bed. He gripped the edge of the tarp and pulled it away in a flourish.

Inside the cart were two massive wooden chests. The light of the torches danced along the brass frame and lock on each.

"Open the chests," Rubens demanded.

"I don't have the keys. The instructions state that Hargrave will open them when he arrives."

"What instructions?"

Uncertain of how long the ruse could continue, Vic reluctantly dug out the missive Ian had prepared and held it out. Rubens lowered his blade and snatched the parchment. He then slid the blade into the scabbard, unfolded the paper, and held it up to the firelight.

The ground shook as a thump echoed from the castle grounds. The sky lit up with a flash of orange as an explosion rattled the ramparts. Rubens and his men all turned toward the gate. Shouts and cries echoed from the keep.

The wooden chest nearest to Vic opened. A dwarf armed with an axe climbed out. From the other chest came a man gripping a crossbow. At the same time, the riders masking as Torrigan's men spurred their horses forward while drawing their weapons.

The dwarf leapt from the wagon with a roar while chopping downward. Rubens spun around as the axe blade cleaved into his head. The man was dead before he hit the ground.

Vic lunged for the gap behind the wagon seat as the other guards drew their weapons. He found his mattock handle, pulled the weapon free, and brought it around in one smooth motion. The pick drove into the side of the nearest enemy, tearing his gut open while sending him spinning to the ground.

A furious battle ensued with Vic battling a swordsman while the dwarf beside him fought a man wielding a halberd. A crossbow bolt suddenly struck the dwarf in the shoulder, the impact causing him to drop to one knee. Vic blocked a sword strike from his attacker and then kicked out to the side, driving his heel into the leg of the other enemy. The man staggered as his halberd came down, narrowly missing the injured dwarf.

The six rebels on horseback, led by Essex, reached them. Four of them surrounded the other group of four guards, swords flashing and clanging against each other while cries rang out. The fifth rider, the only elf in the party, leapt from his horse and landed in the back of Dennard's wagon. He then raised his bow, nocked it, and began to loose, targeting the guards stationed at the top of the wall.

The tarps in the rear of the other two wagons flipped up and a quartet of men climbed out of each. The warriors brandished swords while the others wielded hammers, fire pokers, shovels, and other common tools.

Vic caught an overhead sword strike with his mattock handle. He then twisted and yanked his mattock toward him, hooking the enemy blade and tearing it from his grip. Dennard appeared from the side and swung, the hammer he wielded striking the man full in the face. The gang member crumpled to the ground, joining his fallen brethren. Panting from the brief and furious fight, Vic spun and found only his companions still upright. No guards were visible at the top of the wall, yet the gate remained closed.

A quartet of men in black appeared just on the other side of the bars. Each gripped a crossbow, took aim, and loosed.

Vic ducked and rolled as the horse beneath Essex released a high-pitched squeal. With a bolt in its neck, the horse bucked and thrashed. Essex managed to leap off and land beside Vic just before his horse spun and ran off. A bolt sailed between Vic and Essex, missing them both before striking a wagon.

As Vic regained his footing, an arrow struck the elf in the wagon bed beside him. The elf clutched at the fletching sticking out from his chest and fell between the two chests.

"Behind the wagons!" Essex shouted.

Scrambling after the man, Vic rounded the wagon and fell to one knee.

"Where is that boy?" Essex asked. "We need to get inside quickly, or this is all for nothing."

An enemy archer stood on the wall, took aim, and loosed, forcing Vic to duck as the arrow sailed just over his head. Lacking ranged weapons or a means to get into the castle, they were helpless to fight back.

"Ian and Revita will not let us down," Vic said in the most confident tone he could muster.

CHAPTER 24
RESILIENCE

Ian.

The voice seemed distant.

Ian.

It was a female voice.

"Wake up."

Ian opened his eyes to find Revita leaning over him, her face shimmering in warm light. His head throbbed. "Can you get up? We have little time and need to open the gate."

With a hand pressed against his head, Ian sat up. Across the yard, an inferno raged. A significant portion of the first floor and part of the second-floor wall were destroyed. Flames licked the third floor and the nearest tower, while the area beyond the missing walls was ablaze. Screams and shouts carried over the roar of the inferno, and silhouettes moved about inside the keep.

Revita gripped Ian beneath the arms and pulled him to his feet. He staggered, his surroundings tilting from side to side.

"Are you well enough to run?" she asked.

He nodded. "I have to be."

"Let's go."

She ran off, and Ian followed. Nausea twisted his stomach. The world bobbed and wobbled with each step as if he were drunk. The desire to just fall to his knees and rest tugged at him, but he shoved it aside with the single thought that his brother needed him. For all those times Vic had saved Ian, this was the chance for Ian to be a hero. He would not...could not fail.

They rounded the castle and the front gate came into view. Eight men stood between the outer wall and the castle, all armed and blocking the road while loosing arrows and bolts through the closed portcullis. The castle front door opened and men stumbled out. Some helped companions struggling to stand while others fell to their knees and coughed. Smoke poured from the entrance.

"I need to get to the gate tower," Revita said. "Can you do something about the guards in the way?"

Ian's role in the plan was critical, so he nodded numbly, determined to do his part despite the fog in his head. He strode toward the men while drawing in raw energy that pulsed through him, the buzz of it, combined with his rattled brain, causing him to stumble to one knee.

Revita rushed forward and gripped his arm. "Are you alright?"

"I..."

Ian's response was interrupted when door at the base of the tower to his right burst open and men in black rushed out.

"Intruders!" The dwarf at the fore of the group shouted.

The guards near the gate and those who had escaped the fire turned toward Ian and Revita. More men in black emerged from the tower door, their numbers rapidly exceeding two dozen. Suddenly, Ian found himself trapped between the two groups of enemies and the castle's outer wall.

"We have trouble, Ian." Revita tugged at his arm, pulling him up. "You need to act, now."

A towering bald man in black emerged from the crowd of enemies and pointed at Ian. "Grisgon, Nicks. Kill them."

Ian blinked as he realized the imposing man was the leader of the criminal gang. Worse, with thick shoulders, a barrel chest, and standing well over six feet tall, the man appeared as powerful as anyone Ian had ever met.

"Aye, Creskin," Replied a dwarf gripping a crossbow.

"You've got it, boss," added a lean man with a short bow.

The dwarf took aim at Ian while the man with the bow targeted Revita. With a gap of only twenty feet between the bowmen and their targets, they were unlikely to miss.

Driven by urgency, Ian cast a spell, but the construct dissolved before fully forming. He squinted, concentrating while trying a different spell and choosing the one he knew best.

The bolt and arrow launched toward them and shattered just an arm's length away when striking the invisible shield.

"What the blazes?" the dwarf exclaimed.

"Loose again," the group leader demanded.

While the archer drew another arrow, the dwarf cranked his crossbow and loaded another bolt. The second volley shattered as well, causing mutters among the guards.

Ian channeled more magic into the shield, moving it a few strides away while bending it into a half circle between them and the enemy. "Head toward the wall." He focused on his spell with everything he had. His grip on it felt tenuous, as if it were a slick fish flopping in his hand in an attempt to escape.

When Revita faded from his peripheral vision, Ian began to retreat. The two enemies reloaded and loosed, the arrow and bolt again shattering when striking the shield.

Creskin swore and pushed the dwarf aside. "If you can't do it, we will."

The crew leader drew a longsword and stomped forward. A beat later, a dozen others broke away from the group to follow the big man. Weapons brandished, they stalked toward Ian and Revita as they backed away.

"There is nowhere to go, you little runt." Creskin sneered while glaring at Ian, his pace gradually closing the gap between them. "This fire is your doing. I am going to rip you open from your head to your arse."

Ian's heel struck the wall, and he stumbled against it. Creskin roared, burst forward, and the others charged in. The leader smashed into the invisible shield as if it were a wall of brick. He staggered backward, his eyes rolling while blood spurted out from his nose. Four others in the front of the pack collided with the shield with similar results, two of them crying out as the men behind them accidentally ran them through with their swords. The rest stopped short of the shield and gathered around Creskin, who shook his head to clear it.

The big man scowled and eased forward with his sword extended before him. The blade hit the shield and slid upward until his other hand reached it.

Palm pressed against the invisible wall, Creskin said, "There is something in the way." He stepped back, snarled, and launched a thunderous, overhead strike. The sword bit into the shield, the pressure of the blow causing Ian to struggle to maintain his spell.

"We need to get the gate open," Revita reminded him.

Creskin turned toward the others. "Whatever it is, I felt my sword damage it. Hit it with everything you've got."

The gang members who had held back drew their weapons and rushed forward to join the fight.

Ian spoke between clenched teeth. "Give me just a moment."

The surviving enemies, some with hammers, one with an axe, and the rest wielding swords, spread out around Creskin and wound back. Before they could strike, Ian thrust the shield forward with everything he had. The shield plowed into the enemies and blasted them backward. Creskin and his men fell to the ground, some as far as ten strides away. More than one weapon found the flesh of the person wielding it or bit into a nearby companion. Cries, groans, and screams came from the men, many bleeding, a few unconscious, and more than one with broken bones.

His magic expended, Ian's shoulders slumped, and he fell against the wall.

"Are you alright?" Revita asked.

"I am spent." He leaned against her, using his weight to shove her toward the gate. "Run!"

When she bolted ahead, he ran after her with one hand against the wall to help keep himself upright.

~

REVITA RACED along the castle wall, watching the guards inside the gate. Half of the men stood in a cluster while discussing the situation. The other half repeatedly took aim and sent arrows and bolts between the portcullis bars. A fire raged inside the castle, and Revita suspected her companions had dealt with the guards outside its walls.

One of the men looked in her direction, his eyes widening before he shouted, "They are going for the gate!"

The guards, now numbering north of twenty including those who had escaped the fire, turned toward her. A half dozen broke off from the others and ran toward the gate tower door. It immediately became obvious that she would reach the door too late. Worse, Ian trailed behind her, and he didn't appear in any shape to fight. She made a fist, and the ridge of spikes on her bracer stood on end. Her timing would need to be exactly right. As the lead enemy reached the gate tower door, Revita flung her arm out.

The six spikes launched out in a fan of fury. The first struck the lead man in the shoulder, causing him to twist. He tripped and fell head-first into the door before crumpling to the ground. The second man in, who stood a few inches shorter than the first, was even less fortunate. The spike plunged into his throat, causing him to drop his sword and clutch at his neck while falling to his knees. The third spike missed altogether, while the fourth and fifth hit one man in the chest and bicep. The final spike struck a dwarf in the forehead, snapping his head back. He staggered two more steps before collapsing.

With four of the men down, two remained. One altered his angle and came at Revita, while the other went for the door, which was blocked by the unconscious form of the first enemy.

The attacker rushed in with a sword and swept his blade, intent on removing Revita's head. She dropped low and drove her fist into his crotch, eliciting a grunt. The man doubled over while bringing his sword down at an angle. She rolled to the side, came to her feet, and backed a few steps.

One guard dragged his unconscious companion from the door while the one with a blade in his chest and arm staggered to his feet.

The enemy before Revita, his face red with one hand pressed against his injured groin, growled, "You die now, wench!" He stalked toward her with his sword held before him.

Revita raised her bracer, as if to protect herself. With her other hand, she pressed the gems inside the bracer and waited.

The recalled spikes tore from the flesh of their enemies. One blasted through the leg of the man trying to open the door. Three others plunged into the back of the enemy stalking her, emerged from his torso, and latched back onto her bracer to join the others. The man at the door screamed and fell to one knee while the other simply toppled over.

She ran toward the door, leapt, and kicked the man with the bloody thigh, driving her heel into his chest. He tripped over a downed guard, struck his head on the wall, and lay still. Without pause, she grabbed the door and yanked it open. Ian rushed in behind her as she raced up the stairs.

"I'll lock the door," he said while pulling it closed.

Taking two stairs per stride, Revita ascended at a run. Five landings and dozens of stairs later, she emerged at the winch room to find it empty and the door to the top of the wall standing open. A guard stood just outside the door with his back facing her as he loosed arrows at Vic and the others.

Revita ran through the door, leapt, and kicked with both feet. Her heels struck the archer in the upper back. As she fell to the floor, the man flipped over the wall and disappeared. Without pause, she rolled, shot to her feet, and darted to the winch, which she began cranking. The rattle of chains and creaking of gears echoed in the empty room. *It's now up to Vic and Essex.* She just hoped the latter was as good as he claimed, for her sake and Vic's.

CHAPTER 25

A HEROIC EFFORT

Vic and the other rebels huddled behind wagons, using them for shelter as Creskin's men loosed arrows and bolts through the portcullis bars and from the top of the wall. Their lone archer, an elf, lay dead as did both of Dennard's horses, each with multiple projectiles jutting from their bodies.

The remaining archer atop the wall suddenly flipped over the edge and plummeted. A brief cry preceded a sickening crack when he landed head-first on the gravel. He did not move.

The portcullis then began to rise.

"It's opening!" Dennard exclaimed from Vic's side.

"Ian and Revita did it," Vic said in relief. As the minutes after the explosion had worn on, even his faith had begun to wane.

"Ready yourself," Essex shouted.

As the gate continued to rise, so did the adrenaline pumping through Vic's veins. He gripped his mattock while waiting for the call from Essex. When the gate was five feet off the ground and still rising, the call came.

"Charge!"

Vic and the other rebels, led by Essex, bolted toward the rising gate. Five enemies holding crossbows stood just inside the gate while a larger group waited in a cluster beyond them. Those in the front took aim and loosed. A bolt sped past Vic and struck someone behind him. The man cried out, but Vic did not, could not look back. He was focused on the guards urgently attempting to load their crossbows.

Essex reached the gate first but ran wide of the enemy's front line. He swept his sword out as he raced past them, slashing the midriff of the enemy on the right, tearing his stomach open and causing him to drop his crossbow.

Vic reached the gate a second later. Still running, he swung upward, targeting a loaded crossbow as the enemy raised it. The mattock struck with a crack, causing the crossbow to flip backward. The bolt loosed and launched straight up, where it shattered off the stone arch above the portcullis. Like Essex, he continued forward, focused on the cluster of enemies ahead.

When Essex drew near, Creskin's men braced themselves with weapons held before them. The enemy in the lead made a wide slash, but Essex slowed and deftly dodged the attack before following with a thrust, skewering the attacker's stomach. A man to his right raised his axe and chopped down, targeting Essex's extended sword arm. Vic's shoulder smashed into the axe wielder, knocking him back and causing the blow to miss. He then kicked out and drove his boot into the knee of another enemy before urgently blocking a sword thrust from a third man.

The other rebels reached the group and engaged. Weapons ranging from swords to shovels and fire pokers flashed in the firelight. Clangs of metal on metal were joined by grunts from the effort expended in the fight. Cries and screams of agony echoed above the din. In rapid succession, Vic blocked attacks, kicked, buried his mattock pick in the hip of an enemy, and spun away. The gang member fell into another and were swarmed over by men with hammers and shovels. Backing a few steps to catch his breath, Vic found himself at the edge of the fight, facing two gang members.

The man on his right came in with a sword thrust. Vic twisted around the attack while launching a sideways swing. His mattock struck the hand gripping the hilt, and the sword went spinning off into the night. The other enemy swung his cudgel low, striking Vic's leg. He cried out and fell to one knee. The man came in with a knife aimed at Vic's face. Vic bent his neck to the side, causing the blade to miss. The enemy followed with a knee that struck Vic in the forehead. His head snapped back, his surroundings spun, and spots danced before his eyes. As his vision cleared, he found himself lying on the ground with the attacker standing over him. Knife in his grip, the man raised his arm, ready to drive the blade down, but the fog in Vic's head made it difficult to react.

Suddenly, Dennard appeared behind the man with his hammer held high. The hammer came down as the knife plunged toward Vic. With a crack, the hammer struck the back of the man's head, and the man fell forward, altering the knife's path. The blade nicked Vic's ribs and buried in the gravel. Pain flared from the cut as the enemy collapsed across Vic's body. The back of the man's head was a nasty, bloody mess.

Dennard stood over Vic, panting. "Are you well?" He bent, gripped the dead man's jerkin, and pulled him off Vic.

A groan escaped Vic as he sat up. His hand went to the pain in his side and came away bloody. "Well enough. Thanks."

"Glad to help." Dennard extended a hand toward Vic, offering to help him up, unaware of the enemy behind him.

"Look out!" Vic shouted.

Too late.

A sword tip burst from Dennard's chest as Vic stared in horror. The blade withdrew. Dennard fell to his knees, teetered for a beat, and toppled over.

The swordsman was tall and lean, his blade dripping with crimson. He lunged toward Vic and thrust.

～

WHEN FINISHED CRANKING THE WINCH, Revita locked it in place. A hand touched her shoulder. In a flash, she drew her dagger, spun, and lunged. Just in time, she altered the angle of the strike and missed stabbing Ian by a breath.

"What the blazes?" he exclaimed. "You could have killed me."

"Never sneak up on a thief," she warned. "Unless you wished to get stabbed."

Ian frowned. "I'll pass on the stabbing." He nodded toward the winch. "Are you finished here?"

"Yes. Now, let's see how the fight fares."

She led him out the door and onto the wall. They walked out past the tower and peered over the wall, down into the castle yard.

A furious fight was taking place three stories below where the rebels were facing men in black. The blue sizzle of sparks drew her attention as Vic dispatched an enemy with his enchanted weapon. A pair of enemies came at him, forcing him backward as he blocked attack after attack.

"I am going down there." Revita turned toward Ian. "Stay up here, where you are out of harm's way."

"I..." He closed his mouth and nodded.

She darted back into the tower and sped down the stairs. Three rapid flights later, she unlocked the tower door, threw it open and strode out into the chaos.

Weapons clashed, blood splattered, and men screamed. She searched through the fracas for Vic but could not find him. Through a gap in the fight, she spied Dennard moving a dead man aside to reveal Vic, lying on the gravel.

Revita circled the edge of the fight and was forced to dive when a sword swept toward her. She rolled and came to her feet as Dennard crumpled to the ground to reveal a tall man with a bloody sword. The enemy made a move toward Vic. Without hesitation, Revita drew her dagger, flipped it in her hand, and launched it in a single fluid motion. The blade struck Vic's attacker in the throat. He lowered his sword and staggered while his free hand clutched for the blade in his neck. The man fell to his knees and landed face-down in the gravel.

She ran over and knelt beside Vic. "Are you alright?"

"Well enough. Thanks," He nodded. "Dennard..."

"I know. He isn't the only one. Half our men are down."

Vic reached for his mattock, gripped the handle, and climbed to his feet while wincing and holding his side with his other hand.

"You are bleeding," she said.

"I am aware." His eyes widened. "Oh, no."

Revita spun around and discovered the source of Vic's concern.

Creskin stood across the yard with his sword in hand. The big man shouted orders while the men around him rose to their feet and gathered their weapons. A third of them still lay on the ground, but what remained outnumbered the surviving rebels two to one. Worse, the other fight was not yet finished.

"Maybe we should run," Revita suggested.

His lips tight with anger, Vic shook his head. "We win now, or we die."

"I was afraid you would say that."

Creskin raised his sword in the air and bellowed, "Kill them!"

Revita, with her dagger still in the dead man's throat, made a fist with her right hand. The spikes of her bracer popped up as she readied herself.

~

IAN WATCHED the battle from the top of the wall. Despite the glow of firelight flickering across the castle yard, it was difficult to see exactly what was going on. Even when Revita rushed out of the tower, he soon lost her in the chaos of silhouettes fighting for their lives.

Movement far across the castle yard drew Ian's attention. Those who had survived Ian's magic attack gathered while a big man at their fore waved a sword and issued orders. The man's size made his identity obvious. Creskin had survived, and he was furious. The huge man thrust his sword toward the night sky, shouted, and charged with his entourage close behind.

It was immediately apparent to Ian that too many enemies remained. Vic, Revita, and the others were doomed unless he acted.

He drew in his gift, the energy pulsing through him causing his head to buzz with euphoria. With the desire to end the battle as expeditiously as possible, he crafted the most powerful spell he knew, a spell he had only just recently discovered. He thrust his hand toward Creskin while channeling every last ounce of magic he could muster.

A bolt of white lightning blazed across the distance and struck Creskin in the chest. The man froze in place, his body aglow with raw electricity until his hair and clothing burst into flames. Rather than release the spell, Ian fed it. The energy passed through Creskin, split and struck the two men just behind him. Again, and again, the lightning forked and arced from enemy to enemy in a spreading fan of death until all fifteen enemies were held in a static death lock. Clothing, hair, and anything else that could burn caught fire. Only then did Ian relent.

The electricity fizzled out, the castle yard falling dark other than the flames coming from Creskin and his crew. As one, all fifteen men collapsed to the gravel. Dead.

When the magic fled, his energy expended, Ian slumped to his knees, only the arm draped over the wall holding him up. He closed his eyes, took a few deep breaths, and raised his head to peer toward the castle yard and see what had become of the others.

The fighting in the castle yard had stopped. In the middle of those still standing was a cluster of men with their hands raised and empty. Those surrounding the men held weapons while staring up at Ian. In fact, everyone stared up at him, many with their eyes wide.

Vic thrust a fist up at Ian. "We did it!" He spun around while lifting his mattock in the air. "We won!"

Shouts of victory rang out. Ian grinned in relief as the last bit of energy left him. His eyes rolled up, and he slid into darkness.

CHAPTER 26
THE KING RETURNS

Two days after her first attempt to visit with the elves who lived outside the palace – a quest abandoned the moment Fastellan rode into Havenfall – Rina returned to the city. This outing proved more fruitful. She visited various shops, engaged with shopkeepers, and asked numerous questions of each. The more she spoke Elvish, the greater her confidence in the use of the complex language. To her surprise, the afternoon passed swiftly, and suddenly, the sun was approaching the western horizon.

Filling the afternoon by speaking with others helped to quell Rina's loneliness. In addition, she had learned more about Sylvan culture in that afternoon than in all the time that had passed since Shria-Li's disappearance. Thus, with a full heart and an empty stomach, she headed back to the palace, feeling better about herself than she had in quite some time.

As the sun edged behind the mountains to the west, the scattered clouds above the city turned pink. The air smelled of flowers in full bloom, the temperature comfortable. Rina waved at the people she passed. Some even waved back. When she arrived at the palace promenade, the guards greeted her with nods and smiles. She climbed the stairs, passed the fluted columns bordering the front entrance, and entered the receiving hall. As she traversed the corridor leading to the tower where she lived, she hummed to herself. A curved staircase took her up a four-story ascent. At the top, she entered Shria-Li's apartment and stopped cold.

She was not alone.

"Your Majesty," Rina said. "What are you doing here?"

Tora-Li turned an arched brow toward Rina. "Since when do queens answer to servants?"

The queen's harsh tone caused Rina to wilt. She dipped a curtsy, her gaze dropping to the floor. "I apologize, My Queen. I was startled to find you in my chambers."

"*Your* chambers?" An incredulous edge darkened Tora-Li's tone. "As I recall, these quarters belong to the princess and heir to the Sylvan throne...unless you have convinced my husband to replace his own daughter with a *human girl*."

Rina flinched at the accusation. She shook her head. "I would never...could never do such a thing. Shria-Li is my friend. I want her safely returned as much as anyone."

"Yet, you were the last to see her and the one to find the rope that led to her supposed escape."

The conversation had taken a dark turn and left Rina unbalanced. "When I went to bed that night, she was here and all was fine. I woke to..."

"Leave off!" The queen snapped. "I have heard your story before. For a time, I chose to believe it, but I now find myself in doubt. You have no proof as to what happened, yet thus far, I have found no means to disprove your claims. Regardless, your presence causes my wounded heart to fester."

"I never meant to cause trouble." The queen's anger pressed against Rina until she fought for breath. "It was not my idea to come here in the first place. I am only trying my best to do as you and Fastellan wish."

"You mean *King* Fastellan?"

The situation continued to spiral downward. Rina's reply was meek and barely audible. "Yes, Your Majesty."

Footsteps and the chime of armor coming from the staircase drew the attention of the two females. Chavell stopped outside the open chamber door. "Pardon, My Queen."

"What is it, Captain?"

"I have a message from the king."

"Go on."

"He wishes to meet you in the Garden of Life at nightfall. In private. He is currently donning his armor."

"His armor?" The queen grimaced. "He is leaving again?"

Chavell shook his head. "I do not know."

Tora-Li glanced toward the window. Purple clouds clung to the darkening sky as daylight eased into dusk. "Tell him I will be there after I finish up here and then stop by the kitchens to speak with the staff."

The captain of the guard dipped his head. "Thank you, Your Majesty." He then turned and descended.

When Chavell's footsteps had faded away, the queen turned toward Rina. Her nostrils flared as she inhaled deeply and then exhaled. Her lips pressed tightly together, and Rina feared what was coming next. That fear was realized when the queen issued a final command.

"For some reason, my husband defends you, claiming he is responsible for you being here in the first place, something I have been against from the onset. Well, I am here to inform you that your time in Havenfall has come to an end. Sleep well tonight. Visit the kitchens in the morning for provisions, and then my guards will escort you to the other side of the river. Where you go after you leave, I do not care. I only want you out of the city. Forever."

Rina's jaw worked, but tears emerged rather than words. With her posture stiff, Tora-Li walked past her and faded down the stairwell. Distraught, Rina fell onto her bed and wept. She cried for a solid minute, wallowing in her own sorrow until a voice inside her head told her to be strong, to seek a solution rather than drown in self-pity. That voice belonged to her best friend. *Ian would find a way, but he is not here.* She sat up and wiped her eyes. *It is up to you, Rina. Fix this.*

Rising, she left her room and headed to the balcony. There, she stepped out beneath the darkening sky and peered down into a garden bathed in golden light. At first, she only found shrubs and shadow until she spotted an armored male standing beside the pool that surrounded the Tree of Life.

He was alone.

Rina burst back inside, darted for the doorway, and raced down the stairs. Time seemed to slow, her feet moving as if they were in a pool of molasses. She knew Fastellan would help her if she could just speak to him before the queen did. She reached the bottom, rushed out the door, and took the last flight of stairs down to the garden. With her skirts in her hands, she scurried along the curved, downhill path, toward the pool, not slowing until he came into view.

"Fastellan," Rina said between gasps. "I must speak with you."

The king glanced in her direction, his face shadowed by his helm.

He abruptly turned his back to her, his voice low and gruff. "Why are you here? I am waiting for the queen."

She took a few strides toward him. "I need to speak with you."

"You must go," he said in a harsh whisper. "Now!"

Rina did not understand why he wanted her to leave so badly, but she could not give up. Not yet. She took a step closer. "The queen wants me away from the city. She is banishing me. You must stop her."

Over his shoulder, he hissed. "Foolish girl! Why would I care what becomes of you?"

She froze. "How can you say that?"

From across the garden came the queen's voice. "Fastellan?"

"The queen comes," he snapped. "Go!"

This was Rina's last chance. She could not give up. Moving closer, she rounded him and stopped. It was not Fastellan's face.

"Evarian?" Rina jerked and then froze in shock.

Evarian sneered and lunged toward her. A knife flashed in the golden aura of the tree before it plunged into her stomach. Sharp, terrible pain shot through her. She stumbled backward and clutched at her midriff. Her hand came away slick with blood, which is when she saw Tora-Li standing a quarter of the way around the pool, her gaze fixed on Rina.

"Help!" Rina croaked as she staggered and fell off the blade. She landed on her hip with one arm supporting her and the other hand pressed against her wound.

Evarian followed Rina's gaze and spun to face Tora-Li.

The queen turned and ran with Evarian giving chase.

"Guards!" Tora-Li cried. "Help! Guards!"

Tora-Li disappeared behind shrubs blocking Rina's view. Evarian rounded the pool and raced after her.

Again, Rina was alone.

The hand holding her up slid out, her body lowering until she lay on her side. The Tree of Life stood resolute, the light emanating from it speaking of hope. The irony struck Rina as her life slipped away.

CHAPTER 27

HEALING

A bitter chill had Rina huddled into a ball and shivering. It was dark, her surroundings masked by an impenetrable murk. Where she was or how she had gotten there, she could not recall. She could not remember anything other than the heat of agony turning to a chill like no other she had ever felt.

A soft light appeared in the darkness. She was drawn to that light, gave herself to it, and the light began to thaw her frozen body. It grew warmer and warmer, filling her with life until she felt like she could fly.

The light had a voice, which called her name, "Safrina."

She did not know how to reply.

"Safrina. Come back to us." The voice crooned.

Rina opened her eyes to find herself lying beneath the Tree of Life. A female elf with streaks of gray in her brown hair knelt beside Rina. Despite the gray, her face was smooth and wrinkle free. A stride away, Fastellan stood behind the elf woman, looking down at Rina. The queen stood at his side.

"What happened?" Rina asked in a weak voice.

Fastellan replied, "You were attacked."

"Attacked?"

"Evarian. He pretended to be me."

Memories rushed in - the king's armor, the flash of a knife, intense pain.

Rina tried to lift her arm but found it bound. Raising her head, she peered down to find a web of vines covering her arms and torso, holding her tight against the ground. The vines were the source of the warmth she felt.

The unknown female elf put her hand on Rina's forehead and gently lowered it back down. "You must remain still for now. Your wound was significant and would have been fatal had more time passed before I arrived."

"What are you doing to me?"

"Healing you. Here, beneath the tree of life, the process is faster and more effective, but it still requires time."

Tora-Li said, "This is Fi-Ara. She is as skilled a healer as you will find among our people. Listen to her, and you will soon be well."

Rina gasped when she realized what had transpired. "Evarian was going to kill you."

The queen nodded. "I am afraid so. Had you not intervened, I would be lying in your place without a healer to save me."

Fastellan added, "It was as you warned me. Evarian hatched a plot and convinced Chavell to assist him, and while I had taken steps to ensure I was protected, I never suspected he would target my wife.

"Chavell was sent to find the queen and have her meet me in the gardens. At the same time, he ordered the guards to keep anyone away while Evarian waited for Tora-Li to show. From a distance, with him wearing my armor, anyone would think it was me standing in the garden. He stole my armor from the cleaner, intending to kill her and place the blame upon me."

"Why would he do such a thing?"

"Evarian wished to oust me, and when Chavell refused to have me murdered, he sought to darken my name instead with the shame of spousal murder. Among Sylvan people, such a vile deed is considered an unforgiveable offense." Fastellan turned to Tora-Li. "You should tell her."

The queen nodded. "I thank you for your actions. Had you not been so bold, I would now be dead. For this, I am indebted to you."

Hope bloomed in Rina's chest. "Does that mean I can stay?"

Fastellan glanced at the queen before responding. "I am afraid that your presence here still causes my wife too much grief." He looked down at Rina. "However, we have come to an agreement. I must soon return to Shadowmar to address the final details of the castle's construction. When I do, you will ride with me. There, you will stay to manage the staff as a caretaker when neither Tora-Li nor I are there." He sighed. "I am sorry, but that was the best I could do for you."

Fastellan had told Rina she would soon join him at Shadowmar, and she had often wondered at how he would make that possible without notifying or upsetting Tora-Li. The king using that plan to satisfy the queen's desire to see Rina gone offered a brilliant resolution.

Fi-Ara looked over her shoulder, up at the king and queen. "It would be best if she rested. It will speed up the recovery. At this rate, she should be as good as new by morning."

"We had best be going, then." Fastellan held out his elbow, allowing Tora-Li to wrap her arm in his. "Rest well, Safrina. We leave for Shadowmar the day after tomorrow."

The king and queen turned and walked away, leaving Rina and the healer alone in the peaceful garden.

CHAPTER 28
LIBERTY

On the peak of an impossibly tall mountain, Ian stood, overlooking the world. From his perch above the scattered clouds, he turned slowly, observing all that existed as if he were a god.

Forests, mountains, and grasslands dominated the landscape. Amid them all was the sea, vast yet confined, trapped by land yet untamable. It was a glorious sight that lifted his spirits and made him feel invincible.

A flash of light drew his attention to the northern horizon. There, a darkness loomed, a storm that felt like a weight upon the world. Lightning danced amid those clouds as they roiled. The storm moved south, engulfing a mountain range and obscuring it from view. It raged across a desert, gaining momentum as it darkened the land.

Something shook Ian. He stumbled, thinking the earth beneath him quaked.

A voice called out, and his name echoed across the mountainside.

"Ian," the voice said again, somehow sounding much closer as Ian was yanked from his perch.

He floated up into the sky while the world below dissolved. Eyes opening, through the blur of drowsiness, he saw a face staring down at him.

"Vic?" The name slid past Ian's lips as a whisper. Speaking with force required too much energy.

His eyes reflecting concern, his brother nodded. "I am here. I've been here the whole time."

"What happened?"

"We found you unconscious and unresponsive."

"The castle?"

"Yes. We did it...you did it. Creskin is dead. His crew is finished."

Ian looked to the side. He was in a small room with two beds including the one in which he lay. "Where am I?"

"Jasper's Inn. The room and food are free for as long as we need." He reached for a bowl and held it in his lap. "Are you hungry?"

"What is it?"

"Porridge. Cold porridge by now."

"Ugh."

"Yeah. I agree. If you need to eat, I can get you something else."

"That might be good. Water would be even better."

"Oh. Of course."

As Vic poured water from a clay jug into a cup, Ian propped himself on his elbows. He blinked as the room tilted.

"Drink." Vic handed him the cup.

With eagerness, Ian wet his dry throat, took a breath, and continued until the cup was empty.

"Much better," he said as he laid his head back down. "How long was I out?"

"The castle was taken the night before last."

"Two days?"

"Well, it is late morning, so much of the day remains."

Ian's dream stuck with him, along with the sensation of something horrible coming soon. "I need to reach Havenfall."

"As you have said."

When Ian threw his covers aside and sat up, Vic gripped his wrist.

"What are you doing?" His brother demanded.

"First, I am going to the privy because my bladder is about to explode. Then, I am heading to the harbor to find a ship."

"You need time to recover." Vic's tone made it clear that the matter was not up for discussion. "The ship can wait until morning."

"You don't understand."

"I understand that you place your entire quest in jeopardy if you cannot function. Revita told me of how you were struggling to use your abilities. If you aren't recovered, how will you survive when you encounter trouble?"

The point Vic made was fair. Ian had struggled. His head needed to be clear, and that began by treating his body properly.

"Besides," Vic said, "If you agree to wait until morning, Revita and I will depart with you."

The prospect of companionship alone was worth the extra night. To have them at his side when he next ran into trouble was beyond enticing. "Very well. I will rest and recover today while you secure a ship for an early departure."

"Agreed."

"Now, let me go before I wet myself."

Vic shifted his grip from Ian's wrist to his hand, stood, and helped Ian to his feet. The room tilted before righting. Ian's legs shook. *I need food.* He then recalled how sick he was on his last sea voyage. It would be difficult for him to keep food down while aboard, so a day of sustenance and rest were, indeed, a good idea.

He walked to the door, opened it, and continued down the corridor leading to the inn's back door.

～

Vic followed Ian out of the room and stopped to watch as his brother shuffled down the hallway with one hand pressed against the wall to brace himself.

As Ian stumbled out the back door, Vic called out, "I'll order you some food. Meet me in the dining room."

The door slammed closed, the corridor falling silent. Satisfied, Vic headed down the corridor and turned to take the route leading to the inn's dining hall. Since it was mid-morning and in between breakfast and lunch, the room was quiet and vacant apart from a pair of men seated beside the front window. Choosing a table in the far corner, Vic crossed the room and settled on a seat facing the door. During his time with Revita, he had adopted some of her habits, one of which was being intentional about his position in any public space. Being able to see who entered and exited the building was simply good sense, especially considering that criminals controlled the city. *Not any longer.*

The knowledge that he had been instrumental in eradicating the gangs run by Creskin and Lokix gave Vic solace that countered the sense of loss hanging over him. Everyone involved in the capture of Bard's Castle had known the risks and had accepted them. Freedom was priceless, and if the cost paid required a few lives to liberate the city, so be it. While Vic went into that fight prepared to die, he hadn't considered how it might feel to see Dennard killed in the process. *He was a good man,* Vic thought. *He saved my life even after I betrayed him just days earlier.* A wave of guilt twisted Vic's stomach when he recalled Dennard mentioning a wife and a son. *Dennard's death was my fault. I should never have involved him. I need to find a way to help them.*

"What's wrong?" A familiar voice asked.

Vic looked up as Revita sat beside him. "I was just thinking about Dennard."

She looped her arm inside of his and pulled herself against his side.

The contact gave him comfort. "Yes, he was a good man, but his death was not your fault."

"But…"

"Dennard involved himself because he cared. Don't belittle the sacrifice he and the others made that night by linking them to your actions. All of them, like us, went in with the same goal and awareness of what it might cost us. Fate, luck, and skill all played a hand in who survived and who did not. From what I recall, it wasn't your sword that ended Dennard's life."

"No. I guess not."

"Then, allow Dennard to rest in peace with the knowledge that he saved the city he once loved."

Vic stared into her eyes. "You sometimes bewilder me, Vita. You behave like you are selfish and detached from others, but your actions say otherwise. One day, you ruthlessly kill a pair of toughs even though you know I wish otherwise, and on the next, you risk your own life to save another person. Now, when I am at my lowest, you hold me up and force me to look forward rather than dwell on regret." He then remembered the other issue troubling him. "There is one last thing, though."

"Which is?"

"We need to find Dennard's widow and see that she and her children are sufficiently cared for."

"Oh. That." She nodded. "We will think of something. I may be many things, but I would never allow children to suffer like I did."

He lifted his hand to her cheek. "I am blessed to have you at my side."

She gripped the hand against her cheek, held his thumb, and bent it backward.

"Ouch," Vic groaned as his thumb threatened to break.

Revita hissed, "This pain is nothing compared to what I will do if you ever tell anyone such things about me." She let go and smirked while he rubbed his sore hand. "But I will agree with one point."

Frowning in pain, he asked, "What is that?"

"You are blessed to have me at your side."

Despite himself, Vic laughed. "You are incorrigible."

"And don't forget it."

They were both laughing as Ian approached the table. "What is so funny?"

"I was just telling Vita that..." Vic gasped when she elbowed him in the ribs, right into his still raw wound. It felt as if she had driven her dagger into his flesh, the agony causing him to take repeated shallow breaths while holding his hand against his side.

"Oh." Concern softened her eyes as she rubbed his arm. "I forgot. Are you alright?"

"I will be, eventually," he groaned. "You may have reopened the wound, though."

"I did warn you."

He chuckled, which caused his stabbing pain to flare again.

Ian sat across from them. "I feel like I missed something."

A heavy-set man wearing a stained apron approached the table. "What can I do for my favorite customers?"

"Hi, Jasper," Vic said. "My brother is starved and needs something solid in his stomach. Do you have anything other than porridge for him?"

"Terese and I have been preparing meat pies. The oven is warm. I'll throw one in for him. What about you two?"

Vic nodded. "I could eat."

"Already?" Revita asked. "You had breakfast just two hours ago."

"That was two hours ago." He grinned.

She rolled her eyes. "Fine. Make it three."

"And water," Ian added. "Lots of water."

"A jug of water and three meat pies are on the way." Jasper said with a nod.

The big man turned away as a dwarf came in the front door. Ian recognized him as one of the warriors recruited by Essex.

"Are ye Jasper?" The dwarf asked as he approached.

"That's me."

The dwarf swung a loaded pack off his shoulder, reached in, and pulled out a sheet of parchment, which he handed to Jasper.

"What is this?" Jasper asked.

"Post this and be sure your patrons read it." The dwarf spun and stomped out the door.

Jasper looked over the paper and grunted. He then shuffled to a nearby post and pushed against the paper until the nail sticking from the post punched through it. The innkeeper then lumbered into the kitchen.

"What was that about?" Ian mused aloud.

"Let's find out." Revita stood and walked over to the post. After a few seconds, she returned. "Essex is holding an assembly later today and requests all citizens to attend."

"I suspected something like this would come soon." Vic said. "Where and when?"

"Everyone is to meet in the harbor square an hour before nightfall."

"What is this about?" Ian asked.

"The future of Bard's Bay," Vic replied.

Jasper emerged from the kitchen with three mugs and a brown jug. "Here's your water. The pies are in the oven." He set the mugs and jug on the table. "Just relax. They will be out soon."

Parched, Ian grabbed the jug and lifted it. His hand shook as he tried to pour. He downed the contents of the mug and poured another but could not stop shaking. *I need to eat.*

"I hope those pies come soon," Ian said. "I am ravenous."

~

A SOLID AND tasty meal was not all Ian needed to recover. Weary, he excused himself, returned to his room, and lay down. Sleep claimed him soon afterward. Hours later, he woke to the late day sun streaming through a gap in the curtains. *I slept most of the day,* Ian realized.

The door opened and Vic walked into the room. He stopped and looked down at Ian in concern. "I hope I didn't wake you."

Ian sat up and rubbed his eyes. "I was already awake."

"How are you feeling?"

"Better. What time is it?"

"Late afternoon. In fact, Revita and I were about to head to the harbor square for the assembly. I thought I would check on you before we left."

Ian swung his feet off the bed and stretched. "I'll join you."

"Are you up to it?"

Rising to his feet, Ian took stock of himself. "The shaking and dizziness seem to be gone. Food, water, and rest appear to have made a substantial difference."

Vic clapped Ian on the shoulder and flashed a smile. "Good to hear it, because I have secured us a ship bound for Hooked Point and the captain agreed to drop us off on the way. We are to be at the docks at first light."

"How much do I owe you?"

"The fare is already covered."

"You didn't have to pay. I have coin I was to use to get me to Havenfall."

"I didn't pay. Essex did. It was your cut from the spoils reaped from retaking Bard's Castle."

"Oh. That is fine, I guess." Ian stood over the vanity. A bowl of water and a tower rested on top of it. "Just give me a moment to clean up." He furrowed his brow. "Did Essex say what the assembly is about?"

Vic smirked. "Let's just head down to the square and find out."

Ian narrowed his eyes. "What are you hiding?"

"I have no idea what you are talking about." Vic opened the door. "Revita and I will be waiting downstairs."

With a sigh, Ian bent over the bowl and began to splash water on his face.

∽

IAN AND VIC followed Revita along the shadowed streets of Bard's Bay. Clusters of people walked ahead of them. A bald man stepped outside a bakery just ahead. The man flipped the sign in the window, pulled the door closed, and locked it before turning and heading down the street. Other shops they passed were already closed, including a few inns despite the upcoming dinner hour. The doors of those establishments all displayed the same missive, requesting the people of Bard's Bay to join the assembly.

The buzz of a teeming crowd came from ahead and only grew louder until Ian, Revita, and Vic reached the end of the street where it connected to the harbor square.

The square, three hundred feet long and half as wide, was thick with people. There were so many, Ian wondered where they had been while he traversed the abandoned streets just two days prior.

Revita pointed. "Let's move close to the wall."

She led them along the edge of the crowd, toward the wall that separated the city from the waterfront. A few strides from the wall, she turned and began winding through the gaps between people. As he walked past, Ian heard mutters of rumor and conjecture. The explosion Ian had triggered had shaken the entire city, and while many citizens had seen the castle on fire, they were still guessing at what exactly had happened and how it affected them.

Just before reaching the open harbor gate, Revita approached a pair of armed guards standing beside the gate tower door. She spoke to the men, who moved aside before she opened the door and began up the stairs.

Ian shot a questioning look at the guards. Rather than reply, they motioned for him to go inside, a sentiment that was further urged by Vic's gentle push from behind.

Confused, Ian entered and headed up the stairs. "Where are we going?"

Revita spoke over her shoulder. "To the top of the wall. Isn't that obvious?"

"Why?" Ian rounded a landing.

"It'll be easier to see from up there."

"No. I meant to ask why they allowed us past them."

She continued her ascent as if she had not heard him.

They emerged at the top of the wall, the sun in the western sky forcing Ian to squint as he gazed over the harbor. A rumble came from below the wall, drawing his attention to a carriage approaching from the east as it followed the road between the wall and the docks. The carriage slowed when it reached the gate. To Ian's surprise, the driver guided his team through the gate. Moving at a slow walk, the carriage entered the square, forcing the crowd to part just to avoid being trampled. The carriage continued across the square, beyond the shadow of the wall, and stopped while bathed in the amber light of the late-day sun.

The carriage door opened. A man stepped out, his athletic physique covered in black armor with silver plates on the chest, shoulders, and forearms. He wore a sword on his hip and a striking, red cape on his back.

Even with his beard gone, his face shaved clean, and his new garb, Ian recognized the man as Captain Essex.

Essex rounded the back of the carriage, grabbed the rail, and climbed up. He stood on the carriage roof with sunlight glinting off his armor. Arms raised, he turned slowly. The crowd quieted until only the soft rush of the surf could be heard.

Arms lowered, Essex spoke in a loud, firm voice. "Good people of Bard's Bay, I ask for your undivided attention.

"My name is Miles Essex. Many of you know me as captain of the guard for our former ruler, Commander Kaden. While Kaden had his faults, he made an effort to uphold the law and protect his subjects. The prison break and subsequent conflict that saw Kaden deposed also turned Bard's Bay on end. Since that time, honest citizens have been held hostage by fear and oppression as criminal groups ruled the streets, the riverfront, and the harbor. Thanks to the sacrifices of a few brave warriors, that reign of terror has ended."

The statement stirred murmurs amid the throng.

Essex paused to allow the murmurs to quiet before forging ahead. "Five days past, a confrontation between two criminal gangs took place. This conflict left Guy Lokix and his henchmen dead while reducing the numbers of Cully Creskin's crew. As you know, Creskin's influence over the city and the harbor was significant. So, when a small group of courageous citizens approached me with a plan to oust Creskin and his followers, the opportunity and need were too compelling to ignore. I had no choice but to join their righteous cause.

"I gathered the last few of the guards who were once under my command, joined a small team of civilians consisting of traders, laborers, and shopkeepers, and we set our plan into action. I suspect everyone in the city heard the explosion two nights past. That blast and the resulting fire eliminated half of Creskin's Crew. A bold and creative assault executed by our small squad of rebels saw Creskin and his remaining hoodlums dead or surrendered. By dawn, the castle was ours and only one criminal gang remained, which is why I sent Torrigan Slystone a gift along with a note. The gift was Creskin's head. The missive informed Torrigan that his head would be next if he and his lackeys did not leave Bard's Bay. Shortly after daybreak, dockworkers reported Torrigan and twenty some others boarding a ship bound for Greavesport.

"Bard's Bay is truly a free city once again."

The crowd cheered. Essex grinned and nodded while turning slowly, seemingly savoring the moment. This continued for some time before he raised his hands. The noise eased and once again, Essex addressed the audience.

"As proven by recent experience, a civilized society is dependent on laws to protect her citizens. Rule of law requires someone to govern and brave warriors to enforce those laws. In this, there can be no debate. To guide Bard's Bay as she recovers from a time of darkness, I have agreed to become her ruler. From this point on, until the people of Bard's Bay tire of my rule, I will fill the role under the title of Commander.

"The laws and tax rates that were in place under Kaden are officially reinstated." When mutters arose, Essex raised a hand, quelling them. "Nobody wishes to pay taxes. However, such is required to ensure your safety. Just remember that those taxes are but a fraction of the onerous protection fees forced upon you by Creskin, Lokix, and Torrigan. Murders, assaults, and thefts will become a fraction of what we have experienced of late. Ships will deliver goods without exorbitant prices, sailors will spend their time and coin at our inns, and travelers will once again feel welcome. With your help, our fair city can once again thrive. However, this cannot happen unless I can rebuild the city guard. I ask for able bodied citizens to join me. You will be armed, trained to use your weapon, earn a fair wage, and have the option of free room and board in what remains of Bard Castle. Those interested need but visit the castle tomorrow morning when recruitment opens.

"Lastly, I wish to acknowledge those who made this monumental change possible. A revolution cannot occur without courage, risk, and sacrifice. When this assembly concludes, I invite you all to join us for a special funeral on the waterfront as we honor those who gave their lives. The families who survive those heroes will be compensated with a sizable portion of the coin recovered from the castle, which is significant.

"Before that can happen, I wish to give special thanks to the brave individuals who began this crusade. If you turn and look upon the city wall, you will see Vic Carpenter and Revita Shalaan. Neither is a resident of Bard's Bay, but when they witnessed the disease infecting our city, they were compelled to seek a cure. This began with them tricking Creskin into attacking and slaughtering Lokix and the Southside Blades. With the riverfront freed from Lokix and one fewer gang to contend with, they approached me with their scheme to go after Creskin. I will admit, I thought it impossible at first. How could fewer than thirty people, half of whom have never wielded a weapon in their lives, hope to overthrow a criminal gang four times their count? Well, I was not convinced until I was introduced to Vic's brother. Without the devastating magic of this...this wizard, I would be dead and Creskin would have remained in power.

"I present to you the hero who saved Bard's Bay, Barsequa Illian." Essex pointed toward the top of the wall, where Ian stood. "His friends call him Ian."

Ian blinked as a strange feeling came over him. Never before had anyone proclaimed him a hero.

A crowd exceeding two thousand people began to clap and chant his name. "Ian! Ian! Ian!"

Vic and Revita each grabbed one of Ian's wrists and raised his hands toward the sky. The cheers grew louder, and Ian's pride swelled until he feared his chest might explode. He beamed back at the adoring crowd.

It was the greatest moment of his life.

CHAPTER 29
THE VALE

Ian stood at the ship's bow, his knuckles white. He held onto the port side rail as if he would plunge to his doom if he let go. His power and the knowledge he had gained did nothing to combat the turmoil in his now emptied stomach. Thus, he watched the distant coastline ease past while praying his seasickness would soon do the same.

To the southwest, brown cliffs and rocky points met the white of crashing waves. Forest-covered hillsides and open meadows stretched beyond those cliffs. The aqua blue water between the ship and shore completed a stunning view that almost made Ian's discomfort worth it. Almost. Scattered, puffy clouds gently floated north, driven by the same southern breeze that filled the ship's sails. One of such clouds crept across the sun, casting Ian and the ship in shadow.

Since their departure shortly after dawn, Ian had remained on deck, much of that time alone while Vic and Revita retreated to their cabin. He had no desire to go below deck, not after he had walked in on Revita during their last sea voyage. It wasn't that he found her naked body unpleasant. Quite the contrary, and the image of her shapely, lithe body remained fixed in his memory. Even focusing upon that memory caused his own body to react, which is what he wished to avoid.

It was late afternoon when the shoreline to the southwest abruptly changed from rocky cliffsides to gorgeous beaches. Thick green foliage waited beyond the beach, its color distinctly different than the forest that had dominated the hillside up until that point. The lush land extended to the north and west as far as Ian could see. The view was even more beautiful than the prior coastline, but while Ian stared at it, he felt as if he were being watched, as if the land itself were alive.

"Wow," a familiar voice said from beside him. "I can see why you are still out here."

Ian glanced at Vic, who gazed into the distance. "The scenery has helped ease my discomfort."

"How are you feeling?"

Ian took stock and realized that the queasiness in his stomach had been replaced by hunger. "I think that the sickness has passed."

"Are you ready to eat, then?"

"I think it best if I wait a bit."

The ship's heading altered. The captain issued orders, causing the sailors to scale the rigging and trim the sails.

Ian frowned. "We are heading toward shore."

"It does seem that way." Vic peered over his shoulder, toward the quarterdeck. "I am going to go speak with Captain Resnik."

When Ian released his grip on the rail, he opened and closed his hand to loosen his cramped fingers. "I'll go with you."

They walked along the rail, passed beneath the mainsail rigging, and rounded a pile of crates secured by netting before reaching the quarterdeck stairs.

Vic climbed up. "Ho, Captain."

Resnik was a ruddy-faced man in his thirties. His wispy red hair fluttered in the breeze, as did his thick red beard. The man wore a long black coat over a cream-colored tunic. His dark blue breeches were tucked into boots folded over at the top. With a bulbous nose and squinty eyes, few would call him handsome.

"Why if it ain't my young passengers. Where's that pretty lass of yours?"

"She is still below deck," Vic explained.

"Ah. Well, ya might want to pay her a visit and let her know yer voyage has come to an end."

Ian turned toward the bow, still pointed toward the landmass to the southwest. Beaches and jungle stretched for as far as he could see. "I don't see any signs of civilization."

The captain chortled. "Nor would ye be expected to, not on this shore. Not in the Vale."

The Vale, as Ian recalled, was a lush valley that covered much of the southwest shore of the Inner Sea. Most concerning was its reputation. Like the Agrosi, the Vale was a place of great danger, where creatures of magic stalked the land.

"But we were to travel to Havenfall," Ian argued.

"By ship, that would be a trick indeed. You see, Havenfall is many miles inland. I have never been there, but the stories claim that it is the most elegant city in the world, placed on the edge of a towering bluff and overlooking a pair or waterfalls."

Ian then remembered Truhan making a similar statement. "A river runs from those falls, all the way to the sea."

"That's right."

"The mouth of that river is where you are to bring me."

"I am afraid that will not happen." He pointed toward land. "This will have to do."

"You intend for us to walk all that way?"

"Walk, run, crawl. How ya do it don't matter to me." The captain shrugged. "I agreed to take yerselfs to the Vale. That be the beach ahead. From there, yer on yer own while me and my ship and crew continue to Hooked Point." The man pointed. "Now, be about yer business, so I can focus and not run aground. There be reefs in these waters."

Ian and Vic exchanged looks of concern before descending to the main deck. There, Ian stopped. "If we are to land soon, I think I'll visit the galley. It would be best if I had some food in my stomach before we are off the ship. I'll see if I can get some rations to take with us as well."

"Good idea. I am going to share the news with Revita. We will gather our things and meet you on deck."

As Vic walked off, Ian glanced toward shore. Again, he felt as if something was watching him.

～

THE LONGBOAT LURCHED as it splashed down into the aqua blue water. Ian gripped the rail as the vessel rocked from side to side. The two sailors in the longboat disconnected the winch lines, settled on the middle bench, and set an oar in place. In sync, as if rehearsed, they then began to row.

Captain Resnik and the rest of the crew stood at the ship's rail, watching as the distance between them and the longboat lengthened. The crew's behavior and expressions aroused concern, further spurred by the spat between Resnik and the sailors before launching the long-boat. Not one crewmember would volunteer to tender Ian, Vic, and Revita to shore. When commanded by Resnik, nobody moved. The captain then offered bonus pay for anyone who volunteered. Stern and steadfast glares were responses he received. Finally, Resnik resorted to choosing two men and issued threats of violence against them if they did not comply. All of this, alongside the white-eyed looks among the crew, had Ian concerned.

When the longboat was a few hundred feet from the ship, Ian flipped his feet over the bench, and faced the bow while examining the approaching shoreline.

White sand extended in both directions as far as the eye could see.

Palm fronds and thick undergrowth dominated the landscape beyond the beach. He then spied a split in the beach where a stream met the sea. *At least we will have access to fresh water.* The realization offered solace, yet he had no idea how long it would take to reach Havenfall or what dangers lurked along the way.

The longboat passed over the dark shadow of a coral reef then slid between a pair of black rocks jutting up from the water. Fish were visible in the clear shallows below the boat as it neared shore. A wave and one last thrust from the oars gave the craft a final push. When the wave receded, the bow settled on the sand.

"Get out." A sailor snapped in a firm tone.

Vic climbed past Ian, placed a foot on the rail, and jumped down into the wet sand. A wave rolled past, shifting the craft and washing over Vic's boots until it reached his ankles. He darted up the beach and onto the dry sand.

Revita, moving with balanced ease, stepped past Ian and hopped onto the beach the moment the wave withdrew. That left Ian alone with the two sailors. He cast the men a glance. Both had their backs to him, each warily looking over their shoulder. Their eyes flicked left and right, searching the shoreline while white knuckles gripped the oars.

Ian stood and threw his arms out when the boat rocked. He wobbled while placing his foot on the rail. When he stepped forward, intent on using the foot on the rail to push off for a leap, the craft came loose from the beach and slid backward, out from beneath him. Ian fell face-first onto the wet sand. A wave crashed in as he tried to push himself up. The water, cool but not cold, flowed right up his robes and caused him to gasp and scramble up the beach.

Vic chuckled and Revita laughed hysterically while Ian slogged into the dry sand. He raked sand out of his short beard and dusted it off his chest. He was wet from his torso to his feet. Water had even filled his boots. Only his head, his back, and the pack on it had been spared. He looked back at the bay to find the longboat twenty strides into the water and retreating. The two men rowed with urgency, their expressions landing somewhere between determined and desperate.

When Vic's chuckling settled, he clapped a hand on Ian's shoulder. "Are you alright?"

Ian frowned. "They didn't even laugh."

"Who?"

"The sailors. They didn't laugh. I fell in the water right in front of them, yet they did not laugh."

Revita held a hand to her stomach. "That was the funniest thing I have seen in a long time."

Staring toward the longboat, Vic grunted. "Huh. I see what you mean."

Disconcerted, Ian added, "The way the crew reacted to coming ashore was odd."

Revita snorted. "Odd? The thought of doing so scared the piss out of them."

"Which is why we need to remain alert and watch for trouble."

"I am a thief," she reminded him. "I always watch for trouble."

"I just hope we don't find any." Ian began walking along the beach. "I saw a stream up shore. Let's go fill our waterskins. I also need to empty my boots and wash the sand off."

The three of them walked along the beach. A quarter mile later, the shoreline curved away from the bay and the stream came into view. The waterway was fifty feet across where it met the sea. The fresh water flowed fast before meeting the churning waves. Inland from where Ian, Vic, and Revita stood, the stream cascaded over and through a cluster of rounded rocks sticking above the water's surface.

Ian turned and began an uphill trek. "Let's go upstream, beyond the brackish water."

"Brackish?" Revita asked.

"Yeah. Where the fresh water mixes with the salt water. You don't want to drink salt water, do you?"

"I'd rather not."

"You've never heard of brackish water?"

"I am a city girl, Ian. The wild...well, I've not spent a lot of time in the forest. The trek to and from Ra'Tahal last autumn was my longest."

Ian reached the top of the rise and stared upstream. The waterway ran along a ravine and created a gap in the forest, allowing him a distant view to the west.

An escarpment ran along the horizon, the east-facing cliffside masked in shadows. While difficult to judge the distance, the light haze between Ian and the cliffs left him guessing that it had to be forty or fifty miles away. Ian then recalled Captain Resnik mentioning Havenfall's location atop the edge of a bluff. A sigh slipped out as he realized how far they had yet to travel just to reach the cliff. How far north they would then have to go to reach the waterfalls, he had no idea.

"Why the sigh?" Vic asked.

Ian pointed. "See that cliffside?"

"Yeah."

"Resnik mentioned Havenfall being built upon a bluff like that."

Vic grunted. "That's quite a journey yet."

"And we have no idea what obstacles lie between here and there." Ian squatted over the rushing water and scooped two handfuls to his face. The water offered a cool and refreshing contrast to the warmth of the afternoon sun.

A low, rumbling growl came from the opposite side of the stream. Ian froze.

Branches snapped as the thuds of something heavy came toward him.

"Hide!" Revita hissed as she ducked between two massive shrubs.

Vic grabbed Ian by the arm and yanked him into motion as he followed her. They huddled behind the shrubs and squatted while the footsteps drew nearer.

The trees across the river parted and a glorious, legendary monster emerged.

The creature stood six feet tall with a body one and a half times the length. Its feline eyes flicked up and down the waterway while it lifted its nose in the air. A thick, fluffy mane of orange fur covered its neck while shorter, darker hair coated the rest of its body and legs. Webbed wings of dark red scales opened and closed as it stood there. A tail the color of blood stains curled up from its backside. A stinger the size of a dagger blade opened and closed at the end of the tail. Ian had never seen such a beast, but his research had included a thorough study of a bestiary of monsters. Upon sighting the Manticore, a creature rumored to haunt the Vale, Ian knew why the sailors had behaved as they did.

The manticore walked through the long grass bordering the stream and stopped with its massive forepaws at the water's edge. Talons, each black as night, an inch thick, and four inches long, dug into the riverbank as the beast bent its neck. It opened a massive maw, giving a brief glimpse of sharp, white teeth. A tongue, pink and as thick as Ian's wrist, flicked out and the manticore began to lap water.

Ian's pulse hammered in his ear while a voice inside him screamed for him to run. Another, wiser voice answered with a different command. *Don't move.*

A full minute, among the longest minutes of Ian's life, passed before the manticore lifted its head and sniffed the air. A breeze came off the sea, blowing inland. Ian prayed that the scent he and the others might exude was carried with that breeze and away from the Manticore.

The monster opened its mouth and snarled. It then crouched and leapt, straight toward Ian's hiding place. The beast flapped its wings, banked right over Ian, and soared into the sky. It sailed toward the sea, banked again, and flew northwest. Only when it had passed beyond their field of view did any of the three humans move.

"What in the blazes was that?" Revita stood while staring in the direction of the monster.

"A manticore." Ian was surprised that his voice remained stable. "They are vicious creatures and meat eaters. Worse for us, they are known to attack anything that moves when they are hunting."

Vic stepped through the shrubs and stood at the stream's edge. "It is gone, now. It might be best to fill our skins and get moving before it comes back."

"Where do we go from here?" Revita squatted beside Vic and uncapped her skin.

Ian pointed west. "See that escarpment in the distance?"

"Yeah."

"That is where we need to go." Ian squatted and dipped his water skin into the stream. He tilted it, bubbles emerging as the air was replaced by water.

Revita arched a brow at Ian. "Do you even know where we are?"

"I do."

"Well?"

"We are in the Vale and must cross it to reach our destination.

"The Vale? I have heard it referenced when others are reciting tales of legend."

"Yes. And now, we need to navigate this wild valley while hoping we avoid encountering any more of those legends." Ian had no idea if it were even possible.

CHAPTER 30
VANISHING

Vic extended his arm and used his mattock to push a palm frond aside. He stopped just beyond the palm and held it in place while Revita and Ian walked past him. They stood on a rock shelf with the stream ten feet below them. A tributary rushed in from their left, tumbling down a rocky hillside. To the right, across from the main artery was foliage. The day had waned as they traveled and shadows now lurked in all directions. The sky above remained blue, but it would not last long.

"What do you think?" Vic asked.

Ian surveyed the area and pointed across the stream. "I have been thinking we needed to cross for a while and was waiting for the right time. Now seems as good as any."

Revita looked down. "The current is pretty strong here and I don't see any rocks showing above the water. You don't expect us to swim, do you?"

"No. I will get us across."

She arched a brow. "Magic?"

He nodded but his gaze remained fixed on the opposite side of the stream. "I'll send Vic first. Then you, Revita."

"What do you need us to do?" Vic asked, uncertain of what Ian had proposed.

"Stand still." Ian held a hand out toward Vic and nodded. "Take a step toward me, Vic."

When Vic lifted his foot, it settled on something invisible. He stepped up and found it solid with just a little give. He floated out over the gap while water raged through the crevice some fifteen feet below. When he reached the far bank, he stepped off into a cluster of ferns and turned to look back across the ravine.

Ian turned to Revita. "Ready?"

"Just don't drop me."

Rather than reply, Ian simply pointed toward the ground between them. She stepped onto the invisible platform, her feet hovering a foot off the ground. As Ian moved his hand, she floated out over the ravine and continued toward where Vic waited.

Once Revita was across, Ian set his brow in determination, backed up a few steps, and burst into a run. At the edge, he leapt with Vic and Revita looking on. It was an odd sensation for Vic to witness his brother seemingly leap across a gap of more than twenty feet. Ian's landing, which included him rolling to a stop a foot off the ground, was even stranger to witness.

Ian got his feet beneath him, stood, and straightened his robes. "Is everyone ready to continue?"

Vic glanced at Revita, who shrugged. Ian's magic remained a bizarre and unknowable thing, but it had also begun to feel far less shocking than he would have guessed. Still, he was impressed. "You amaze me, Ian."

His brother turned toward him. "How so?"

"You can do things that seem impossible."

Ian shrugged. "I was gifted this ability."

"But the magic is the least of it." Vic clapped his brother on the shoulder. "The way you carry yourself is different. You seem far more confident than the awkward boy I remember. It makes me proud."

In response, Ian beamed. "Thank you, Vic. I am proud of you, too."

Revita snorted. "When you two are through gushing at each other, maybe we could resume this journey. It is getting dark."

Vic lifted his gaze to the sky. "Good point." Daylight was fading fast. "We need to seek out a place to stay the night. We've been lucky to avoid any trouble since our encounter with the manticore, but something tells me that traveling the Vale in darkness would be a bad idea."

Ian nodded. "Agreed." He pointed northwest. "Let's continue along the stream while looking for a good place to camp."

Again, Vic took the lead with his weapon in hand.

It had been decided at the onset that Vic would go first, not because he knew where he was going, but rather for defense purposes. His weapon required him to be close to an enemy while Revita's blades and Ian's magic were best used at range. Vic, knowing he was the strongest of the group, readily accepted his position at the fore. Doing so best fulfilled his inner desire to protect the people he loved by increasing the odds of him drawing the attention of any monster they happened upon.

As they had throughout much of the afternoon, they climbed an upslope. The elevation had gradually risen since leaving the beach, yet the surrounding forest, thick with trunks, branches, leaves, and fronds, made it difficult to see anything beyond their immediate surroundings. All the while, the day waned until shadows reduced even that narrow field of vision.

The trio crested a rise and entered a grove of trees with bare, barkless trunks rising some fifty feet before branching out to thick umbrellas that blotted out the sky. Gloom engulfed Vic and the others, the limited visibility forcing them to slow. Still in the lead, Vic walked while waving his weapon in front of him to cut through any spider webs, something he had learned to do early in their trek.

Pale light appeared through the trunks ahead, beckoning Vic. He headed toward the light until the trees fell away, and he stepped out onto a shelf of rock.

The dim aura of dusk blanketed the sky, the brightest of stars piercing that blanket. The moon, half masked by shadow, was a beacon to the east while the towering cliff to the west had turned to a dark silhouette. In between, the jungle canopy extended across the Vale, something the rock shelf allowed for them to look down upon for the first time. Vic eased toward the edge of the rock and peered down. To the west, he found nothing but a sheer drop exceeding a hundred feet. To the right was a hillside covered in rock, shrubs, and trees. Revita stood to one side of Vic, Ian to the other as they all surveyed the area.

"It looks like we are forced to go back down," Vic noted.

"I'd rather not do so in the dark," Ian said. "To be honest, I am exhausted."

"I am tired as well." Vic glanced toward the grove of trees behind him. The nearest tree was twenty feet away. "This rock shelf has enough space to safely light a fire. Let's see if we can scrounge up some dead wood, and we will camp up here for the night."

"Agreed."

Revita produced her light disk. "Let's find some wood, then." She walked back into the forest with the disk held before her.

In short order, they each gathered an armload of broken branches and then returned to the shelf of rock. There, Vic broke branches into sections from one to two feet in length, arranged some of them in a pyramid, then set the remainder a few strides to the side.

He stood and dusted his hands off. "Alright, Ian. Give us some fire."

Ian held a hand toward the pile of sticks. A cone of flames burst forth, its bright light illuminating the area. Seconds later, the cone doused, and only the bonfire remained. Vic arched a brow at Revita, who nodded, acknowledging that she was also impressed by Ian's abilities.

They arranged themselves around the fire and ate trail rations while sharing sparse conversation. Soon after, Ian lay down with his cloak over him and his pack under his head. Vic, tired as well. did the same while nestling beside Revita. With his arm around her, they both faced the flagging fire in silence. The orange of simmering coals was the last thing he remembered before he drifted off to sleep.

~

AN EERIE SCREECH woke Vic with a flinch. Revita rolled over and shot to a crouch with her dagger in hand. In the darkness, she appeared as a silhouette over him, unmoving. As quietly as possible, he rolled to his hands and knees before rising to a stance with his mattock in hand. There, he spun slowly while peering into the night.

The fire, now burned off, was nothing but smoldering, black coals. The moon had crossed the sky and now hovered above the cliff to the west. A light breeze stirred his hair and chilled his bare skin. The valley stood to one side, the shadowy grove of trees to the other. The gentle swaying of branches among the trees was the only sign of movement.

"Do you see anything?" he whispered.

"No," she hissed. "What made that sound?"

"I have no idea. Ian, do you know?"

Vic turned toward where his brother had been sleeping.

Nobody was there.

Panicked, Vic spun around, searching for him. "Ian?" He waited a beat and raised his voice. "Ian?"

There was no answer. A lump formed in his throat and rapidly dropped until a heavy weight bogged down his stomach. He cupped a hand to his mouth and shouted into the night. "Ian!"

The echo of his own voice was the only reply.

CHAPTER 31
CAPTIVE

A tickle caused Ian to squirm. An itch then bothered him, further drawing him from his slumber. He tried to scratch the irritated area but found his arm unable to move. Alarmed, his eyes flashed open.

Pale moonlight shone down on him. In the moonlight stood a tiny humanoid figure, just inches from his face.

Ian lifted his head to find other tiny people climbing on him with a thin cord trailing behind them. That cord was wrapped tightly, binding his arms against his torso. Just a few strides away, Vic and Revita lay on their sides, unconscious and in the same position they were in when he had fallen asleep. *I am still asleep, and this is a strange dream*, he told himself. It was not the first time he had experienced a dream that seemed to mix with reality. He closed his eyes again and screamed in his own head, *wake up!*

When he opened his eyes, the strange, tiny people were still there and had gathered before his face. A female broke from the group and strode toward him. Her body glowed with a soft aura, her movements flowing and graceful. It was a strange yet mesmerizing thing to see. As she drew close, he noticed wings akin to a dragonfly, semi-transparent and as long as she was tall, attached to her back. Those wings fluttered, lifting the tiny woman into the air. She floated up and hovered above Ian's face. Tiny sparks of golden light trailed her like stars that appeared and faded. *It is a fairy*, he thought. *What a strange dream.*

The fairy began to circle in the air, moving faster and faster, filling the air with sparks of light. She then dove toward Ian's face and drove her fist right into his nose. He yelped in pain even as his surroundings were engulfed by a flash of white.

∾

A JOSTLING CAUSED Ian to open his eyes. Stars dotted the sky above, battling the light of the half-moon. He lay on his back while the powerful sensation of his strange dream lingered. When he attempted to roll onto his side, he found resistance.

A nasal voice said, "Lie still, human."

Ian lifted his head and looked down to find his torso bound by thread. Even more troubling, the campsite was gone, and he was moving through a forest of dark tree trunks rising from a field of ferns. He was only inches off the ground.

"What is happening?" Ian asked in panic.

"You are to stand trial before our queen." The voice came from beside him, but Ian could see nothing.

"Trial? What queen? Who are you? Where am I?"

"Hush. You are our prisoner. We will ask the questions when it is time."

"Prisoner? Why?" As if the entire situation were not bizarre already, it felt strange speaking to someone Ian could not see.

"For violating our most sacred law. I warn you again, you must remain silent or you will be sorry."

Again, Ian told himself that he was dreaming. Desperate to wake, he twisted his wrist and grabbed a chunk of his thigh, pinching it. Pain flared, but he did not wake. He was already awake!

A streak of golden light shot past him, twisted around a tree trunk and wound past another. The spark of light then made a sharp turn and raced back until it came to a sudden stop just a few feet above him. Ian blinked at the glowing figure, its wings buzzing noisily.

"A fairy?" Ian said in shock.

"I am a fairy. What of it?" She hovered above him with her fists on her hips. Her voice and her willowy frame were distinctly female.

"I...just have never met a fairy before."

"Of that I have little doubt." The way she said it reeked of disdain.

"Why do you say that?" The dark forest continued to slide past Ian.

"You are human," she said in a haughty tone. "Humans know nothing of magic, so they seek to erase it from the world. This is why humans are not welcome in Fae Gulch."

"Is that where I am headed?"

"Yes."

"But you just said I was not welcome because I am human."

Her face pinched and she darted toward him, stopping inches from his nose. "Do not try to twist my own words upon myself, human!"

She flipped, extending her leg, Her toe struck Ian in the tip of the nose. The impact stung and also caused a tickle. He gasped as the tickle continued to build until he sneezed.

The sneeze launched the fairy, her glow like a shooting star as she streaked through the forest gloom. Some twenty feet away, she caught herself and then darted back to hover above Ian.

"You will pay for that, human." The fairy waggled a finger at him.

"I couldn't help it. You made me sneeze," he argued.

"Your attack on me will be but another reason for Queen Tanaya to sentence you to a painful, horrible death."

"Queen Tanaya?"

The fairy darted in, landed on his forehead, and grabbed him by the eyebrow hair. She then pulled upward. Hard.

"Ouch." Ian winced.

The fairy laughed. "You can expect far worse if you ever use the name of our queen again." She stood between his brows and leaned over to glare into his eye. "And you had best behave and show the queen the respect she deserves."

"I will. I swear."

With a firm nod, The fairy launched back into the air, her wings buzzing.

"I am Ian," he said, hoping to ease the tension. "What is your name?"

The fairy narrowed her eyes. "Why do you want to know?"

"Because giving one's name is the polite thing to do."

She pressed a finger to her chin, appearing to contemplate his request until she nodded. "If it is the polite thing to do, I will share my name. Everyone knows that I am polite."

"Oh, yes," Ian cooed. "You've been nothing but polite to me."

The fairy smiled, seemingly oblivious to Ian's sarcasm. "My name is Avi."

"Hello, Avi. It is nice to meet you." Ian still didn't understand what was happening, but he figured that treating the fairy well couldn't make the situation any worse.

"You are pleasant, for a human. It is too bad you will soon be dead." She launched upward, rolled backward, and sped off into the darkness.

His gaze followed her twisting, turning trail of light and then it disappeared. Confused as to what became of her, he stared at the last spot he had seen her while his body continued across the forest floor, straight toward that same location.

When he drew near, he realized that the trees were bound together by a woven wall of vines. Massive, threatening thorns jutted out from the vines, and he was heading straight toward them. When he tried to squirm free, his bonds tightened. Then, just as he was about to plow into the thorns, the vines before him retracted and unwove. Pale light emitted from the opening. Without any way to stop himself, Ian slid through the gap in the vines. The moment he was past, the web wove back together, sealing the opening in seconds.

Soft, warm light bathed the trees around him. Seeking the source of the light, Ian lifted his head and gasped in wonder.

The thick trees ahead stood some forty feet tall while surrounded by a wall of vine-connected trees twice the height. The surrounding forest remained dark, but the shorter trees in the middle shone with a warm phosphorescence. Amid the trees were three-story-tall mushrooms in a range of colors including yellow, pink, orange, and green. Tiny doors and windows adorned the trees and mushrooms alike.

Ian was carried down a golden trail, past flowers in full bloom. Butterflies flitted past and the hum of bees came from nearby. Birds tweeted as if it were the middle of the day rather than the deep of night. In the light of this amazing grove, it felt like daytime.

The trail wound around a tree with a stump twenty feet in diameter. When they cleared the tree, they were met by a female with a willowy build. Wings as long as her own height, somewhere above five feet, stretched out from her back. Pale green gossamer clothing covered just enough of her body to prevent Ian from blushing. Her near nudity caused him a few seconds of distraction before he recognized her.

"Avi?"

She stood firm while Ian was carried toward her. "You are now in Fae Gulch. Take care to behave, or your death will be long and painful."

Ian's movement stopped at her feet. It felt strange to have her stand over him after she had been only a few inches tall during their prior conversation. Rather than ask how she changed her size so quickly, he held fast to the subject of their conversation. His life. "And if I comply?"

"Then, I will urge Queen Tanaya to sentence you to a painless execution." She pointed toward the ground. "Set him down but leave him bound."

The pressure on Ian's backside shifted as the little people supporting him stepped to the side. They dropped him and he fell the last few inches, smacking the back of his head against the ground in the process.

"Oof," Ian grunted. Pain came from the back of his head, causing his temples to thump.

Tiny people dressed in leaves stood to either side of him. There were six in total, each glaring at Ian as if he had ruined their dinner. *I hope I am not dinner.* The thought was more disturbing than any other aspect of the strange experience.

Avi said, "Thank you, brownies. You may be on your way."

A tiny male figure spoke with a nasal tone. "What about me?"

"What about you, Lint?"

"I was witness to his crime." He thumped his chest. "I can testify to his guilt."

"Fine. You will join us as we go visit Tanaya."

The little man leapt three feet in the air and pumped his fist. "Yippee!" He landed and thrust a finger at Ian. "You will suffer, human!"

"Brownies..." Avi sighed. She then pointed at Ian. "Time to stand."

"How do you expect..." Before Ian could finish the sentence, he began to rise.

Avi, her face etched in concentration, pulled her hands toward herself while sparks of white light swirled around Ian. He soon found himself three feet off the ground. She then rotated her hands, and Ian's body mirrored the action until his feet hovered inches above the path. When Avi dropped her hands, the sparks of light faded and Ian fell to his feet.

Standing upright, Ian again tested his bonds. He strained until the threads bit into his flesh. They held fast. When he reached for his magic, he found nothing, which was the most troubling thing of all...until he remembered Vic and Revita.

"Where are the other humans?" Ian asked.

"Your companions were sleeping last I saw. I must say, you were easier to abduct than I anticipated." The fairy waved. "Follow me. Just remember that you promised to behave and to show respect."

With gliding, effortless strides, she followed a winding path through the glowing trees and oversized mushrooms. Ian followed, his strides limited by the bonds around his upper legs. The tiny brownie, Lint, ran, skipped, and hopped while circling around Ian, seeming to keep up with ease and displaying far too much delight about Ian's impending execution.

The trio soon came to a narrow stream meandering through the otherworldly village. An arched bridge took them over the stream. Once across the bridge, Ian spied a new spectacle through gaps in the trees.

A castle made of pink-tinted crystal drew his attention and held it fast. Elegant spires capped by purple cones thrust up from the structure. The stream curved and ran along the castle's outer wall. A drawbridge made of golden, glowing wood stretched over the stream. Avi made straight for the bridge, her gliding strides carrying her across it with ease. At the same time, Lint hopped, skipped, and even did a cartwheel as he crossed the bridge. Their stunned and overwhelmed captive numbly followed along.

The trio passed beneath the outer wall and entered a lush garden split down the center by a path of golden bricks. The sweet scent of flowers taunted Ian as he walked through the garden and stared up at the structure above him. The central keep stood three stories tall while the towers surrounding it stretched two to three times that height. Gold and green ivy graced by purple flowers clung to the castle towers. Shadows lurked behind the narrow windows lining the keep and dotting the rounded towers. High above, the night sky had begun to lighten, signaling morning's approach. Like the drawbridge, the keep's main entrance stood open. Avi and Ian climbed the stairs while Lint hopped up one stair at a time before darting ahead in obvious excitement.

The castle interior was even more amazing than the exterior. Stunned, Ian stopped just inside and gazed across a massive chamber with a ceiling three stories above.

Shards of crystal jutted up from the floor, reminding Ian of massive canine teeth. The shards glowed in a myriad of pastel colors. Ferns, flowers, and mushrooms covered much of the interior floor while paths of gold, silver, and bronze-tinted flagstone meandered across the interior garden. The narrow paths branched, intersected, and led to arched doorways cut into the walls along each side of the room. A broader path snaked and climbed toward the center of the room, leading uphill and stopping before a dais that overlooked the entire chamber. Upon the dais, seated on a sparkling, iridescent throne was a fairy wearing a crown of glowing Ivy.

Pain flared as something struck Ian's ankle. He looked down to find Lint glaring up at him.

"Keep moving, human," Lint demanded in his squeaky voice. "The queen is waiting."

Avi paused halfway between Ian and the dais, where she waved for him to follow.

Still bound from his waist to his shoulders, Ian crossed the room and joined Avi as she ascended the gentle upslope. The floor leveled some twelve feet above the entrance. Avi stopped a few strides before the dais. Ian settled in beside her while Lint stood at her other side.

"My queen," Avi curtsied while speaking in a cooing tone. "We require your audience and wisdom in a most serious matter."

The queen glared at Ian, her porcelain face unreadable. "Welcome, my daughter. I see that a brownie and a human have joined you. The former is unusual to enter my court. The latter is unprecedented. I pray you have good reason for this breach of etiquette."

Avi's prior confidence faltered. She glanced down at Lint. "I will allow the brownie to explain."

Lint hopped forward, stood between Ian and the dais, and bowed. "Queen Tanaya. I am blessed by your grace and am grateful for your audience." He pointed at Ian. "This...human," he snarled, "Has violated our most sacred law."

The queen arched her thin brow. "Fire?"

"Yes," Lint hissed. "As I witnessed personally, this warlock conjured flames and set sleeping wood ablaze. This fire burned atop Black Bluff for any to see. Of course, I was appalled by this atrocity and immediately set out to find a protector of the forest. Avi was kind enough to join me and five of my kin as we set out to apprehend the vile firebrand and deliver him to you for sentencing."

Tanaya turned her attention to Ian. "Is this true? Did you bring fire to the Vale?"

"I..." Ian stammered. "I did not know."

The queen snapped, "Ignorance is no excuse!"

"But, but, but we only burned some dead wood. No trees were harmed. I swear."

"Wood can only die if burned. The wood you used was merely asleep and would one day wake again in the form of a new tree."

Confused, Ian grasped for another argument. The queen spoke again before he did.

"Since we have a witness and you admit to the crime, you are clearly guilty. As written millennia ago, the crime of bringing fire to the Vale requires a punishment of death."

Desperate, Ian strained against his bonds but to no avail. He opened himself up to his magic but found it blocked once again. He was about to turn to run when the queen thrust her hand toward him. Golden sparks shot toward Ian, swirled around him, and lifted him into the air.

"I will make this quick and painless, human." Tanaya spoke firmly, but there was a sadness in her eyes. "This is my gift to you."

Ian's eyes widened in fear of what would come next.

"Wait!" a female voice echoed throughout the chamber.

A female elf emerged from a door at the side of the chamber. The presence of an elf was surprising.

The fact that Ian recognized her was even more shocking. "Shria-Li?"

CHAPTER 32
FAE GULCH

Shria-Li strolled along a path leading toward the dais at the heart of the throne room. She was shocked to see a human in the Vale, let alone in the hidden home of the Fae. More startling, the young man knew her name. "How do you know me?" She asked.

"It is me. Ian. We met in Ra'Tahal."

As she drew closer, she realized it to be true. "I apologize. I did not recognize you at first. You humans age so quickly and with the beard, even more so. "

"Good morning, Cousin," Queen Tanaya said.

"Greetings, Your Majesty," Shria-Li stopped at the side of the dais and dipped her head. "May I ask what magic you intend for this human?"

Golden sparks swirled about Ian as he was held suspended a foot above the floor.

The queen said, "This human has been found guilty and must pay for his crime."

"What crime?"

Ian shook his head. "I didn't know. I swear I meant no harm." He sounded on the edge of crying.

"As I said," Tanaya glared at him. "Ignorance is no excuse."

Shria-Li sensed the queen losing her patience and sought to intervene. "I apologize for the interruption, but may I *please* know what crime he has committed?"

Avi stood straight with her chest thrust out. "This human has brought fire to the Vale."

"Fire? Was anyone harmed or killed with this fire?"

The brownie standing beside Avi thrust a finger at Ian. "He fed a sleeping tree to the flames."

Closing her eyes while stifling a sigh, Shria-Li considered how to respond. The world outside the Vale used wood to feed flames. The Fae's belief that fire consumed the tree's soul was bizarre and something she struggled with despite living among them for over a full season. *They know nothing of souls, she reminded herself. They don't understand.* Still, she could not allow the execution to continue.

Opening her eyes, Shria-Li spoke boldly. "Ian is my friend. He visits the Vale and Fae Gulch under my protection. To harm him would be a direct affront against me."

Tanaya lowered her hand. The magic swirling around Ian disappeared. He dropped to the floor, stumbling before righting himself. His arms remained secured to his sides by strands of fairy thread.

The queen gave Shria-Li a look of warning. "Do you understand what that means?"

"I do."

"You are willing to pay for his crimes?"

"I am." Somehow, the quiver of fear that turned in her stomach did not affect the resolve in her voice.

The room fell silent other than the tapping of Tanaya's fingers on the arm of her throne. Finally, she nodded. "I choose to modify the sentence I have issued. This human is to remain under the watch of our cousin, Shria-Li, until he departs the Vale. During his stay, he is to hold fast to Fae law and any subsequent violation will be met with swift justice...to him and to his protector." With the last, the queen's eyes stared into Shria-Li's. In that look was a silent plea. *Please do not allow this to pass.*

Shria-Li bowed. "As I have witnessed time and again since my arrival, Her Majesty displays the honor, hospitality, and sense of justice that the Sylvan value so highly."

"Well said, cousin."

The queen seemed satisfied, so Shria-Li turned her attention on Ian. "Are you well?"

"Well enough. I can't tell you how happy I am to see you."

"I can guess." She glanced toward Avi. "You may free him from his bonds."

Avi shot a questioning look toward Tanaya. When the queen nodded, the fairy relented with a sigh. "Very well." She gestured toward Ian, spun her hand in a circle, and the thread swiftly unwound from his body. It floated through the air and wrapped around Avi's torso until it appeared as a belt made of silver thread.

The brownie crossed his arms over his chest, frowned at Ian, and then jumped. As he landed, Lint stomped both feet, right onto Ian's toes.

"Ouch!" Ian yanked his foot back and then hopped on the other foot. "What was that for?"

The brownie thrust a finger up at Ian. "You ruined my fun. I have always wanted to see a human die, and now I will have to wait."

"I am sorry to disappoint you, but I have important things to do, so I cannot die just yet. The entire world is counting on me."

"What is this?" Shria-Li asked.

"I..." Ian glanced toward the brownie glaring up at him. "Perhaps we can have a private conversation?"

Tanaya nodded. "I think it best if you and Shria-Li are on your way."

As Ian made to move, Avi snatched him by the wrist. "I found him. If he is to live, he should be mine."

"What?" Ian blurted.

The queen smirked. "You desire him as a consort?"

"Consort?" Ian's voice rose an octave.

"I have never had a human," Avi looked Ian up and down. "I have heard interesting stories and would like to see what is true and what is not." The fairy gave Ian a naughty smirk and squatted. She grabbed his robes with one hand, raised them, and reached up underneath with the other.

"What are you doing?" Ian exclaimed.

He tried to back away but the fairy had a firm grip on his robes. What else she might have a grip on, Shria-Li could only guess.

Avi's eyes grew wide. "Oh, my!"

Ian froze while gasping for air, his eyes bulging even more than Avi's.

Shria-Li covered her mouth to avoid laughing. Ian's cheeks were already red and his eyes appeared haunted. Steeling herself, she hardened her expression before lowering her hand. "I am sorry, Avi," Shria-Li said, "As his protector, I cannot allow you to claim him as a consort unless he is willing."

Avi turned toward Ian with hope in her eyes. "We could have so much fun together."

"I...I..." Ian appeared to have a difficult time getting the words out before he said, "I thank you for your interest, but I have other commitments."

The fairy dropped her hand and let go of his robes. Ian stumbled backward while holding his hands to his groin as he tried to cover his obvious reaction to her advances.

Avi stood, crossed her arms, and stuck out her lower lip. "I never get to have any fun."

Tanaya, covered her smirk and gestured toward Shria-Li. "It would be best if you and your guest left us alone, cousin. I would speak with these two in private."

"Yes, Your Majesty." Shria-Li dipped her head and waved for Ian to follow. She then marched off to the door at the side of the room, careful not to look backward so she might allow Ian time to regain his dignity.

~

A CURVED staircase illuminated by the soft pink glow of its crystal walls took Shria-Li and Ian to the tower's upper reaches. Six flights up, the staircase opened to a circular chamber ten strides in diameter. A three-foot-tall mushroom with a flat top and a pair of white toad stools sat below a window at one side of the room. From the vaulted, cone-shaped ceiling dangled a hammock made from woven fairy thread. The room was otherwise bare, making it a simple setting surrounded by otherworldly beauty.

Shria-Li sat on one of the toad stools and gestured toward the other. As Ian sat, she lifted a gourd from the table and tipped it up. Golden liquid poured out of the gourd and into a cup made from a pomegranate shell.

"Here," she handed the cup to Ian. "Drink."

He sniffed the cup. "What is it?"

"The Fae call it nectar. It is a mixture of juices from their gardens." She poured another, set the gourd down, and sipped hers to show him it was safe. The contents were sweet and made her tongue tingle.

Ian drank, his eyes widening before he swallowed. "It is...strange."

"You'll find that it rejuvenates your body. The Fae consume nothing else and it sustains their lives far beyond even that of a Sylvan."

"But elves live for hundreds of years."

"And Fae for thousands."

Ian whistled. "I cannot imagine. Eighteen years seems like a long time to me."

She smiled. "You humans are like falling stars shooting across the sky. You blaze through life, bright and wild, and then rapidly fade away."

"It all comes down to perspective, I guess." Ian glanced out the window. "This place is so strange. It doesn't seem real." He looked at her. "Why are you here?"

I am here because I don't wish my curse to destroy my people. Shria-Li told herself that every day, lest she give in to her longing to return home. *What should I tell Ian?* He was the first to ask since she made her decision. In contrast, the Fae seemed to simply accept her presence, even Queen Tanaya.

"I...left Havenfall last autumn. Alone, I journeyed into the Vale. As you likely have discovered, it is a wild and dangerous land. Even aware of this, I sought to brave it, for I saw no other choice. Four days into my expedition, as the last moments of daylight fought against the oncoming night, I happened upon a trio of werecat cubs. While the young are not dangerous, adult werecats are another story. The pack, including the parents of those cubs, emerged from the forest and had me surrounded. Knowing that the adults will do anything to protect their cubs, I thought myself doomed. Then, a spark shot across the clearing, circled around me, and continued, moving faster and faster. Golden light bloomed and I found myself in another part of the forest. The glowing form flew around me one last time and then stopped just inches before my face. The light came from a tiny female who fluttered in the air. She introduced herself as Exi and asked if I was Sylvan. I gave her my name and she brought me here, where I have lived ever since."

Living among the Fae had forced Shria-Li to master their language, which was remarkably similar to Dwarvish, the language which Ian was speaking. As far as she could tell, only an accent and a smattering of words were different between the two.

Ian frowned. "Why did you leave Havenfall?"

Hesitating, Shria-Li looked down at her hands, still cupping the pomegranate shell. She had yet to share her reason with anyone. Not having to speak it aloud helped make the situation seem less real, the consequences less terrifying. She lifted her gaze to meet his and forced herself to say the words.

"There is a dark prophecy as old as our people. It foretells the end of the Sylvan. I left Havenfall in hope of preventing this nightmare from coming to fruition."

His eyes dropped to the table. "I know something of prophecy, so I understand taking actions that might lead toward a better outcome. In fact, I am here because of prophecy as well." Ian looked into her eyes and spoke with violent passion. "I must reach Havenfall or our world is doomed. A darkness comes, one that erases all life in its path."

His words sent a chill down her spine, for they sounded familiar. "Why Havenfall?" She dreaded what his answer might be.

"I seek something called the Paragon."

"The Paragon?" Shria-Li repeated the word while trying to recall any mention of it in her studies. "I have never heard of it."

"Few have. In fact, the person who can lead me to it is dead."

Another chill. Her voice dropped to a whisper. "Dead? Who?"

"King Gahagar. You see, prophecy claims that Havenfall is the home to one who can speak with the dead. I seek this person so they might ask Gahagar's spirit what became of the Paragon. However, time is short, and should I fail, I fear the calamity that will follow."

Shria-Li's throat tightened, and her hands trembled. Her breath came in gasps as she gathered the courage to speak a truth she had denied since discovering it. "I am the death speaker."

CHAPTER 33
THE DEATH SPEAKER

Ian gasped at Shria-Li's revelation. "You are the death speaker?"

His journey had been fraught with unexpected twists and turns. While he felt no foreign hand guiding him, he had somehow navigated his way through those events and ended up here. Incredibly, fate, destiny, luck, or some hidden power had brought him straight to the single person he had been seeking despite her hiding in a place he could never have found on his own. *If Lint had not seen me light that fire, I would have passed by Fae Gulch without knowing it was there or that Shria-Li was living within it.*

The elf princess stood, crossed the room, and stared out the window. "I wish it were not true, but I am the one who can talk to the dead. It was my birth and the discovery of my ability that the dark prophecy mentions. It connects me to the end of my people. This is why I fled Havenfall...and why I cannot return."

Ian stood and held his hands out as he pleaded, "You must help me. If you do not, your people, mine, and all others are doomed."

She spun around. "This prophecy you speak of...Where did you learn of it? How do you know it is true?"

"Much has occurred since we last met. I am not the same person I was a year ago. Like you, I have abilities that make me different."

She narrowed her eyes. "What sort of abilities?"

Ian opened himself to his magic and prepared to cast a spell. His surroundings blurred and wavered as if he were staring into a pond, the reflection on its surface disturbed by a tossed stone. Confused, he stepped back with his head on a swivel. Other than Shria-Li, everything around him had a milky and instable appearance.

"What...what is happening?" he stammered.

"Are you well, Ian?"

"This place...there is something wrong."

"It is a place of magic."

Ian stared at the wall as it shifted and wavered. While the bizarre, disorienting image troubled him, there was something about it that demanded his attention. Without consciously doing so, Ian slid into meditation. The image began to flake away like layers of rotting flesh. At the core of the image was something shocking. A construct unlike any Ian had seen before.

It began with a completely original core made of swirled lines intersected by geometric shapes. The core created a feeling of depth while previous construct types appeared flat. Rather than made of runes or patterns, the two rings surrounding the core contained imagery. The inner of the two rings appeared crystalline. The outer was made of woven bands of pale light. Ian focused on the core, fighting against a sense of distortion as he memorized its pattern.

A hand shook him, drawing him from his meditation. His magic slipped away. The construct and the strange, milky images around him solidified.

"Are you well, Ian?" Shria Li stood at his side with her hand on his shoulder.

He nodded. "I am fine."

"I was concerned. You were silent and staring at the wall for minutes. You seemed distant, as if you could not hear me talking to you."

"I saw something." He pressed his hand against the wall. It felt solid.

She glanced at the wall. "What did you see?"

"I am not certain. It seemed as if the walls were not real."

"How could you possibly know that?"

His head snapped toward her. "What?"

"What do you know of Fae magic?"

"Nothing. I didn't even know fairies existed until an hour ago."

"You may have noticed that Tanaya referred to me as her cousin."

"I did notice and thought it a bit odd."

"Long ago, back at the dawn of the first age, elves and fairies were one people. Legend says that our god, Vandasal, chose to divide our races into three, creating elves, dark elves, and fairies. Each was gifted with a different magic. We Sylvan were graced with the gift of nature. The Drow were given the abilities of warrior blood and song. The Fae were blessed with the power of illusion."

"Illusion? Avi's magic was real enough for me."

"Oh, their illusions are as real as anything you have known, but they do not suffer the rules placed upon the physical realm. As you have noticed, their magic is quite powerful, but such power comes with a cost. You see, fairies do not have souls. They live for many centuries, sometimes thousands of years, but when they pass, that is the end. Period."

"No soul?" Ian had long prayed to good spirits, the souls of his ancestors. One day, when he passed from this world, his soul would join theirs in the afterlife until he was chosen for rebirth. "That is horrible."

"I find it sad, but we each have abilities and burdens unique to ourselves. The Fae are no different in that regard."

"So," Ian considered what he had learned. "This palace is an illusion?"

Shria-Li smiled. "Impressive, isn't it?"

"That means..." Ian's eyes opened wide. "That means I have discovered another use for my magic."

Her smile melted. "Magic? Humans possess no magic."

"That is what I was trying to show you. I can wield magic. It is how I lit the fire that caused me trouble with the Fae."

She crossed her arms over her chest. "That is impossible. Humans have no god. They are an ungifted race."

He sighed. "You don't believe me."

"I like you well enough, but you cannot change the laws set by the gods long, long ago."

Ian sat on the toad stool and rested his head in his hands.

Shria-Li slid onto the other stool. "Why is this so important to you?"

"I was trying to explain about the prophecy. I experienced it myself."

"What?"

"This prophecy. I saw it. Felt it. A darkness is coming."

She frowned. "Prophecy magic is rare, Ian."

"Rare or not, you must listen to me. I need your help. The fate of the world may depend on it."

For a quiet moment, she stared into his eyes, as if measuring him. "You truly believe this, don't you?"

"Of course. I would show you, but my magic behaves differently in this place."

"Why do you need to show me?"

"I need you, Shria-Li. I need to find the Paragon and the only person who knows where to find it has been dead for six years. Only you can get me the answer I need."

A long stretch of silence passed before she replied. "I must admit that your ability to identify Fae magic as an illusion is concerning. On the off chance that what you tell me is true, I will walk you out of Fae Gulch. In the forest, I will give you another chance to convince me.

Should that happen, I will join you. If I remain unconvinced, I will return here, and you will go on your way. However, I believe I could request someone to guide you. The Vale is a dangerous place to travel alone."

Ian shot to his feet, panicked as he suddenly remembered last seeing Vic and Revita lying on the other side of their campfire. "I was not alone. My brother and his female companion are out there somewhere and likely looking for me. We should go."

She stood with Ian's cup in her hand. "Drink the rest of the nectar. It will help to sustain you."

Ian took the cup and downed the sweet contents. Again, his tongue and throat tingled as the nectar made its way to his stomach. He set the cup down. "Now?"

Shria-Li smiled. "Your conviction is inspiring. Come. Let us go and secure an escort."

~

OUTSIDE THE FAIRY CASTLE, Ian followed Shria-Li along the meandering path through the exotic gardens of Fae Gulch. She walked right up to a golden mushroom that stood a few inches taller than she or Ian. The mushroom's bulbous head spread out like an umbrella, its stem thicker than most tree trunks. Windows peered out from the stock and head of the mushroom, each only a few inches tall and half the width.

"Hello." She patted on the mushroom, causing its rubbery skin to quiver. "Is anyone home?"

A tiny face appeared at a window at eye level. The brownie wore a smock and a frown, her hair tied back and fists on her hips. Despite her obvious displeasure, she nodded to Shria-Li. "Greetings, Princess."

"Hello, Mistletoe. I am seeking your youngest son."

The little brownie woman scowled. "What has that no good, wander-about Lint done this time?"

Shria-Li smirked. "Nothing bad. I simply request his assistance."

Mistletoe snorted. "Whatever you have planned, I hope it includes pounding some sense into that empty gourd of his." She turned and shouted over her shoulder. "Lint!"

A distant voice replied, "What?"

"Get up here! Now!"

Moments later, Lint appeared in the room beyond the window. "What is it, Mother?"

"The elf princess is here looking for you."

Lint walked up to the window, his eyes hardening when he saw Ian. He tore his gaze from Ian to Shria-Li. "Why are you protecting this *human?*" He snarled the last part.

"Ian is a friend and my guest. I know that you are angry about his use of fire, but what you perceive as a crime is not only common in the human world, it is expected. Yes, fire can be destructive when unchecked, but when used properly, it can provide warmth, comfort, and is frequently required for preparing meals. Would any of those things be considered a crime?"

The brownie frowned. "I suppose not." He thrust his finger at Ian. "But he violated our laws!"

With an eye roll, Shria-Li sighed. "Which he never denied. Since, Queen Tanaya has placed Ian under my care, I will ensure he commits no further crimes."

Ian nodded eagerly. "You will see no more fire from me, not until I am far from the Vale."

Lint crossed his arms. "Fine."

Shria-Li pressed onward, "With that behind us, I have need of your services."

He blinked. "Me?"

"You seem to spend a lot of your time away from Fae Gulch."

He thrust his chest out proudly. "I know the Vale better than anyone else."

"Which is why I need your help." She put a hand on Ian's shoulder. "Ian needs a guide to help him find his way out of the Vale safely."

The brownie's chest deflated. "You want me to travel with *him*?"

"I do."

Lint shook his head. "No."

Mistletoe punched him in the arm.

"Ouch!" he flinched away from her.

"The princess is Queen Tanaya's special guest!" Mistletoe hissed. "You had better honor her request or you will find a new mushroom in which to live."

"But mother..."

She thrust a finger into his chest. "Don't *but mother* me. You do nothing around here, disappear for days on end, and then return to eat my cupboard bare before you leave once again. For the first time in your life, someone important has need of something you can provide. You *will* do this."

Lint took a deep breath, huffed, and made fists at his sides before turning from the window and stomping out of sight.

Mistletoe watched his retreat before turning back toward the window. "I apologize. Lint has always been a wild one, but beneath his bluster, he has a good heart. He will not fail you in this."

"Thank you for convincing him, Mother Mistletoe. Have a good day."

The brownie woman gave a firm nod, turned, and walked off. The door at the base of the mushroom opened, and Lint emerged.

"I am here," he said. "Let's go, so this human will be far from my people before he brings fire again." Without waiting, he headed down the path, toward the glade's edge.

In a soft voice, Ian asked, "He isn't going to be trouble, is he?"

"He is only a hand-span in height. How much trouble can he be?"

Ian followed her while casting one last glance back at the brownie's mushroom home. Lint seemed emotional and unpredictable. Even if the brownie did not already hate Ian, he would have concerns.

CHAPTER 34
HIDDEN DANGERS

Rapid, urgent strides carried Vic through the shadowy forest. He wound his way through a legion of bare, smooth tree trunks, his eyes searching the surrounding area for signs of Ian's passing but finding none. Completing his loop, he headed toward daylight. A shelf of black rock came into view. At the edge of the rock, Revita stood in the light of the morning sun staring out across the valley below. Usually, Vic's heart leapt at the sight of her, but in this case, it sank like a boulder dropped into the sea.

She spun around with her dagger ready as he emerged from the woods. "Oh. It's you."

"Any sign of Ian?" he asked, expecting the worst.

"Sorry."

He walked past the blackened coals of the dormant fire from the prior evening and stopped at the edge of a steep drop. Treetops spread out in all directions. Far to the east, the sea lay beneath a haze of white. To the west, a towering cliff loomed in the distance.

Vic spoke without turning toward her. "I searched the wood from here back to the stream. Other than evidence of our passing through late yesterday, I found nothing."

She stood beside him while rubbing his arm. "Perhaps he climbed down."

He silently thanked her for not suggesting that Ian fell. Still, he needed to know and there was only way to be certain. "Let's climb down."

It was a decision that had been delayed, because a climb back up would be difficult and he had hoped Ian might wander back to camp if given time.

Revita sheathed her dagger. "Lead the way."

Vic walked along the edge while looking down, seeking an ideal place to begin his descent. He then came to a crevice cut through the rock shelf. It was twenty feet deep and ran down at an angle as it cut into the cliff wall.

"This will do. Follow once I reach the bottom of this gap."

He sat on the edge, turned, and began to scale down. Moments later, his feet touched down on the crevice floor and Revita followed. Confident in her ability and knowing she would not need assistance, Vic resumed his descent, working his way along the sloped bottom and then down the channel carved into the rock face. The going would be slow, but he was determined to find his brother.

~

SHRUBS, long grass, and scattered trees covered the uneven ground at the bottom of the bluff. A wall of jagged rock rose a hundred feet above Vic, who walked parallel to the cliff side, searching in desperation. Finally, the wall of rock receded to reveal a ravine. A creek ran along the base of the wall and flowed northeast. Unblemished slopes of mud and grass bordered the water. No footprints were visible in the mud and the opposite side of the ravine appeared too steep to ascend. Hope darkened to despair. Deflated, Vic sat on a fallen log above the stream and stared into space.

Revita knelt in front of him and took his hands. "I am sorry, Vic."

"He's not dead, Revita," he croaked. "I know he is out there alive. Somewhere."

She gave him a sad smile while caressing his cheek. "Somewhere."

Lightning shot overhead and struck the opposite wall of the ravine. Shards of rock burst from the point of impact and rained down on the forest floor, some of which tumbled into the creek below him.

Vic shot to his feet and peered toward the sky. There was not a cloud in sight. "That was not natural."

"What if it came from a monster?"

"What if it was Ian?" He decided he could not avoid taking the risk. "Come on."

Swift strides carried Vic through the forest as he headed in the direction of the blast. His fast walk turned to a run as he shot between shrubs, leapt over fallen trees, and ducked below low branches, barely slowing while counting on Revita to follow. A few hundred feet later, he burst into a glade. A hill stood across the glade. Trees dotted the hilltop. Standing among those trees were two people having a quiet discussion. One of them was instantly familiar. Relief washed over Vic upon seeing his brother.

"Ian!" Vic shouted with a wave to draw attention.

Ian turned and called out. "Vic! I am glad I found you."

Revita came to a stop beside Vic. "Found us?" She squinted. "And where did the female elf come from?"

"Let's find out."

As the two of them climbed the hillside, Ian and the elf continued their discussion, which concluded just as Vic and Revita drew near.

"Vic, Revita," Ian said. "This is my friend, Shria-Li."

The elf's almond eyes examined Vic before shifting to Revita. "I am pleased do meet you."

Then, Vic saw something that made him stop cold. "Is there a little man standing on that log, or am I imagining it?"

The small figure waved a fist in the air and responded in Dwarvish, "I am no little man. I am a brownie!"

Ian gestured toward the small being. "This is our guide, Lint."

Revita burst out laughing. "Its name is Lint? Did he fall out of your pocket, then?"

Vic, still plagued by concern for his brother, said, "We woke to find you gone and thought something bad had happened to you."

"Something did happen," Ian replied. "At first, I thought it bad as well, but Shria-Li saved me. Better yet, I found what I was seeking."

"But we have not yet made it to Havenfall."

"True, but the death speaker was here in the Vale, and she has agreed to join our quest."

Vic noted the concern on Shria-Li's face. "You?"

"I am the one Ian was seeking."

Ian gave a firm nod. "Now, we must make haste for Ra-Tahal. It is quite far and it will be a difficult journey. I hope we will not be too late."

Shria-Li turned to gaze northwest, her eyes distant. "There is another way."

"Another way?"

The elf woman's brow furrowed. She chewed on her lip in apparent contemplation until her expression turned to resolve. "We must go to Havenfall and speak with my father. If we can convince him of the dire nature of our quest, he can help us reach Ra'Tahal in a fraction of the time."

Revita narrowed her eyes. "Havenfall is in the wrong direction. This would only be possible with some sort of..."

"Magic."

Ian arched his brow. "What sort of magic is this?"

"I cannot say." Shria-Li gestured to the brownie. "Do you know a way up the cliffside that bounds the western portion of the vale?"

Lint puffed up proudly. "Of course, I do."

"Take us there."

"Follow me!" The brownie hopped off the log and raced down the hillside.

~

A SENSE of accomplishment fueled Ian. The first goal of his quest had been achieved. Not only had he located the death speaker, but he had convinced her to join him. Best of all, she was someone he genuinely liked and believed he could trust. The journey he had begun alone now included four others, which seemed to reduce the burden of responsibility that had weighed upon him at the onset.

The brownie, Lint, seemed tireless as he repeatedly darted forward, paused for the others to catch up, and was off once again. He leapt over logs and up boulders with ease and seemed to take delight in every aspect of traveling. The defensive and often abrasive nature Lint exhibited in Fae Gulch were gone. Instead, he laughed, giggled, and released whoops of joy that seemed to lift everyone's spirits.

Then, his demeanor changed as they approached a dark copse of trees.

Lint thrust a palm behind him and waited for the elf and three humans to stop. He then held a finger to his lips and slunk off into the shadows.

Ian exchanged glances with his brother and the two females. "Do we wait here?" he whispered.

Shria-Li shrugged. "I do not know."

"I say we wait," Revita suggested. "If he wants us to follow, he will come back."

A growl came from the dark wood, the sound too close for Ian's comfort. Branches broke as something suddenly trampled through shrubs. A squeal rang out. Snarls, growls, and more squeals followed, along with the noise of a scuffle.

Concerned for Lint, Ian bolted past Vic and charged into the woods. He raced past trees, leapt through shrubs, and continued toward the sounds. Light from a clearing came into view. In that light, something large tromped around as it violently shook the body of something far smaller. The large creature had the head, wings, and claws of an eagle, but its body was striped and covered in fur. Ian froze at the sight of the griffin, for the monster was the size of a horse and far, far more deadly. The others gathered around him to watch through the trees as the fight ended and the griffon began to eat.

Tense moments passed with a concerted effort to remain still and silent. Then, the griffin raised its head, burst into a run, and took flight. It circled once and then flew off to the southeast. Only when it was over a mile away did anyone move.

They walked through the woods and stepped out to stare down at the torn, bloody corpse that had become griffon fodder.

The dead animal had a head resembling an oversized jack rabbit, but the creatures spotted body and long, elegant legs spoke of another creature of legend.

"A jackalope." Ian recognized the creature from his studies.

Vic stared down at the corpse. "Another creature from fireside tales. I wonder if all of those stories are rooted in truth. I used to doubt such things, but the more I see, the more I realize that there is much to the world I have yet to discover."

Shria-Li nodded in turn. "I, too, find that the world outside of Havenfall is not as I expected. Even the Vale is not the dark and twisted land the Sylvan claim it to be. There is beauty and harmony to balance the danger and deadly magic."

The torn, bloody remains of the animal left Ian wondering if he could have done something to save it. "Tell that to this poor creature."

Revita shrugged. "How is this any different than a squirrel becoming a meal for a hungry wolf?"

"That is true," Vic said. "Hunters and prey exist everywhere. The creatures may be more exotic here, but the circle of life remains the same."

Lint emerged from the shadows and hopped on a rock. "If you humans are through babbling, we should keep moving. We've a long way to go if we want to reach the escarpment before nightfall."

The elf princess pointed ahead. "Lead on, brave brownie."

Lint grinned, leapt off the rock, and ducked into the long grass. Ian followed the wiggling grass stocks as he trailed the tiny brownie.

Without forest to block the view, Ian surveyed his surroundings. Colorful butterflies flitted from flower to flower. Trees of various shades of green bordered the glade while rolling, wooded hills were visible beyond the trees. In the distance, the towering escarpment watched over the valley. All of this took place below a cloudless sky and painted a picture worthy of framing, the beauty belying the inherent danger of the Vale. The dichotomy created an odd mixture of emotions within Ian, trapped between wonder, anxiety, and sorrow – the latter for the jacka-lope. He could not stop thinking of himself in the position of the poor animal, desperate to survive and praying for someone or something to save him, only to die a horrible death.

At the far end of the glade, they came upon a large bank of shrubs covered in raspberries, round, ripe and begging to be picked. His hunger along with the allure of the plump, red fruit made them too compelling for Ian to ignore. He broke from the others, approached the shrubs, and reached for a berry.

"No!" Lint's shout was like a needle bursting the bubble of enthrall-ment around Ian.

With his hand hovering inches from the berry, Ian asked, "What's wrong?"

The berry trembled and hundreds of black thorns popped out from it, making it appear as a red and black burr with the nearest spike less than an inch from Ian's fingers.

He yanked his hand back and gaped. "What is it?"

"You are lucky, human," Lint said. "Those are known as bait berries. Only, taking this bait is deadly. Those thorns are poisonous and will kill something far larger than you in mere minutes."

The idea horrified Ian, who backed from the bush to join his companions.

Following Lint's lead, they circled the bank of bait berry shrubs, careful to remain at a distance. Beyond the shrubs, the brownie led them up a slope shadowed by trees thick with purple flowers. The wind caused the branches to waver and the flowers on them to make a tinkling sound akin to tiny bells. As they passed beneath these branches, the three humans and even Shria-Li stared up in wonder.

A few hundred feet later, the trees ended at a pit dirt, six feet deep and twice the diameter. Beside the pit, a fallen oak tree lay at the edge of a clearing, the tree's roots still clinging to the dirt that had come with them to create the hole in the ground. They circled the dead tree and entered an open meadow that stirred additional curiosity.

Trees encircled a glade half a mile across. Flowering shrubs occupied the outer third of the glade while long grass covered the middle third. The inner hub of this giant wheel was nothing but dirt surrounding a tree made of strange, twisted branches that formed a massive globe atop a thick, gnarled trunk. Lint hopped on top of a rock amid the flowers and stared toward the tree while Ian and his companions gathered behind him.

Vic whistled. "That is the largest weeping willow I have ever seen."

Ian added, "Are those apples among its branches?"

"Those are not apples, and this is like no other willow." Lint pointed. "Watch."

A tiny, dark shape flew in from the east, slowed, and hovered just beyond the tree as it eyed a large, red fruit.

"Poor thing." Lint shook his head.

"What's wrong?" Ian asked. "Is that bird dangerous."

"It is not a bird, nor is it the source of danger."

The tree suddenly lashed out with a long whip-like branch that wrapped around the flying creature. High-pitched squeaks of terror carried across the meadow and sent chills down Ian's spine.

Lint sighed. "The widow willow has claimed another victim."

"Victim? What will it do?"

"The tree always devours its prey."

The small creature flapped in desperation, shrieked in terror, and tugged at Ian's heart. Before he even realized it, Ian was dashing through the flowers, straight toward the carnivorous tree. Vic and the others shouted Ian's name, but he barely heard them, for his thoughts were elsewhere.

An innocent creature, too naïve to understand the danger, was about to die a horrible death, just like he could have if he had touched the bait berry before his friends intervened. This creature had no friends, so Ian sought to fill that role.

He burst from the flowers and raced across the grassy patch as the tree loomed closer. The willow appeared huge from a distance, but now he realized that it was even larger than expected. The upper branches of the globe were hundreds of feet above while the tree's shadow covered the entire bare inner third of the meadow, making its diameter about three hundred feet. The dark red creature flapped its wings, struggled, and thrashed as the branches wound about its little body. Ian felt as if that was happening to a piece of his heart.

Magic flowed into Ian as he neared the end of the grassy patch. He cast a construct of hardened air and formed it into a thin band that launched toward the willow. The air sliced through the thin, vine-like branches in a spray of leaves. A violent creaking came from the willow as the creature bound in its branches fell toward the ground. The tree shuddered, bent, and hundreds of thin branches whipped outward, straight toward Ian.

With urgency, Ian crafted a new construct and prepared to wrap a shield about himself, but the tree was too quick. The branches wound around Ian's wrists, yanking his arms wide before another encircled his waist. He was lifted into the air and drawn toward the tree. The globe of branches parted to reveal the tree's trunk, a hundred feet away. A massive knothole in the trunk opened to become a dark, gaping maw with Ian heading straight toward it.

CHAPTER 35
EATEN ALIVE

"Ian!" Vic shouted as Ian raced toward the monstrous willow tree.

When Ian did not slow, Vic glanced toward Revita and burst into a run. While in a full sprint, he untied his cloak, slid it off along with his pack, and reached for the weapon on his back. Just as he pulled the weapon free, he glimpsed Revita from the corner of his eye as she kept pace with him. He did not look in her direction, but her presence added comfort despite the incredibly insane thing he was about to do.

Ian reached the willow and used magic to cut through the branches holding the struggling creature. The tree reacted by attacking Ian, lifting him into the air, and pulling him toward it.

Vic and Revita charged in without slowing. A tree bough bent and vine-like branches lashed out. Vic dove in one direction, Revita in the other. Both rolled as branches slapped the barren ground, just missing them. They came to their feet and charged forward. Other boughs shook and branches slapped down behind them.

As Vic drew near the gnarled, twisted tree trunk, he wound back and swung his mattock with all of his might. The claw end drove into the ten-foot diameter trunk with a crack, splitting bark and sending wood chips scattering. Blue sparks sizzled along the bark around the wound. The tree shuddered, its branches waving wildly. Vic yanked the mattock free, wound back, and took another swing.

～

REVITA STOOD BESIDE VIC, facing away from the tree trunk. She held a dagger in her left hand while the spikes of the bracer on her other arm stood on end. Her breath came in gasps from the run, and her heart hammered from adrenaline.

The tree flailed while Vic fought it. *We are fighting a tree.* The realization came in an odd, detached manner. *People would think we were insane if we told them about this. Maybe we are insane.*

The boughs above Revita cracked and bent downward. Long, leafy strands swept above the ground and stretched inward, straight toward Vic. As the tree wrapped its tentacles around Vic's legs, Revita slashed with her dagger and followed with the sweep of her bracer. Both sliced through the thin, wiry strands, severing them and freeing Vic. The damaged shoots yanked back and other branches shot toward them both.

Slashing with fury, Revita's dagger and bracer spikes sliced through dozens of strands before one wrapped around her left wrist and another found her right one. Branches wound around her legs and waist. The tree lifted her off the ground, flipped her upside down, and swept her away from the trunk.

With her view inverted, she shouted, "Vic! Watch out!"

He tore his mattock from the tree and spun around as dozens of vine-like branches thrust toward him. They snapped around his arms, legs, and waist while others found the mattock handle and tore it from his grip.

~

SHRIA-LI STOOD over Lint as the two of them watched in horror. Ian was somewhere inside the massive willow while Vic and Revita tried in vain to stop the monstrous tree from consuming him. Desperate thoughts screamed in her head. *What can I do? Ian is my friend. He needs help.* Then, in the silent moments between such thoughts, a deep, booming voice replied.

Why do you wake me from my slumber?

She lurched in shock. *Who said that?*

A branch snapped behind her, causing her to spin around in alarm. The dead tree at the edge of the tree line wobbled. *It is I, the once mighty oak. Please, allow me to sleep. It is not yet my time to return.*

The Sylvan people possessed varied abilities. Some could heal wounds. Some spoke with beasts. Some foretold the future. And then, there were the cultivators, who could influence plants and trees, urging them to grow and flourish. Among all the elves with these/such skills, she had never heard of any having ever had a conversation with a tree, and surely not a tree that lay dead. Amid her doubts and confusion, she found possibility.

I saw you move. Can you help my friends? The willow will kill them.

The tree's deep voice rumbled in her head. *If I do this thing, I can return to my slumber?*

Yes. I promise.

The oak branches, thick, twisted, and bare of leaves, bent and pushed the trunk up off the ground. Twigs snapped, branches creaked, and the tree itself groaned like a weary elder rising after a long nap.

Lint gaped as the once mighty oak stood, the tree's upper reaches a hundred feet above them. "Now, this is something I have never before seen."

Shria-Li pointed toward the willow. "Save my friends."

The tree turned, its branches spinning overhead. It then lumbered across the meadow with its roots snaking across the ground.

The brownie looked up at Shria-Li. "You command trees?"

"Dead ones, apparently." In truth, she was as surprised as him.

"Alright, then. I guess it's a fight." The brownie whooped and ran off.

Without a weapon, Shria-Li had no idea how she would fight a tree. Even with a weapon, the concept seemed ludicrous. Yet, she ran off after the dead oak come to life.

When the oak reached the barren meadow interior, the willow lashed out. It's leaf-covered shoots wrapped around the oak's meaty branches, but the oak continued forward. The willow boughs bent with the oak and then willow branches began to snap.

The brownie burst into the area and darted past the oak as it headed straight for the willow trunk.

Shria-Li slowed and followed in the oak's wake, uncertain of how to help but determined to do so.

$\sim$

EXTERIOR WILLOW BRANCHES handed Ian over to interior ones, each time yanking his arms around by the wrists and making it impossible for him to concentrate enough to form a construct. The massive knothole in the trunk spread wider, the opening easily big enough to engulf Ian as he continued straight toward it. Again, and again, he was passed from branch to branch and carried closer to the dark opening while he thrashed and tried to free a hand.

Vic appeared below him and attacked the tree, causing the branches holding Ian to tremble and loosen their grip. Repeatedly, he hammered at the tree while Ian tried to break away. Just as Vic's efforts began to seem promising, the tree got ahold of both him and Revita, then Ian's journey toward its trunk resumed. The last, innermost layer of branches wrapped about him and shoved him into the willow's mouth. Just in time, Ian tore his wrist free and cast a spell as he was tossed into the gaping maw.

~

REVITA FOUND herself strung up with her arms and legs spread out and her face toward the ground, ten feet below. Beside her, Vic writhed against his bonds, but to no avail. What had been a wild and chaotic scene became outright bizarre when a dead tree came across the meadow, straight toward her. She didn't know if that was a good or bad thing, but she had no intention of being caught in between two behemoth trees.

She twisted the wrist still gripping her dagger. The blade severed the bonds tied to that arm, freeing her so she could then slash at those holding the other wrist. Her upper body dropped and she swung by her ankles.

"Arrgh!" Vic cried out in frustration. He craned his neck toward her. "Can you do something?"

"On it." Revita bent at the waist, reached past her own feet, and slashed.

Her dagger cut through the bonds holding her left leg, causing her to drop sideways. She swung and bent again, this time lunging for the other side. Her dagger sliced through the final branches, releasing her. She fell, twisting with the momentum and landed on her side, the impact driving the wind from her lungs. Turning onto her back to stretch her battered muscles, she spied another cluster of branches thrusting straight toward her. Again and again, Revita rolled, dodging the strikes. She reached Vic's fallen weapon, grabbed it, and shot to her feet.

"Vic!" She called out as he was lifted toward an opening in the branches.

He strained against his bonds, the branch growing taut before it snapped, freeing his right hand, which he held toward her. "Throw it."

Revita would have one shot, but the situation was desperate, so she took aim and tossed the mattock.

~

STRAINING AGAINST HIS BONDS, Vic tried desperately to break loose. His right hand came free as the willow lifted him toward the opening in the branches. Revita launched his mattock into the air. Spinning while it ascended, the weapon lost momentum at the top of its arc, an arm's length below Vic. He reached out with his freed arm just before it fell.

Vic caught the mattock handle and was yanked up into the willow's interior. A thick branch came within reach, giving him a target. He swung the mattock. The claw end of the weapon sliced deep into the branch. The tree shook violently. His bonds were suddenly loosed and Vic plummeted through branches that slapped at him. He landed at an angle, a few strides away from the tree's trunk, with his feet striking first, his back and then head immediately after. Spots invaded his vision and the world went dark.

~

SHRIA-LI STOOD at the edge of a strange but frightening battle. The dead oak tore through the attacking vinelike branches, while the willow boughs shook and thrashed. Oak twigs and leaf-covered willow shoots littered the ground. Vic fell from the tree and lay still while Revita rushed to stand over him, using her blades to fend off attacks. She reached down with one hand and grabbed his wrist, dragging him while slashing at whip-like branches with her dagger.

Lint was nowhere to be found.

Then, the willow tree shook mightily. Again and again, it trembled

315

as if it were at the center of a tremendous earthquake. A horrific, high-pitched groan came from the willow, the ominous sound causing Shria-Li to back away.

~

IAN FORMED a shield around himself as he fell into the dark maw in the willow's trunk. The opening closed behind him as Ian fell. He landed on something soft and lay there, wrapped in his shield and surrounded by darkness. It was strangely silent. Then, something began pressing against the sides of his shield. The pressure came from dozens of points, as if he were caught between the gears of a mill. As the pressure grew, Ian was forced to feed magic to his shield. He feared if it continued, the outcome would be very ugly. So, he crafted another construct, this time of air, and he fed it with every ounce of magic he could muster.

The pressure of the teeth was replaced by that of the surrounding air. The tree's interior seemed to expand from the force of Ian's spell. The tree shook and a terrible creaking arose from its bowels – a scream unlike any Ian had ever heard. Still, he kept feeding his spell. Cracking, snapping, and creaking noises came from all directions. A bone-rattling tremor shook the tree and Ian alike. Then, the tree trunk exploded.

~

REVITA DRAGGED Vic across the ground, trying to get away from the tree. Fifty feet away from her position, the dead oak battled the larger willow in a strange conflict of nature. *Strange? A carnivorous tree fighting a dead one is beyond strange.* Still, things had gone wrong and escaping was preferential to dying in what seemed to be a losing battle. So, she urgently towed Vic away from the tree.

The willow ceased attacking Revita and Vic. She made use of the respite by biting on her dagger blade and grabbing ahold of him with both hands to quicken her pace. His unconscious body left a track across the dirt until she reached the grassy area beyond the willow's reach.

There, she stopped, dropped his wrist to the ground, and wiped her brow. She pulled the dagger from her teeth and glanced toward Shria-Li, who stared toward the willow with wide eyes. "Was that thing your doing?"

"What do you mean?" The elf woman turned toward her.

"The dead tree." Revita pointed toward the oak.

"Yeah. I guess." The way Shria-Li replied made it sound as if she was as surprised as anyone.

Revita shook her head, still panting from her exertion. "I didn't know such a thing was possible."

"Me neither."

Vic opened his eyes and squinted up at Revita. "Vita?'

She knelt beside him. "Are you alright?'

He raised his head and sat up. "I think..."

The willow exploded.

Branches, bark, and leaves pelted Revita and the others, forcing them to spin away and curl up. As the initial wave of debris settled, she turned to find leaves and chunks of the tree twirling in the air high above. The oak remained standing with half of its massive branches broken off and scattered across the ground behind it.

A distant cry of terror carried on the breeze. Curious, Revita shielded her eyes and peered toward the heavens, seemingly the source of the sound. Amid the fluttering leaves and debris raining down was a tiny, flailing body. *Lint.* The brownie plummeted from a terrifying height, his screams growing steadily louder as he drew near the ground. Revita reacted.

Natural quickness, combined with skills honed from years of training with knives, took over. She darted forward, dove, and snatched Lint by the legs before landing on her free arm and rolling onto her back. She held the brownie above her and paused for a breath.

Lint's eyes bulged in fear and shock, his tiny breaths coming in gasps. His eyes closed and then opened to stare down at Revita. "You saved me."

Revita sat up and set him down beside her. "Yeah. I thought it preferable to cleaning up the mess you'd make if you splatted across the ground."

"I can't believe a human would do that for a brownie."

She pulled her feet beneath her, stood, and dusted the dirt off her clothing. "It was not a big deal."

"It means everything to me." The brownie dropped to his knees. "I owe you my life."

"Listen, pipsqueak. You don't owe me a thing."

"My existence would have ended if not for you." Lint lowered his head to the ground. "From this moment forward, I am your faithful servant until you pass from this world."

Revita looked toward Shria-Li. "Is he serious?"

The elf woman nodded. "I am afraid so."

Vic climbed to his feet and slowly spun, his gaze sweeping the meadow. "Ian?"

Like Vic, Revita glanced around. Other than the oak, the only thing standing was the willow stump, still intact from the ground to a point ten feet up. Beyond that, nothing remained. Amid the broken branches, chunks of tree trunk, and leaves, there was no sign of Ian.

Agony twisted Vic's face as a tear tracked down his cheek. He wobbled and then fell to his knees. Holding his face in his hands, he wept.

Vic's pain and loss tugged at a part of Revita that she thought lost forever. His sorrow became hers, and she felt compelled to comfort him. Silently, she knelt beside Vic, wrapped one arm around his head, the other around his shoulder, and she pulled him to her breast.

CHAPTER 36
COMPASSION

In the low hollow of the tree trunk, Ian lay still while his body slowly recovered from the strain of his spell. The mid-day sun shone down on him, its warmth soothing after the terrifying ordeal. Daylight gave shape to the willow's innards. While Ian lay on a strangely smooth and soft wooden surface, hundreds of wooden spikes, many of them broken off, lined the sides of the hollow. Those spikes had tried to grind him to bits and would have succeeded if not for his magic. The mystery of how a tree devoured an animal or person had been solved, but given the circumstances, Ian would have been fine not knowing.

He sat up then stood but he still could not see beyond the surrounding wall of cracked and splintered wood. Using the spikes for footing, he climbed up and out of the hollow. Taking care to avoid splinters, he swung a leg over the upper edge and then the other. Dangling by his hands, he glanced over his shoulder. The ground waited four feet below, a fall unlikely to injure himself so long as he did it correctly. He let go, his feet hit the ground, and he bent his legs with the impact while rolling backward.

Completing a somersault, Ian rose and looked around but saw nobody. *Did they leave me? Do they think I'm dead? Did the explosion kill them?* Those troubled thoughts and others ran through his mind. Then, Ian saw a small red and black creature lying near the edge of the grass surrounding the dirt field. He ran over to it, slowing as he drew near.

The beast had a long neck, snake-like tail, and wings larger than its foot-long body. Black scales coated its underside while its head, wings, and back were a dark red. A crest of small spikes ran from the top of its head, down its back, and along its curved tail.

"A tiny dragon," Ian muttered.

The miniature dragon moved as it made a rasping gasp for air before it shuddered and fell still.

Concern for the injured creature tugged at Ian's heart. He fell to his knees beside it and placed a hand on its body. Beyond the scaly hide, warmed by the midday sun, Ian felt a weak heartbeat. He opened himself to his gift, closed his eyes, and attempted to will the energy flowing through him to help the creature. Nothing happened. He closed his eyes and slid into meditation, allowing the peace and harmony of his silent surroundings to calm and sooth him.

～

Vic still mourned for his father and for the friends he had lost over the prior year. He missed his mother and prayed she was still safe. She had made Vic promise he would watch over Ian and ensure nothing bad happened to him. While he knew it was impossible to guarantee his brother's well-being, Vic had vowed he would do everything he could to keep that promise so long as they traveled together. And now, he had failed. Ian was gone, and the realization was a crushing weight upon Vic's soul.

With his face in his hands, he sobbed while praying it was not real, that Ian was not dead. A small part of him appreciated Revita's attempt to console him, but he didn't want to be consoled. He deserved to suffer for his failure. *I should have found a way to save him.*

The brownie's small, nasal voice cut through his sorrow. "Look! It's Ian!"

Vic lifted his face and wiped the tears blurring his eyes.

Far across the meadow, beyond the huge stump of the destroyed willow, a person knelt on the ground with his back to them. Although he did not move and his face was not visible, there was no doubt in Vic's mind as to who it was.

Hope flared within Vic's chest. He pulled away from Revita and stood. "Ian!" His shout echoed across the open space.

Ian remained still with no reaction at all.

Worries resurfaced, clouding Vic's hope. He broke into a run, taking care to hop over broken branches while dodging tree trunk remains. The sprint across the meadow seemed to happen in slow motion, the time passing slowly although he only had to cross a few hundred feet. Vic drew near Ian, his gaze affixed on his brother.

Ian's eyes were closed, and he appeared frozen but unharmed. On the ground beside him was a miniature red and black dragon, eyes closed and motionless with Ian's hand resting on it.

"Ian?" Vic spoke in a quiet voice.

There was no response.

He considered shaking Ian but was concerned that he might disturb something important. Thus, Vic stood over his brother and wiped the tears away with the back of his sleeve.

~

Shria-Li followed Revita and Lint across the open space. The brownie seemed focused on Revita, circling her feet and repeatedly glancing up at her, but she appeared to ignore him. As those two headed toward Vic and Ian, Shria-Li approached the dead oak.

The tree spoke in her mind. *Are your friends now safe?*

They are. Shria-Li noted the jagged remains from where major branches had broken off the oak. *I thank you for your help and am sorry that you were injured.*

It is of no concern. There is no pain in death, only numbness.

That eases my conscience.

I may return to my slumber as I await my rebirth?

Yes, you may, I am grateful for your efforts and I wish you a pleasant slumber.

The oak swayed toward the willow stump and then tilted back. Creaking and crackling, it toppled to the ground. Branches snapped at impact and the tree bounced and rocked before settling.

Sleep well, mighty oak. Shria-Li headed off to join her companions.

～

THE ZEPHYRS of his own internal harmony enveloped Ian as he drifted in the serenity of meditation. In the back of his mind, he remained aware of his contact with the tiny dragon. Through that contact, he tried to extend his will toward the injured creature but found resistance. That resistance seemed to have a shape to it. He pressed his will against various areas, seeking a soft point. Drawing upon more magic, he used that energy to bolster his will and to apply more pressure. The barrier flexed, bent, and snapped. Ian's consciousness flowed through the opening and into the tiny creature.

Agony and weariness washed over Ian. His breath felt ragged, his throat constricted and painful. His leg hurt badly, his body bruised. Darkness pressed in from all directions and threatened to consume him.

Ian channeled energy through the connection, feeding the foreign, battered body he now occupied. The dragon responded by drawing in a deep breath. The pain eased. Another consciousness seemed to waken. That consciousness touched Ian's awareness and something strange happened. Foreign thoughts came at Ian like a storm, wild and uncontainable. Hunger, fear, fury, and a fight for survival...all came in a flurry of waves washing over him. Fearing he would lose himself, he pulled his awareness back to his own body.

Ian opened his eyes as the dragon did the same. He pulled back as the dragon rolled to its belly. The creature stood, its wings extended for balance. It drew in a deep, rasping breath and shook as if it were a dog attempting to dry itself. The tiny dragon then turned toward Ian and squawked.

A strange sensation came from the back of Ian's mind, a warmth he could only call love.

The dragon hopped onto his lap and rubbed against him while snorting.

Ian then realized his companions were standing over him, staring in confusion and wonder.

"What is it doing?" Vic asked.

Ian tentatively stroked the dragon from the top of its head down to the back of its neck. A quiver of pleasure came from the back of his mind. "The dragon is thanking me for saving it."

Lint laughed. "That is no dragon. It is a fire drake. Dragons are far, far larger and they never come to the Vale."

Revita asked, "Why not?"

"Simple. Dragons breathe fire, and fire is not allowed here. The forest's magic affects dragon magic, causing their breath to remain nothing but air. As you might guess, dragons do not like not being able to use their fire, so they avoid the Vale." The brownie pointed at the creature in Ian's lap. "Drakes are not as smart. Some end up here not realizing that their fire breath will not work. Like this one almost did, most end up dead." Lint scratched the mop of hair on his head. "To tell you the truth, I haven't seen a fire drake in many years, and I thought they might have all died off."

Ian continued to pet the fire drake during the discussion. All the while, a low purr came from the beast while the sensations of pleasure and contentment echoed in the back of Ian's head. *We are connected, you and I,* Ian thought. The creature did not reply.

Vic put a hand on Ian's shoulder. "I thought you were dead."

Looking up at him, Ian nodded. "I feared the same, and it was a close thing."

Revita said, "I can't believe you risked yourself for that overgrown lizard."

"He is no lizard." Ian gazed down at the creature while still petting it. "You heard Lint, he is a fire drake and may be among the last of his kind. How could I allow him to come to such a dire end?"

"Well, now that this is over, perhaps we should gather our things and move along."

Lint chimed in. "You heard my mistress. Let the drake go, and we will be on our way."

Ian arched a brow up at Revita. "Mistress?"

She sighed. "Lint, I told you..."

"You may tell me to do anything you wish, mistress."

"Don't call me that."

"What should I call you?"

"My name is Revita."

The brownie shook his head. "No. That wouldn't be right."

She smirked. "Fine. Call me goddess."

With a serious expression, Lint nodded. "As you wish, my goddess."

"Revita..." Vic chided.

She nudged him. "Are you jealous that I have an admirer?"

"Him? He is smaller than my...Ouch!" Vic yanked his foot back after the brownie stomped on it.

Lint shook a finger at Vic. "You had better show my goddess respect, or I will end you."

Revita laughed aloud. "I have wondered what it might be like to have boys fighting over me, but this is nothing like what I expected."

Vic grimaced down at Lint. "That is because one of them is a delusional little imp who might find himself squashed flat if he keeps it up."

When Lint scowled and waved a fist, Shria-Li stepped between him and Vic. "That's enough." She pointed across the meadow. "Vic, please go get our packs. Once you return, we will resume our journey. Standing here arguing is wasting time we may not have."

Vic shot Lint one last glare before walking off.

Shria-Li turned to Revita. "If Lint is going to obey you, perhaps you should stop him from antagonizing Vic."

The thief sighed. "I suppose you have a point. It was fun for a moment, though."

Ian lifted the drake as he stood. The creature climbed up his robes, turned, and settled on his shoulder.

"I have never seen a drake do that before," Lint said.

"He likes me," Ian said.

"How do you know it is male?"

"I just do." Ian reached up and ran the back of his hand along the drake's stomach. A buzz of pleasure came through the connection, joining the creature's rasping breaths.

Shria-Li asked, "Why does it make that wheezing noise?"

"His throat was damaged in the fight with the willow. He has a tough time breathing." Ian had no idea if the injury was temporary or permanent. Regardless, the creature did not seem able to properly protect itself until it was healed. "I am taking him with us."

Revita frowned at the creature. "Are you certain it is safe?"

"He will listen to me. It will be fine."

Vic approached with packs on both shoulders and another in his arm. "Are you alright?" He gulped. "I thought you were..."

Ian gripped his brother by the wrist. "I am fine," he reassured Vic. "Don't worry about it."

His eyes shifted to the creature on Ian's shoulder. "What is that thing?"

"This is a fire drake. He is coming with us," Ian said. "In fact, I am going to name him... Lionel."

"Lionel?" Vic frowned. "Like your friend who drowned in the river five years ago?"

Ian sometimes still missed his boyhood friend but not as much as he missed Rina. Still, naming the drake after Lionel seemed the right thing to do.

"Yes." Ian reached out, took his pack from his brother, and tossed it over his left shoulder. "Come along, Lionel. We are going on an adventure together." He began across the clearing.

Lint darted past Ian while the others trailed behind him. The party, now consisting of six, left the glade and resumed their northwest trek.

CHAPTER 37

THE ESCARPMENT

S hadows amid the forest thickened as the day waned. The lack of sleep the prior evening, compounded with a long day of travel, numerous harrowing events, and the heavy use of his magic left Ian weary and longing for rest. Complaints about the situation never crossed his tongue. This quest was his burden, and he refused to stop unless the others demanded it as well.

The fire drake spent much of the afternoon riding on Ian's shoulder. Twice, it took flight but never strayed far from him. All the while, Ian sensed Lionel in the back of his head. The feeling was powerful enough that he could point in the creature's direction without looking. Ian found the sensation both strange and comforting.

Throughout the day, Lint led the party as they wound their way across the Vale. Despite his tiny legs, the only signs of the brownie tiring came in the form of reduced exuberance when compared to the blatant enthusiasm he exhibited during the first hours of the journey. Now, with the scattered clouds overhead tinted with the pinks and oranges of sunset, Ian and his companions followed the brownie through a grove of trees covered in long, dark green leaves with silver underbellies. At the edge of the grove, the view expanded for the first time in over an hour.

They strode into an area blanketed by ferns that reached Ian's waist. The open space stretched west until coming to a steep cliffside rising hundreds of feet before leveling. Rocks, trees, and shrubs, all darkened by shadow, covered the daunting, steep slope.

Lint stood on a log and announced, "As promised, I have led you to the escarpment." The brownie pointed toward the cliff wall. "The way up lies ahead. It will be difficult, but it is scalable, even for you humans."

Shria-Li stared north. "The home of my people lies at the top of those falls."

Ian followed her gaze and squinted as he tried to see through the failing daylight. Through the gloom, he spied two shimmering ribbons running from the top of the escarpment to the valley floor. The falls were easily five miles distant, if not farther away. The sky to the north, beyond those falls, was darkened by rainclouds.

"Are you ready to begin our climb?" Lint asked.

Ian blanched. He already struggled against the fog of exhaustion hanging over him. The idea of climbing a steep and dangerous slope in the darkness while attempting to remain awake and alert was down-right terrifying. His reluctance to speak up about his condition caused him to hesitate. Before he could object, his brother saved him.

"No," Vic said. "Our quest, regardless of urgency, will have to wait another night. We need to rest before we tackle something so extreme."

"Besides, Shria-Li said. "It looks like rain is heading this way. I can't imagine being caught halfway up during a downpour."

"Goddess?" Lint asked. "What would you have of me?"

"I agree with the others," Revita said. "We should rest and begin our climb at sunrise."

"Very well." Lint gestured. "As I recall, a spring lies just north of here. We can visit it for fresh water and then find a place for you soft humans to shelter from the rain."

The brownie hopped off the log and headed north, below the cliff-side with Ian and the others trailing him. Even when Lint was lost in the shadows and foliage, the shake and tremble of the ferns disturbed by his passing informed Ian as to his whereabouts. A few hundred feet later, they came to a rivulet, turned, and followed it toward its source. The ground began to rise with rocks and flowers amid the ferns. The ferns opened to a pool twenty feet across and half as wide. Just above the pool, water trickled from a dark opening in a wall of rock.

Ian squatted just below the spring, uncorked his empty waterskin, and dipped it below the surface. The water was cold and promised to be refreshing. When the waterskin was full, he raised it to his lips and took a long drink. Lionel, resting on his shoulder, leaned in and bumped his hard nose against Ian's cheek.

Lowering his skin, Ian glanced toward the fire drake. In the back of his head, he sensed the creature's urgency and desire for something. "Are you thirsty?"

A spike of excitement came through their bond.

Ian lifted the waterskin to the dragon's snout and tipped it up. The dragon drank eagerly, lapping and gulping while water spilled down its snout and body, and onto Ian's robes. When the dragon's emotion shifted to satisfaction, Ian lowered the skin, dipped it in the water, and filled it again. He stood to find the others capping their skins. Thunder rumbled, drawing his attention north. The clouds were far closer and rain was only minutes away.

"If you are finished, there is a recess beneath the rock not far from here," Lint said. "It might make a good place to get out of the rain."

"Show us," Revita replied.

The brownie turned from the pool and headed south with the rest of their group trailing. Two minutes later, they came to a dark cavity beneath a rocky overhang. The alcove ran only a dozen feet deep, but the ground was bare and would protect them from the rain.

The group sat beneath the shadow of the overhang, opened their packs, and began to eat. The rations Ian had packed before leaving the ship were nearly gone. As he chewed on a strip of dried jerky, he broke off a piece and gave it to Lionel. The drake gnawed enthusiastically on the meat while a wave of pleasure came through their bond. Ian shared the rest of the dried meat, and when even that was gone, he moved on to his last pieces of hard, crusty bread, again sharing it with his pet.

Then, it began to rain.

Rain patter filled the air, and water tumbled down the cliffside to drip and feed rivulets just outside of the alcove. Yet, Ian and his companions remained dry.

There was little conversation and no mention of a campfire, although Ian longed for one and suspected Vic and Revita felt the same. After Lint's previous reaction to fire, Ian didn't even wish to broach the subject. With the food gone and night darkening their surroundings, Ian lay down on his side, his head resting on his bunched-up cloak. Lionel curled up with his body pressed against Ian's chest. Ian pulled out his cloak, draped it over the two of them, and slid into the deep sleep of exhaustion.

~

A RUSTLE CAUSED Ian to stir. Again, he heard the sound, drawing him from his sleep. He opened his eyes to the pale light of dawn. A rustle came from his pack, which was a stride away and moving. A black and red body backed from the pack. When Lionel pulled his head out of the pack, a strip of dried meat dangled from his mouth.

"Hey!" Ian snatched for the meat, but the drake jumped backward, beyond his reach. "Give me that."

Rather than obey, Lionel eagerly chomped on the meat, jerked his head back, and the rest disappeared into his mouth. With a sigh, Ian grabbed his pack and began to dig through it.

Revita, who lay with Vic, lifted her head. "What's all the noise?"

Ian discovered that the last of his food was gone. He grimaced at Lionel. "Someone decided he was hungry and was quite selfish about it."

Satisfaction came through the bond as Lionel swallowed the last of the jerky. A nasty, ripe odor then struck Ian, causing him to cover his nose with his cloak.

"Yuck!" Revita blurted. "What is that stench?"

Ian shook his head, his voice muffled by the cloak held against his face. "It wasn't me." He pointed toward Lionel. "It was him."

Vic pinched his face. "How can something so small create a smell so nasty?"

Revita sat up with her hand over her mouth and nose. "I think I am going to puke."

Ian waggled a finger at Lionel. "No more jerky for you, not if it does that to your system."

The drake blinked at him and dropped its head in shame.

A wave of motion passed through the brush just outside the alcove where they had slept. Lint emerged from the shrubs and stopped a few feet away. "It is about time you soft humans woke."

Ian glanced over at the elf princess as she sat up and rubbed her eyes. "Shria-Li was sleeping as well, yet I don't hear you calling her out for it."

"The princess has earned my respect, as has the goddess." Lint beamed at Revita. "Good morning, Goddess."

She glared at him. "It is too early to be so chipper, Pipsqueak."

"Early is good in this case. You've a long climb ahead and one I believe you would prefer to finish as soon as possible. It will be a hot and sticky day after last night's rain."

Vic stood and dusted himself off. "The brownie makes a good point.

We should get moving. The escarpment faces east, and we will be exposed to the morning sun for most of the ascent."

With a sigh, Ian forced himself to rise. There was only one way to reach Havenfall at this point, and that meant going up.

∾

A BEAM of early morning sunlight forced Ian to squint. He passed through the sunbeam and returned to shadows cast by trees a few hundred feet to the east.

Lint stopped and stared up at the cliffside with a grin. "Here it is."

Ian and the others followed the brownie's gaze. The ominous escarpment loomed over them like a threat of death to any who should attempt to defy it.

Vic frowned while surveying the daunting incline. "This doesn't appear any easier to scale than the rest."

"Do you not see the trees on this part of the cliffside?"

Trees with long, sinuous branches clung to the slope.

"What of them?"

"Those are snaking jacks. Their vines extend many times the height of the tree, and they are quite strong."

"You want us to use vines to climb the escarpment?"

"Do you have a better idea?"

When Vic shot him a questioning look, Ian shrugged. "We need to get up there, at least according to Shria-Li."

The elf woman nodded. "A brief visit to Havenfall will prove valuable to the quest. We could find ourselves in Ra'Tahal as soon as tomorrow."

With narrowed eyes, Ian asked, "How is this possible?"

Shria-Li shook her head. "I cannot say, not until I have my father's consent."

Revita smirked. "It appears that the elves hold secrets of their own."

"We all have secrets, Revita," Ian noted.

"True, but mine are not so elaborate."

"If we are going to do this, the sooner we begin, the sooner we finish." Vic set his jaw and began climbing the slope, still damp from the prior evening's rain.

Rather than follow his brother, Ian allowed Revita to go next while he turned toward the forest to the east. *Lionel*, he sent the thought out like a call. He sensed the fire drake's direction but found it difficult to determine the distance. A quiver of satisfaction came through their bond. Moments later, Ian sensed the drake drawing closer.

A winged silhouette burst from the trees and flew across the field of ferns. The drake spread his wings and dove toward Ian. The distance closed rapidly, and Ian feared he might be subject to a violent collision until the drake turned toward the sky, flapped mightily, and then settled on his shoulder. Lionel's face appeared wet. Ian slid a finger along the drake's snout and smelled it. A sweet yet sour scent tickled Ian's senses.

"You found a pestle berry tree," Ian noted. The drake puffed up his chest and a sense of pride came through their bond. "Did you bring any for me?"

The drake's eyes widened before it dropped its head in shame.

Ian laughed and pet Lionel's head. "Do not worry about it. Just think of me next time."

Turning, Ian found the others ascending the hillside with Vic in the lead and Revita following. Lint's head poked up from the pack on Revita's back. Just below Revita, Shria-Li drew near the end of the first vine, found another foothold, and continued upward.

With a sigh, Ian gathered his resolve and scrambled up the hillside with Lionel squawked, fluttered his wings, and took to the sky. When Ian reached the first snaking vine, he grabbed ahold and tested it. The vine was thicker than his thumb and thirty feet long. It held when he gave it a hard tug. Shria-Li was already beyond that vine scaling up the hillside with the help of another, some fifty feet above him.

Pulling himself up, hand over hand, Ian climbed the steep upslope until he came to the end of the first vine. He reached over, grabbed another vine, and continued his ascent.

~

WEARY ARM MUSCLES tensed and knotted as Ian pulled himself along a particularly steep section of the escarpment. The toes of his boots found tiny lips of rock, which he used to push himself up. The vine dangled from a tree hanging over him, the base of the tree blocked from view by a shelf of rock. His brother's face appeared above him as he peered over the ledge.

Vic extended his arm. "Grab my wrist. I will pull you up."

The idea of getting help was more than enticing. A year ago, there was no way Ian could have made such an onerous climb. His training had boosted his strength and endurance significantly. Even then, he flagged behind the others, particularly his brother. His exhaustion made it easy for him to set his pride aside and accept help.

Ian lunged and latched onto Vic's wrist. In turn, Vic gripped his arm and began to lift. Aided by the slim purchase of Ian's scrambling feet, Vic pulled him up and over the edge. Ian rolled to his back and lay there, gasping for air while his heavy arms throbbed from the effort. He rested while staring up into the blue sky until a shadow passed over him. Lionel drifted in and landed beside Ian's head. The drake then bent and licked Ian's face, forcing him to push the creature away, but Lionel persisted, coming after him with a sense of excitement coming through their bond. Finally, Ian gave in, sat up, and pulled the drake onto his lap. He stroked the head and neck of his overly loving companion while staring out at his elevated view.

The lush green of the Vale stretched out before him with seemingly endless treetops blanketing the valley. Miles to the north, a river snaked eastward. In the other direction, the escarpment gently curved to bound the south end of the valley, many miles away.

The weary group of Ian and his companions rested on a rock ledge six feet deep and twenty feet in length. Vic stood, staring out into the distance while Revita and Shria-Li sat on rocks, both with their waterskins in hand. Lint was nowhere to be seen.

Ian pulled his own waterskin out and gulped down half its contents. He capped it, turned, and stood beneath the light of the mid-morning sun. The escarpment loomed above him without a clear end in sight. He sighed. "I hoped we were near the top."

Lint appeared on a boulder ten feet above. "You are halfway up, you lazy human. There is much yet to do and the day advances."

Ian frowned at Revita. "Can you do something about his sharp tongue?"

She shrugged. "I find it entertaining and prefer he remains as is."

Lint beamed. "Thank you, goddess."

"Besides, I like having an admirer who thinks of me as a goddess."

Vic turned toward her with a frown. "I admire you."

She patted his cheek. "Which is why I keep you around."

Despite her light tone, Vic did not appear happy. He turned and began climbing the hillside. Rather than go last this time, Ian set off after Vic, leaving Lionel behind. Concern came through the bond, but Ian responded with an image of the drake taking flight and waiting for him somewhere above. Focused on each handhold and toe placement, he scaled a rocky section in his brother's wake. Thirty feet up, he reached the next vine, gripped it, and continued his ascent. All the while, the knowledge that slipping would result in a deadly fall lurked at the edge of his awareness.

CHAPTER 38
A BITTERSWEET RETURN

With her stomach tied in a knot, Shria-Li led her companions through a forest of massive oak and maple trees. A bed of fallen leaves from prior seasons covered the ground while an umbrella of green leaves and dark branches blotted out the mid-day sky. Nobody spoke. She suspected this was because they were weary from the taxing ascent of the escarpment. Her own silence was due to something completely unrelated.

Birds hidden among the branches above serenaded the quest party, their happy tune all but drowning out the crunch of dead leaves beneath each footstep. In the past, Shria-Li had often found peace and solace in birdsong, but today she barely heard it due to the conflicting emotions warring inside her.

The Sylvan viewed prophecies as messages from their god, Vandasal. Such warnings were to be heeded and respected. Now, she found herself trapped between two such prophecies. One warned of the death speaker's arrival – an event that would precede the end of Haven-fall and the Sylvan people. The other, delivered by Ian, demanded they seek out something called the Paragon with the hope of staving off some sort of apocalyptic fate for not only the Sylvan, but other races as well. The first prophecy had caused Shria-Li to flee her people in the hope of protecting them. The latter required her return, albeit brief, so she and her companions might find a way to spare them. Caught between these nebulous threats, she sent a prayer to Vandasal and forged on.

However, her worries extended beyond prophecy.

Her return would require her to face her parents. Questions would be asked. Demands would be placed upon her. Rather than bend to their will, she would need to stand up to them for the first time. She needed to convince them of the urgency and critical nature of their quest. Should they deny her, she would be forced into a situation she wished to avoid.

The rush of water rose above the din as daylight peered through gaps in the trees ahead. The knot in Shria-Li's stomach tightened, for she knew what that meant.

They emerged from the forest and came to a dirt path that ran from east to west. Beyond the path, the ground sloped down to a river hundreds of feet wide, the water flowing eastbound with vigor. A quarter mile downstream, the river split around an island connected to each bank by a pair of alabaster bridges that were impossible to miss in the midday sunlight. In the past, those bridges stood two stories above the river. Now, the waterline ran a mere foot below the base of the bridges, something that caused her immediate concern. *Why is the water level so high?*

Scattered, towering trees thrust up from the island. Sunlight glinted off their golden leaves, making it appear as if they were made of precious metal. Amid the trees stood the city of Havenfall, her pale arches, glass domes, and narrow spires calling to Shria-Li. After many years of longing for freedom to explore the world, she now felt an unexpected warmth in her chest. *I am coming home.*

A whoop came from Lint as he burst into a run. The brownie raced along the dirt path and faded from view. Moments later, he reappeared on the rail of the nearest bridge, where he stood and stared toward the fabled city.

Motion at her side drew Shria-Li's attention to Ian, who walked stride for stride with her.

Ian appeared transfixed as they rounded a bend and approached the bridge. "I never imagined it would be so beautiful." The drake on his shoulder made a gurling coo as if he agreed.

A visit to Ra'Tahal the previous summer was Shria-Li's only experience outside of Havenfall other than her recent stay in Fae Gulch. Both places displayed beauty in their own way – the dwarven citadel was constructed with precise craftmanship to create a practical and daunting fortress while the fairy village was akin to a dreamlike song from a distant land and a time long forgotten. Havenfall's nature landed somewhere in between, but neither could compare to the hope and grace the Sylvan capital inspired.

As they crested the bridge, Lint hopped off the rail and grabbed ahold of Revita's pack, which he climbed up until he sat on her shoulder.

The brownie grinned broadly. "I have forever wondered what it might be like to visit Havenfall. Little of it can be seen from down in the Vale. I did not realize the city and trees would be so...grand."

Ian noted, "The leaves on the trees... They look like gold."

"Yes," Shria-Li stared at the glittering leaves, hundreds of feet above. "Of course, they only appear that way. I would not wish to be standing beneath such a tree if leaves of metal fell from that height."

Revita snorted. "They'd likely slice you bloody on their way down."

"Huh," Ian grunted. "I suppose they would."

The bridge ended and brought them to a broad path made of pale, crushed rock. The path ran on a gentle, uphill slope, toward the center of the island city. Flowers and shrubs covered in berries bordered the path and surrounded the base of the first, golden-leafed tree. Tiered structures made of smooth, pale stone stood amid the foliage. Elevated bridges connected buildings to each other and to higher levels of the island. They climbed stairs, passed beneath arches, and crossed squares graced with spectacular fountains and faceless sculptures dedicated to the Sylvan god, Vandasal.

Elves, male and female, paused to stare, as did their human slaves. Shria-Li wondered if their curiosity was due to the sight of their princess, who had been missing for half a year, or if it were the strangers in her group that drew their attention. She suspected that none had seen a brownie or a fire drake before and doubted any foreign humans had visited Havenfall in over a century. Visitors of any kind were rare, and the varied races, weapons, and general appearances of her companions added to their mystery.

Climbing another tier, they rose above the city and entered the wooded area at the center of the island. The trickle of water flowing down the aqueduct beside them was a low, gentle harmony to the tweeting of birds in the trees above. The trees parted to reveal the sprawling palace Shria-Li called home.

The path meandered through flowing shrubs, sculpted junipers, and pillars of quartz gleaming in the sunlight. It then brought them to a courtyard garden hundreds of feet in diameter and surrounded by arches. Flowers and shrubs of various shades of green filled the garden, the ground sloping down from the palace to a glass-like pool of water at the center. The pool encircled a small island upon which stood the most stunning element of the glorious palace.

A massive, towering tree thrust up from the island, stretching toward the heavens and gleaming with twinkling, golden light. The tree was the largest of its kind, its lowest branches a hundred feet above the ground, the tree's pinnacle ten times that height.

Shria-Li paused to allow her friends a moment to drink in the view before speaking. "This is the Tree of Life. It is sacred to my people. It has been long said, so long as the tree thrives, so will the Sylvan."

Vic gaped up at the spectacle of nature. "How old is the tree?"

"They claim it is as old as the Sylvan people, and our history stretches back for two thousand years."

While the others appeared enthralled by the tree, Ian stared toward the palace with a strange look on his face.

"Are you well, Ian?" Shria-Li asked.

His response was a single name and one unexpected. In a tone thick with emotion, he croaked, "Rina."

Shria-Li followed his gaze but saw nobody. "Did you see her?"

"Yes." Ian shook his head. "I mean no." He stared into the distance. "Not now, anyway. I saw her here during my prophetic vision. Then, she was somewhere else. A castle in the mountains."

A chill wracked Shria-Li's spine. It wasn't that she did not believe Ian's ability to foretell the future, but until that moment, doubt had lingered. *He knew Safrina was here, something nobody could have known.*

Ian's next words came out as little more than a whisper. "Something horrible is going to happen in that castle."

His ominous prediction caused Shria-Li's hair to stand on end. "What is going to happen, Ian?"

His breath came in shallow gasps as he stared into space, reliving some traumatic moment. Vic watched his brother with his brow furrowed in concern while Revita arched a brow at Shria-Li and shrugged.

Her need to know forced Shria-Li to try again. "Ian," she said softly. "What is going to happen?"

"Your father will be there, at the mountain castle, with Rina," he said. "Together."

"Together?"

"Then, he is gone. A monster appears and latches onto Rina and..." A tear tracked down his cheek. "The castle overlooks a chasm. Nobody could survive that fall." He sobbed. "Oh, Rina."

Shria-Li was stunned. Yet, despite everything else, she could not believe it was true. *Father would never lay with a female other than mother...and certainly not with a human.* She pictured Rina's golden hair, large blue eyes, and glowing smile. Those features, along with a lean frame made her as beautiful as any human Shria-Li had ever seen, but Rina was not Sylvan and for that alone, it could never happen. *Ian must be mistaken. Father knows the scripture of Vandasal as well as anyone. He would never betray his god.*

Would he?

A male voice came from behind her, speaking Elvish. "Princess."

Shria-Li spun around to find four palace guards, three males and one female, standing a stride away. The males held spears, the female a bow. All stood at attention with their jaws set and lips tight.

"Good day, Askan," Shria-Li said to the one who had spoken.

Askan, a tall male elf only a few decades older than Shria-Li, his shoulder-length brown hair held back by a simple leather band, gave a slight nod followed by a terse reply. "We have been searching for you."

Shria-Li had expected as much. "If I caused you or the other guards trouble, I apologize."

From the start, she had known that her flight from Havenfall would come with consequences. She suspected that her father had been furious and her mother overcome with worry, but she had fled to save them and her people. Despite her initial conviction, as time went on, Shria-Li worried that her leaving would change nothing. It was her birth that would precede the end of the Sylvan. Nothing in the prophecy said it was due to her presence or her use of the dark ability. Thus, her joining Ian on his quest had not been as difficult a decision as she had let on.

The tightness in Askan's face seemed to ease. "The past is the past, Your Highness. We are now pleased to see you safely returned."

"And I am glad to see that all is well in Havenfall."

Askan's eyes flicked to the guard next to him. "Yes. Um. Well enough, I suppose."

His reluctant reply aroused concern. "What happened?"

He shook his head. "Nothing to worry about." The guard looked at Ian, Vic, and Revita. "Who are these humans? More slaves?"

"These are my friends, and I would have you treat them as such."

"Very well. We will see that they are properly taken care of while you are with your mother." Askan stared hard at Shria-Li. "We are to bring you to her straight away. Our orders are strict in this matter."

Shria-Li had expected as much but she noted a discrepancy. "What of father?"

"He is away, but I strongly suspect he will wish a private audience with you upon his return." Askan turned toward the other guards. "Take them to the guest quarters while I deliver the princess to Queen Tora-Li."

Yara-Ji, the female guard, nodded. "Yes, Squad leader."

Revita asked, "What is happening? I speak little Elvish."

"I am to meet with my mother. Meanwhile, these guards will escort you to a room where you may rest."

"What about food? I am starving."

"Same here," Vic added.

Shria-Li turned to Yara-Ji and shifted back to Elvish. "Please see that they are fed. Climbing the escarpment has left us all weary and starved."

The guards shared a worried glance with Yara-Ji asking, "You came from the Vale?"

"Yes. That is where I spent the last two seasons." Shria-Li headed toward the palace stairs. "Come along, Askan. It is time I face my mother."

~

AT ASKAN'S SIDE, Shria-Li crossed the palace entrance hall while heading toward the throne room. Both had remained quiet since leaving the garden. They approached a doorway bracketed by armed guards, one of whom opened the door, allowing them past.

Two small trees with glowing bark and sparkling, golden leaves illuminated the throne room. The branches of those trees extended toward the other and wove together to create a pair of seats elevated above the ring of benches surrounding the trees. While one throne sat empty, her mother occupied the other. Before them stood a pair of female elves, one of whom held her palms out in supplication while addressing the queen.

"...refuses to lend us a single rain dancer. Meanwhile, River's End drowns."

The other elf shook her head. "You don't understand. We've only two rain dancers beside myself, and it has taken all our energy to keep the spring storms from overwhelming Havenfall. Winter storms left the Silver Mountains thick with snow, but King Fastellan demanded action so he could complete construction at Shadowmar. The warm weather and rains we sent westward to melt the snow came at a cost. Now that snowmelt has raised the river to dangerous levels. The rushing waters surrounding our fair city threaten to override the riverbank, to wash out the roads, and to engulf our fields. My team and I must remain vigilant and guide all precipitation away from the region. Even last night, a storm came in and we were barely able to divert it so it struck south of the city rather than adding to our problem. We cannot spare a rain dancer until the water has subsided and the danger has passed."

Queen Tora-Li leaned forward, her expression intense. "Three rain dancers are all that remain?"

"Yes. We lost Aemon and Pursa-Kai this spring. Both were in their fifth century. I feared that their bodies could not handle the stress placed upon them, and we said as much to King Fastellan, but he would not listen. Then, the Roc attack claimed Varrelan two weeks ago." She shook her head. "We are now down to three and are so exhausted from our efforts, we've not even had time to grieve his loss."

The other elf woman sighed. "What are we to do? River's End is small compared to Havenfall, but we are still your people."

"And the Sylvan will not abandon..." The queen stopped in mid-sentence while staring toward the doorway. She shot to her feet. "Shria-Li!"

Treating her mother's reaction as permission to approach, Shria-Li descended the sloped floor. "Greetings, Mother. I do not mean to interrupt."

"Nonsense." Tora-Li turned toward the other two females. "Listen, Gia-Wey. The people of River's End need not fight this disaster alone. We will send help. Just give me a day to think on a solution."

"Thank you, Your Majesty."

"Now, I ask you both to leave, so I may speak to my daughter. Alone."

As the two females turned from their queen, Shria-Li climbed the dais.

Tora-Li called out. "Askan. Close the doors behind them. Nobody is to enter until I give you leave."

"Yes, my queen." When the room cleared, Asken closed the door behind him, and an uncomfortable silence settled in like a tree shedding every leaf at once and blanketing the chamber.

Shria-Li had been schooled in the proprieties of court since birth, and she knew the right to speak first fell upon the queen. So, she endured before her mother's steely glare and remained still despite her eagerness to flee.

Tora-Li closed her eyes and sighed. "I prayed every night that Vandasal would keep you safe." When she opened her eyes, the steel was gone. "How could you hurt me so?"

Prepared for anger, Shria-Li felt blindsided by guilt brought on by her mother's sorrow. "My leaving had nothing to do with you, Mother."

"My daughter disappears without cause or a goodbye and strolls back in half a year later to tell me it is none of my concern? Where was she while I tossed and turned all night, consumed by worries of what had become of her? I wept until the tears ran dry, but it had nothing to do with me. Your father and I forced the palace guard and Valeguard to search day and night for weeks on end, but it had nothing do to with me. How can you say that?"

It was Shria-Li's turn to sigh. "I am sorry if I caused you pain, Mother. I accepted the risk of hurting you when I departed, but you always said that pain is something royalty must endure for the good of the people."

"And how did the Sylvan benefit from the disappearance of the crown princess?"

Shria-Li turned away in shame. "It was the prophecy. What happened with Pansara frightened me to the core. I sought to prevent the prophecy from coming to fruition. If the dark ability meant doom for the Sylvan, then removing the one cursed with it might give them hope."

Tora-Li stood, approached Shria-Li from behind, and softly gripped her arm. "The prophecy, which may or not be true, indicated that your ability was a sign, not the cause of whatever might come next."

"I realize that...now." A tear ran down Shria-Li's cheek. "Before I fled Havenfall, my thoughts and emotions were a twisted mess. Time has allowed me to sort through everything. It has given me perspective."

"What perspective?"

"It has allowed me to see that any ability can be used for good or bad. While my talent is different, it is not a blight for myself or for my people."

Her mother gripped Shria-Li by the arm, turned her around, and peered into her eyes. "I tried to tell you as much."

"I know, but sometimes, you have to work things out for yourself."

"Very well." Tora-Li hugged her. "I am just glad to have you back home."

Shria-Li returned the embrace, relishing the contact and drinking it in as if using it to fill a well she could feed off in the coming days. Force of will and sheer determination allowed her to say the next sentence. "I must leave soon Mother."

"What?" Her mother stepped back. "Where would you go? Why?"

"Much has occurred since I left the city. Our prophecy is not the only one warning of a dark future. There is another prophecy that mentions the death speaker. This one requires my abilities to locate something called the Paragon. Without it, I fear that Sylvan and the rest of the world are at significant risk."

"Where did you hear such a thing?"

"From a friend who has the gift of prophecy. That friend and others are now here in the palace as my guests. Together, we intend to leave for Ra'Tahal tomorrow."

"Who is this friend?"

"He is a human and the same young man who was acting as court translator for King Arangar when father and I visited Ra'Tahal last autumn. Now, he is something more."

"Does this young man have a name?"

"His name is Ian, but he also goes by the name Barsequa."

Tora-Li arched her brow. "Gifted one?"

"I was taught that humans do not possess magic, Mother, but he wields frightening power that is unlike anything I have ever seen."

"And this...human, he can foretell the future?" Tori-Li did nothing to mask the doubt in her voice.

"He claims that something dire is coming, and if he does not succeed in his quest, the entire world is at risk."

"You believe him?"

"I do." Even Shria-Li had doubted until reaching Havenfall. "That belief was fortified when we arrived here. Ian claimed he had seen Havenfall and the palace in a vision. In a vision, he saw Safrina in the palace garden."

"He knows Safrina?"

"They are friends."

"How did he know she was in Havenfall?"

"That is just it, mother. He could not have known, which validates his visions."

Tora-Li turned sharply toward her daughter. "What else did he say about the girl?"

"He claims that the location of his vision shifted to a castle in the mountains." Shria-Li paused to consider how to say the next part. "Father was at this castle with her until Safrina was attacked and killed by some sort of monster."

The queen's eyes widened, her hand covering her mouth.

"What is wrong, Mother?"

"Your father. He is away on Mount Shadowmar. He left a week back to address the final details of the mountain fortress. He took Safrina with him, claiming that she was no longer needed here with you away. She is to join the staff at Shadowmar Castle."

Shria-Li blanched. "By Vandasal's breath, Ian's vision was true. That means..."

Something bad was going to happen. Safrina was Shria-Li's friend. If she was truly at risk, she needed to be warned. Shria-Li then wondered what role her father played in Ian's vision.

CHAPTER 39
CONFRONTATION

Lying upon a soft, white cloud, Vic floated high above the world. The lush green of the Vale blanketed the ground below him while the sun's soothing rays shone down on him. That warmth and comfort eased his weariness, filling him with peace and contentment.

A jostling caused him to stir. He opened his eyes to a tray ceiling stamped with exotic patterns. A sunbeam streamed through a gap in the curtains, its low angle informing him that the afternoon waned.

Revita lifted her head from his chest and gave him a sleepy smile. "Did you sleep well?"

Surprisingly, he felt more refreshed than anticipated. "It may have been the best nap I have ever taken."

"The bed is soft." She ran her hand across the mattress. "I would love to have one like it for myself."

"The bed is nice but holding you while I sleep is what made it special."

She climbed up his chest and gently kissed him. He gave in to her soft, warm lips while his blood heated and other parts of his body began to stir. Too soon, she pulled away and stared down at him.

"I don't see Ian. Perhaps we could..." She flashed a naughty smirk.

Vic glanced toward the glass door, through which sunlight streamed in. The door stood open a crack. "I think Ian is on the balcony."

"He has seen me naked. I suspect he has seen you that way as well."

The implication caused Vic to blush. "I can't have him walk in on us while we are...compromised."

Her twinkling laughter filled the air. She held his chin between a finger and thumb while staring into his eyes. "It is so fun to embarrass you."

"I am not embarrassed."

"If your cheeks were any redder, I'd think someone had just slapped you silly."

"Well, I am glad you are entertained by my need to maintain just a bit of propriety. I only ask that you limit your teasing while others are around." It was not the first time he had asked this of her.

Her smile slid away, her expression serious as she stared into his eyes. "Does it injure your pride so badly?"

"I am who I am, Revita."

"As am I." It was not the first time she had said as much.

"Then, we must meet somewhere in between."

After a silent beat, she kissed him gazing into his eyes. "I can do that."

He smoothed her raven locks. "Your hair is still a bit damp."

She smiled. "A bath was necessary. You seemed to enjoy it as well."

His pulse quickened as he recalled the experience. "It is something we should do more often."

"Agreed." She slid off him and sat on the edge of the bed, the light, wispy dress given to her by the chambermaid clinging to her lithe frame. While Vic found it odd seeing her in a dress, she looked more beautiful than ever. "However, there are times when a woman needs privacy." Rising to her feet, she stretched. "And now is one of those times. When I am through, I will see if our clothes are dry."

As Revita headed out the chamber door, Vic sat up, his altered angle giving him a better view through the glass doors. Sure enough, Ian stood outside, leaning against the balcony railing, his back to the doors.

Vic worked his shoulders, still a bit sore from the grueling climb up the escarpment earlier that day. The clean tunic he had been given was tight across his chest, shoulders, and arms due to his physique being a bit thicker than that of elves. He stood, pulled the curtain aside, and stepped out to join his brother, who was dressed in pale green robes provided by the palace staff.

Warm afternoon sunlight bathed his upper body while the marble railing cast a shadow from his stomach to his feet. Vic leaned against the rail, his elbow touching Ian's as he gazed out over the city of Haven-fall. Sunlight gleamed off glass domes, white arches, and the water flowing down a myriad of aqueducts. Towering trees of gold stood amid the buildings in a glorious marriage of nature and civilization.

"This is a sight to behold," Vic said.

Ian stared out into the distance. "Which is why I have been standing out here for the past hour."

"You couldn't sleep?"

"I slept for a time, but Lionel was restless."

"Where is your little friend?"

Ian pointed south. "That way, in the forest we passed through after we reached the top of the escarpment."

The certainty with which Ian said it made Vic reflect on how his brother had behaved since finding the injured fire drake. Lionel followed and obeyed Ian as if they had been together for decades. What Vic had at first thought to be Ian being too soft of heart turned out to be something profound.

"What is it like?" he asked.

"What do you mean?" Ian glanced toward Vic.

"Lionel. He is more than just a pet, isn't he?"

"Oh. That." His gaze distant, Ian explained, "I can feel him at all times. He is like another presence in my head. Simple things like hunger, fear, anger, and contentment come through that connection. In return, I can sort of communicate with him, but it is not through language. It is through feelings and images. How well he understands, I am not certain." He smirked. "Sometimes, I think he understands perfectly, but he is stubborn and chooses when he wants to obey."

The fire drake reminded Vic of the dragon egg he had found and visited repeatedly the prior year. Then, the lava pool below the egg was disturbed, the egg cracked, and hatchlings emerged. *Those dragons responded when I spoke to them.* Vic thought he had established some connection with the dragons, but it was nothing like what Ian described. *Maybe I was just fooling myself.*

"He returns." Ian disturbed Vic's musings.

"Where?"

Extending his arm, Ian pointed south. "There."

Vic stared in that direction but saw nothing. Then, a tiny spec appeared. The spec grew larger as it reached the city's edge. Flapping wings became discernable. Guards appeared on a terrace below. In Elvish, commands were issued. The guards raised bows and nocked them. Vic gasped in concern as they took aim at the approaching fire drake.

"No!" Vic bellowed.

His cry went unheeded, but he was not the only one who reacted.

A single command rang out. The thwaps of bows releasing followed. The arrows shot into the air but before they reached the drake, they shattered. Splintered bits of wood tumbled from the sky.

Ian shouted something in Elvish. The guards turned toward him and lowered their bows. Lionel flew in, banked toward the balcony, and landed on Ian's arm. With a wave to the guards, Ian turned toward Vic.

"That is why I was waiting for him," Ian explained. "I was afraid of how the guards might react."

Vic nodded. "They are responsible for protecting the palace. They could not know if the drake were friend or foe."

When Ian bent his elbow to his chest, the drake hopped onto his shoulder. "Now that he has returned, let's go inside. I would like to sit for a bit before dinner."

The guest chamber included two beds, each large enough for two, along with a table, four chairs, and a nightstand. The door to the adjoining bath chamber stood open, the recessed bath visible through the doorway.

Ian set Lionel on the back of one chair while he plopped down in another. Vic pulled out a chair across from him and sat while Ian poured liquid from a clay jug, filling two cups. They both drank water infused with fruit, slightly sweet, slightly tart.

Staring across the table, Vic frowned in thought. "Why do you continue to wear robes? When you were Devigar's apprentice, I assume it was expected, but you are court translator no longer."

Ian looked down at the robes and gave the pale fabric a tug. "Like a warrior dressed in armor, this garb is best suited for what I do."

"What does that mean?"

"Hmm." Ian rubbed his bearded chin. It had grown in and made him look years older than the teen Vic remembered from their last days in Shillings, before their lives were turned on end. "Let us begin with air," Ian said. "It can penetrate clothing, but tight layers stifle it. If you wear leather, like your jerkin or Revita's coat, air is greatly restricted, which is why leather can be so warm. You might sweat beneath the leather, but that perspiration has no chance to cool since the access to air is limited."

"What does air have to do with anything?"

"Magic is much like air. You cannot see either one, yet they are all around us. To use magic, I must have unfettered access to it. Robes are loose and unrestricted, and that allows magic to flow better. Tight clothing would reduce my access to magic like a beaver's dam slowing a river's flow. Armor would be even worse, choking it off until I could access only a fraction of my power."

"Huh," Vic grunted. "That actually makes sense."

Ian smiled. "I am glad you think so."

"You were always the smart one, Ian. With all that has happened, and for all the responsibility you place upon yourself, well, I want you to know that I am proud of you."

Ian stared across the table in a long moment of silence. His gaze lowered while he fiddled with his fingers. "I have always looked up to you, Vic. I wished to be like you, but no matter how hard I tried, I am not you."

"You should be yourself, Ian."

"I know that...now. This past year has been difficult, but somewhere in the mess we both had to wade through, I found myself." He lifted his gaze to meet Vics. "But that would not have been possible without your support. I wanted to thank you for everything you have done, including joining me on this quest. It would be far more difficult if I had to do this alone."

Vic reached across the table and gripped Ian's hand. "You are not alone. Remember that, and while you are at it, share your burdens rather than carrying them yourself. We will find the Paragon, and after that, we will figure out what happens next."

The door opened and Revita walked in with Shria-Li a step behind.

"Look who I found." Revita tossed a pile of clothing onto a bed. She once again wore her own breeches, tunic, boots, and leather coat. "Our things were dry, so you two can get changed."

Shria-Li said, "When you are dressed, meet Revita and me at the bottom of the stairs. We are to dine with my mother."

When the two females left the room, Vic stood, pulled his breeches from the pile, and began to undress. "If we are to dine with the queen, we should not keep her waiting. Besides, I am starved."

Ian leaned toward Lionel and stroked his head. "Remain here. Sleep. I will be back soon." He then rose and began to undress.

~

A COZY BIT of warmth came through Ian's connection with Lionel. When he left his room, the fire drake was curled up on a pillow, his eyes at half mast, his hunger sated. Ian tried not to dwell on the creature killing and eating other animals. Through their connection, he had the sense that Lionel's latest meal had been an unlucky squirrel. He hoped his own fare would be something more appetizing.

With Shria-Li in the lead, Ian, Vic, and Revita traversed a corridor lined by arches on one side, through which the palace garden with the massive, golden tree at the center was visible. As he strode down the corridor, Ian found himself staring out toward the garden once again. The tree emanated a subtle yet looming presence as if it were sentient. *Trees cannot think, can they?* Considering all Ian had experienced over the past year, he no longer had confidence in knowing what was possible and what was not.

The corridor ended as they passed beneath another arch and strolled out onto a terrace blanketed in shadow. The last moments of sunlight shone upon cone-capped towers high above them. A marble railing surrounded the terrace while golden-leafed trees stood just beyond the railing, their branches shadowing the outer portion of the terrace. The tree bark appeared to emanate a soft, golden aura amid the shadows.

At the center of the terrace stood a table made of dark wood. It had a live edge that curled and bent without a single straight section and ten chairs made of thin, twisted shoots surrounded it. A pair of humans stood between the table and the railing, each holding a glass carafe filled with red liquid.

Shria-Li stopped beside the table and gestured toward an open chair. "Ian, you can sit here, beside me. Vic and Revita should sit across from us. My mother will claim the seat at the head of the table."

They all settled into their assigned chairs. The human servants approached the table and began to fill goblets. When Ian lifted his and sniffed it, a fruity bouquet tickled his nose. A sip confirmed it as wine, smooth and warming his throat while leaving a slightly bitter aftertaste on his tongue. Before he could even set the goblet back down, a female elf trailed by a pair of guards glided out onto the terrace. A crown made of twisted, golden twigs rested amid hair so pale it was almost white. A dress of silver and white hung on her willowy frame, its skirts flowing as she approached the table.

"Mother." Shria-Li nudged Ian and stood.

Ian rose to his feet and whispered harshly. "Stand up."

Vic and Revita stood and turned toward the queen.

"Hello, daughter," the queen said in Elvish. She stopped at the head of the table and spoke in the human tongue. "Welcome to my daughter's companions."

"Thank you for your hospitality, Your Majesty," Ian replied in Elvish. He then shifted to human as well. "I am Barsequa Illian."

"Barsequa..." She arched a brow at Shria-Li, who nodded. The exchange was not lost on Ian. The queen then added, "That is an Elvish term."

Ian nodded. "I am aware." He pointed across the table. This is my brother, Victus Carpenter. The woman is Revita Shalaan."

Tora-Li nodded. "Please, sit. We can talk while we await our meal."

The queen settled in her chair, and the others did so as well. A servant poured wine into her goblet and backed to the rail.

"It is rare for us to have visitors," Tora-Li said. "Even less common for them to be human."

Vic said, "Havenfall is unlike any city I have seen. How many people live here?"

"Perhaps ten thousand in total, half of which are human."

A cloud darkened Vic's expression as his gaze met Ian's. Neither had to say it aloud, but it was clear that the queen referred to human slaves.

Oblivious, Tora-Li continued. "Roughly half of the Sylvan population lives in Havenfall. A quarter live in River's End while the rest are scattered throughout the realm."

"Why are there so few?" Ian asked.

"At our peak, over a millennia past, our numbers exceeded thirty thousand. Our lives may be long compared to humans, but our births are few. At the end of the first age, war gripped the land and our people suffered greatly for what was gained. Yes, the Sylvan control the western lands and Havenfall is the jewel of the crown upon our head, but the cost was too great. Twenty centuries have passed since that war, and our population is barely a third of what it once was." Tora-Li's brow furrowed at her daughter. "I thought you had another in your party. A brownie, I believe."

"Yes," Shria-Li nodded. "Lint is quite exuberant. I thought it best if he kept himself occupied, so I offered him the opportunity to explore the Garden of Life while we dined. I just hope he stays out of trouble."

Tora-Li turned her gaze toward Ian. "And what of the tiny dragon the guards reported?"

"That is Lionel. He is my companion. I assure you, he will not harm anyone."

The queen seemed to consider Ian's explanation before nodding. She opened her mouth to speak but stopped short when a tall, male elf emerged from the archway. With a lean yet muscular build and impeccable posture, he projected his exalted position even if you ignored the twisted, golden crown nestled in his platinum hair. His angled eyes sparkled like the sun, his skin flawless, his features sculpted and so handsome, even Ian found him attractive.

Ian burst to his feet and blurted, "King Fastellan."

The others stood in response to the king's appearance.

Fastellan's eyes widened, and he exclaimed in Elvish, "It is true! My daughter has returned!"

With a pained expression, Shria-Li greeted him in her native tongue, "Hello, Father."

Fastellan strolled toward the table, rounded it, and wrapped his arms around his daughter. "I...we feared what had become of you."

In a soft voice, she said, "I am sorry. I did not mean to worry you."

He released her and looked from Vic, to Revita, and then to Ian. "Those two, I do not know, but is this one not Devigar's apprentice?"

Ian replied in Elvish before she could speak. "I was, but Devigar is dead and I am no longer a slave." He knew he should hold back but could not when images from his vision flashed before his eyes. "Where is Rina?"

Fastellan glared at Ian. "I am king here. You have no right to demand questions of me."

Tensing, his fists clenched, Ian spoke with tight lips. He fought against the urge to use his magic, which required all of his discipline. "Where is Safrina? I know she was here. I know she was with you."

The king blinked and glanced toward his wife.

Tora-Li arched a brow. "Why do you not answer the boy?"

Fastellan's eyes flicked from side to side before he nodded. "She is well. I have moved her to Shadowmar Castle. I needed someone to manage the castle staff, and she was available."

The king's acknowledgement revealed a truth Ian had long suspected. "You abducted Rina from Ra'Tahal and brought her here."

"How dare you accuse me..."

Ian thrust a finger at the king while releasing a tiny bit of his magic.

Without physical contact, the king staggered backward and then rubbed his chest. "How did you do that?"

"I am asking the questions," Ian growled. "I can do far worse if pressed."

Four guards rushed in, two with bows aimed at Ian, the others gripping spears.

Still holding his magic, Ian formed a shield and launched it toward the guards. The blast sent the guards sprawling. He then turned back toward the king.

"Have your guards stand down. I don't wish to hurt anyone."

Fastellan stared at Ian with wide eyes.

Shria-Li put a hand on Ian's arm. "Ian. Please don't do anything rash."

"I am here to talk." Ian did not look at her, keeping his attention on Fastellan. "Your father can provide answers, or he can choose violence. The latter proves his guilt."

Tora-Li stood and crossed her arms while staring at her husband. "Answer the boy."

The king huffed. "Fine. I took Safrina to spite Arangar."

"Who is now dead."

"As I have heard."

Ian pressed the king. "Yet, you did not return her. Why?"

Fastellan gestured toward Shria-Li. "She was my daughter's personal attendant."

Ian turned towards Shria-Li. "Is this true?"

"Yes." There was shame in her tone.

The sting of betrayal was like a dagger to his trust. "You did not tell me."

"We had other worries. I did not think..."

"For two days?" His volume increased as his anger swelled. "Even when we arrived in the palace garden, I shared my vision about her and you said nothing."

The elf princess lowered her gaze. "I...apologize."

Ian turned his anger back on the king. "Your daughter has been away for half a year, yet Safrina remained with you here. Why not return her to Ra'Tahal?"

"I hoped for Shria-Li's return. When time passed and she did not, I decided to take Safrina to Shadowmar."

Ian believed as much, but it did not answer everything from his vision. "What of the monster?"

The king frowned. "Monster? What monster?"

"Half man, half bull."

"A minotaur?" The king snorted. "They are pure myth. Not even the Vale is home to such creature."

The last question, the one Ian was reluctant to ask, hung in the air like a noose, tightening around him and demanding he not ignore it. The question emerged as a tentative whisper. "Is Safrina your...lover?"

Shria-Li's eyes widened. Her mother gasped.

Fastellan blanched, his reply little more than a whisper. "How could you know?"

CHAPTER 40
A PAINFUL TRUTH

Shock held everyone motionless, including Ian. *What came over me?* He hadn't meant to say those things, but as the words began to come out, they gained momentum and continued until the ugliest accusation was revealed.

Tora-Li took a step toward Fastellan and lashed out. Her palm struck his cheek, the slap like a thunderclap amid the silence. She spun on her heel and walked away.

Fastellan's shock turned to a glower, which he directed at Ian. His nostrils flared, and Ian prepared himself in case the king did something rash. Instead, Fastellan stomped off with his fists clenched at his sides. His guards, now recovered and still holding their weapons ready, followed in the wake of their queen and king.

Shria-Li grabbed Ian by the arm and spun him toward her. "What were you thinking?" She hissed.

He blinked as guilt washed over him. "I just..."

"You were thinking only of yourself!" she snapped. "You certainly did not consider what this might do to my family or to my people."

He stiffened. "Rina is my friend." Then he thrust out his chin in accusation. "I thought you were as well."

Shria-Li exhaled in frustration. "I apologized for not telling you about her sooner Ian, but what difference would it have made? She is not here any longer." She pointed toward the doorway. "They are not just my parents. They are the king and queen of the Sylvan. Do you know what you've done?"

"I revealed the truth. Don't you think your mother had the right to know?"

Shria-Li covered her eyes and sighed. Lowering her hand, she stared toward the dark archway leading away from the terrace. When she spoke, sorrow had replaced the anger in her voice. "I suspect my mother already knew. Their marriage was not one built upon love. It was a sacrifice both made for the good of my people. For many years, I have known this. There is no affection between them, only a pragmatic division of responsibility that relies on respect for each other. That respect is now destroyed."

"But if your mother knew..."

She turned toward him, her volume rising again. "Don't you get it, Ian? Some things can be ignored so long as they remain unsaid. You blurting it out in front of the guards and staff makes it too real. Even worse than my father betraying his oath of marriage is him doing so with a human."

Ian stiffened. "I thought you were above such bigotry."

"I have nothing against humans, Ian." She shook her head sadly. "If you believe otherwise, our friendship was built on lies."

"What, then?"

"The scriptures of Vandasal are quite specific in this matter. It is forbidden for a Sylvan to couple with a human. If that has happened...I fear the price my father must pay for his transgressions." She turned away. "Now, if you will excuse me, I must attempt to clean up the mess you have made."

With a deep breath of courage, Shria-Li headed off to find her parents, leaving the three humans alone with the two servants.

In Dwarvish, Vic asked, "What was that about? I didn't understand a thing you said."

Revita snorted. "Whatever it was, they are pissed. That much is certain."

Ian realized that the entire confrontation had taken place in Elvish. He then remembered the reason for their journey to Havenfall. *We need Fastellan's help to reach Ra'Tahal.* Now, the king likely wished Ian dead and is unlikely to listen if Ian tried to explain the urgency of his quest. *What have I done?*

⁓

After finding the royal chambers empty, Shria-Li descended to the palace main floor and hurried down a long corridor. When she reached the entrance hall and spied a quartet of guards posted outside the closed throne room doors, she turned in that direction.

"Are my parents inside?" She asked as she drew near.

"Ah, Princess." A male guard named Harrisol thumped his fist against his chest. "We were strictly told to allow nobody past."

"I see. What if I order you to step aside?"

Harrisol appeared to consider the issue before replying, "The king's orders were quite clear."

"I am going in and you will need to use force to stop me."

The guard glanced toward his cohorts and then moved his spear aside. "I trust you will explain what happened."

"I will shoulder all blame in this matter." She walked past him, pushed the door open, and stopped just inside the doorway.

Her parents stood on the dais, in the soft golden glow of the tree and thrones. Both with their backs to the entrance, Tora-Li facing away from Fastellan. The king said something to the queen, his volume too low for Shria-Li to interpret from across the room. The tension was palpable from a distance, reinforced by Tora-Li's refusal to face him.

After one last breath of courage, Shria-Li headed along the downslope, toward the dais. As she drew closer, her father's words became intelligible.

".... marriage was a sacrifice for our people."

Without turning around, Tora-Li replied, "I know that better than anyone, since you have said as much from the start."

"Then why are you so upset?" He threw his hands up in frustration.

She spun toward him. "I knew you might find a mistress, and I was willing to look the other way, willing to pretend all was well if that happened. But you have not just betrayed me in this. You have betrayed your god."

"Let's be honest. Vandasal does not care about me or my indiscretions."

"So, that gives you free reign to do as you wish? You would toss aside thousands of years of belief just to suit your own desires?"

Fastellan pulled his crown off and ran his hand through his platinum hair. "I realize that scripture dictates we remain true to our race, but those laws were crafted by a priestess, not by Vandasal himself."

"Blasphemy," Tora-Li spat. "If Valaria heard you say that, she would have you standing before the tribunal."

Shria-Li decided it was time to intervene. She climbed the dais. "Mother. Father. I must apologize for my friend's inappropriate behavior."

Her mother snorted. "The one guilty of impropriety stands before you."

Fastellan turned toward Shria-Li. "I...am sorry you and your mother had to find out this way. I had hoped to spare both of you the pain by removing Safrina from Havenfall."

His poor attempt to explain his actions only caused more pain. Tears blurred Shria-Li's vision. "Why, father?"

He moved closer and took her hand. "I never wanted to hurt you, your mother, or our people, but the heart feels as it feels. The moment I saw Safrina, I was smitten. It was as if our pairing was written in the stars. Against this, I knew no defense."

Tora-Li hissed. "She is *human*."

He fired off a heated retort. "Human or not, she is special."

Caught between the pain of her friend pursuing her father and her father's betrayal against her mother, Shria-Li did not know what to say. *Safrina, why?* Yet, she was young, barely an adult while Fastellan had lived many times her eighteen years. *This is father's fault.*

Tora-Li closed her eyes and exhaled before opening them. "I need some time alone. I think I will visit the temple." She walked past Shria-Li and headed toward the door.

Silently, Fastellan watched his wife leave the room before turning to his daughter. "How did your companion discover this...secret?"

Numbly, Shria-Li replied, "He has the gift of prophecy and saw it in a vision."

Fastellan snorted. "He is human. How is that possible?"

"I wondered the same, still his ability cannot be denied. In fact, this human wields magic unlikely anything I know. I suspect his abilities outstrip a Drow singer. They might even match what can be achieved through the Staff of Life."

Upon mentioning the magical artifact, Shria-Li glanced toward the gap between the two thrones. There, the staff stood upright with one end planted in a hole in the dais.

Fastellan rubbed his jaw. "If what you say is true, and this boy has the gift of prophecy, something significant has changed."

"That is why I am here, Father. Ian and I crossed paths in the Vale. He was searching for me, for my abilities. He seeks something called the

Paragon." She watched him closely to see if he recognized the term, but there was no reaction. "He believes that this thing he seeks can counter a dire prophecy. The Paragon's location is known only to Gahagar, who is dead. Only one who can speak to spirits can garner the information Ian requires. It is why I agreed to join him on his quest."

His brow furrowed. "This prophecy he claims to follow…. What does it foretell?"

"The end of humans. The end of dwarves. The end of the Drow and even the Sylvan." The last bit came out as little more than a whisper, as if saying it aloud would make it come to pass.

"But why come here?"

"How soon this end comes, we do not know. Ian claims that every day is critical. Gahagar lies in the Hall of Ancients in Ra-Tahal. A journey from the Vale to the Tahal capital would take a week or longer. I sought a faster route, so we climbed the escarpment to come here."

He narrowed his eyes. "You wish to use the portal stones."

"I do."

"Our ability to translocate is a secret we Sylvan hold close, known only to the royal family and a handful of others. You were sworn to never reveal the portal stones to another."

"I have not broken that pledge. I did not tell them how we could travel such a distance in such a brief time. I simply informed them that it was possible, but I need your help."

Her father tented his fingers and tapped them against his lips in a long moment of silence before he said. "No."

"But I just…"

"You ask me to violate Sylvan law for someone who just blew up our lives for no reason other than to reveal the truth. Worse, he did so in front of palace guards and servants. Whispers and rumors will swirl among our people. Doubt and distrust will follow. He is not trying to save the Sylvan. He is trying to destroy us."

He stomped toward the chamber exit.

Shria-Li called out, "We could blindfold them. They need not know anything..."

The king opened the door and slammed it behind him, leaving her alone in a silent, empty chamber.

She mulled over what her father had said and while she agreed with much of it, she knew Ian meant no harm despite his actions. While her father was too upset to do the right thing, Shria-Li could not allow her people to suffer because of his wounded pride. She would do her part to help Ian, even if it meant her betraying her own father.

A memory replayed in her mind, one that occurred two decades earlier yet felt like yesterday.

~

Shria-Li, with her father's hand on her shoulder, entered the throne room. Morning sunlight streamed through glass panels in the dome overhead. The chamber was empty.

"Come, daughter," Fastellan walked her down the slope, toward the dais.

He climbed up and approached the gnarled wooden staff standing between the two thrones. The moment his hand touched it, the staff came to life, emitting a gentle hum while pulsing with a golden aura.

Fastellan turned toward her while cradling the staff in both hands. "This is the Staff of Life. It is our most sacred possession. This was a gift from Vandasal, which he carved himself from the Tree of Life. We are a people of magic. It is in our blood and often exhibited through talents that make us unique while strengthening our society. Like us, magic flows through this staff, but its might is vast and capable of things we still do not understand. However, the staff requires a bond. Without that bond, it is nothing more than a piece of wood.

"Since our god named the Sylvan and gifted us the staff, each king and queen has passed this bond on to their children. Today, I wish to extend the bond to you. If something dire ever happened to your mother and I, you would pick up the staff, don a crown, and lead our people."

Shria-Li shook her head. "I don't want anything to happen to you or mother."

"Perhaps nothing will. We can only pray that it is so. However, wishes do not dictate reality. Should I neglect to pass the bond to you, the staff will be beyond your ability to claim. Our people would suffer its loss, which is something I cannot allow. We must serve our people first and foremost. So, today, you will bond with the staff. It is our responsibility to ensure the future, and this is required to do so."

While the thought of her parents dying disturbed Shria-Li, particularly since she had yet to reach her majority, she understood duty. It was among the first words she had been taught. "What do you require of me?"

"Stand before me, but do not touch the staff until I tell you to."

She moved closer while eying the staff, its golden glow pulsing like a heartbeat.

He closed his eyes. The hum of the staff lowered in tone, the rising and falling glow slowing until it remained dim. Without opening his eyes, he said, "Grip the staff, Shri."

Tentatively, she reached out. Her fingers wound around the staff, tentatively closing around it. Finally, she squeezed.

A tingling sensation shot up her arms as the staff glowed brightly. Raw power flowed through her veins, so intense she thought they were on fire. She tried to release the staff, but her fingers refused to obey. Her heart raced as if she had sprinted for miles, the thump of it like a drum in her chest. The pain receded, as did the light emitted from the staff. As her pulse slowed, the glow from the staff rose and fell in time with her heartbeat.

Her father opened his eyes and removed his hands. "The staff is now yours to command should the need arise."

Shria-Li stared down at the staff with numb detachment, for her thoughts were clouded by the presence of another – the Tree of Life itself. It felt as if she were connected to nature, something that existed before the races of magic, before humans, even before the creatures that wandered the wild. She was part of the vast, eternal existence from which all living things were born. Beyond all of this, a strange yet comforting power thrummed in her bones and left her believing that she could accomplish anything.

"Let it go, daughter. "Fastellan reached for the staff. "While the staff will be yours one day, that day has not yet come."

With bitter reluctance, she released her grip. Disconnected from its power, she was fragile and alone once again.

～

THE MEMORY FADED but the longing it brought on did not. Determined and willing to bear the consequences, she crossed the dais, reached for the Staff of Life, and wrapped her fingers around it. The staff bloomed with light and it filled her with energy. A faint whispering echoed in her head as the staff taunted her to use its power. Images flashed in her head, ranging from her calling powerful storms to sprouting thousands of vines that would rise up and strangle her enemies. It required focus and applied will for Shria-Li to shun those images and regain control over the staff.

She turned toward the door and crossed the room before stopping. *Remain silent*, she issued a mental command. *And dim your light.*

The staff's aura quelled until it appeared like nothing more than a mundane wooden shaft. Shria-Li opened the door a crack and peered out. A cluster of four guards stood in the center of the otherwise empty hall. With the staff held at her side, she slipped out the door and headed straight for the stairwell at the side of the room, careful to use her body to shield the staff from view. When one of the guards glanced in her direction, she waved as if nothing were amiss. He gave a nod of acknowledgement and turned back toward the others to rejoin the discussion. She reached the staircase and hurried up, intent on finding her companions.

CHAPTER 41

THE PORTAL STONE

A sharp pinch of the ear woke Ian. He shied away, opened his eyes, and rubbed his ear. "Ouch."

He lay in his bed in the guest suite he shared with Vic and Revita. Light emitted from the golden trees seeped through the open curtain and gave shape to his surroundings. The door stood open a few inches, the corridor outside dark. Lionel was curled up against his side, snoring as usual.

A quiet voice came from beside him. "The princess says you are to get up."

He turned to find Lint standing on the bed. "You didn't have to pinch me."

"Hush!" The brownie glanced toward the door. "We are not to wake anyone."

"What time is it?"

"An hour or two until dawn."

"Don't you ever sleep?"

Lint laughed. "Brownies are strong. We do not need sleep like you weak humans."

Ian glanced over to the other bed. The covers were pulled back, the bed empty. "Where are my brother and Revita?"

"They are visiting the palace kitchen."

"They are eating without me?"

"Not to eat, you fool," Lint snapped. "They are getting provisions."

Ian pulled back the covers and swung his legs off the bed. The hard stone floor was cold beneath his bare feet.

"Get dressed," Lint said. "You are to meet the others downstairs." The brownie hopped across the mattress and nudged the sleeping drake with his foot. "Wake up, you overgrown lizard."

Lionel opened his eyes and snapped at the brownie. Lint yipped and leapt off the bed, narrowly missing getting chomped. He landed on the floor, giggled, and scurried out the door. Through their connection, Ian sensed Lionel's irritation.

"I know. Lint can be annoying." Ian sighed. "It looks like sleep will have to come later." He bent and reached for his boots. "Time to go join the others."

⁓

"I don't suppose there is any way you can breathe quieter," Ian whispered to Lionel, who sat on his shoulder. The drake's rasping breath continuing to rumble in Ian's ear was his only response.

Ian, Vic, Revita, and Shria-Li stood in the shadows of an arch while peering out into the Garden of Life. Together, they waited.

Lint suddenly appeared on the path below, some thirty feet away. The brownie waved and then darted off.

"That's the signal." Shria-Li headed toward the stairs. "Let's go."

Ian, like the others, ducked as the party hurried along the garden path. Dark foliage ranging from four to six feet tall bordered the path, providing cover. All the while, the massive, golden tree at the garden's center looked down on them. When they reached the far edge of the garden, Lint appeared in the middle of the path, waving his arms over his head.

"Get down," Lint hissed.

Everyone stopped and crouched. A male voice arose, gradually growing closer. A female voice responded, both speaking Elvish. The pair of guards crossed the path not more than a dozen strides away. When the voices faded, Lint rushed to the intersection, looked both ways, and waved them forward.

The path soon turned to a downslope and ran beneath one of the aqueduct channels. The palace fell behind and they entered the city. Holding to the darker, less traveled streets, they navigated across Havenfall until the bridges came into view. By then, the soft twilight of predawn had masked all but the brightest stars.

Standing amid a grove of trees, they gathered around Shria-Li. "Remain close to me while we cross. The bridges have wards that prevent unwelcome guests from entering the city at night."

She then walked out to the same bridge they had crossed the prior day. With the staff held before her, Shria-Li led them over the arched bridge and to the south bank. Their brief stay in Havenfall had come to an end. Despite the contentious nature of the meeting with Fastellan, Ian was disappointed that he would no longer be able to enjoy the beauty of the Sylvan capital. He turned and caught a final glimpse of Havenfall's tallest spires against the early morning sky, holding on to the image. Then, the surrounding trees masked the city as the party continued westward.

~

AN HOUR LATER, after following a narrow, rarely traveled trail, Ian and his companions came to a thick copse of golden trees. A wall of vines connected the trees, reminding Ian of the border surrounding Fae Gulch. As with the fairies' home, the obstruction was daunting and suggested they go around. Just when he was certain the route was impassible, Shria-Li turned sharply, followed a narrow gap between trees, and then turned again. A clearing became visible through a gap in the trees. The party walked through the thick wood and emerged in a meadow a hundred feet in diameter. In the center of the meadow was a circular stone platform standing some three feet above the forest floor.

"This is it," Shria-Li said as she stared at the platform.

"This is what?" Revita asked. "It looks like a stage. Do you plan to perform for us?"

The elf princess ignored the quip. "A portal stone stands before you. Few have seen them and fewer understand their intent. I am sharing a great secret, one I beg you to keep."

Ian asked, "What does it do?"

"Nothing without the key, which I hold in my hand." She lifted the staff and it bloomed with golden light. "There are portal stones throughout the southern realm. The magic in the staff, combined with a portal stone, makes translocation possible.

"What the blazes is transitation?" Revita asked.

"Translocation," Shria-Li corrected her. "As for what it is, you will soon find out. Follow me."

They crossed the meadow and climbed up onto the platform. Even Lint, who stood no more than six inches tall, leapt onto the three-foot-tall portal stone. He then marched across it, his chest thrust out proudly as he followed Shria-Li toward the platform's center.

A myriad of runes and lines were etched into the stone surface, reminding Ian of a giant construct. He found himself intrigued by the pattern, its design both foreign and familiar. He squatted near the platform's edge, transfixed as he examined the complex carvings. The movement caused Lionel to scurry across his upper back, moving from one shoulder to the other. Mesmerized by the design etched in the stone, Ian barely noticed.

"Ian." Shria-Li said. When he did not reply, she said it louder. "Ian!"

He tore his gaze from the runes and looked up to find the others standing around a small hole in the platform's center. "Yes?"

"Come closer."

With reluctance, he kept his attention on Shria-Li while crossing the stone and stopping a stride from her. "What now?"

She lifted the staff. "Watch."

The butt of the staff slid into the hole. A click resounded.

Light flared from the staff, and the runes etched into the surface of the stone began to glow. The surrounding forest shimmered and brightened until white light enveloped both the portal stone and the people standing on it. The light faded, and the area around the portal stone came back into view.

Rather than a forest of golden trees, oaks with green leaves and brown bark surrounded them. While the forest had been still when they first climbed onto the portal, a stiff breeze now ruffled Ian's robes, tousled his hair, and rustled the leaves of the surrounding trees.

Ian spun around, trapped between wonder and confusion. "Where are we?"

"Roughly an hour south of Ra'Tahal."

His head snapped toward her. "We traveled a thousand miles?"

"Yes."

Revita whistled. "Now, *that* is a good trick. What else can you do with that twisted stick in your hand?"

"I suspect I only have hints of what the Staff of Life can make possible." The elf princess frowned at the rod of golden, twisted wood. "The staff urges me to test its might. It requires willpower to ignore its whispers."

"First, you talk to dead trees. Now, you tell me that stick whispers to you." Revita shook her head. "You elves are strange."

Lionel squawked and an urge came through Ian's connection with the creature.

"Fine," Ian said. "You can explore the new forest. Just don't get into trouble."

The drake took flight, rising as he circled above the portal stone. When he was above the trees, he faded from view.

"We should get going." Shria-Li crossed the stone and hopped off with the staff in her grip. "If we leave now, we can join the dwarves for a late breakfast."

Intrigue, wonder, and curiosity caused Ian to hold back while the others headed across the clearing. Through force of will, he set his feet moving, jumped off the stone platform, and hurried to catch up. All the while, the concept of translocation magic haunted him, demanding he study it for a deeper understanding.

∼

THE MORNING ADVANCED as Ian and his companions followed a lightly used trail heading northeast. All the while, the wind grew stronger. The thick oak and maple branches above wavered in the gusts, causing the leaves to swish noisily. The trail intersected with a broader path, where they turned north. Minutes later, the rush of running water rose above that of the rustling leaves. The trees parted to reveal a scene Ian recalled well, although over half a year had passed since his last visit.

The Wellspring River flowed in from the east, passed beneath a stone bridge, and continued westbound for another quarter mile before abruptly dropping out of sight into a valley a thousand feet down. As they neared the bridge, the roar of the falls arose above the din, reminding Ian of the gorgeous vista that lurked just beyond his current view.

As they climbed the arching bridge, Ian admired the structure's crisp and clean lines, perfectly bonded sections, and the ornate sculptures rising from it. The bridge was a prime example of dwarven craftmanship, practical, precise, and impeccably constructed. As he reached the bridge's apex, an even more impressive sight came into view.

A massive, sprawling citadel stood at the edge of a drop, overlooking the valley and the falls. Towering walls, a hundred feet tall and made of gray stone, surrounded the fortress. Multi-tiered, rectangular stone structures and blocky towers rose above those walls. The citadel loomed like a sleeping giant, yet Ian was certain that the dwarves would be monitoring their approach.

A gravel road took them past the last clump of trees, crossed a field of yellowed grass, and brought them straight to the city gate. The massive, black iron portcullis remained closed while the dwarven guards standing beyond the gate watched in silence. Most guards wore a mixture of plate and leather armor, some with silver studs protruding from the leather, while others were garbed in chainmail. All were armed, their weapons ranging from swords to axes and crossbows.

Ian stopped fifty feet from the gate. "Hold on."

"What is it?" Shria-Li asked.

"I should go first. I hold no weapon, so it will appear less threatening. Besides, some of them may recognize me, and that will allow me to explain before someone makes a rash action that they might later regret."

"Good idea."

Ian approached the gate and held his arms out. "Ho! Don't attack. I am unarmed."

A dwarf with wings on his helmet called out, "What is your business, Human?"

Lowing his arms, Ian continued toward the gate. "My business is with King Korrigan. He is a friend."

The dwarf narrowed his eyes. "You have a familiar look."

"I should. I was Devigar's apprentice."

"Ah. That is right. Ian-something."

"I am now called Barsequa Illian, but my friends still refer to me as Ian."

The brows of the dwarf standing beside the first shot up until they were masked by his helm. "The wizard?"

"The very same."

One dwarf elbowed the other. "The boy used magic to disarm an entire squad of Drow. I saw it myself."

Ian rolled his eyes. While the result was on point, the recount was inaccurate at best. "You know my name. May I have yours?"

The dwarf with the winged helm said, "I am Sergeant Sandokar. The inland gate is my responsibility."

"And you appear to be doing a fine job." Ian figured a compliment would help to improve the dwarf's disposition.

"Many thanks."

Gesturing toward his companions, Ian said, "My friends and I request shelter and an audience with King Korrigan. We come in peace and will cause no trouble."

Sandokar pointed at Ian's shoulder. "What of the little dragon?"

"He is my companion and does as I say...more or less."

The sergeant craned his neck to peer past Ian. "Is that an elf in your company?"

"That is Shria-Li, princess and heir to the Sylvan crown."

"And..." The dwarf squinted. "Is there a tiny little man with you as well?"

"His name is Lint. He is a brownie from the Vale. The two humans were among our team when Arangoli, the Head Thumpers, and I infiltrated Ra'Tahal to free it from Rysildar and the other Drow. They are heroes, and I suspect Korrigan would want you to treat them as such."

"Hmm. So, you say." Sandokar tugged at his thick, black beard before arching a brow. "What if we declined to allow you entry?"

Ian frowned. "I would hate to use my magic and ruin this impeccably crafted portcullis."

"Huh," Sandokar snorted. He then erupted into deep, bellowing laughter. "Right you are. T'would be a shame, indeed." With one hand to his belly as he chortled, he looked up at the gate tower and made a waving motion.

The portcullis began to rise, so Ian motioned for his companions to come over. By the time they joined him, the gate was open. Ian led them inside.

The dwarf sergeant's laughter quelled. "While I must take you at your word about you meaning no harm, I hope you will understand if I escort you to the central keep."

"As I expected," Ian admitted.

Sandokar spoke briefly with the other guards on duty, pointed to three of them, and then turned toward Ian. "Follow me."

The sergeant took the lead while three armed guards fell in behind Ian and his companions. The group, consisting of four dwarves, three humans, an elf, a brownie, and a fire drake, headed down the narrow streets of Ra'Tahal.

The interior of the fortress, bustling with dwarves going about their daily business, was just as impressive as the exterior. The citadel's outer walls were thirty feet thick, with homes and shops built right into the foundation, utilizing the space in a way that was both practical and efficient. Its buildings were crafted of the same crisp, clean lines leaving no gaps or imperfections between the stone blocks from which they were assembled.

Sandokar escorted the visitors through the citadel, past outdoor markets and open shop doors, through narrow alleys and across catwalks over pools of water. The street ended at an open square with the central keep looming over it. In the shadow of the keep, twenty-four armored dwarves stood in columns with their chests and chins thrust out. Before them stood a dwarf with a scar on his cheek and a frown amid his braided beard. Like many others, he wore armor made of a mixture of leather and plate. Unlike the others, he cradled his helm in one arm, leaving his bald head exposed. Ian recognized the lead dwarf immediately. *Vargan.*

"This concludes the morning exercise," Vargan shouted. "You may retreat to the barracks. Those scheduled for duty are to report straight away. The rest of you, we will gather here an hour before sunset to practice battle formations." He waved. "You are dismissed."

The dwarven soldiers visibly relaxed. They broke into small groups, their chatter buzzing as they headed down a side street. As Vargan watched his men retreat, Sandokar approached him from behind.

"Captain," Sandokar stopped three strides from Vargan. "We have visitors who wish to see His Majesty."

Vargan turned as he replied, "The King is busy..." His eyes widened. "Ian! Vic! Revita!"

Ian said, "It is good to see you, Vargan."

The dwarf lumbered over and opened his arms to hug Ian. When he drew near, Lionel craned his neck forward and snapped. The dwarf yanked his hand aside just in time, causing the drake to clamp onto his bracer instead.

"Argh!" Vargan blared as he flailed with the drake dangling from his forearm while flapping its wings.

Ian cast a hard thought, *Let go!*

Lionel released his grip and hovered in the air in front of Vargan as the dwarf backed away.

Come, Ian sent through his connection with Lionel. *He is a friend.* Although the sensation coming from the drake was one of reluctance, the creature flew a tight circle around Ian and settled on his shoulder.

"I am sorry about that." Ian gave Lionel a sidelong look. "He is a bit overprotective."

Vargan warily eyed Lionel while rubbing his bracer, the leather indented by teeth marks. "What is that thing?"

"This is my companion, Lionel."

"A dragon?"

"He is actually a fire drake," Ian explained. "I would hug you, but as you can see, Lionel gets defensive."

"I'll say. That thing nearly bit my finger off."

"Again, I apologize."

Vargan turned to Vic and Revita. "What about you two?"

Revita grinned. "I won't bite you, but I can't speak for Vic."

Vic gave her a wry smile. "You can't fool Vargan. He knows you are more likely to bite than I am."

The dwarf grinned, stepped in, and wrapped an arm around each of them. They returned the embrace for a beat before pulling away from him.

"You two look well." He turned to Vic. "I am surprised she hasn't stabbed you by now."

Vic grinned. "It's not as if she hasn't tried."

Revita rolled her eyes. "Oh, please. If I wanted to poke you, I could have done so a thousand times over."

"Well, I am thankful you haven't wanted to in that case."

She smirked. "I have thought about it a few times, so I suggest you don't upset me too much. I would hate to mess up that pretty face of yours..." her gaze lowered. "Or anything else."

Vic's eyes widened. "You wouldn't."

Vargan laughed heartily. "Oh, I have missed you three." His laughter calmed, and he turned his attention to Shria-Li. "I see you brought an elf with you, and a little man as well."

"The elf is Shria-Li, daughter of Fastellan and Tora-Li."

"A princess?"

"Yes, and we need to speak with Korrigan about an urgent matter."

"Your visit is well-timed. I was to break my fast with Korrigan after the morning training exercise, which just finished." He nodded to Sandokar. "Thank you, Sergeant. You may return to your post. I will assume responsibility for our guests."

Sandokar and the guards from the gate turned and faded down the street while Vargan led Ian and his companions to the keep's entrance. They stepped inside and went straight for the staircase near the door.

As the home of the king, his family, the council, other clan leaders, their servants, and their personal guard, the keep was the largest building in Ra'Tahal. It stood twelve stories tall, its form blocky with the upper eight levels indented from those below. Balconies jutted out from the upper stories, providing a spectacular view of the citadel and the valley stretching out below it. While Ian had never lived in the keep, he had visited it on numerous occasions, so it was not unfamiliar.

The procession climbed a staircase illuminated by windows above each landing. Upon reaching the top floor, they traversed a long corridor lined by tapestries. The hallway ended at a square chamber occupied by four armored dwarves bracketing a pair of ornate doors stained black. Vargan gestured as he approached the guards. Two of them responded to the wordless command by opening the doors and standing aside.

Ian and his companions stepped into a dining hall with a high, coffered ceiling supported by dark-stained oaken beams. Colorful murals of past battles covered the recessed, flat surfaces between the beams. Paintings and sculptures decorated the walls on three sides, while the fourth was covered in diamond-paned windows facing west.

In the heart of the chamber was a long table surrounded by chairs to seat twenty. Warm light emanated from torches mounted to posts along the edge of the room. The two dozen candles on the chandelier of dark beams and black iron above the table remained unlit. Dark blue marble tiles with gold and white striations covered the floor, completing the scene.

Korrigan sat at the far end of the table, his attention fixed on a missive in his hand. The king wore a tunic made of red and black panels while the golden crown of his station rested on the table beside his empty plate. The chair to his right was the only other with a setting in place, leaving the rest of the table empty.

Vargan cleared his throat.

When the king lifted his gaze, his brow furrowed. "Ian?"

Ian grinned. "Have you missed me?"

Korrigan burst to his feet and crossed the room. Knowing what was coming and wishing to avoid a repeat of what happened with Vargan, Ian reached up and clamped a hand over Lionel's eyes. The drake squirmed in response while Ian sent assurance through their bond. The dwarf king wrapped his arms around Ian, squeezed, and lifted him from his feet.

Ian laughed despite his constricted chest. "Alright. You can put me down."

The king set him down and turned to hug Vic and Revita. When finished, he stepped back with a big grin. "I was hoping you'd come and visit us."

The smile on Ian's face slid away. "I wish otherwise, but we are not here for pleasure."

Korrigan glanced toward Shria-Li. "Isn't that the elf princess?"

"It is. The small one is a brownie named Lint. The creature on my shoulder is a drake named Lionel. We have come on urgent business."

The king nodded gravely. "Urgency seems to be the flavor of the day."

"Why do you say that?"

He crossed the room and lifted the parchment from the table. "This missive is from Fandaric. It appears there is trouble plaguing Clan Argent."

The hair on Ian's arms stood on end. "What happened?"

"Ten thousand Drow are camped in the pass north of Domus Ra."

Ian shot a worried look at his companions. "So many? Are they invading Clan Argent's lands?"

"Not yet, but the situation troubles me."

"What are you going to do?"

"Arangoli and the Head Thumpers are on their way to Talastar now.

Rumor has it that the city was abandoned, so I sent them to investigate. I suspect they will follow the trail to the Drow and will contact Clan Argent at that time. I will send a messenger to share that information with Fandaric. For now, I am hoping that will satisfy his concerns, but I also ask that he alert me if the Drow show any signs of aggression."

Ian glanced toward his brother and Revita. "I hope this has nothing to do with my vision."

"Your vision?" Korrigan's brow furrowed. "What vision?"

A rumble came from Ian's stomach, the noise echoing in the silent chamber. "Sorry."

The dwarf king rubbed his bearded chin. "Perhaps we should sit. We will eat, and you can explain why you have come to Ra'Tahal. I would like to hear more about this vision and what it has to do with the Drow."

Korrigan called for breakfast before reclaiming his seat at the table. Vargan sat beside him while the others each claimed an empty seat. All the while, a lump of worry rested in Ian's throat.

CHAPTER 42
WINNIE

"...W hich is why we require access to the catacombs below the Hall of Ancients."

Ian finished his tale, having laid it all out for Korrigan and Vargan. The two dwarves had asked only a few questions during Ian's story. Both appeared to listen intently and neither exhibited the doubt Fastellan had made so evident. With nothing remaining to say, Ian glanced down at his plate. Half of his meal sat untouched. His stomach was much stronger than it had been prior to his transformation, but dairy products remained problematic, so rather than eat the cheeses on his plate, he began to feed them to Lionel. The drake hummed in satisfaction with each bite taken.

Korrigan arched a brow at Vargan. "What do you think?"

"Hmm." Vargan tugged on his braided beard while staring into space, "I am not one for prophecy, but Ian certainly believes it, and I trust him. If this has anything to do with the Drow leaving Talastar, I suggest we help in any way we can."

Korrigan arched a brow. "Even though the catacombs are sacred and nobody outside the clan is allowed entry?"

"You worry about upholding tradition?"

"I worry that a display of preferential treatment toward my friends might look bad to the clan. When those friends are three humans and an elf, and the favor they ask goes against the tenets of our priesthood, my worry is tripled. I cannot afford a rebellion."

Vargan snorted. "We are dwarves and too practical to rebel over such a trivial issue."

"Trivial to you," the king replied. "It may not be so trivial to High Priest Chogar."

"I'll admit, Chogar is a stodgy old sot."

"And one with enough influence that I would prefer his approval."

"So, go get it and be done with it."

Korrigan sighed. "I hope it comes that easily." He turned to Ian. "If this situation is as urgent as I believe, we cannot afford to dally. I will set aside my court appointments for today and, instead, go speak with Chogar straight away. Give me until noon to convince him. Meet me at the hall then, and I will escort you into the catacombs."

"You are coming with us?" Ian asked.

"If the princess can truly converse with the dead, I would very much like to hear what Gahagar the Impregnable has to say." Korrigan stood. "Vargan, go speak with Bucklegon about assigning Ian and his companions sleeping quarters."

"That is not necessary," Ian said. "We will stay at Devigar's Tower while we are in the citadel."

"Oh. Of course." Korrigan raised a finger. "However, that tower now belongs to you, Ian. Devigar is gone and after his betrayal, I prefer not to hear his name."

"I apologize." Ian shrugged. "Old habits, I guess."

Korrigan smiled and clapped him on the shoulder, only to yank his hand away when Lionel snapped at him. He rubbed his hand, gave the drake a wary look, and then turned his gaze toward Ian "Despite the circumstances, I am thankful for your visit. I will see you at noon."

The king walked off.

Vargan trailed behind the king before stopping at the door. "You know your way around, Ian. I trust you do not need me."

"We will be fine," Ian reassured him.

"In that case, I need to make my rounds. I will see you later."

Left all alone, Ian stood. "Let's go visit Winnie."

The elf and the brownie followed closely behind Ian while Vic and Revita brought up the rear. As Ian recalled what happened before his departure from Ra'Tahal the previous autumn, his anxiety steadily rose. He was about to face Winnie for the first time since they kissed. How will she react? Regardless, Ian feared it would be an awkward meeting, but he was an adult, and he told himself that he could not avoid such things.

～

A SQUAT, cylindrical tower stood above Ian and his companions. Memories and emotions consumed Ian's thoughts, beginning with the day he had stood in the same spot with Korrigan at his side a year prior – the same day he had been introduced to Devigar. The elderly dwarf had been his master, his tutor, and guide as Ian adapted to life among the dwarves.

As Chancellor, Devigar had held a position of power. As translator, he also manipulated discussions between the king and foreign powers. Even that paled in comparison to his ultimate duplicity, when Devigar schemed with the Drow singer, Rysildar, to assassinate King Arangar and the Council. After Ian was wounded and Devigar expressed concern for him, the old dwarf revealed his role in the plan and explained that it was a sacrifice intended to help his people. Good intentions or not, Ian experienced the sting of Devigar's betrayal as much as anyone who survived that day.

All this passed through Ian's head in seconds. The memories and emotions from that time reminded him of just how much he had changed since then. While the tower had been his home for nearly half a year, just as much time had passed since he had last visited it. The day he left with Truhan to begin his training was when Winnie kissed him. He still did not know how he felt about her, and he worried about how she might react after not hearing from him for so long. *Will she be angry? Does she still care about me?* Questions, concern, and doubt held him in a trance until Lint spoke and broke the spell.

"Why are we standing here?" he asked. "Is it customary among the dwarves to stare at a door before opening it?"

Ian looked down at the brownie, who grinned at his own sarcasm. "Sorry. I have memories of this place." A gruesome image of his stomach torn open, his torso matted with slick blood, flashed before his eyes. "Some of those memories are...not good."

"Well, when you are through remembering, let us know."

Ian sighed. "Let's go in, but first, I think it best if I do something about Lionel."

Eyes closed in concentration, Ian thought. *Go. Explore the area. Return to this tower when you are finished.*

The drake leapt off Ian's shoulder, flapped its wings, and sailed up into the sky. Having dealt with Lionel, Ian walked up to the door and knocked. Technically, the tower belonged to him, but he had been away for quite some time and thought it would be rude to walk in on the person who lived there.

Anxiety caused Ian to fidget. For all of his might, there were areas where he lacked confidence. Women securely owned the top position on that list. The door opened, and he held his breath when he saw who stood in the doorway.

Red, curled locks cascaded over her shoulders, the color a striking contrast to her green dress. The dress hugged her voluptuous figure in a way that tugged at Ian's attention, making it difficult for him to avoid staring. His heart hammered against his chest as if it wished to escape. Somehow, he managed to speak despite the distractions.

"Hello, Winnie."

"Ian." Her green eyes sparkled as a smile turned up her full lips. "It is good to see you."

"May we come in?"

She looked past him, her gaze passing over each of his companions. "I know Vic and Revita, but who are the elf and the...little man?"

Lint waved a fist. "I am a brownie, you stupid human!"

"You will have to excuse Lint," Ian said. "He is prejudiced against humans and reacts that way when called one. The other is Shria-Li."

Winnie blinked. "The princess?"

"Yes."

She hastily curtsied. "My apologies, your highness."

Shria-Li waved it off. "There is no need for titles."

"Please," Winnie stepped aside. "Come in."

Ian gathered himself and walked past her.

The interior of the tower's main level was illuminated by sunlight streaming through narrow windows, the curtains all pulled open. Fresh, yellow flowers in a vase on the table gifted the room with a sweet aroma, a drastic change from the old, musty scent of parchment Ian remembered.

Winnie led them to a sitting area with a sofa and three chairs. "Would you care to sit? I can make some tea."

"Tea would be nice," There were things Ian needed to say, but he could only do so in private. He turned to his companions. "You four, wait here. I will help Winnie in the kitchen."

With Winnie in the lead, Ian crossed the room. A staircase curving along the tower's outer wall took them to the second floor. They passed through a doorway, into the tower kitchen. Cabinets ran along the wall on one side. A table and four chairs occupied the other. A long counter stood in the middle while a five-foot-tall brick oven waited at the far end of the room. Winnie approached the oven, slid a leather mitt on one hand, and opened the door. She stuck a poker inside and stirred the coals at the bottom. Orange glowed amid the shadows. She then shoved two birch logs into the coals. The bark began to smoke and curl. The orange sparks along the edges then turned to flames.

Meanwhile, Ian lifted the tea kettle from a shelf, walked over to the pump sticking out from the wall, and began to raise and lower the lever. Water poured out in bursts, slowly filling the kettle. He handed the filled kettle to her, which she then hung on a hook over the flames.

Turning from the oven, Winnie removed the mitt. "Would you care to sit while we wait for the water to boil?"

"Good idea." Ian walked over to the table and pulled out a chair.

Winnie sat across from him, shyly staring at her hands on the table while her fingers stroked one another. She then broke the silence. "I... I hoped you might visit sooner."

He sighed inwardly. "It is not that I didn't want to come back."

Her gaze lifted to meet his eyes. "You seem different. Older."

"And you look even better than I remember." The compliment came easy because it was true.

She beamed. "You are too kind."

Ian wanted to impress her and ensure she realized he had grown in more ways than she might guess. "I am trying to act like the man I want to become. That includes expressing myself rather than holding back, as I have done in the past."

Winnie bit her lip in a moment of contemplation. She then reached across the table and held his hand. "I have missed you."

A fleeting thought of Rina passed through Ian's head and was quickly erased by the girl sitting across from him. His pulse thumped when he stared into her emerald eyes. "I have missed you as well."

She beamed.

"How have you been faring?"

"Well enough. The dwarves are nice to me, and King Korrigan has visited me twice, just to ensure I have everything I need. I have made friends with some of the female dwarves, and we get together now and then to chat, but most of the time, I am alone."

"I know what you mean." Ian squeezed her hand. "My training was very isolated. For most of the past two seasons, Truhan was my only companion. And there were full weeks when he would leave me all alone." The memory of his aching loneliness brought him to the edge of tears. "Living in such isolation leaves one with little to do other than study and practice their art."

"Art?"

"In my case, that is magic."

Her gaze dropped to the table. "This magic...it is what you used to kill Rysildar?"

The image of the Drow singer flying out the window flashed in Ian's head. The dark elf's twisted corpse followed. There were times when that corpse spoke to him in his nightmares. The memory sent a chill down his spine.

"Yes."

Winnie lifted her head and stared into his eyes. "I thank you again for rescuing me. I feared..."

"I know." He patted her hand. "What of you? What have you been doing?"

"Not much." She shrugged. "Few people visit the tower, so I have taken up reading."

"You have?"

"Devigar left so many books. I thought to improve myself."

"His books are all written in Dwarvish or Elvish."

"I have learned much of Dwarvish, but the Elvish titles are beyond me."

"Still, I am impressed."

Her smile lit up the room.

Ian pushed past his reservations and forced himself to venture into more difficult territory. "I have a confession. When back in Shillings, I considered you as little more than a young woman seeking a husband to provide for her."

The smile slid off her face. She lowered her gaze in shame. "I would be lying if I said otherwise."

"Yet, you do not seem so dependent now."

"I try...but it is so lonely." Her voice cracked.

Ian pulled her hand close and held it tightly. "I know." The words emerged as little more than a whisper.

Winnie's gaze remained fixed on Ian as she rose to her feet, rounded the table, and stood over him. She bent, cupped his chin, and kissed him. Stunned, Ian did not react.

She pulled back. "I am sorry..."

He burst to his feet and snatched her hand before she could back away. "No. I...liked it. I like you."

Winnie eased closer until their lips almost touched. They remained there, two breaths mixing as one until Ian could stand it no longer. He pressed his lips against hers and wrapped his arms around her lower back. She melted into the kiss and returned his embrace, pulling him tightly against her. The contact and heat of their embrace sent his pulse racing.

A soft whistle came from the kettle, but Ian ignored it. The whistle grew louder until he was forced to pull back and glance toward it. Steam puffed from the kettle's snout.

His breath in gasps, Ian said, "We should bring the others their tea."

She gripped his chin and turned his face toward her. "I want you, Ian."

"Want me?" He blinked. "For what?"

In a throaty voice, she urged him, "Let's go to your bedroom."

"My bedroom?" He gulped at the implication. "What about the others?"

She gave him a naughty smile. "They are not invited."

He blushed. "No. I mean..."

Winnie stepped away and smoothed her dress, his gaze followed her hands as they flowed over hills and valleys. The sensuality of the simple action caused his body to further react. He could not imagine saying no to her request.

After a firm nod toward him, she spun around and slid the leather mitt on her hand. "We will bring them the tea, tell them that we have something to discuss, and then we will retreat to my room." Reaching into the oven, she lifted the kettle off the hook. With her free hand, she pointed. "Now, grab three mugs from that cabinet. You'll find bags of tea in the one below it."

The woman walked out of the room. Ian stood frozen for a beat before he rushed over to the cabinet, snagged three mugs, and dropped a tea bag into each. He then hurried downstairs, eager for what would come next.

CHAPTER 43
GHOSTLY WHISPERS

Ian slid his arms into fresh robes. These ones were black and lacked the tears his gray ones had endured over the past week. He cinched a red, silken sash around his waist and turned from the wardrobe pausing to appreciate the view.

On a bed in a room on the fourth level of his tower in Ra'Tahal lay a woman with only a thin sheet covering her naked body, giving him a not-so-subtle reminder of what treasures hid beneath the covers. Her red locks lay strewn across the pillow below her head, her gaze fixed on him while sharing a lazy smile.

Winnie rolled to her side and propped her head up with an elbow on the pillow. "I must admit that the second go was far better than the first. It leaves me wondering what heights we might achieve with a third run at it."

Ian blushed at her forwardness. "I am sorry about the first..."

"No. As I said, I expected as much. You are eager and unexperienced in this." She smirked. "However, you proved to be a fast learner. That much is certain."

His cheeks reddened further. He was unused to discussing this particular topic, yet her easy manner in the bedroom made him take a bold route with his reply. "As you may recall, fast was my problem the first time around."

Her laughter filled the air. She slid her hand across the bed. "Are you certain you don't wish to give it another go?"

An internal war waged within. One part of Ian urged him to accept her invitation. Another part reminded him of the dire nature of his quest, along with his appointment with Korrigan. He glanced toward the window. The building next door lacked a shadow, which meant that the sun was high overhead. "I cannot. I am to meet King Korrigan at noon."

She sighed. "I thought you might say that."

Ian sat on the bed, leaned in, and gave her a kiss. He ran his hand through her hair as he stared into her eyes. "I will come back soon, perhaps yet today. The future is uncertain, but if I ignore my duty, there may not be a future for you, for me, or for anyone else."

Winnie stared at him in concern. "Do you speak of war?"

"Worse than war. These monsters..." his vision flashed before his eyes. "They kill without care or cause. It does not matter if you are an elf, dwarf, or human, a man, woman, or child. They care not for gold or jewels. You cannot reason with them. They will sweep over the land and deliver death to anyone in their path."

She squeezed his hand. "You are scaring me."

"I am scared as well." He bent, picked his boots off the floor, and began to slide them on. "This is why I must put my own desires aside. My abilities, these feats I can perform...they come at a price in the form of responsibility. If my magic might prevent these monsters from slaughtering innocents across the realm, I must set all else aside and focus on that objective."

"And King Korrigan can help?"

"In truth, it is King Gahagar who can help."

She cocked her head. "I have heard that name. He was king before Arangar, but I thought he was dead."

"He is." Ian stood and walked to the door, where he paused to look back at her. "Be well, Winnie. I will be back. Perhaps today. If not. Soon. I promise."

Ian stepped out into the fourth-floor common area, took a deep breath to fortify his resolve, and headed for the stairs.

When he reached the main floor, he found Vic sitting on the sofa with Revita beside him. In the chair across from them was Shria-Li with her staff balanced across her lap. Lint sat on the edge of a nearby stool, kicking his legs in the air like a child in a swing.

"I was wondering when you'd come back down," Vic said.

Revita arched a brow. "Did you enjoy yourself?"

Ian's cheeks grew warm, and he sought to change the subject when a knock came from the door. He hurried over, thankful he didn't have to reply to Revita's question.

He opened the door to the king and a pair of dwarf warriors. "Korrigan," Ian said, "We were just leaving to meet you."

"I spoke with the high priest." Korrigan explained, "It took some convincing, but he agreed to allow you and Shria-Li to enter the catacombs, under my watch. The others are to remain here."

"But they would be no..."

Korrigan interrupted by thrusting a palm toward Ian. "I do not wish to create friction with the priesthood. It will be the two of you and that is all."

Ian turned toward his brother. "I am sorry..."

"We heard." Vic gave Ian a nod. "Revita and I will wait here and try to keep Lint from getting into trouble."

"Alright." Ian waved. "Come along, Shria-Li. We have a dead king to visit."

With the Staff of Life in her grip, she walked over.

Korrigan said, "You won't need a weapon. Where we are headed, you'll find nothing but long-dead dwarves."

"The staff goes where I go." The way she said it left no room for argument.

The dwarven king shrugged. "Suit yourself."

~

THE HALL OF ANCIENTS was a multi-tiered building in the citadel's eastern quarter. Towering columns crafted of sparkling white marble stood along the hall's facade. The beauty of the columns created a stark contrast to the stern, gray stone from which the rest of the keep was built.

With Korrigan on one side and Shria-Li on the other, Ian climbed the stairs and approached the entrance doors. A quartet of dwarven guards moved aside and opened the door for their king and his guests.

Once inside, they crossed an entrance hall encircled by gilded pillars. Tapestries of golden threads woven in intricate designs hung from the walls while a massive, elaborate chandelier of sparkling crystals dangled above the center of the room. Black marble tiles with gold and white striations stretched across the hall, leading them to a set of ornate doors plated in gold.

Ian pulled a door open and held it for his companions before following them inside the Hall of the Ancients.

Sixty feet up, murals of legendary battles adorned the coffered ceiling. Marble columns rose to support a balcony three-quarters of the way around the room. A short run of stairs carved into half-circles rose up to a round floor made of black and gold marble tiles. Upon a raised dais at the far end of the room stood an ornate, golden throne covered in red, padded cushions. The room was vacant, its interior illuminated by sunlight streaming through stained glass windows high above.

Korrigan ascended the platform in the middle and then continued onto the dais. He circled behind the throne and paused. "We dwarves might be boisterous on the outside, but inside, we hold many secrets. The entrance to the catacombs is among those secrets. You must swear not to tell anyone of what I am about to reveal."

"I swear," Ian nodded toward Shria-Li, who echoed his words.

The dwarf king dug into his pocket and pulled out a ring with a ruby cut into an eight-pointed star. He slid the ring on a finger and pressed the ruby into a recess on the back of the throne. A click resounded. The throne and the marble tile it was secured to slid forward to reveal a staircase leading down into darkness.

Korrigan began descending, paused six stairs down, and fumbled with something in the shadows. Light bloomed from a lantern in his hand. "Come along." He and the light continued downward.

"You go first," Shria-Li said. "I will follow."

Ian began down the steep staircase. He put his hand on the sides and ducked to get past the floor above then continued down, taking care with each step. His history of falling in such situations was warning enough. He did not want to tumble down on top of Korrigan.

Thirty-two stairs later, Ian reached the bottom and stood in a small chamber bordered by three arched doorways carved into stone. In the light of Korrigan's lantern, Ian noted Dwarvish script etched into the wall beside each doorway. When Shria-Li reached the bottom, Korrigan led them through an archway and down a tunnel of rock.

Dirt crunched beneath their feet as they walked past dark alcoves occupied by caskets. Above each alcove was a carving depicting a crest and the name of the dwarf buried there. The tunnel intersected with another, where Korrigan turned without pause. Repeatedly, the dwarf king led them down branching paths. He stopped outside an alcove and held the lantern up. Carved into the wall above the alcove was the name Arangar Handshaw.

"Here lies Arangar," Korrigan said gravely.

Ian stared at the casket, made of smooth, white stone. The image of a hammer was carved into the side of the casket. The former king was responsible for Ian's abduction and the enslavement of his entire village. Yet, Ian felt sorrow for the king. He had witnessed Arangar's murder, and despite his obvious faults, he had never wished him dead.

"You missed Arangar's funeral, Ian," Korrigan spoke in a solemn tone. "I thought you might wish to visit him for a moment, since you knew him."

Ian nodded. "Thank you."

"Come. Gahagar awaits just ahead." Korrigan led them down the tunnel, passed through another arched doorway, and entered a six-sided chamber with no other way out. Dark alcoves were cut into five walls while the arch they had just passed beneath marked the sixth. "This chamber holds the remains of Gahagar and his ancestors, who ruled for a thousand years before Gahagar was even born. His reign alone lasted for over five hundred years. While no other dwarf has lived and ruled for so long, Arangar's reign lasting only five years was both tragic and rare for my people."

Ian glanced from tomb to tomb. Deep underground and surrounded by corpses long dead, Ian felt as if ghosts lurked in the shadows. The hair on his neck stood on end, and he longed to draw upon his magic should something malevolent lurk in the darkness.

Despite the tightness in his throat, he asked, "Which crypt is Gahagar's?"

Korrigan pointed straight ahead. "The greatest king who ever lived lies there, waiting for you."

After all he had been through to get to this point, Ian was suddenly overcome by uncertainty. *What if I was wrong? What if my vision was nothing but my imagination? What if there is no paragon?* Doubts raged inside him until that uncertainty turned to guilt. If the entire quest was unnecessary, he had wasted Korrigan's time. Worse, he had caused Shria-Li to betray her parents by stealing the staff and using the portal stones.

A hand gripped his arm. "Are you well?" Shria-Li asked.

He nodded numbly. "I just hope..." *What do you hope, Ian? If your vision was true, the world would be in peril. If it was a lie, you are a fool and a burden to your brother and your friends.* "I hope we can discover the truth."

"I hope I can do this," Shria-Li said.

He turned toward her. "You don't sound confident."

"I barely comprehend my...ability. What if I fail?"

Her self-doubt was evident and reminded Ian of himself. Encouragement from others had helped him in the past, so he sought to do the same for her now. "I have faith in you, Shria-Li. A twist of fate brought me to Fae Gulch, so I might find you. That could not have been pure chance. Your ability was intended for this. It is why you stand here today and why we will succeed."

She nodded. "I will do my best."

The elf princess closed her eyes. A heavy quiet hung over them, the kind of silence that can only be experienced when deep underground and isolated from the world of the living. Uncomfortable minutes trickled past while Ian waited for something to happen. Nothing did.

Shria-Li opened her eyes and shook her head. "I am sorry."

Ian frowned. "But you only stood there, doing nothing."

"I thought to reach out with my mind, like I did with the dead oak in the Vale."

Korrigan snorted. "Dwarves are not trees."

"I suppose not."

"I have never heard a tree speak, so trying to have a conversation with one would seem foolish. Dwarves, on the other hand, we are a loud lot."

"Hmm," Ian rubbed his jaw, noting that his whiskers were close to an inch long and still growing. "What if Korrigan is right? What if you need to tap into your ability but speak aloud when doing so?"

"I will try." Shria-Li set her jaw while staring at the casket. "Gahagar. Wake Gahagar. I need you to wake."

Silence. Then, the casket shook. It shook again. The lid, made of carved stone and weighing twice Ian's weight, slid aside. Skeletal fingers covered by bits of gray flesh wrapped around the casket's edge. The lid flipped up, toppled to the floor, and broke into a dozen pieces. A corpse sat up, its face sunken in. It turned its bulging eyes toward them. Despite himself, Ian backed away from the horrific creature.

"Why have you woken me?" the creature croaked.

"Are you Gahagar the Impregnable?"

"I was...once...until I was betrayed."

Korrigan frowned. "Betrayed by who?"

"It was Fandaric and Kobblebon. They poisoned me. Among the clan leaders, only Arangar remained loyal."

The gasp from Korrigan was sharp and thick with shock. "Treason!"

"Yes, young Korrigan. Treason in the highest degree."

Making a fist, Korrigan growled. "I will see those two hanged."

"No." The corpse shook its head. "Do not sow strife among the clans. Seek unity. It will be necessary for what comes."

Ian asked, "What comes?"

"I...cannot say."

Remember why you came here, Ian. "We need your help, Gahagar. We seek to spare the living from a rising darkness. This cannot happen unless we find the Paragon."

"The Paragon? I have not heard anyone speak of the Paragon in a long, long time."

"Where can we find it?" Ian urged.

"I feared what might occur if others discovered the Paragon's capabilities. Thus, I sent the Paragon south, deep into the Glacia."

"The Glacia?" The region had come up in Ian's studies. That land stood a great distance to the south, far beyond even Shillings and

Darristan. There, it was so cold, winter never relented its grip, covering the land in perpetual ice and snow.

"Seek the Tower of Solitude," Gahagar said. "There, you will find the Paragon."

Ian frowned. "I have never heard of such a tower."

"It is far beyond civilization. You will find it on no map. The tower stands over a river of fire deep in the heart of a land of ice." The corpse of Gahagar shuddered. "I tire and must sleep."

Shria-Li glanced toward Ian, who nodded. "Thank you, great king. You may return to your slumber."

The corpse lay down and the chamber fell still.

"That was incredible." Korrigan shook his head. "I'd never had believed it if I had not seen it for myself." He then frowned at the shattered stone on the floor. "That will send the priesthood into a fit if I don't deal with it straight away. Come. I need to speak with the stone shapers and have a new lid crafted." The dwarf held his lantern up and headed toward the tunnel.

As Ian and Shria-Li fell in line behind Korrigan, she said, "We now know where to find this Paragon."

While she was correct, he worried about how long it would take to travel to the distant south and locate the fabled item. Time was the enemy, but it was an enemy Ian could not see or fight.

CHAPTER 44

PORTALS

The Staff of Life hummed in Shria-Li's ear. Since the moment she had touched it back in Havenfall, that soft song persisted. At first, she found it mesmerizing. Then, it became annoying. Now, after a full day of its persistent humming, it brought her comfort.

She led Ian, Vic, Revita, and Lint back down the same forest path they had taken early that day. Through gaps in the trees overhead, she caught a glimpse of red and black as Lionel circled above them. The path took them through a dense section of wood and then opened to a clearing to reveal the portal stone.

Without pause or word spoken, they all climbed upon the portal stone and gathered near its center. Ian peered up toward the sky until Lionel soared in from the northeast. The drake dove toward the stone, circled once and lightly settled on Ian's held out forearm.

"Alright," Ian said. "We are all here."

Shria-Li held the staff ready. "Here we go."

In her head, doubt lurked. *I hope I remember this right.* She placed the staff in the slot at the portal stone's center. The staff glowed with bright, golden light that flowed and swirled about her head. In her mind, she recalled a map her father had once shown her. That map marked the locations of stones across the southern realm. From it, she focused on the southernmost marking and willed the staff to take her there.

The runes and lines etched in the top surface of the portal stone began to glow. Their surroundings shifted and blurred to white.

~

IAN FELT a shift and queasiness in his stomach. The white surrounding him and his companions turned to a blur, which then solidified to a forest made of thick tree trunks so dark they were nearly black. Needles covered the bows high overhead. Although the clearing and surrounding forest were covered in shadow, the sky above remained blue. The air felt cool, as if the heat of the day could not penetrate the forest. In contrast to the unwelcome sensation coming from the trees, birds hidden in the branches serenaded their arrival.

Both Vic and Revita turned slowly while peering into the surrounding forest.

He said, "This wood is darker than the last. It feels...old."

Shria-Li replied, "It is old. This wood is also unused to strangers."

"Where are we?" Revita asked.

"This portal stone is the most southern of any I know about. It is in the heart of a forest that surrounds a solitary mountain. The Glacia begins somewhere south of this wood."

During the entire conversation, Ian examined the lines and runes marking the stone below their feet. From the moment he stepped on the first portal stone, he had been drawn to the design on its surface. The two translocations only increased his interest, and he now found it too compelling to even turn away – not until he had memorized every line.

"What is it, Ian?" Shria-Li asked.

He squatted and ran his hand over the runes. "This pattern. It is powerful."

Lint scoffed. "It is a bunch of lines carved into rock."

"No, this design tells a story written in a language you do not understand."

"And you do?"

Ian stood and backed from the portal stone's center while continuing to examine the runes. "I think I do."

Shria-Li asked, "What does it mean?"

"I believe that this is a construct, despite it having only a single layer. While the magic you use to power it is foreign to me, the construct is akin to others I know."

Revita looked at Vic. "Do you have any idea what he is talking about?"

"Not a clue," Vic admitted.

She shrugged. "Well, at least our journey south will be far shorter than we feared."

"Your journey..." Shria-Li took a breath and gave a firm nod. "I wish you luck on your quest."

Ian looked up from the portal stone to meet her gaze. "You are leaving us?"

"The staff does not belong to me. It belongs to my people. I must return it, and myself, to Havenfall. If something dire is coming, as I fear, we must prepare."

The elf princess had a critical role in Ian's quest, but now that they had spoken with the ghost of Gahagar, her task was complete. "I understand." He knew what it was like to be concerned about others and feeling responsible for them. "What about Lint?"

The brownie piped up. "I go with the goddess, even if she travels to the end of the world."

Revita frowned at Lint. "I didn't think being called a goddess would get old, but I was wrong."

"What do you wish me to call you, mistress?"

"Revita would be fine."

"Are you certain?" Lint sounded doubtful.

"If I am saddled with you, yes."

"Saddled?" The brownie put his hand behind his back. "I don't feel any saddle. Besides, you are too big to ride on me. Are you going to wear a saddle?"

She sighed and shook her head.

Ian approached Shria-Li and clasped her forearm. "Thank you for everything. I could not have done this without you."

She gripped his forearm in return. "Your quest is not yet finished, but I was glad to help as much as I could."

"I pray we see each other again."

She nodded. "If Vandasal wills it."

He turned from her, crossed the stone, and hopped down to join the others. They backed away from the platform as Shria-Li thrust her staff back into the center slot. A golden glow arose and grew brighter until Ian had to raise his arm to shield his eyes. The light suddenly dimmed. When he lowered his arm, the portal stone stood empty.

"What now?" Revita asked.

"Our destination lies to the south, but it will be dark soon," Vic said. "We risk getting lost without the sun to guide our direction."

"Give me a moment." Ian lifted Lionel from his shoulder and tossed him in the air. The fire drake circled around the clearing as it ascended. With his eyes closed, Ian extended his awareness through their connection until he saw through Lionel's eyes.

The drake rose up above treetops, the view expanding far beyond their immediate surroundings. Up and up, Lionel continued and through his eyes, Ian surveyed the countryside.

The sun, appearing like a massive ball of warm light, hugged the flat, western horizon. Distant, purple mountains ran along the northern edge of the forest while a solitary mountain peak covered in white thrust above the woods to the east. To the south, the treetops extended for many miles.

Ian opened his eyes. "We are near the heart of a giant forest."

Revita snorted. "I didn't need magic to tell you that."

He sighed. "My point is that we are unlikely to find a better location to camp before nightfall. As Vic said, traveling at night risks us getting off track, getting injured, or worse. So, I suggest we scavenge for some dead wood, build a fire, and camp near the portal stone for the night. We can head out at first light."

"Agreed." Vic took Revita's hand. "Let's go find some wood."

As the couple walked off, Ian turned toward the empty platform. Rather than joining them to search for wood, he climbed back onto the portal stone and resumed his study of the massive and intriguing construct.

TWO BODIES COVERED by dark cloaks lay beside a mound of blackened coals. Just a stride to the other side of the dormant fire, a drake slept curled up beside a pack and an abandoned cloak. Flocks of birds hidden in the surrounding woods sang of the impending sunrise. Ian ignored it all. In the gentle twilight of predawn, he stood upon the portal stone, again studying the lines and runes marked on its surface.

The construct tantalized him unlike any other. All night, it had haunted his dreams and left him tossing and turning, repeatedly disturbing Lionel, who lay at his side. When the first moments of daylight finally began to brighten the night sky, he quietly rose and climbed upon the portal stone.

The layout of the construct was distinctly different than the others he had studied. Memorizing the pattern required time and focus. He was determined to do so. It had become an obsession. Why, he could not say.

Vic's voice rose above the birdsong. "Ian?"

He glanced over to find his brother standing beside the platform. "Good morning."

"When did you wake up?"

Revita sat up and stretched. "Too early if you ask me."

Ian glanced up toward the pale blue sky. "Maybe an hour ago." It was difficult to be certain. "I found myself unable to sleep."

Vic looked down at the portal stone. "It is this pattern, isn't it?"

"Yes," Ian admitted.

"Well, I hope you are almost finished. We have a long way to travel and should leave soon."

"You two eat. Let me know when you are ready."

"Very well." Although Vic didn't say it, Ian heard the concern in his voice. "Where is Lint?"

"Exploring," Ian replied without looking away from the markings that held his curiosity hostage. "He said he would return at sunrise, so he should be along anytime."

As Vic and Revita dug into their packs, Ian focused on the portal stone's design. The increasing light made it easier to see. He ran his fingers down the lines and across runes, memorizing each twist and turn. With him focused, time passed quickly.

His study of the portal stone was interrupted when he saw boots standing just a few strides away. He looked up to find Vic standing over him.

"What is it?"

Vic said softly, "We need to leave, Ian."

"But you were to eat and wait for Lint to return."

"We did eat, and Lint came back fifteen minutes ago."

Ian looked up to find the treetops brightly illuminated by the sun. Narrow sunbeams peered through the trees to the east and shone across the clearing. He stood upright and gave a firm nod. "I think I am ready."

"Very well. Grab your pack and we will leave."

"That is not what I meant."

Vic frowned. "What, then?"

"I am ready to test this new magic."

"What new magic?"

"You will see." Ian jumped off the portal stone and walked across the clearing.

Stopping just shy of the tree line, Ian turned toward the clearing and Vic, who still stood on the platform a hundred strides away. Ian's gift flowed in, and he used a trickle of it to recreate the pattern marking the portal stone. Rather than the construct holding in place as a flat disk, it bent and wavered. At first, Ian fought to hold it flat. When that proved difficult, he did the opposite and encouraged it to expand. The disk folded as it expanded, its lines bending until they met each other. The completed construct appeared as a sphere the size of a pumpkin. Ian stared in wonder as the strange globe of glowing, intersecting lines and runes hovered in the air before him. Since it was three dimensional, it differed from the design on the portal stone, yet it was also the same. Notably, it felt right to Ian and was even more intriguing than the original design. *I must test it, but I need to give it direction, so the portal knows where to take me.*

Ian focused on a location far across the clearing, picturing it firmly in his mind while channeling his magic through the construct. A ribbon of light cut through the air before him and then spread until it became a perfect circle six feet in diameter. The opening was akin to peering through a glass tube with light shimmering at the edges. Beyond the portal, a dark forest lurked. Far across the clearing, a similar portal shimmered at the forest's edge.

With a breath of courage, Ian stepped through the gateway and emerged at the opposite side of the glade. He turned and released the spell. The portal disappeared with a pop.

"Ian!" Vic cried out, jumped off the portal stone, and ran toward the far end of the clearing, where Ian had just been standing.

"Here!" Ian shouted.

Vic stopped and spun around, his eyes gaping. "How?"

As Ian headed toward the center of the clearing, a grin spread across his face. "I did it. I have discovered a new way to travel!"

CHAPTER 45
PLUNDER OR BLUNDER

Arangoli lay awake. Having slept a fair portion of the previous day, in addition to much of the night, he was no longer tired. Idleness ate at him. It always had. Worse, it was his own idea to bribe Kasgan into sailing to Talastar rather than travel inland. *It will save us time,* he told himself. Again. Ships travel faster than going on foot, and even if they had horses, animals tire and they would make no progress while sleeping. A ship continued to sail throughout the night. *I wonder how far we are now.* Kasgan had promised the trip from Sea Gate would take no more than six days. Five if the winds were favorable. He looked up at the cabin's outer wall and found the light of early dawn outside the small porthole. *Finally.*

He swung his feet off the bed and sat up, taking care not to bump his head on the upper bunk. From beneath the bed, he pulled out his boots and began to slide them on.

A voice came from the upper bunk. "Can't sleep either?"

"'Morning, Paz." Arangoli spoke softly to avoid waking Rax and Gortch. "I've been awake for hours."

"Same here." Pazacar slid off his bunk and dropped down beside Arangoli. "If you are going on deck, I will join you."

Arangoli pulled his cloak off the bed and put it over his shoulders, choosing to forego his armor. "Get yourself dressed, then."

Moving with haste, Pazacar did just that and was ready in less than a minute.

Arangoli opened the cabin door and led Pazacar toward the stairs. They emerged on deck and stood beneath pale blue skies. The cloak of night still clung to the western horizon, far across the Endless Ocean. Many miles to the east, land stretched for miles, the hills and mountains appearing purple against the aura of the rising sun.

A sailor climbing the mainmast rigging paused and called out, "Sunrise, Captain!" He then resumed his climb toward the crow's nest.

Arangoli turned to find Kasgan standing below the quarterdeck. The captain closed the door to his cabin and waved. "Ho, Goli! Paz!"

The three dwarves moved toward each other and converged on the starboard side of the ship.

Kasgan said, "It appears to be another beautiful day, gents. If the winds hold and we encounter no rough weather, I'll have you in Talastar late tomorrow."

"Thank Vandasal," Arangoli said. "No offense, captain, but I am not cut out to be cooped on a ship. The idleness is driving me crazy. Now, if we hadn't run out of ale..."

Kasgan grunted. "Isn't drinking what got you into trouble back at Sea Gate?"

"That was wine. I'll admit it is best if I avoid it from now on."

"Aye," Pazacar agreed. "Ale on the other hand, is a gift from the gods. I think it unwise to upset deities, so ale is perfectly acceptable."

Kasgan laughed and patted Pazacar on the shoulder. "Well said, Paz! Truth to tell, since I've thirty barrels of wine on board, I am glad you are avoiding it. You drank my three barrels of ale in our first day out of Bard's..."

411

The man in the crow's nest called out. "Ship sighted! Starboard side and coming in fast!"

Arangoli, Pazacar, and Kasgan all stepped to the starboard rail and peered into the distance. The sun edged over the land to the east to reveal a white sail ten miles away. It only took a moment to determine its heading.

"Pirates!" Kasgan hissed. "She means to catch us."

"Can you outrun her?"

"Perhaps. Sunstreak is fast, but we are at the point where the coast begins to recede east. If we remain parallel to land, that'll take us right into her path."

"The other choice?"

Kasgan grimaced. "Sail out into the open sea."

"Which will cost us time."

"A day at least. Perhaps longer."

Arangoli could not stand the idea of an extra day on board, let alone two. "If you hold your heading?"

The captain seemed to measure the enemy vessel and her speed before replying. "The ship will catch us eventually. My guess, sometime this afternoon."

Arangoli turned the situation over in his mind. It only took a moment for him to make his decision. "In that case, hold your heading. Sail as fast as you can while I meet with my squad. When we have a plan formed, I'll let you know what you need to do."

Kasgan frowned. "I hope you know what you are doing."

"Sailing is your job. Mine is dealing with bullies. These pirates might pray on merchants like you, but they haven't seen the likes of us. Let's see if we can turn their quest for plunder into a deadly blunder."

~

ARANGOLI CROUCHED on deck while peering between a cluster of crates secured to the foremast by netting. To the starboard side, a ship sailed toward Sunstreak, as it had since early morning. Now, beneath the midday sun, the black flag atop the ship's mainmast was easily visible, as was her crew. With the ship no more than a few hundred feet away, Arangoli was able to count eighteen crew members on the enemy craft. If others lurked below deck, he wasn't certain. The plan he and his squad had hatched should work regardless...unless things turned in an unexpected direction. As a warrior, he was trained to expect the unexpected, but the uncertainty that came with such turns gnawed at him like a host of hungry termites feasting on a mighty oak.

"What do you think?" Gortch stood a stride away, pretending to mend the netting.

Rather than wearing his armor, which waited in his cabin, Gortch was dressed in a tan tunic and brown trousers. The tunic was stretched to the point of shredding, the trousers bunched at the bottom since they were made for a taller person. Both had been borrowed from one of the sailors and the outfit made him look like he was just another member of the crew.

"The ship will close the gap in just a few minutes." Arangoli thought it best to remind Gortch of the plan, since he would lead the Head Thumpers while Arangoli was away. "When they board, you are to continue to play the part of sailor until the shouts arise and the pirates onboard this ship react. That's when you dig out your weapon and lay waste."

"No quarter?"

"Only if they throw down their weapons. Distraction and surprise give us an advantage, despite their superior numbers. Besides, who knows how skilled they are in battle? I'd rather not risk any of you or Kasgan's crew because we were too soft."

Gortch gave a grim nod. "It will be done as you say."

The gap between the ships narrowed, and Arangoli decided it was time to act. "I had best get below deck."

"Luck to you and Rax."

"Thanks. Same to you and the others."

Staying low, Arangoli crept over to the open hatch and climbed down the ladder, into the shadows of the ship's hull. He pulled the hatch closed and secured it. When he reached the bottom, he turned to find Rax standing two strides away.

"How's it look?" Rax asked.

"As we expected. I count eighteen crew members on the enemy ship. There are likely to be a few hiding below deck as well."

"So, we'll be outnumbered."

"We are always outnumbered. However, that's not the worst of it."

"What, then?"

"They have a catapult mounted to the bow and a ballista at each rail."

Rax whistled. "I'd hate to see what damage a catapult could do to a ship."

Arangoli felt the same way. "Maybe we can figure out a way to use it against them."

"The plan calls for us to only..."

"I know the plan, but plans change in battle. You know that as well as anyone."

Gortch's voice came through the lattice in the hatchway above. "They are readying grappling hooks."

"It's almost time." Arangoli opened and clenched his fist while steeling himself for what must be done.

Rax turned to the barrel beside him and hefted the pack resting on it. His bow and quiver lay on the neighboring barrel. "I'm ready."

From above came Gortch's voice. "They have us hooked and are reeling us in."

"Let's go." Arangoli crossed the storage room and approached the hull door.

He undid the latches, opened the hull door a crack, and peered through the gap. Daylight greeted him, along with the rush of water. The pirate ship, its hull painted black, was no more than fifteen feet away. Ocean waves crashed against the hulls of both ships, sending a spray of salt water into the air, some of the drops coming through the doorway.

Peering up, Arangoli spied four ropes spanning the gap between ships. Pirates at the other ship's rail pulled on those ropes, drawing the two ships together. The distance between the two ships closed until the railings bumped against one another. By then, the pirate ship hull was only eight feet from where Arangoli stood. It might still be too distant for him to reach, but that was why he had asked the crew to leave a rope dangling from a cleat on the deck above. The rope had been fed through a gap in the rail and hung directly over the hull door, its tail end bouncing on the waves below.

Arangoli swung the hull door wide open, grabbed the rope, which was wet, and pulled it into the hull. He wound the rope around his left arm once and gripped it firmly. With his other hand, he pulled Tremor from the harness on his back and held it ready.

Shouts came from outside as pirates leapt from one ship to the other. Dozens of footsteps thumped on the deck above. Considering the shouting and stomping around, Arangoli hoped they wouldn't hear what he was about to do.

With a running start, he leapt out the hull door, swung toward the opposing ship, and came around with his hammer. It struck the hull with force. At contact, a thump released from the weapon. The wood cracked and a dent appeared. His momentum took him back to the open hull door, where he regained his footing, gathered himself, and launched again.

The second blow landed a foot below the first, cracking wood again and leaving a dent. On his third swing, he aimed higher. Tremor hit true, this time leaving a hole the size of his head while a crack connected the hole to the dent below. His momentum again took him back through the hull door but this time, he slid his hammer into the harness on his back, darted forward, and launched with all his might. He swung outward, raised his feet, and thrust. His boots crashed through the hull, and he shot inside the other ship. The rope slipped from his hand, and he fell on his side with an "Oof."

Ignoring the pain in his ribs, Arangoli pushed himself to his hands and knees while surveying the area. He was alone in a cargo hold amid barrels and crates. A beam of sunlight shone down through the lattice of a trap door in the ceiling and onto the ladder below it.

"Thank the gods." He stood as Rax readied to make the leap.

With a jump and a swing, Rax came at the opening with a hand extended. Arangoli grabbed the dwarf by the wrist, catching him.

"Take the rope." Rax urged.

Reaching down, Arangoli grabbed the rope's tail. "Got it."

When Rax let go, Arangoli reeled the rope in and tied it to a post.

Moving quickly, Rax lowered the pack from his back and began digging through it. He pulled out a jug and handed it to Arangoli, who ran over to the ladder. He climbed to the top, unlatched the hatch, and lifted it up a few inches. The ship's bow appeared empty while pirates were clustered mid-deck, along the port side rail. With nobody looking in his direction he opened the hatch fully and climbed out. He crouched behind the cluster of barrels beside the foremast and uncorked the jug. The odor of kerosene wafted out. Upending the jug, he poured the contents on and around the barrels. Rax joined him with another jug, which he dumped down the base of the foremast.

"Hurry and light the fire," Arangoli hissed.

With a flint in one hand and a striker in the other, Rax held them near the foremast. "I'm working on it." He dragged the striker across the flint. A spark shot out but was swiftly snuffed by the wind.

Worried they might be seen, Arangoli spun slowly, searching for anyone he may have missed until he spied something of interest on the bow, just a few strides away. At a crouch, he approached the catapult, examining it. The base was bolted to the deck, which made it impossible to turn but also kept it in place regardless of the weather or its load. The launch arm was already cranked back, but the projectile basket was empty.

A shadow moving at his feet was his only warning.

Training and experience set Arangoli into motion. He dove aside and rolled as a scimitar swept over him. After another roll, he came to his feet and drew his hammer. Standing before him was a tall man with thick arms and a barrel chest. His head was shaved, his face sporting a black goatee surrounded by tattoos that formed a strange pattern resembling magical script. The pirate lunged and slashed. Arangoli hopped backward, beyond the blade's tip. Before the man could turn his wrist for a backswing, Arangoli burst forward with a downward strike. The man hastily raised his sword for a block that resulted in a deflection. The hammer missed the man, the change of direction altering the momentum and causing Arangoli to stumble into the rail. He caught himself as the man launched an attack intended to remove his head from his body. Dropping to one knee, Arangoli launched a sweeping counterstrike. The pirate leapt to avoid it, but the hammer struck his boot, knocking his feet from under him.

"Goli!" Rax called out. "Let's go!"

Fire blazed along the foremast and the surrounding barrels. Shouts rang out, as pirates on both ships turned toward the flames. Cries of alarm were joined by calls to put out the flames. Arangoli glanced toward the other ship's foremast to ensure the Head Thumpers responded.

Gortch flipped the crate beside him over and Fesgar burst out from it. He tossed Gortch his mace and thrust his short sword into the back of a nearby pirate. From various points on the ship, dwarves emerged from hiding spots and attacked the distracted pirates.

The distraction almost cost Arangoli his life when the pirate he had been facing sat up and slashed low. Arangoli jumped onto the catapult and scrambled over it as the bald pirate climbed to his feet. The man scowled and climbed onto the contraption to follow. Arangoli wound back, causing the man to hesitate just long enough. Rather than launch an attack at the pirate, he targeted the catapult release. The catapult arm, a thick beam twelve feet long, shot forward while the pirate was standing with a foot to each side. The beam plowed through the man, lifted him into the air, and sent him flying over the prow.

Arangoli turned to find pirates racing toward him. The hatch door stood open and Rax was nowhere to be seen. He darted toward the hatch, hoping to reach it before the first pirate intercepted him. A tall, lean pirate with long strides closed in with a sword in his hand. Without slowing, Arangoli jumped high, folded his arms in, and plunged through the hatch as the tall pirate's sword swept overhead. Arangoli's feet struck the ladder three quarters of the way down, and he landed on this side.

The pirate stopped over the hatch and shouted. "They are down below!"

The lean man began climbing down as Arangoli regained his feet. With a wide swing, his hammer struck the ladder full on, shattering one of the poles in a spray of splinters. The pirate fell and landed on his back. Arangoli wound back and delivered a hard kick to the man's head before rushing across the hull, toward the opening. He peered outside to find Rax in the doorway to the other ship's cargo hold. The lines had been cut, the two ships parting. A pair of pirates fell into the water while shouts, cries, and the clang of steel on steel came from the skirmish above.

"Toss me the rope!" Arangoli bellowed as he slid his hammer into its harness.

Rax gathered the wet rope tail into a ball, wound back, and threw it. The rope swung out, uncoiled, and Arangoli snatched it by the end. He pulled it tight, grabbed ahold with both hands, and prepared to jump.

A massive explosion shook the pirate ship, the hull filling with a ball of flames. The force of the blast sent Arangoli tumbling out of the opening. The sky, the ship, flames, and smoke swirled around him as he somersaulted toward the water. The rope pulled taut, yanking his arms upward, and altering his fall. He slammed into Sunstreak's hull, his feet and lower legs splashing into the water. There, he dangled while his body spun toward the enemy ship. Flames engulfed most of the forward third of the pirate vessel. The upper portion of the bow was gone, and the burning foremast had fallen at an angle across the ship's deck, leaving the upper portion jutting out toward Sunstreak. Screams rose above the roar of the flames and the rush of the water. A burning pirate launched himself over the edge, his arms flailing as he plunged into the rough sea. A wave crashed into Arangoli, coating most of his body with seawater. He gasped and blinked while dangling with his legs still submerged.

"Goli!" Rax shouted from above. "Climb up!"

With determination, Arangoli reached up with one hand and clamped onto the rope. He pulled up and extended his other arm. Tired and wet, he reached and pulled again and again until Rax gripped him by the wrist. The skinny dwarf strained to lift as Arangoli pulled himself up. Stumbling backward, Rax lost his grip and fell onto his backside. By then, Arangoli rested on his stomach with his upper body inside the ship. He clawed his way forward a few feet more and then rolled onto his back. Air filled his lungs in ragged gasps. His arms felt like lead, his body soaked.

"I would hate to be on that ship," Rax said.

Gathering himself, Arangoli sat up and peered out the open hull door.

The pirate ship had fallen behind Sunstreak, a hundred feet away, the distance growing. Flames raged on the front half of the ship. The pirates on board pulled buckets of water from the sea, passed them along, and tossed the water on the fire. Their efforts appeared to have little effect.

"That explosion nearly got me." Arangoli said.

"I wonder what was in the barrels we set on fire."

"Naphtha. Kerosene. Whatever it was, that ship is done for." With a groan, Arangoli stood. "Close the hull door. Let's see how the others fared."

Arangoli staggered to his feet and limped across the cargo hold, toward the ladder. His ascent to the ship's deck was slow and labored. At the top, Arangoli flipped the hatch open, stuck his head up, and peered around. A dead pirate lay just a few feet from the hatch, and two more were in a pile beside the foremast. Of Gortch, or the other dwarves, he saw no sign until he climbed on deck and stood.

His nine dwarven companions stood at the starboard rail, along with most of the ship's crew. Arangoli and Rax crossed the deck, and just before they reached the others, the burning ship, now a quarter mile behind them, exploded.

Bursts of flame and black smoke came from multiple locations while debris sprayed out in all directions.

"That's the end of that ship," Arangoli said.

The others turned around.

Gortch looked him up and down. "You're wet."

"We had some trouble. How did you all fare?"

"A few scrapes and cuts on our end." Gortch gestured toward the corpses. "Five of the pirates did not make it back to their ship."

"In this case, it appears that they were the lucky ones." Arangoli turned and limped off. "Now, if you will excuse me, I need a change of clothes and a nap." The boredom he had experienced during the bulk of the voyage suddenly sounded appealing.

CHAPTER 46
A CLEVER SOLUTION

For a full day, Ian, Vic, Revita, Lint, and Lionel traipsed through the dark forest while maintaining a south heading. On numerous occasions, Ian had used gateways to help their advance, but he soon found out that the spell was taxing and would not work unless he could firmly picture his destination in his mind. Unless he had a clear line of sight over a decent distance, he saved his energy and they continued on foot instead.

Although it was early summer, the weather was pleasant for traveling, the coolness of the shadowy forest nicely balancing the effort required to tread uphill. In fact, the incline persisted throughout the day and by the time orange and pink shades began to color the clouds overhead, Ian guessed that they had gained a few thousand feet in elevation. As the sky darkened, the air cooled, and soon, Ian's breath visibly swirled in the air with each exhale.

By the time they entered a small glade and approached a rockpile surrounded by long grass, daylight had waned to the point where Ian could not see more than a dozen strides away.

"Lint," Ian called out. "We need to stop."

The brownie's voice came from the darkness ahead. "But it was just getting interesting."

"Traveling in the dark is too dangerous. Besides, I am exhausted."

The grass rustled ahead of Ian and Lint emerged a stride away. "You humans and your need to sleep."

"Yes. We know. Brownies are above resting. You can sleep when you are dead."

"You are learning the way of things."

Vic stood at Ian's side while surveying the area. "We can make camp here near the rockpile and resume travel in the morning."

Ian rubbed his hands together. His fingers were numb. "It is cold."

"We need a fire. Revita and I will look for wood while you two wait here."

Too exhausted to argue, Ian sat on a boulder with his back to the rockpile.

Lint climbed onto the boulder behind him. "You are a strange human."

"You think *I* am strange?" Ian found the concept ironic.

"Humans don't possess magic. Yet, you can do things I cannot otherwise explain."

"I realize that my abilities are uncommon among humans."

"It's not just that. Your magic feels foreign. Unnatural. Elves, dwarves, fairies, and other races possess magic, but their abilities all feel the same. Yours is different."

"What magic do brownies possess?"

"Brownies *are* magic." He thumbed his chest "We are like a spark that burns bright until it expends and fades."

Ian was uncertain how to take that. "Well, my magic, like my body, requires time to recover. This is why we sleep."

A nearby growl came from the darkness. A dark shape burst from the grass, launched toward Ian, struck him in the chest, and flipped him backward, over the boulder. As Ian fell to the ground, he thrust his hands toward his attacker, gripping a handful of fur. Lionel squawked and launched himself into the air. Ian landed hard, the back of his head striking the ground. Pain shot through his brain. The edges of his vision blackened while claws dug into his chest.

The wolf standing over him snarled and snapped, its eyes like dim, amber coals within the darkness. Teeth flashed and the creature drooled on him but Ian kept his arms straight while holding fast to the wolf's chest fur. Having grown up in wolf country, Ian had been taught from an early age about rock wolves. They earned the name from jaws powerful enough to split stone. If the wolf clamped its jaws on any part of your body, the fight would be over.

A flash of amber illuminated the night. Flames billowed from Lionel's open mouth and licked the wolf's dark fur, causing the creature to spin away from Ian. The fire burst faded. The drake flew in with his legs extended and struck. Lionel's claws latched onto the top of the wolf's head. The wolf yipped and snarled while thrashing and trying to bite its attacker. Lionel flapped his wings rapidly while holding tight and keeping his body elevated.

Ian rolled away from the fracas and scrambled to his feet. Before he could act, Vic burst from the darkness, rushed in, and swung. His mattock drove into the wolf's back and sparks of blue sizzled near the wound. The beast shrieked, staggered, and fell onto its stomach as Lionel flew off into the darkness. Vic tore his mattock free and swung again. The weapon struck the wolf's head with a crack, ending the struggle.

Vic stood over the wolf, panting while gripping his mattock.

Revita rushed in with wood in her arms. "What happened?"

"This wolf attacked Ian." Vic peered out into the night. "They run in packs, so there may be others out there."

Ian rubbed his chest. It was sore and likely punctured from the animal's claws. His head ached as well, but things could have gone much worse. *Lionel,* he sent the call out, suddenly concerned for the drake. He then sensed Lionel's approach. The drake flew in and landed on the rocks beside him.

Reaching out, Ian caressed Lionel's head. "That's a good boy," he crooned.

Lint hopped on top of the boulder where Ian had been sitting prior to the attack. "That was fun." Words poured out of him in a steady stream. "I have never seen an animal like this one. It tried to eat Ian's face, which is gross. Who would want to eat a human? Yuck."

Vic stood beside Ian. "Are you alright?"

"I am fine." Ian rubbed his sore chest. "Nothing more than a few bumps and bruises, thanks to you."

"I should not have left you alone."

"I wasn't alone. Lionel was here, and his intervention saved me."

"His flame was the beacon I needed to find you." Vic turned to Revita. "Let's build a fire. Rock wolves hate fire, so that should keep them away."

Using the wood Revita had gathered, Ian created a pyramid of dead branches while Vic used his mattock to clear away the surrounding grass, flowers, and weeds. Ian then stepped back and casted a spell. Flames engulfed the pyramid of branches for a few seconds. When the spell ended, a fire continued to burn.

"Ian, you stay by the fire and watch for trouble. Revita and I will find more wood. When we come back, we can settle in for the night."

As Vic and Revita walked off into the darkness, Ian put his back to the rockpile searching the glade for any signs of movement. All the while, a troubling emotion he thought he had overcome clutched at his confidence. His magic often made him feel invincible, but the wolf's surprise attack had nearly cost him everything. An image of him lying on the ground with his throat torn out flashed before his eyes. Cold and scared but refusing to admit it to anyone else, Ian hugged his arms tightly and stared into the night with his fire drake at his side.

~

THE NEXT DAY of traveling through the dark forest passed in a similar manner to the first. A lack of visibility again limited the use of Ian's gateways, so most of the distance was covered on foot. In addition, he began to worry about their provisions. Korrigan had filled their packs with dried meat, fruit, and bread, but that food would be exhausted in a few days and they had yet to even reach the fabled ice fields of the Glacia. As the day went on and they continued to trudge south, Ian considered the problem and how he might use his magic to overcome it.

He had determined that the portals he cast would take him to a location if he could picture it well. However, he had no idea if there was a limitation regarding distance. Thus, he decided that they would stop early, so he might perform a test.

It was late that day, with the sun ready to set in the west, that they came upon a massive pine with a dark alcove in its ten-foot-diameter trunk. The recess was large enough for Ian to stand in. More notably, a unique knot jutted out from the recess. To Ian, the knot looked like a 12-pointed star.

"Let's stop here," Ian said abruptly.

Vic and Revita turned toward him while Lint climbed on a fallen tree and put his hands on his hips.

"It is still daylight," the brownie said. "Don't tell me that you are too tired already."

"No. I want to try something." Ian concentrated on the tree as he spoke.

Vic looked up at the big tree. "I hope you don't want me to chop this tree down. Not only would it be a shame to kill such a glorious tree, it would take forever to hew through that trunk."

"No. It's nothing like that."

Ian fixed the tree firmly in his mind. He then thought back to his room in Devigar's old tower. The time he had spent there with Winnie remained near the forefront of his thoughts, but he was forced to push images of her aside and think about the room itself – the furniture, the crack in the ceiling, the direction the windows faced. With the room firmly in his mind, he cast the translocation construct. A ribbon of light tore through reality and separated to reveal the exact view pictured in his mind. Resolute, Ian stepped through and allowed the gateway to snap shut.

～

VIC WATCHED as his brother stepped through a shimmering hole in the air and disappeared. The opening snapped shut with a pop. The forest fell quiet.

Lint threw his hands up. "How are we ever going to get anywhere if you humans keep getting distracted?"

"The pipsqueak has a point," Revita said. "Where did Ian go? This ridiculous quest was his idea. He had better not have left us to the wolves."

Angry at the accusation, Vic turned toward her, his tone terse. "Ian would not do that. After everything we have been through, you have no right to question his loyalty."

"Then, what is he doing?"

"I...don't know," he admitted. "Just sit tight and wait until he returns. I am sure he will explain what this is about."

So, they stood in silence. Waiting. Meanwhile, the shadows thickened as the sun set somewhere beyond view. As the minutes passed and night darkened the sky, Vic grew increasingly anxious.

"How long do we wait?" Revita asked. "Should we just build a fire here?"

"I don't know," Vic admitted.

Just as he was about to walk over to where Ian had been standing before he disappeared, the air shimmered, split, and a gateway opened. Warm light flickered from the gateway.

Ian stepped out and flashed a grin. "How would you like a hot meal and a soft bed for the night?"

Vic blinked. "Where were you?"

"Come along. I'll show you." Ian stepped back through, fading from view.

Lint whooped, raced past Vic, and rounded the gateway before leaping out of sight.

Taking Revita by the hand, Vic walked past the edge of the gateway, so he could see through it. A bed, a desk, and an open door were visible through the opening. The room was illuminated by indirect torchlight coming through the open doorway. The couple stepped over the shimmering rim and into a bedroom.

Ian, who stood to the side of the room, lowered his hand and the gateway popped out of existence. Lint was nowhere to be seen.

"Where are we?" Vic asked.

"We are back in my tower in Ra'Tahal."

"What?" Vic asked, "We are back where we started? Why would you do that?"

Ian gripped him by the wrist. "Easy, Vic. I can bring us right back to where we were when morning comes. That is what I was testing."

"I see." Revita nodded. "You can bring us back here each night and then we can continue our journey the next morning. Clever." She pointed. "What happened to the table?"

Vic followed the gesture and realized that the small table in Ian's room was now split down the middle, the two halves tipped in toward each other at an angle and ready to fall if anyone should move either piece.

Ian explained, "I discovered that gateways slice through more than air. Considering how it cut through the table like that, I will have to be careful not to open a gateway near anybody." He walked through the open doorway. "Enough about the table. Let's head downstairs, where Winnie is preparing dinner."

When Revita moved to follow Ian, Vic gripped her arm, stopping her. She turned toward him and arched a brow in question, but Vic waited until Ian was beyond earshot.

"See," he whispered. "I told you he would not abandon us."

She sighed. "It's not that I truly believed he would. He is like you and tries far too hard to be a good boy."

"Why'd you say that, then?"

"I don't like it when others change plans and don't explain themselves first."

"Really?" He smirked. "I find that ironic."

"Yes. I know I am guilty of the same thing, but I am a thief. It is what we do."

"So, you are faulting Ian for this behavior because he is an honest person?"

She shrugged. "Basically, yes."

Vic rolled his eyes. "Are all women this complicated, or are you special in this regard?"

"Both, I suspect. Come along. I am starved." She walked out, leaving him alone.

Vic glanced around the dark room and realized how nice it would be to sleep in a warm, soft bed. That, along with a belly full of freshly cooked food, lifted his spirits. He stepped out into the torchlit corridor and descended to the second floor.

CHAPTER 47

RIVER OF FIRE

S atisfied and proud of his cleverness, Ian trailed behind Lint, Vic, and Revita.

His latest gateway had returned them back to where they had ended the journey the prior day, over a thousand miles south of Ra'Tahal. With buoyed spirits after a solid night of sleep, a warm bath, and a hot meal, they set out at a good pace to continue their journey.

By mid-morning, the trees thinned and gave way to sprawling, uphill fields. Sporadic stands of trees and wayward pines dotted the open surroundings. The expanded view allowed for their travel to accelerate as Ian wove gateways from hilltop to hilltop. Each leap covered miles as they tracked south beyond any map he had ever seen.

Fierce winds blew across the open land, leaving them thankful for their cloaks. The hours seemed to trickle by, and the sun's path across the sky slowed. Then came the snow and ice.

At first, it was nothing more than patches of white on the south side of any tree or rock cluster. Not long afterward, snow and ice dominated the landscape. As the day waned, Ian became weary and he required rest before he would attempt another gateway. All the while, the weather grew steadily colder.

When the sun was near the horizon and Ian's body and mind were ragged from the steady use of his magic, he memorized a spot where jagged, gray rock jutted up from an ice-covered hillside. Only once that spot was firmly etched in his mind did he open a gateway back to his tower in Ra'Tahal. Ian and his companions hurried through, and when Ian allowed the portal to fold, a weakness overcame him, his knees folding as the room spun. Thankfully, Vic was there to catch him and help him into bed. Lying there in his clothes, Ian slid into sleep in seconds and did not wake until morning.

~

RESTED, fed, and wearing an extra layer of clothing, including mittens to keep his hands from freezing, Ian and his party set out for another day of travel.

Privately, Ian worried about finding the Tower of Solitude. The Glacia seemed endless, its white landscape stretching from horizon to horizon. With each new hilltop he crested, he prayed for some sign to inform him that they were on the right path. *What if we missed it by twenty miles and have already passed it?* Considering the vastness of the ice fields, he worried that they might be a hundred miles off course, which would only grow worse with each new leap.

Six hours into the fourth day of travel, they stepped through a gateway and onto a white slope below a rocky crag. They trudged along the hillside, the snow coming to their knees and filling Ian's boots. He suffered in silence rather than complain. Ahead of them, Lint skittered along the surface of the snow, which left Ian jealous. He suspected he could figure out a way to use his magic to replicate that act but chose to save his energy for gateways. The steady use of such taxing magic had cost him the prior day, and he did not want to push himself too far, fearing he might send himself into a coma.

They rounded the rocky spire, climbed a small rise, and stared out across the frozen wasteland. For the first time in hundreds of miles, something new graced the view.

A thick column of white rose above the ground to the southeast, beside a range of snow-covered mountains. The column broadened as it climbed in elevation, masking the stratosphere across the southern horizon. A faint warm glow illuminated the bottom of the column.

"What do you suppose *that* is?" Vic asked.

Ian frowned in thought. "Steam, I believe." He then recalled Gahagar's final words. *The tower stands over a river of fire deep in the heart of a land of ice.* "It must be the river of fire. Heat like that would melt snow and ice and turn it to steam."

"River of fire?"

"It was something Gahagar mentioned when we asked where to find the Tower of Solitude. He said it stands over a river of fire." Ian pointed toward the mountain with its upper reaches masked by white clouds. "That is a volcano."

"We are going toward an active volcano?" Revita asked.

"Yes."

The target location was too distant for Ian to see clearly, so he turned his gaze on the flatlands between them and the mountain range. Amid the snow drifts, he spied a dark overhang. With that location pictured firmly in his mind, he crafted a gateway.

~

THE WIND TUGGED at Ian's cloak, forcing him to hold it close as he trudged through the snow. Steam covered the sky above, masking the sun. The odor of sulfur tainted the crisp, clean winter air that had dominated their surroundings the prior two days. Steam swirled around them, reducing visibility to no more than a dozen strides. The steam left their skin, hair, and clothing damp. The air began to warm, and an amber glow loomed ahead. The snowpack eased with exposed rock becoming common. The steam parted to reveal what lay ahead. Everyone stopped to stare.

They stood a few hundred feet above a narrow lava flow. To the east, orange, fiery tracks ran down a mountainside of black rock surrounded by ice and snow. The molten stream flowed past and tracked west until fading into a deep chasm. A half mile beyond the lava flow stood a tower. Sunlight reflected off the ice coating the tower, making it appear as if it were crafted of glass.

"The Tower of Solitude," Ian said. "We found it."

Revita grunted. "I'll admit, I doubted if the tower even existed. For once, I am glad I was wrong."

Lint, who had been riding in Revita's pack, peered over her shoulder. "A river of fire. It is horrible. How far does it run? What if it flowed all the way to the Vale? Can anything stop such a frightful monstrosity?"

Ian said, "It is lava, Lint." He pointed. "The flow comes from that volcano, but the molten rock originated from deep underground."

The brownie's eyes somehow widened further. "What other horrors lurk deep underground?"

It was a strange question yet something about it was familiar. Ian tried to recall what, but it was as if it were a memory just beyond his reach.

Vic pointed. "Ian. Can you get us to the other side? From my previous experience with lava, I can tell you we don't want to get too much closer."

"Give me a moment."

Ian surveyed the upslope beyond the lava flow. Amid the jagged, black rock and ice, he spied a unique formation midway between the lava and the tower. The rock looked much like a gopher on its hind legs, except this rodent stood eight feet tall and was made of stone. He concentrated on the formation and cast his spell. A gateway opened before him. He stepped through, moved aside, and waited for the others. When everyone was across, he released the spell and turned toward the tower.

The structure was massive, easily eight times the size of his tower in Ra'Tahal. Hundreds of feet of gray stone thrust up toward the sky. Ice and snow covered much of the tower, giving it a glossy sheen. Icicles lined the bottom of every protruding feature. The tower's uppermost levels were obscured by steam.

"Let's walk from here," Ian suggested. "I think it best if I save my energy in case my magic is needed once inside the tower."

They set off toward the solitary fortress. As they walked, Ian wondered who built such a massive structure so distant from civilization. The tower, hidden deep in a frozen wasteland, was surely intended for its inhabitants to be isolated. When he considered the bleak surroundings and lack of potential visitors, the tower's name suddenly made sense.

The closer they got to the tower's base, the larger the building appeared. However, there was no door visible, and the only windows Ian could see began a hundred feet up.

"Let's circle the tower and look for a way inside," Vic suggested.

Heading in a counter-clockwise direction, the small party slogged through snow and across ice-coated rock. Like the northern face, the east revealed no entrances. Continuing, they worked their way around the southern side when a mighty roar came from high above, the sound echoing across the empty landscape. Ian backed from the tower while peering up into the mist-covered upper reaches. A dark shadow moved within the mist. The silhouette took shape, and what it revealed caused Ian to stagger backward and fall into the snow.

A dragon swooped down and banked above them with its webbed wings extended. The monster was as big as a house, its wingspan as long as a ship. Iridescent purple scales covered its head and neck while its body, tail and wings were a silvery black. The dragon shot out over the frozen plain south of the tower, turned again, and came toward them. It released another mighty roar, opened its mouth, and a cone of flames burst forth.

Ian scrambled to his feet and dusted the snow off his backside. There was nowhere to hide, and the creature was too fast to outrun. While Vic and Revita were armed, their weapons were unlikely to be effective against such a mighty beast, so Ian drew in his magic, cast a construct, and unleashed a deadly spell.

A bolt of lightning shot toward the dragon, striking it full on. The electricity fizzled and faded away, leaving the dragon unharmed. The monster dove toward them with its talons extended, but Ian was so shocked about his spell failing, he did not react. Black claws as big as a longsword came toward him at a terrifying speed. He was about to die.

CHAPTER 48

HATCHLING

The dragon sailed in with its wings arched and talons extended. Vic prepared to dive out of the way when he noticed Ian frozen in place. With a lunge, Vic drove his shoulder into Ian. They both toppled to the snow as the dragon's claws raked across the ground, right where they had been standing.

Vic rolled off Ian, reached over his shoulder, and pulled his mattock from its harness. Rising to his feet, he spun around in search of the monster and found it banking a half mile away.

Revita appeared at Vic's side. "You don't intend to fight that thing, do you?"

"I'd rather not, but unless we can get out of here, I don't see another option."

Ian sat up. "My magic didn't affect it."

Lint scrambled onto the rock beside Ian. "Dragons are immune to elemental attacks."

"They are?" Ian blinked.

The brownie snorted. "Everyone knows that."

"I didn't know." Ian climbed to his feet and peered up into the sky. "Lionel is up there."

"The drake?" Vic glanced away from the dragon as it rounded the tower. "Where?"

"In the mist above us."

The dragon faded behind the tower.

"While it is out of sight, run!" Vic shouted.

They took off running the way they had come but only made it a few dozen strides by the time the dragon reappeared, coming straight for them. The dragon dove low and leveled with its wings spread wide, just above the ground. It was a few hundred feet away when a small, dark shape dropped from above and landed on the dragon's head.

"Lionel!" Ian shouted.

The dragon roared, rose, and turned while the drake clung to its head. Both creatures sailed up into the mist, disappeared briefly, and then reappeared with the dragon diving downward in a rapid spin. Lionel's grip broke free and the momentum sent him sailing off into a freefall. The drake spun and spun while plummeting toward the ground. Just a few dozen feet from splattering on the rocks, Lionel extended his wings, banked, and leveled. The dragon turned and sped after the tiny drake.

Vic shook his head. "Lionel is in trouble, but at least the dragon is distracted."

"For now," Revita added.

"We need to help him," Ian said while watching the large monster chase the smaller one.

"How? We can't even help ourselves."

Ian's brow furrowed, his face taking on a familiar look.

"What is it, Ian?" Vic asked.

Seemingly ignoring Vic, Ian spun toward Lint. "You said that dragons are immune to elemental magic. What about other magic?"

The brownie scratched his head. "Well, some magic can affect them, otherwise they would be able to bring fire to the Vale."

"Right." Ian turned again, set his jaw, and closed his eyes.

"What are you doing?" Vic asked.

"Reaching out to Lionel."

"Why?"

"I need him to bring the dragon back this way."

Revita blurted "What? Why would you do that?"

Vic gripped her hand and spoke softly. "Ian has a plan."

"What plan?"

"We will see."

"You know I hate not knowing the plan," she growled.

"Yes. Now, hush and wait until he tells us what to do."

The drake, with the dragon close behind, turned back toward the tower. The dragon opened its mouth wide and blasted forth a cone of fire. Just before the flames reached him, Lionel turned again, this time heading straight toward Vic and his companions. When Lionel dove toward the ground, the dragon followed. The small creature leveled just before impact. The dragon did the same. All the while, they closed the distance, causing Vic to tense and ready himself to dive aside again. Lionel sped right between Ian and Vic. The dragon tucked its wings in and opened its maw while heading right toward Ian.

At the last moment, Ian thrust his arms forward and opened a gateway. The edges spread and expanded to thrice the size of any he had created before. The dragon flew through the gateway and reappeared a quarter mile away. It crashed into a boulder that gave the impression of a gopher on its hind legs. The boulder shattered, the force of the impact, sending shards of rock, ice, and snow spraying through the air. The dragon skidded and tumbled before coming to a stop a few hundred feet later.

Ian lowered his arms, the portals snapped closed, and he collapsed.

Vic took one look at his brother, lying in the snow, and weighed his options. Should the dragon recover, they would all be dead, Ian included. Thus, Vic burst into a run toward the downed creature, covering the four-hundred-foot gap at a full sprint.

The monster opened its eye as Vic drew near. When he was a few strides away, Vic wound back, prepared to drive his mattock right into the monster's slit pupil.

A voice echoed in his head. *Please, do not hurt me.*

Stunned, Vic stumbled and fell to the ground, causing the pick end of his weapon to plunge into a narrow gap in the rock, wedging itself. Vic looked up as the dragon raised its head and turned its massive snout toward him.

He urgently thought, *Please, do not hurt me.*

The dragon blinked.

Vic yanked his weapon but it held fast in the narrow fissure. He gripped it with both hands and pulled backward. When it broke free, he stumbled a few steps and landed on his backside. The dragon's massive, slit pupils remained fixed on Vic. The creature still lay on its stomach, a dozen strides away – close enough to roast Vic alive if it chose to do so.

Again, he tried. *Did you hear me?*

The dragon spoke aloud. "I hear you, human. How can this be?"

"I..." Vic stammered as he scrambled to his feet. "I don't know."

The dragon pushed itself up from the ground and stood over Vic. Its shadow blotted out the sky. "I would have your name."

Happy to talk to the massive creature rather than fight it, Vic complied. "I am called Victus."

"Ah. The name of a champion."

"I...suppose." Vic asked. "What is your name?"

"Umbracan is my name, given to me by Vandasal himself."

If I keep the dragon talking, perhaps it won't eat me. "You were named by a god?"

"Named and given the responsibility to protect the Tower of Solitude."

"Protect the tower from whom?"

"I do not know. I was told to ensure that nobody enters...or leaves."

"Why?" Vic was genuinely curious.

"Again, I do not know. However, I find such duty exceedingly tiresome."

"You could just leave."

"And go where? We dragons are unlike other creatures. Our lifespans greatly exceed those of humans or even elves, but we require purpose. Without purpose we wither and slide into endless slumber." The dragon glanced toward the tower. "It has been pleasant speaking with you, human, but it is now time for me to eat you and your companions. I do hope you understand."

"Wait!" Vic blurted. "Why would you eat us?"

"I told you. Protecting the tower is my purpose. It was assigned to me shortly after I hatched last autumn."

Vic flinched. *It cannot be, can it?* He asked, "You hatched last autumn?" He recalled four dragons emerging from the egg in the secret chamber beneath Ra'Tahal. "Were there three other dragons?"

"My siblings. How did you know?"

"I was there. I visited your egg every day until a tremor caused the tunnel to collapse. Rocks fell from the cavern ceiling, stirring the lava pool and creating a tremendous heat. That is when the egg cracked and four dragons emerged."

Umbracan bent its neck and brought its snout within a few feet of Vic, who stood still despite an urge to back away. The dragon's nostrils flared as it sniffed. Its eyes narrowed before it pulled back and tilted its head. "It is you."

"What is me?"

"I remember you. You kept my hatchlings and I company. This is why your thoughts can touch mine. We are bonded."

Bonded? Vic wondered exactly what the dragon meant.

Yes. Bonded. The dragon's voice echoed in Vic's head.

"What does this mean?" Vic asked.

"It means that I am not going to eat you. Frankly, humans are quite unsavory anyway."

"Oh. Well, I would hate to give you indigestion."

The dragon chortled, the sound frightening rather than soothing.

Despite his nervousness, Vic held his ground and continued their discussion. "My companions and I have traveled far in a quest to find the Tower of Solitude. How do we gain entrance?"

"You wish to enter the tower?"

"We must."

"But I explained my purpose to you. I am to prevent such a thing from occurring."

Vic needed to convince the dragon, knowing that Ian would never give up his quest, not after coming so far already. "Listen. We do not do this on a lark. Within the tower is something called the Paragon. Whatever it is, this thing is important. We must have it. The fate of the world depends on it."

"The world?" The dragon cocked its head again. "What danger could threaten the entire world?"

Ian's voice came from behind Vic. "A darkness comes. A vile army of monsters that will sweep over the land if left unchecked. They are mindless and driven by a hunger for destruction rather than intelligence."

The dragon narrowed his eyes. "Who are you, human?"

"I am Barsequa Illian."

Vic added, "He is my sibling."

"Your name means Gifted One does it not?"

"It does."

"Then it was your magic that caused me to crash."

Ian held his hands out. "I was only protecting myself and my companions."

"And this enemy you say will blacken the land? From where do they come?"

Ian stared into space. "They will sweep down from the north, but these creatures seek darkness. I believe they come from...somewhere deep underground. They are called orcs."

"Orcs?" the dragon's nostrils flared and a puff of smoke billowed from them. "Vile creatures. But are you certain they are orcs?"

Ian said, "These creatures are sort of like humans but with black, leather-like skin. Their movements are quick, their talons dripping with poison."

"Definitely orcs." The dragon stared at Ian for a beat and then turned back toward Vic. "The way into the tower is hidden at the base of the fire mountain. When the sun nears the western horizon, its rays shine through windows on the upper floors of the tower. That light refracts through a crystal in the tower and is magnified into a single sunbeam. Follow that ray of light, and you will find a tunnel entrance. That tunnel leads to the warrens beneath the Tower of Solitude. At the heart of the warrens is a lift that rises to the tower's interior."

Vic frowned, fearing a trap. "Why did you reveal the location of the entrance?"

"Dragons are reclusive, yet we abide other creatures and acknowledge their place in this world. Orcs do not belong. Their mere presence is a blight that stirs anger and hatred within even the most placid of dragons."

"You hate orcs?"

"We do."

"You want us to succeed?" Vic asked.

"I do. In fact, should you survive your visit to the tower and emerge with your prize, I will join your quest. Together, we will defeat this army of darkness." The dragon reared up and thrust its chest out. "Now, go. I must return to my duty as the tower's protector. Do not come near it again, or I will be forced to slay you." Umbracan tilted his head, his words echoing in Vic's mind. *When the time comes for us to battle, call out to me. I will come. I welcome this new purpose.*

Vic replied, *I pray it will not be required, but I would feel blessed to have such a glorious warrior on my side.*

Well said. Be well, Champion. Umbracan stretched its wings out, flapped them, and lifted into the air. The dragon hovered above Vic for a moment and then sailed off toward the tower. It circled twice while ascending before it slid into the steam-covered upper reaches and was gone.

CHAPTER 49
HIDDEN ENTRANCE

The afternoon waned slowly while the sun gradually migrated from its apex, toward the horizon. Ian had listened closely to the dragon's instructions, memorizing every word. In fact, he had recited the entire sequence a dozen times over, telling himself that he had to wait. There was no rushing the sun. Yet, the forces of evil were not held back by such restrictions. How many lives would be lost because of this latest delay?

After the dragon flew off, Ian and his party marched east and settled in at the foot of the mountain. A hundred feet away, lava flowed down the hillside to join the glowing, amber river crossing the plains. Even at that distance, the warmth of the molten rock helped to balance the chill breeze coming across the ice fields.

Little was said during this wait. Concern for what unknowns lurked in the massive tower consumed most of Ian's thoughts while the memory of the dragon encounter and the worry about the time slipping by occupied the rest.

"Look!" Lint cried out, interrupting Ian's musings.

The brownie stood on a jagged, black boulder ten feet up while pointing to the south. Ian, Vic, and Revita all rose from the rocks they were seated upon and rounded the boulder.

To the west, beyond the tower, the sun hovered above the horizon, its rays bathing the tower and the cloud of steam above it. A bright white light came from the shaded side of the tower, three quarters of the way up. That beam shone across the quarter mile gap between the tower and the base of the mountain, where it was lost amid a cluster of rock, ice and snow.

"The dragon's words were true!" The brownie began to dance a jig while singing, "We are going on an adventure! We are going inside the tower! We will find the Paragon, and with it comes unknown power!"

"We aren't in the tower yet." Revita gestured. "Come on down, pipsqueak."

The brownie scrambled along the side of the boulder and jumped when halfway down. He landed in Revita's pack and then stuck his head up over her shoulder. "I am ready!"

"Good. Let's go see if we can find this entrance."

Ian lifted Lionel off his shoulder and tossed him into the air. *Go. Follow the light.*

When the drake flew off to the south, Ian headed in the same direction. Vic walked to one side of him, Revita to the other. They trod through snow in some areas and ice-coated rock in others, all the while heading toward the rockpile with the spotlight shining on it. As they drew near, they were forced to ascend a slippery slope. Ian fell twice, once banging his knee. In the shadow of the tower, the air was cold and growing colder. His hands soon went from chilly to numb, having to use them for support while ascending the slick hillside. Finally, he drew near the rockpile and the beam of light. The outcropping was massive, consisting of more than a dozen boulders, each standing three to four times Ian's own height.

"Do we climb up one of these?" Vic asked.

"I think I see a gap beyond the next boulder," Revita replied.

They navigated around the outcropping. A shadowy gap appeared beneath a tall boulder leaning at an angle against its neighbor. Revita ducked and scurried through with Vic and Ian close behind. Once beyond the opening, they stood to find themselves amid a ring of boulders akin to a massive nest made of rock.

"It's gone," Revita said.

"What's gone?" Vic asked.

"The light beam." She turned slowly while searching her surroundings. "The sun must have dropped too far. We are too late."

A pang of disappointment shot through Ian's gut. He spun around, seeking a doorway but was met by nothing but rock, ice, and snow. Worry, regret, fear of failure, and other troubling emotions waged war as tears threatened to emerge, but those feelings were quelled by a calm sense of pride coming through his connection with Lionel. He turned and spied the fire drake seated on a ledge beside a boulder.

What is it? Ian thought.

The drake hopped off the ledge and dropped from sight.

Ian climbed up a pile of broken rock and snow and found a narrow gap on its backside. He descended carefully and peered behind the boulder to find a dark cave, hidden from view until he stood in that exact spot. Lionel stood at the mouth of the cave, waiting.

"This way," Ian called out.

He eased into the gap behind the boulder and peered into the cave. It was dark and ran downward. How far, he could not tell. The crunch of footsteps and tumbling rocks drew near. Revita stopped beside Ian, reached into her coat, and pulled out a glowing disk. With the light held in front of her, she advanced down a series of cascading rocks.

She paused a half dozen strides away. "I see a staircase around this bend. It curves back toward the tower."

Vic clapped Ian on the shoulder. "Good job. You found it."

"No. It was Lionel who found it." Ian squatted and held his forearm out. Lionel hopped on it. Ian caressed the drake's head and neck as he stood. "You are a good boy." Warmth and contentment flowed through their bond.

"Come along, boys." Revita held the disk up. "Let's see what surprises lie ahead."

∼

REVITA HELD the light disk before her while scanning the dimly lit tunnel. Footsteps, heavy breathing, and the rustle of fabric came from behind her, mostly from Ian with perhaps a little added in by Vic. The former was poor at sneaking while the latter had gained some skill with the benefit of Revita's tutelage. She doubted Vic would ever willingly turn to thievery as a profession, but he had demonstrated enough potential to leave her wondering what he could become if he embraced the role.

At first, the stairs brought them some three stories down below the frozen landscape before the ground leveled into a tunnel that was equal to a castle corridor in its width and height. While the staircase had followed a gentle curve, the tunnel was straight. The smooth walls and lack of distinctive features made it seem as if Revita were running in place. The sensation left her unable to determine how far they had traveled. In her head, she tried to imagine them crossing the gap from the tunnel entrance back to the tower. If nothing else, doing so offered a sense of progress.

An intersection came into view. She slowed as she approached it while examining the tunnel walls, ceiling, and floor for traps. Finding nothing of note, she eased forward and stopped. A corridor ran in both directions. She peered one way, turned, and peered the other.

"Hmm. It seems we have a decision to make."

Ian poked his head around the corner. "Which way?"

"That would be the decision." She frowned in thought. "What did the dragon say?"

"He mentioned warrens beneath the tower."

Vic added. "And a lift at the center of the warrens."

She sighed. "So, it is a labyrinth."

Ian furrowed his brow. "Don't they say to always turn the same way, and you will eventually find the way out of a maze?"

"That is one way." Revita considered the option but she preferred to avoid such tedium. "However, it might take a while. Who knows how many dead ends we will come across."

"What do you suggest?"

We need to get to the center of the maze. Maybe I can find our way to it and save us some time. She turned toward Ian. "Are you still carrying that chalk?"

"It's in my pack," he replied.

"Give it to me."

He dug into his pack and handed her a chunk of white, dusty stone.

Revita bit her lip, made a choice, and drew an arrow on the wall. The arrow pointed left. "We go this way."

With her in the lead, they headed down the corridor. Fifty strides later, they came to a tunnel heading right. She drew another arrow, took that turn, and continued. At each turn, she marked the way while relying on her intuition. Left, right, right, left, left, right, right, left, she continued the pattern, all the while attempting to keep their general heading in the same direction. Twice, they came to dead ends, forcing them to double back. On both occasions, Revita restarted her pattern of two rights followed by two lefts. In her head, she had a sense of their progress, which had slowly but steadily continued toward where she believed the tower to be.

"Do you know where you are going?" Vic asked.

"No," Revita admitted. "However, we haven't gone in a circle. Until we come across arrows on the walls, that much is certain." Moments later, the tunnel terminated. She stopped and sighed. "Another dead end. We are close, I think, but it looks like we have to go back again."

"Wait." Ian froze and tilted his head as if listening.

Revita frowned. "What is it?"

"When I hold onto my magic, I sense a resonance just ahead." He slipped past her and approached the wall at the tunnel's end. With his palms pressed against the wall, he closed his eyes. "Whatever it is, it waits just beyond this tunnel."

"Can you get us through?"

Ian stepped back and frowned. "I do not know, but I will try." He turned toward them. "Back up. This might be dangerous."

Revita arched a brow at Vic, and they both backed down the corridor.

Ian stood on one side of the tunnel, extended a hand, and a portal appeared beside him while another bloomed at the other side of the tunnel. Both gateways intersected the dead-end wall. The portals disappeared, each leaving a gap seared into the wall by portal. He then shifted to the middle of the tunnel, raised his hand above his head, and cast another portal, this time parallel with the ceiling and intersecting the wall. Cold came through the portal, along with the dim light of the setting sun. The gateway closed with a pop, and Ian lowered his hand. Another portal appeared just inches above the tunnel floor and intersected the wall. Like the prior portal, this one peered out into the frozen landscape. The section of the wall blocking the route broke free and fell through the opening. It shattered, split, and crumbled while spilling across the frozen ground. The portal snapped shut. Debris rained down from the ceiling, and dust swirled in the air. Slowly, the dust cleared to reveal the view beyond.

The remaining edges of the old dead-end wall, now cut away clean by the gateways, were roughly two feet thick. Darkness lurked ahead, where a chamber much wider than the tunnel waited.

With the light disk held before her, Revita stepped over the debris, the darkness receding as she advanced. She strode into a chamber carved from rock, twenty strides across. In the heart of the space was a cell surrounded by stone on three sides. Inside the opening was a platform crafted of metal, just inches above the floor. A panel was mounted to a post in the middle of the platform. A pulsing glow came from the panel.

"This is it." Ian walked past her and stopped before the platform.

"This is what?" Revita asked.

"The lift. It is similar to the ones used to travel from upper to lower Ra'Tahal."

"Oh." Revita recalled riding the lift before they left the dwarven citadel the prior autumn. "That one was made of stone."

"Stone or metal, it does not matter." Ian climbed onto the lift. "Get on. We are going up."

Revita and Vic climbed on. Ian held his hand to the panel on the pedestal. Light came from the panel and a hum arose. The lift began to rise, leaving the maze behind and taking them toward the fabled tower.

CHAPTER 50

A MIGHTY HERO

The lift jerked to a stop. Walls of stone surrounded three sides of the platform, and a dark chamber lurked just beyond it. Revita squatted and held her light disk near the floor for inspection. It was smooth and featureless. Walls made of gray bricks stood on either side of her, the gap between the two walls no more than four feet.

Vic whispered. "Is someone standing over there?"

She extended her arm while raising the disk and then just about dropped it when she spied a person standing ten strides away. Pale arms, face, and clothing had her soon realizing the truth. "It's a statue."

"The statue is holding something. What is it?"

She spied a reflection in the statue's hand. "I am not sure."

Ian asked, "Can we get off the lift and find out?"

"I think so. I don't see any signs of traps." As she said it, she stepped off the platform and carefully advanced down the corridor. Even her soft footsteps seemed loud in the quiet confines.

The statue came into view and caused her to frown. As if reading her mind, Vic asked, "Why is there a sculpture of a dwarf so far from their lands?"

The dwarf was life size and wore round spectacles that rested near the tip of his big nose. Rather than dressed in armor, as Revita was used to seeing them, this one wore robes and held a thick book beneath one arm. In the statue's other hand was a ball of glass the size of an apple. While Revita and Vic stopped just shy of the sculpture, Ian slipped past them. He lifted the globe from the stone dwarf's hand and held it up.

"This is a crystal orb. I have seen ones like it before." Ian turned and set the globe on top of a bronze sconce jutting out from the wall across from the statue.

The moment the crystal orb settled on the sconce, purple-tinted light bloomed, emanating from the crystal. At the far end of the corridor, which was a good distance away, a sconce holding a similar sphere shone with a pale purple aura. Across from the far sconce was a statue identical to the one beside Ian. The area in between was empty, but the floor and walls were noticeably different across that span. Square tiles, each a foot wide and just as long, covered the floor while narrow slots dotted the walls. A voice in Revita's head shrieked *beware* – the same voice that had kept her alive through years of risk-laden heists. When Ian began to advance, Revita snatched a hold of his cloak and yanked him backward just as he stepped on the first tile.

A rapid series of thwaps echoed in the corridor. Tiny crossbow bolts shot out from both sides of the corridor and collided with the wall on the other side. Most of the bolts shattered on impact, but a few tumbled to the floor with a clatter.

"What were you thinking?" Revita hissed.

Ian shook his head. "I don't know. I thought it would be..."

She spun him toward her. "No. You didn't think at all." Shaking a finger in his face, she added, "Before you act rashly and get yourself, killed, think of me and Vic. We have no idea what we are looking for or what to do with it when we find it. Even if we found the Paragon, how would we get home without you? What would become of your quest to save the world?"

His gaze dropped in shame. "I guess I am anxious. We are so close."

"Take it from a thief, Ian. Close counts for nothing. Succeed or fail. There is nothing in between."

He lifted his chin and met her gaze. "We will succeed. We must."

"Good. Now, let me think about how to get past this corridor."

When Ian moved to the side, Revita squatted and eyed the tiles that had triggered the trap. First, she needed to decide if the triggers were the tiles, or something else.

"Vic. Come here."

He stood at her side. "Yeah?"

"Don't move from where you stand but drop the head of your weapon on this tile." She pointed to where Ian had stepped.

Vic pulled out his weapon, squatted, and dropped the mattock head to the floor while gripping the far end of the handle. Thwap, thwap, thwap. Darts shot across the corridor. One of the intact darts rolled toward Revita and stopped beside her boot. She picked it up and noticed dark ichor on the end with the damaged point.

"Poison," she announced. "The tips are dipped in poison."

From behind her, Ian said, "So I would have been..."

"Dead." She allowed the word to hang in the air for added effect. "Let's try something more subtle."

Revita slid her pack off her shoulder. Lint hopped out of it and landed lightly on the floor beside her. She reached into her pack, pulled out a day-old biscuit, and rolled it down the corridor. The biscuit crossed the first tile, passed the next row, and settled three tiles away. Nothing happened.

Standing upright, Revita peered into the distance and then noticed a lever just below the bronze sconce at the other end of the corridor. "I believe I know how to disarm this trap."

"Are you going to share it with us?" Vic asked.

She pointed. "See the lever below the sconce holding that orb?"

They both followed her gesture.

Vic grunted. "I see it, but if that disarms the trap, it seems like we are on the wrong end of the corridor."

"*We* are." She looked down at the brownie. "But Lint soon won't be."

Lint looked up at her. "Me?'

"I saved you once. Here is your chance to play the hero."

The brownie beamed. "Me? A hero?"

"You just need to cross to the far end of this chamber, find a way to reach that lever, and pull it down."

After a beat of contemplation, Lint gave a firm nod. "I will save you, goddess."

"I told you not to call me..."

Lint giggled and darted off, running along the seam between adjacent floor tiles. No noise or darts emerged. A few moments later, he reached the corridor's far end and stopped to peer up at the lever. He gathered himself, ran toward the wall, and leapt. For someone standing only a hand-span tall, the brownie's jumping ability was impressive. Yet, a three-foot-high jump added to his six-inch frame still left him short of reaching the lever. Again, he tried. Again, he failed. He backed from the lever while scowling up at it and bumped into the foot of the far sculpture.

Lint spun toward the statue and waved his fist. "Stupid stone dwarf!" He snarled. "How can I be a hero if you are in my way?"

The brownie suddenly froze. He lowered his fist, glanced over his shoulder, toward the lever, and began to chortle.

"What is so funny?" Revita called out.

"The stone dwarf seeks to stop me from being a hero. I will show him."

The brownie backed up, ran, and jumped. He grabbed onto the stone hand holding the book and began to scale the statue's arm. When he reached the shoulder, he stood and eased toward the dwarf's head before disappearing behind it. A few seconds later, the statue rocked forward before tipping back into place. It rocked forward again, balanced on edge for a beat, and then toppled across the corridor with the brownie on its back.

The statue's face struck the opposing wall. The stone spectacles and nose broke off and fell. Shattered bits tumbled across the floor. Lint scrambled up the statue's back and onto its head. From there, he jumped up and wrapped his tiny arms around the lever. It did not move. However, the brownie was not yet finished. He slung a leg over the lever, set his feet on the flat, metal top, and crouched beneath the bronze sconce, which was no more than three inches above the lever. Lint applied pressure against the lever and sconce. The lever moved slowly, one inch, then three, then it suddenly fell the rest of the way. Lint let out a screech and jumped to land on the statue's back. He rolled, tumbled along its spine, and fell to the floor, where he lay. Unmoving.

"Lint!" Revita cried out.

A sense of loss came over her. The brownie was annoying and often distracting, but she never wanted him to die. Since she had first rescued him, he had acted as if she were the sun and the moon, something she found simultaneously irritating and endearing. But if he was dead now… Unfamiliar emotions emerged, beginning with guilt about how she had treated him, followed by sorrow about him dying.

"Can we cross?" Vic broke the silence.

Revita regained her focus. "Try hitting the tiles again."

He extended his arm and dropped the mattock downward. It struck the floor, but nothing happened. Again, and again, Vic tapped tiles while advancing. When it was clear that all was well, Revita bolted past him. She slowed as she neared the far end of the hallway.

Lint lay on his back with his eyes closed.

She squatted beside him and gently reached out. Her fingertip brushed along the side of his face, but he did not move. "I am sorry, Lint. I should have been nicer to you."

Lint's tiny little eyes flashed open. He sat up, wrapped an arm around her finger, and grinned. "Do you love me?"

Revita jerked her hand from him and snapped, "I thought you were dead."

Vic stopped behind her. "I did as well."

The brownie stood and dusted himself off. "Not dead. Just resting." He looked up at the lever. "Being a hero is a lot of work. Are you impressed?"

Despite his little scare, she laughed. "I am mightily impressed."

Ian moved past them and stopped near the edge of the light. "It is another lift."

Revita rose to her feet. Sure enough, a lift waited in the shadows, some twenty feet ahead.

Turning, Ian reached for the glowing orb and lifted it from the sconce. The glow from orb at the other end of the corridor doused, but the globe in Ian's hand still glowed, albeit with a fraction of the light it emitted while in the sconce.

"Come along," Ian said. "Let's see where this takes us."

The party climbed onto the platform and encircled Ian. With the orb held in one hand, Ian placed his other palm on the control panel. The lift hummed and began to rise.

CHAPTER 51
LIFE-LIKE STATUES

The lift hummed, carrying Ian and his companions upward. The dark, deadly corridor and the tipped statue faded away. Stone briefly surrounded the lift before another dark chamber came into view. Ian removed his hand from the control panel. The lift stopped with a lurch.

Light emanating from the globe in Ian's palm revealed a bronze sconce on the wall beside the lift opening. The floor beside the lift was tiled in blue. Beyond the soft, purple aura emitted from the orb, gloom dominated the surroundings.

Lionel began to lick Ian's ear. He flinched away, but with the fire drake seated on his shoulder, it was impossible to get out of Lionel's reach. Finally, Ian clamped his hand over his ear.

"Stop, Lionel."

A sense of disappointment came through their connection. When the drake settled, Ian stepped off the platform and placed the glass ball into the cupped upper surface of the sconce. The orb, and others like it, bloomed with light to suddenly expose their surroundings. He turned slowly while surveying a room of curious design.

It was a sprawling chamber, the ceiling fifteen feet up, the space stretching all the way to the tower's curved, outer wall. White, cylindrical columns evenly spaced between the outer wall and the lift supported the floors above. The chamber's floor was uneven with peaks and valleys throughout, none lower than the azure tiles where Ian stood. Just strides away, the blue gave way to green. Mesmerized, Ian crossed the low floor and stepped onto the green, elevated tiles to test them. Even the raised areas felt solid, so he continued another five strides and stepped up onto a platform. Beyond that shelf, green extended before rising to peaks. Strips of blue meandered through the green, leading to a miniature city crafted of arches and narrow spires. That city sat on the edge of the drop on an island of green.

All at once, the purpose of the room became clear. "Amazing," he muttered.

"What is this place?" Vic asked from beside the lift.

Standing upright, Ian turned slowly while surveying the area. Most of the chamber behind the lift was covered in blue while the area between the lift entrance and the wall opposite consisted of greens and tans before turning brown. When he completed his turn, he found a white region. Amid the white stood a single column, a hand-span tall.

"This is a map of the world." Ian pointed at his feet. "This is Havenfall. You stand on the Inner Sea." His arm swept out. "Greavesport is right in front of you. To the right is Bard's Bay. Far across the room, in the white area, is the very same tower we currently occupy."

Lint's eyes grew wide and he burst into a run. The brownie jumped up a foot-tall cliffside and raced through forests, over the Agrosi, and hopped upon the fifteen-inch shelf representing the bluff where Ra'Tahal was located. "I can explore the entire world!" He whooped, skipped, and spun in excitement before racing off again.

Revita shook her head. "While the pipsqueak acts as if he has discovered a stash of gold, why do we care about this chamber?"

Ian shrugged. "I can't say that we do." He looked around again but found nothing of note. "I still do not know what the Paragon is, but I doubt this chamber is where we would find it. Unless we seek to map out the world and wish to use this place as a reference, I think we are done here."

He climbed down and headed toward the lift.

"Pipsqueak!" Revita shouted. "Come back. We are moving on."

The brownie stopped beside a mountain range that stood four times his height. "But I only just got here."

"Come along...unless you would rather have us leave you behind. In the dark."

"Fine," Lint sighed. His return to the lift was much slower than his boisterous foray across the room. His head and shoulders drooped in disappointment as he walked back to the center of the room.

Ian waited for Lint to climb on the platform before he lifted the globe from the sconce. The room fell dark other than the island of light around him. He stepped on the platform, pressed his hand to the control panel, and it began to rise.

When the platform reached the next floor, Ian stopped the lift and stepped off into a small room with an arched doorway straight ahead – the top of the arch twelve feet up, the opening half as wide. He placed the globe into the sconce on the wall, triggering the spell that caused the orbs throughout the floor to ignite. A few strides carried Ian beneath the arch, allowing him to view the next room while his companions joined him.

The chamber beyond the first arch was shaped like a piece of pie with a bite taken off the tip. The near walls were no more than fifteen feet apart, while the far end of the room was four times the width. Cut into each side wall was an arch leading to another illuminated room. While the architecture stirred curiosity, what occupied the room demanded further examination.

Alabaster sculptures filled the room, each crafted to match the appearance of a different creature. Ian strolled into the room, slowing to examine the statues he passed, each crafted with exceptional skill.

The first statue depicted a werecat with its mouth open in mid-roar. The entire creature was carved from a single piece of white marble except for its eyes – made of emeralds that sparkled in the light of the globes. To Ian's other side stood a rock wolf, its chest thrust out proudly, its snout raised in a howl. The wolf's eyes were topaz with a yellow gleam amid the amber gems. Upon other pedestals were likenesses of smaller creatures ranging from squirrels to rabbits and even rats. Each had jewels in place of eyes, the size of the gems mirroring the scale of the animal. In all, more than two dozen sculptures occupied the chamber, the largest being a moarbear, a fearsome creature whose back was five feet off the floor, its body nearly as wide. The bear was frozen in mid snarl, its jagged teeth bared and appearing like ice picks made of stone. Rubies like oversized cherries occupied the slots where its eyes should be.

With an expression of longing on her face, Revita examined the eyes of each statue she passed. "These jewels could be worth a fortune. Do you think anyone would miss them?"

Vic arched a brow. "Weren't you the one who warned us not to touch anything? Didn't you claim that traps could be lurking anywhere?"

She shot him a look of disappointment. "I hate it when others use my own words against me."

He laughed. "I was just reminding you."

She sighed. "I'll try to restrain myself, but we had better keep moving in case the temptation becomes overwhelming."

The three humans and the brownie moved on to the next chamber. While the statue garden stirred curiosity, that was nothing compared to what awaited in the next room. Like the first chamber, sculptures made of pale stone occupied the otherwise open space. The new chamber was twice the size of the first, the carvings occupying the room also twice as astounding.

A griffin, a manticore, a unicorn, a fairy, and dozens of other magical creatures were spread throughout the area. As in the previous chamber, likenesses of smaller creatures stood upon pedestals. Just as in the prior room, a rainbow of jewels ranging from purple amethysts to red rubies, and everything in between, had been used in the place of eyes. Far across the room, light came through another archway.

"What is this place?" Vic asked.

"I am not sure," Ian admitted. "But whoever crafted these was skilled, that much is certain."

He led the others across the chamber, noting the meticulous detail and skill demonstrated in every sculpture he passed. As he neared the next chamber, he gasped. Just past the archway, he stopped and gaped while his companions gathered around him.

The last chamber consumed half of the third floor, yet it only contained three sculptures. The nearest was that of a giant bird with its wings extended. The bird's body was bigger than a carriage, the tip of one wing reaching the wall adjacent to where Ian stood, the tip of the other wing meeting the tower's outer wall, over a hundred feet away. Ian instantly knew it as a roc. The sight reminded him of his encounter with an actual roc while crossing a bridge over a chasm. He had stood frozen in fear rather than react as he should. His hesitance had almost cost him his life, and he would have died for certain had Truhan not been there to help him.

Ian dismissed the memory, advanced past the Roc statue, and turned his attention on the next behemoth.

A humongous humanoid monster with a thick torso stood in a squatting position. Even then, the monster's head pressed against the high ceiling. Its arms were as thick as wine barrels, its legs like tree trunks. With a bulbous nose and sharp underbite teeth jutting up from its closed mouth, Ian instantly recognized it as a rock troll – another creature that had nearly killed him.

The third and final sculpture was the most glorious of all – a life-sized dragon. While crafted of alabaster stone, the statue was the spitting image of Umbracan.

Ian led the others across the chamber, all staring in awe at each of the three giant monsters. Like Ian, nobody said a word nor did they stray anywhere near the sculptures. It felt as if one might come to life at any moment and attack, and considering the scale of their subjects, surviving such an attack was not likely. When Ian noticed the size of the gems occupying the dragon's eye hole, he glanced toward Revita. If she had been tempted before, she was doubly tempted now, for the jewels in this chamber were massive and undoubtedly worth a fortune.

"Revita..." Vic warned, obviously thinking the same as Ian.

Raw desire tainted her voice as she crooned, "We could buy anything we wanted."

"I don't need anything." Vic grabbed her hand. "I just need you."

She shot him a stern look. "You are trying to disarm me."

He slid an arm around her, pulling her against his side. "I am trying to keep you out of trouble."

Revita pulled away. "Trouble finds me, not the other way around."

"In that case," Ian said, "we will keep moving, so trouble won't find you."

They crossed the room and passed through the next archway to return to the room where they encountered the first group of statues.

Revita said, "This tower shocks me at every turn. Each level has me wondering what we might find next. I have never visited a place that was so strange."

"Who built this tower?" Vic mused. "Why fill it with such strange things? Why bother to construct any building in this distant wasteland anyway?"

"All are good questions," Ian admitted. "And while these sculptures are impressive, I don't see how they are of any use." He looked around the chamber one last time. "We should..." He paused when he saw Lint across the room, staring up at the moarbear statue. "Lint. What are you doing?"

The brownie tilted his head while staring up at the beast. "This is a moarbear, is it not?"

"It is. Why?"

"I feel like this one is looking at me."

Ian sighed. "None of the statues are looking at you."

"Are you certain?"

"Yes, now, let's move along."

Lint glanced over his shoulder, toward Ian, and then turned back to the bear. He walked up to the bear's foot and kicked the bear's paw. The act looked comical and akin to Ian trying to pick a fight with a towering oak tree. What followed was not comical in the least.

The moarbears's ruby eyes began to glow and the statue came to life.

The bear bent its head down, opened its jaw wide, and snapped. Lint yelped and reacted just in time by diving to the side. The bear's snout struck its own foot, snapping off bits of marble and sending tiny shards spraying in all directions. The sculpture raised its head and opened its mouth in a silent roar. It then lumbered forward, after Lint, who bolted back toward Ian and his companions.

The animated moarbear statue plowed through anything in its path, knocking over pedestals and sending sculptures half its size spinning and toppling over. Thumps, crashes, and clatters echoed throughout the room as the bear charged.

Ian opened himself to his magic, drew it in, and prepared a spell. The bear charged into the rock wolf statue, toppling it over. The head broke off and skittered across the floor. Before Ian could release his spell, the wolf's head struck his ankle and sent him tumbling to the ground and Lionel sailing off his shoulder. He landed on his hands and chest, looked up, and found the bear only strides away.

~

WHEN IAN FELL, Vic reached for the weapon on his back, spurred by the urgency to save his brother. He burst forward while driving the mattock forward with an overhead chop. A leap took him over Ian. As the mattock came down, the bear stopped and threw its head to the side to dodge the blow. The mattock missed the creature's head, striking the side of its neck. A crack resounded, sparks sizzled, and chips of marble sprayed across the floor.

The bear swept a massive paw out. Vic leapt, and the paw passed beneath him. He landed and swung again, this time driving the pick into the bear's shoulder, breaking off bits of stone and leaving a thin crack. The animated statue lunged for him with its mouth wide. Unbalanced and desperate to avoid those massive teeth, Vic dove and slid across the floor. Faster than he would have thought possible, the monster spun toward him.

~

REVITA HELD HER DAGGER READY, but what good would a dagger do against a massive bear made of marble? So, she stood aside and prayed that Vic or Ian would find a way to stop the monster, but when Vic went sliding across the floor, she had to act.

The bear spun toward Vic, leaving its back facing her. Without any idea how to fight the thing, she chose another route.

She darted forward, jumped, and landed stomach-first on the bear's back. Moving with haste, she pushed herself up and straddled the monster with a leg to each side. The bear stopped and craned its neck while snapping its massive maw. The bear's teeth came just shy of reaching her when it bobbed and spun into the werecat sculpture, causing it to topple and shatter.

~

Ian scrambled to his feet, ready with his magic, but the lightning bolt he had intended suddenly carried unwelcome consequences. There was no way he could use that spell with Vic and Revita in the way. Lionel circled the upper reaches of the room, his squawking adding to the noise of the ruckus.

As Vic rose to a stance and Revita rode the stone monster as if she were breaking in a wild stallion, Ian struggled to think of a spell to use. The bear chomped, spun, and flailed while Revita held on for her life and Vic dodged around it. Each time the bear spun away from Vic, he would dart in and strike, his mattock knocking chunks off the statue, which seemed to have no effect. All the while, the monster's ruby eyes glowed with malevolence. *Wait.* Ian glanced toward the other creatures, the jewels in their eyes dim and dull. *That's it!*

"The eyes!" Ian shouted. "Target the rubies!"

~

"What?" Vic carefully watched the bear while readying himself for another strike.

"The eyes!" Ian bellowed. "Hit it in the eyes!"

"Oh, boy," Vic groaned. Targeting the eyes meant getting past the monster's massive jaws.

Waiting as the bear spun in a circle, Vic readied himself and darted forward as the bear's head came toward him. He swung. The mattock struck true. The pick end shattered the bear's left eye in a spray of sparks. A massive paw came around and struck Vic's leg, the force of the blow sweeping his foot out from beneath him. He fell onto his backside, struck his elbow on the floor, and pain shot straight up to his hand, causing him to release his grip. The mattock flipped over his shoulder, bounced, and skittered across the floor.

The bear stood over Vic, opened its jaw wide, and came down at him.

~

Revita held on for her life as the bear rocked, spun, and thrashed. While she had distracted the bear sufficiently to help Vic and Ian, she found herself in the center of a fight she could not win.

Ian shouted something about eyes, but she was too busy trying not to get thrown to the ground to pay attention. In her mind, she pictured a two-ton bear made of rock stomping on her as if she were grapes and the bear was making wine. But when the bear spun around and Vic's weapon destroyed one of the rubies, she realized Ian's intent.

She let go with one arm, reached for her dagger, and drew it in one motion. The bear knocked Vic to the floor. Revita flipped the dagger, gripping the hilt with the pommel facing down. She raised her hand as the bear lunged toward Vic. With a hard downward strike, she drove the hilt into the glowing eye. The ruby shattered.

The bear froze in place with its open jaws just inches from Vic's face. The wild, noisy ruckus of the previous minutes turned to silence, disturbed only by panting breaths and the hammer of racing hearts.

Revita sat upright and exhaled as she sheathed her dagger. "That was interesting."

Vic slid from beneath the bear and stood. "A bit too interesting for my liking." He crossed to his fallen weapon and picked it up.

Ian approached from the other direction as Lionel landed on his extended forearm. "Are you two alright?"

She slid off the bear statue. "I might have a bruise or two."

Vic touched the side of his leg and winced. "My ankle hurts to the touch, but I don't think anything is broken."

"Good. I wanted to help but couldn't use my magic without harming you two as well." Ian looked around the room. "This place is a mess."

Lint strolled in from behind Revita. "That was exciting! Do you think any other statues can come to life?"

She waggled a finger at him. "You were told not to touch anything."

"I didn't touch the bear. I kicked it."

Her voice rose an octave "Why would you do that?"

He shrugged. "The elders share tales about moarbears. They are reputed to be fierce and as dangerous as any creature. I had never crossed one before and thought to see how impressive it might be from up close."

"But why did you kick it?"

The tiny brownie stood tall. "To show it that I was not afraid."

Revita slapped her forehead, closed her eyes for a beat, and then spoke in a calm tone. "Touch nothing else in this tower, Lint. Not one thing...unless I give you leave."

The brownie sighed. "Very well."

Ian cleared his throat and waited until Revita turned toward him. "Are you finished scolding your pet?"

"I think so."

"Good, because I'd like to leave this level...unless you still want to steal the eyes off these statues."

"Based on what just happened, I think not."

"Wonderful. Let's take the lift before some other lump of stone comes to life."

They tiptoed through chunks of marble, passed beneath an arch, and climbed onto the lift. When Revita, Vic, and Lint were ready, Ian pulled the orb from the sconce, it's light diming while those in the other chambers turned black. He stepped onto the platform, pressed his palm to the panel, and the lift continued upward.

A stone shaft obscured the recently vacated room. Moments later, the shaft opened to a lit chamber a dozen feet wide and just as long. An open door graced the wall opposite the lift. A wooden chair padded in red velvet stood beside the doorway. In the chair sat a dwarf with a long, white beard, wisps of white hair on his head, and round spectacles resting on his bulbous nose. The dwarf wore midnight blue robes adorned with silver stars. Across his lap lay a gnarled staff carved from wood so dark, it appeared black.

The lift stopped, but nobody moved.

The dwarf lifted his head, planted the butt of the staff on the floor, and leaned forward. From beneath shaggy, white eyebrows, his purple eyes scrutinized the tower's intruders.

Finally, the dwarf spoke in a scratchy, throaty voice. "So, you are the ones creating all the ruckus."

CHAPTER 52

CARETAKER

Ian stood in shock. Considering the tower's remote location, not to mention the structure being coated in ice and protected by a dragon, he had not expected to find a living person inside.

The dwarf scrutinized them with an intense gaze. "Three humans, a brownie, and a fire drake. Interesting." He used the staff to support himself as he stood. "Are you going to stand there like statues, or are you going to introduce yourselves?"

"Statues?" Ian repeated the word. "We are sorry about that."

"Ah. So, *that* was the ruckus. You woke one of my sentinels."

Lint piped up. "It was a moarbear."

"I see. Was anyone hurt?"

"Thankfully, no," Ian replied.

"Hmm. You must be skilled in battle."

"I..." Ian glanced at his brother.

The dwarf waved it off. "Never mind that. I forget myself. You are the first visitors I have had here. My manners have waned during my stay." He held a wrinkled hand to his chest. "I am Parsigar."

"My name is Ian. This is my brother, Vic. This is Revita. The brownie is named Lint. The drake is Lionel."

The dwarf peered over his spectacles. "You must have traveled far. I suspect you are hungry."

"Now that you mention it..." Ian's stomach growled.

"Ha!" The dwarf thrust a finger toward the ceiling. "As I suspected. Come." He turned in a series of tiny shuffling steps. "Let's get you some food."

The old dwarf hobbled through the doorway and faded from view.

Revita whispered, "Does anyone else find this strange?"

Vic snorted. "There is not one thing about this tower that isn't strange. Why should the elderly dwarf be any different?"

Ian shook his head. "It's not just the dwarf's behavior. His mere presence stirs dozens of questions."

"Maybe he will give us answers."

"I hope so." Ian stepped off the lift and crossed the chamber.

A curved corridor waited beyond the room and stretched in both directions. Doorways were visible along the outside of the curve. Glowing orbs resting in sconces illuminated the way. Of the dwarf, Ian saw nothing. However, a mouthwatering aroma hung in the air.

"Where did he go?" he whispered.

An old, scratchy voice came from the right. "Are you coming?"

"This way." Ian headed down the curved corridor and the dwarf came back into view.

"There you are." Parsigar shuffled forward and passed through the doorway at the end of the hallway.

Ian and the others followed him and stepped into a warm chamber with a brick oven, shelving, cabinets, and a counter to one side. A table and chairs stood on the other side of the room. Between the two, purple clouds floating in the soft haze of twilight were visible through a window made of diamond shaped panes.

The dwarf hobbled over to the oven, slid on a heavy mitt, and lifted a pot from a hook inside the opening. He set the pot on a stone coun-tertop and began speaking as he continued to work.

"I must apologize. I did not expect company, so there may not be enough stew to satisfy everyone." Parsigar turned back toward the oven, bent, and pulled a flat tray from the lower opening. A long, narrow loaf of bread spanned the length of the tray. He held it close to his face, closed his eyes, and sniffed. "Mmm. There is nothing quite like the scent of freshly baked bread."

Ian watched the dwarf set the tray on the counter. "Would you care for some assistance?"

"Assistance? After all this time alone? I would not know how to function with anyone else in the kitchen."

"If you don't mind me asking, where does your food come from? I can't imagine anything growing out here in the Glacia."

The dwarf set the bread in a basket and reached for a stack of bowls on the shelf behind him. "Questions are welcome. Answers may be offered, depending on the subject." Parsigar set the bowls on the table and then lifted a ladle from a canister on the counter. "You are a curious one, are you not?"

"I have been told that I ask too many questions."

"Nonsense." The dwarf scooped stew from the pot and dropped it into a bowl. "Inquisitive minds are necessary if the world is to ever advance. Without them, there would be nothing new. The world would just march on, never changing without discoveries or mysteries to unravel." He finished filling the five bowls. "Come and take a bowl. You'll find spoons in the box at the end of the counter. Someone also please bring the basket. It would be a shame if the bread were forgot-ten." He shuffled across the room, heading for the table.

Ian glanced toward Vic and Revita before picking up a bowl, a spoon, and the basket. The scent of the bread mixed with the gently spiced stew taunted him as he joined the dwarf at the table. He sat, broke the heel off the bread, and took a bite. His teeth cut through the crust, to find a soft, warm interior. It was delicious. He broke off a piece of crust and fed it to Lionel, who scarfed it down eagerly. The drake snorted and slurped while a bubble of spit formed on his mouth. Sensing his eagerness, Ian gave his pet another morsel before passing the basket to Parsigar.

When he finished chewing the bread, Ian spooned up a scoop of stew. Steam rose from the spoon, so he blew on it to cool it and then tried a bite. Potatoes, carrots, peas, and some sort of meat combined to make a tasty dish.

"This is wonderful," Ian said as Vic and Revita sat beside him. Lint stood at the far end of the table. "You never did answer my question."

Parsigar set his spoon down. "Where do I get my ingredients?" He grinned and tapped the side of his nose. "That is a mystery I will expose, but not until we finish eating."

While the response left him unsatisfied, Ian noted the dwarf's behavior. In many ways, he was reminded of Devigar. It had taken Ian weeks to learn how to best deal with his former master, but those lessons might serve him well now, which was why he shifted subjects.

"How long have you lived here?"

"Oh, my. It is difficult to say. You see, time functions differently in the tower."

Revita scoffed. "Time is time. Minutes, hours, days, weeks, years... they are always measured the same way. How can it be different?"

"So," the dwarf leaned back. "You are so smart that you know everything?"

"Well, not everything, but I certainly know how time works."

He leaned forward. "Tell me, how long have you been in the tower?"

She shrugged. "Maybe an hour."

"I'd say you've been here thrice that time."

"I don't think so..."

"Not to your perspective, but to the rest of the world."

"I don't understand."

"In truth, I don't fully understand the enchantment either. I believe that a long, long time ago, the tower's owner became weary of how slowly events advanced in the world, so he sped things up inside it. Time here moves at two or three times the rate it does elsewhere."

Ian frowned. "The tower's owner?"

"I am sorry. That is among the questions I cannot answer right now." The dwarf ducked his face into the bowl and began to scoop stew.

Sensing that their host wished to eat rather than answer questions, Ian and his companions did the same. Minutes passed with only the clanking of spoons, slurps of stew, and crunch of bread filling the lack of conversation.

Ian finished, set his spoon down, and picked through crumbs in the basket, which he then fed to Lionel, who gobbled them up in a flash. The drake then hopped off Ian's shoulder, landed on the table, and began to lick Ian's bowl clean.

Parsigar was the last to finish. When through, he pushed his bowl away and dabbed the bits of stew caught in his beard away with a napkin. The dwarf released a sigh of contentment. "A good meal will never grow tiresome."

"I...guess," Ian said, feeling like he needed to respond. With the resumed conversation came an opportunity for him to broach a critical and urgent subject. "We have come here on an important..."

"Stop." The dwarf tilted his head and peered over his spectacles. "One need not be a scholar to guess that you have sought out the tower for some quest you feel is important. It is not as if you were just wandering the Glacia and happened upon it."

"No. I suppose not."

"All things come in time and *when* you do something is often more important than the actions you take. The quest, urgent or not, will have to wait until the time is right."

Frustrated, Ian clenched his jaw. A voice inside him screamed for him to press the dwarf, but another voice calmly told him to wait.

Rather than attempting an exhaustive and possibly dangerous search through the tower, Ian preferred tapping into the elderly dwarf's knowledge to locate the object of his quest.

Parsigar gripped his staff and leaned into it as he stood. "Our meal is spent. Please gather the dishes and bring them this way." He crossed the chamber and stopped beside a copper vat. "Place each bowl in a slot. The spoons go in the middle slots."

Ian stood over the vat and discovered a metal rack inside it. The rack had eight pie-shaped sections. Each was divided into a large outer compartment and a smaller inner compartment. The compartments were a foot deep. The dirty dishes filled up five of the eight slots, each dish joined by a spoon. When finished, Parsigar pulled a lever on the side of the vat. Water rushed in, filling the vat. He then poured white shavings into the water.

"What is this thing?" Vic asked.

"Watch." Parsigar touched a dark sapphire mounted to the side of the vat. Light bloomed in the sapphire. The rack began to spin, stirring the water. Foam bubbled from the swirling water until nothing else was visible within the vat.

Ian understood. "It is washing the dishes."

"Very good." Parsigar smirked.

"Can you do the same with clothing?"

The dwarf's smirk stretched to a full smile. "How intuitive. A similar device waits in the neighboring chamber and is used for that exact purpose." The dwarf turned. "Come. It is time for a tour."

They followed Parsigar into the corridor, where he stopped by the first open door. "This is my bathing room and here I do my laundry."

The chamber was half the size of the kitchen. A bench, a vanity, and shelving with towels resting upon it ran along one wall. The opposite side of the room consisted of a copper tub and a vat similar to the one used for dishes. There was no window, the chamber instead illuminated by an orb by the door and one on a sconce on the far end.

The dwarf moved along while Ian and his companions followed. Bedrooms lurked beyond the next three doorways, the first being the one Parsigar used, the others vacant apart from furniture. The end of the corridor brought them to a sitting room with a fireplace. A fire burned in the opening, but there was no wood visible nor could Ian recall seeing smoke outside the tower.

"This ends the tour of my quarters," Parsigar gestured back the other way. "Now, let us return to the lift, so we may move on to the interesting parts of the tower."

They returned to the lift chamber, gathered on the platform, and waited until Parsigar climbed on to join them.

"If you will, my boy," Parsigar gestured toward Ian. "Take us up one level."

As bidden, Ian placed his palm on the panel. The lift hummed and began to rise.

CHAPTER 53
ANCIENT PROPHECY

Ian, with Parsigar standing beside him, Lint at his feet, and Vic and Revita behind him, stood upon a lift platform that took them to what he counted as the fifth floor. Considering the ceiling heights and the thickness of the structure between each level, he believed that they were now a hundred feet or more above the frozen landscape outside. However, the dark gap between the fourth and fifth level was much more extensive than the previous levels, leading Ian to believe that two entire floors had been skipped.

The view opened to bright light. After his time on the other, dimly lit tower levels, the glare forced Ian to squint. The lift stopped, and Parsigar climbed off. Blinking in the light, Ian followed, took a few strides, and began to slowly turn while surveying a sprawling conservatory that felt like an illusion rather than reality.

Lint whooped, ran off, and disappeared into the foliage.

The ceiling stood some thirty feet up, supported by a dozen columns spaced between the lift and the outer wall. Each column emitted a powerful glow akin to a tiny, cylindrical sun. Surrounding the columns were lush gardens thick with vegetables, shrubs, and trees.

Berries of assorted colors dotted the shrubs while apples, oranges, and lemons dangled from the tree branches. Paved paths ran throughout the area, dividing one garden from another.

The brownie darted across a nearby path and ducked into another garden. Red, ripe tomatoes swayed as he ran through the plant and shot into a grove of beans.

"How is this possible?" Ian asked. "Plants do not grow indoors. There aren't even any windows."

The dwarf turned toward him. "Do you know all things?"

"I...no."

"Then, how do you know what is possible and what is not?"

Ian needed to know. "What about sunlight? Nothing can grow without sunlight."

"While true, these columns simulate daylight, feeding the vegetation."

"What about the tree roots?"

"This entire level is covered in dirt twenty feet deep."

Then came Ian's last question. "What about water?"

"Ah." The dwarf nodded. "I was wondering when you would get to that one."

The light in the columns flickered and dimmed.

Parsigar pointed with his staff. "Everyone, back to the lift."

"What is happening?" Ian asked.

"You will soon find out, but I suggest you do so from the lift."

Disappointed, Ian cast another glance backward and then followed the old dwarf, who trailed Vic and Revita. Just as Ian climbed onto the platform, the columns flickered brightly and then dimmed. Water began to fall from tens of thousands of tiny holes in the ceiling. And, just like that, it was raining throughout the indoor garden. The air drastically cooled, joined by the musty scent of rain.

A tiny yipe came from far across the garden. Seconds later, Lint burst from a blueberry bush and raced down the path leading to the lift.

He hopped onto the platform and stopped with his arms held out, his body stiff.

"That water is c...c...cold," the brownie's teeth chattered.

"You are soaked," Revita noted.

"I hadn't n...n...noticed."

Ian extended his arm toward the gardens until rain pattered off his palm. The falling water was, indeed, quite cold. "Where does the water come from?"

"A question I expected." Parsigar nodded. "An aquafer runs deep beneath the tower. The water is pumped up through tubes built into the outer wall. That water feeds the entire tower, but most of it is used on this floor and the one above."

"What is the one above?"

"Put your hand to the panel, and you will find out."

As instructed, Ian activated the lift.

~

A NEW LEVEL opened outside the lift. It was similar to the one below, but rather than being filled with trees and shrubs, it was covered in grass. Amid the grass were chickens – dozens and dozens of chickens, all pecking away at the grass. The chickens ate in clusters with a watchful rooster beside each cluster. Four chicken coups stood along the outer wall, each with its door open and a ramp leading up into a shadowy interior.

"As you can see," Parsigar said. "These are my chickens. They provide eggs and meat to go along with the fruit and vegetables on the floor below."

Ian looked up and noted the tiny holes in the ceiling. "The rain falls here as well."

"It does. What the grass does not use then filters down to a reservoir between this floor and the one below. It rains down there and feeds another reservoir."

"This is all quite interesting, but chickens and gardens can be found throughout the realm. Why live in this tower so far from the rest of the world?"

"Ah. That question again." The dwarf gestured. "Take us to the next floor. There, I will explain."

As requested, Ian complied. The chamber disappeared and the lift was engulfed by darkness. The dwarf pulled an orb from his robes, its soft light illuminating the area. A dark opening appeared, the lift stopped, and the dwarf stepped off. When he set the orb into an empty sconce beside the lift. Orbs spaced along the walls illuminated a pie-shaped workshop. Vials, crucibles, open books, and tools covered six tables along the wall to the right. Each workbench was crafted of dark wood, thick and heavy. An anvil, a hammer, and a forge stood in the center of the far wall, the coals in the forge aglow. To each side of the forge was a window, the pale of twilight visible outside. Shelving and racks stood along the wall to the left. Strange contraptions, weapons, and artifacts made of metal, stone, and wood filled shelves and racks. An arched doorway nestled between sections of shelving led to another chamber in one direction while another positioned between two workbenches opened to a neighboring room in the other.

"Welcome to my sanctum." The dwarf shuffled to the center of the chamber and stopped. "The hours I have spent here are countless. Nothing in my life has equaled the pleasure or reward of creating."

Vic asked, "What do you create?"

"Things of all sorts. Some are mere baubles with no practical element. Others are useful and sometimes life-altering. I craft items that are harmless while some are dangerous in the extreme. However, after centuries of applying my craft, ideas for new creations now come slowly. My end draws near, and I fear that it will be the result of boredom rather than any physical malady. Either way, I have served my god well and will be rewarded in the afterlife."

"Vandasal?" Ian asked.

Parsigar turned toward him. "I thought humans did not believe in gods."

"I have spent enough time around your kind to know of the god you share with the Sylvan and Drow."

"Interesting." The dwarf gestured toward the doorway to the right. "That room holds the raw materials I require for my work. In there, you will find ore, chromium, vartanium, silver, gold, several types of stone, and even wood in the form of poles and boards." He turned toward the opposite doorway. "However, our destination lies in this direction." He hobbled off while Ian and his companions filed through behind him.

Revita glanced toward the raw material storage room. "Did he say silver and gold?"

Vic took her by the arm. "Let it go, Vita." He pulled her along as he followed the old dwarf through the other doorway.

They entered a library as impressive as any Ian had ever seen. Rows of shelving ran along the walls and throughout the space. The shelves stood ten feet tall and were filled with thick tomes. The chamber encompassed half of the floor while long windows were visible above the shelving. Orbs glowing in sconces at the ends of each row illuminated the space.

To the left side of the room, near the hub at the center of the tower, was a desk. The dwarf made for the desk and settled into the chair behind it with a sigh.

"Your book collection is impressive," Ian said. "But why are we here?"

"You seek knowledge. This study is a center of knowledge."

Excitement stirred within Ian. "We can finally explain why we came seeking the tower?"

The dwarf nodded. "The time has come."

Ian glanced toward Vic and Revita. "A darkness looms – a horde of monsters who will kill and destroy anyone or anything in their path. This evil is upon us. Should it prevail, the races of humans, elves, and dwarves might be extinguished. To stave off this threat, we have come seeking something called The Paragon." He closed his eyes for a beat, praying for a positive response to his next question. "Have you heard of it?"

The dwarf ran his fingers through his white, wispy beard. "The Paragon, you say. That is a term I have not heard in an exceedingly long time."

"So, you have heard of it?"

"I just said as much. Weren't you listening?"

"Yes, I heard you." Ian pressed the dwarf. "Do you know where we can find it?"

The dwarf arched a brow and stroked his white beard. "I may, but before I expose such a long-kept secret, I must know more."

"Very well. Ask anything."

"Where did you hear of The Paragon?"

"In a vision. It was part of a prophecy."

"From what source?"

"Myself, I guess."

"You?"

"Yes."

Parsigar shook his head. "Humans are not beings of magic. Prophecy, like all magic, is beyond them."

"I am different."

"How so?"

Ian crafted a tiny thread of flame that flickered above his palm.

The dwarf leaned forward and peered at the flame through his spectacles. "How did you do that?"

"The same way I can conjure lightning, wind, or a dozen other spells. I told you, I am different than other humans."

"This magic...it is how you were able to reach and access the tower?"

"Yes."

"Ah." The dwarf nodded. "It now makes sense. You are the one."

"The one?"

"There is an ancient prophecy that exists only in this library. You see, it was foretold long, long ago, by a Sylvan seer who revealed this prophecy to her god, Vandasal. What it contained disturbed him beyond reason, so he sought to destroy it. However, all beings, even gods, are limited by the laws of nature. Few know it, but it is impossible for gods to destroy prophecy. They can create it, but they can never destroy it. Unable to erase this prophecy from the world, Vandasal chose to steal it and hide it, here, in this library, far from any civilization and in a tower nigh impossible to penetrate."

Excitement and anxiety twisted in Ian's stomach. When he voiced his request, it emerged as little more than a whisper. "May I see this prophecy?"

The dwarf stood. "I will reveal a portion of it, and you may even comprehend what it says. However, you will stop reading where I say. To know too much of a future connected to your actions would risk everything, for if your choices are not a result of your own free will, they may result in an unpredictable and possibly dire outcome."

The warning reminded Ian of a similar one issued by Truhan. "I understand."

Rather than head into the daunting array of bookshelves, Parsigar turned toward the wall behind his chair. He ran his hand along the wall, passing over the bricks and thin lines of mortar before stopping at a seemingly innocuous place. A small piece of stone sank beneath his fingertips. A click resounded, and the entire brick below his hand slid out from the wall. Parsigar reached into a drawer made of stone and pulled out a book as thick as Ian's wrist. The cover was made of worn, brown leather.

The dwarf turned and held the book before him. Ribbons of yellow, orange, red, green, blue, and purple stuck out from the pages. Choosing the orange ribbon as the starting location, Parsigar opened the tome. The pages crackled and the binding creaked as he laid the book flat on the desk.

"Read this page and the next. You will not continue past the red ribbon." The dwarf cocked his head while glaring at Ian. "Do you understand?"

"I do." Ian wondered at what nuggets he might uncover in the ancient book of prophecy had he been allowed to study it from cover to cover, but time was short, his quest urgent. Even had Parsigar allowed Ian to read more than a few passages, he could not afford such distractions.

"Come. Sit." The dwarf circled the desk in one direction. Ian chose the other before settling in the chair. Parsigar arched a brow. "You do know how to read Elvish, do you not?"

"I do."

"Splendid. Read on but please have the courtesy to translate aloud, so everyone present may gain perspective."

"Very well." Ian focused on the book, found the start of the first paragraph on the left side of the page, and began to read.

"The sun god shall dominate, placing his blessings upon the races of magic and causing them to rise above all others. Elves and dwarves, each given a slice of the world to rule, live in peace and harmony. As time passes, their societies evolve, allowing them to flourish until the era of the great king arrives.

"Invincible and armed with a sword of flame, the great king leads a terrible army, seeking to force the world to bend knee to his might, but his campaign is fraught with obstacles. Weeks become years, years become decades, and still, the king wages war. His quest is destined to fail, for those close to the great king shall betray him. When he slides into endless slumber, his empire shatters. But the great king's war has left a blood stain that cannot be easily erased.

"One with the dark ability shall arise among the Sylvan, foreshadowing an ugly end for the most beautiful race. Among the humans comes another, one who will either save or destroy the world. The long-lived call him Barsequa, the gifted one. His might swells quickly, making him a beacon among men. While the actions of these mortals leave a mark upon the land, the true enemy hides in the murk, for where there is light, there is shadow.

"The dark lord, who was once smitten by his brother, seeks retribution. In the shadows, he schemes, seeking to topple the sun in favor of darkness. Deep in the bowels of the earth, he bends reality and breaks the laws of nature, unleashing a scourge that would wipe out all life if left unchecked.

"Guided by a prophecy of his own making, the gifted one will seek out that which was hidden. A secret long kept shall unleash power unequaled, a light more spectacular than the brightest star. The one wielding the light shall make a choice, and that choice is the most profound of all. The consequences of this decision will affect the world and all possible futures."

Ian turned the page and paused, for the red ribbon lay across the page.

Parsigar reached out and closed the book. "That is enough."

Sitting back, Ian reflected on what he had read. The words of prophecy were indirect, their meanings often buried beneath strange and generic descriptions.

"What did you learn?" Parsigar asked.

"How many times have you read that passage?" Ian was curious, for the dwarf seemed to know it well.

"Oh, I should think over a hundred times by now."

"So, you have an interpretation for it?"

"Do you?"

"I...think so."

"And who is the sun god?" Parsigar stared at him intently.

"Vandasal." Ian recalled the sun representation on statues and tapestries he had seen in Ra'Tahal.

"And you have heard of the dark lord?"

"I have, but in this text, it sounds as if he and Vandasal were brothers."

"Very good. What else can you tell me?"

Ian considered the rest of what he had read. "This text claims that dark lord is behind the horde of monsters."

"And?"

"The prophecy mentions Barsequa. That is a term I have adopted from the Elvish language. It refers to me seeking out that which was hidden."

"The Paragon."

Ian frowned. "It said that The Paragon will unleash a mighty power, which will lead to a choice I must make."

"I am impressed, young man. You truly do have the power to understand prophecy."

"But the decision sounds like it has massive ramifications. If I could read a bit more, I might learn something, so I do not choose wrong."

The dwarf shook his head. "That cannot happen."

"But..."

"No. The choice must be your own and it cannot be made under the influence of prophecy."

"Do you know what it says?"

"I do, and what it exposes is disturbing on one hand, frightening on the other. Since both would be deemed negative without additional information, I fear you might be reluctant to choose at all, which would cause the worst of all results. You must continue toward your destiny of your own volition." His tone left no room for negotiation.

Parsigar rose to his feet and shuffled off toward the doorway.

Ian hurriedly caught up to him. "Where are you going?"

"I am going to do what must be done." The dwarf turned once past the doorway and headed toward the rear of the workshop. Without stopping, he strode up to a stone box beside the wall. When opened, the box revealed a slot dropping into darkness. Ian stood beside Parsigar, watching while the dwarf slid the book of prophecy into the slot. It slid down and was gone.

"Where did it go?"

"Away." Parsigar turned and dusted off his hands. "If it is gone, you cannot be tempted to read further."

Ian blinked. "But, but, what of the other things the book reveals?"

"If the book is meant to be read, it will return when the time is right."

Lifting a palm to his forehead, Ian sighed. "This is not what I anticipated."

"Prophecy offers hints at to what the future might hold, but it does not tell you how it comes to pass."

Ian furrowed his brow. "What does that mean?"

The dwarf held up a finger and smirked. "It means you still have not learned the answer to the question you brought here."

"Where is The Paragon?"

"No." Parsigar shook his head. "That is *not* the question."

"What is the question, then?"

"*Who* is The Paragon.

"Who?" Ian blinked. "The Paragon is a person?"

"Not just any person. The Paragon is a unique person. A special person unlike any other."

Revita huffed. "Enough already. You two keep speaking in circles and I can't take it any longer. Who is the blazing Paragon anyway?"

Parsigar smiled. "I am."

CHAPTER 54
THE PARAGON

"You?" Ian was stunned at Parsigar's revelation. "You are the Paragon?"

During the challenging quest to find the Paragon, never once did he guess it might be a person. *Why is he called The Paragon? How can he help me save the world?*

Parsigar walked past Ian, approached a workbench, and settled on the stool with a deep sigh, "Ahh." The old dwarf rubbed his lower back. "I must say, growing old comes easy but dealing with the consequences requires patience and resilience."

Revita crossed her arms while the toe of her boot tapped on the stone floor. "Funny you should mention patience, because you are trying mine."

The dwarf's eyebrows climbed his forehead. "Whatever do you mean?"

She rolled her eyes. "Listen. We have come a long way and been through a gauntlet of deadly challenges just to find you. Yet, you dole out information in crumbs while we are starved and ready to feast."

Parsigar chuckled. "I forget that you humans flit so quickly through life. Time is a valuable commodity even to elves, but to your people, it is akin to the rarest of precious metals."

"Yeah, metals you seem to spend without care." She made no attempt to hide her displeasure.

"You must forgive me. As I said, I have been here for a very long time. The only other I have spoken to in that span is the one who owns this tower."

Ian frowned. "You mentioned that before. Who owns the tower?"

"Oh, but if you paid close attention, I suspect you might be able to guess."

Their early conversations had, indeed, given Ian clues, but he had doubted where the clues led, thinking it impossible. "Is it, by chance, Vandasal?"

The dwarf grinned. "Oh, you are a clever one."

Vic frowned. "A god lives here?"

"Sometimes. Where he goes when he is away, I have no idea, nor do I profess to understand the way of gods. All I know is that I am forbidden to visit the floors above this one. Those are his and his alone."

Ian guessed that they were more than a hundred fifty feet up a tower that was twice that height. "Could we meet this god?"

"Oh, no," Parsigar shook his head. "That is not for me to say. Vandasal visits me from time to time, but years pass between those visits and each comes of his own volition. Should he appear while you are here, consider yourself fortunate."

"Don't let him distract you, Ian." Revita still appeared frustrated as she turned back toward Parsigar. "This prophecy claims that we must find the Paragon. We have found you. Now, what?"

The dwarf stroked his beard. "I am uncertain, but I suspect you were told to seek me out due to my unique gifts."

"What are these gifts?" Ian asked.

"We dwarves are often born with abilities unique to our race. Some can shape stone with their bare hands. There are those who can influence metals and bend them to their will. Others can imbue objects with any of a myriad of enchantments. A few can even mend flesh to heal otherwise mortal wounds. I am the only dwarf who can do all of these things."

"All?" Ian had lived with dwarves for half a year, and while he knew that some were born with innate magical abilities and that those skills were vital to dwarven society, he had never heard of any dwarf possessing more than one of such skills. "That is why you are called the Paragon?"

"It is. In fact, that name was given to me by Gahagar himself. Tell me, did my king ever accomplish his goal to unite the world under his banner?"

"You do not know?"

"I cannot leave this tower. How could I know anything of the world?"

"Wait. What do you mean you cannot leave this tower?"

Parsigar shook his head. "I promised my king I would not say."

"I am sorry, Parsigar, but King Gahagar is dead. In fact, it was his ghost who told us where to find you."

"Dead?" The dwarf's bushy, white eyebrows climbed his forehead. "How could that be? His armor made him invincible."

Revita replied, "Not from poison."

"Poison? Who would do such a thing?"

"His fellow dwarf kings, Kobblebon and Fandaric."

The dwarf sucked air in through his teeth. "Treason!"

"Aye," Vic shook his head. "Betrayal is the most bitter of drinks."

Parsigar's head drooped. He sat in quiet for a long beat before raising it. "Then, it is over. Even here, where time flows differently, I never expected I might outlive Gahagar. Please, tell me that his betrayers did not acquire the Sky Sword."

Ian said, "As I understand it, nobody can wield the sword."

"What about the secret of his armor?"

"With his dying breath, Gahagar passed the secret on to his most trusted captain, Arangar. What became of it, we do not know, nor do we know where to find the Caelum Edge."

"Well, without the Band of Amalgamation, the sword is safe from causing trouble."

"The band of what?" Revita asked.

"Amalgamation. It is an armband that, when donned, alters normal flesh to hardened metal."

Ian gasped at the revelation. "That is how Gahagar was able to wield the flaming sword. His own body had turned to armor."

"It is true. The band was among my greatest creations, for it made the impossible possible. However, it also forced me into hiding, for Gahagar feared that the forces of darkness might learn of it and come after me. Should evil possess the power that Gahagar controlled, the world would be doomed. Thus, he appealed to Vandasal, who brought me here, to the farthest corner of the world. Rather than languish without purpose, my god bade me to craft traps that would help him protect his home."

"The underground labyrinth?" Revita asked.

"Of my design."

Vic posed, "The deadly corridor on the first floor?"

"Creative, was it not?"

Lint piped up, "And the statues?"

"All my creations." The dwarf seemed pleased with himself. "In addition, Vandasal encouraged me to craft artifacts and weapons of power. Many of them sit on the shelves in this room, but most were claimed by my god. What became of them, I do not know."

Throughout the conversation, Ian had turned the fresh revelations over in his head, which led him to a conclusion. "You must craft something to help me save the world."

"But you already wield magic, do you not?"

"I do, but...I don't know. What if there was something that could make me stronger?"

"An item that expanded your abilities?" Parsigar stared toward the ceiling while stroking his beard. "Yes. I believe that would be possible. However, enchantments require understanding, and I know nothing of your magic."

Since experiencing the prophecy telling him to seek The Paragon, Ian had wondered how it might help him stop the darkness. Now, suddenly, something clicked. With clarity, he knew that Parsigar was the one to help him and that help would come in the form of a unique enchantment.

Ian addressed Parsigar. "We need to return to our people, so we can help them prepare for what comes. Please join us. You can study my magic while I train. Together, we can save the world."

"You suggest that I leave the tower after all of this time?" A tear tracked down Parsigar's cheek. "I could stand beneath the sun and breathe fresh air? I might again see the forests and the sea? I could again walk the halls of Ra'Tahal?"

"Yes." Ian spoke with passion. "In fact, I could bring you to Ra'Tahal right now. You could sleep there tonight and watch the sun rise over the citadel's eastern wall in the morning."

"Tonight? How?"

"Magic, of course."

In silence, Parsigar seemed to consider the idea with Ian and the others watching with a belly full of expectation. The old dwarf gave a firm nod. "Very well. I accept." He stood with a groan. "Give me a few minutes to gather my things." He then hobbled off toward the lift.

Ian remained still for a minute while the realization washed over him. He had done it. The Paragon had been found. Despite his exhaustion after a long and eventful day, the excitement inside filled him with energy.

"Let's go," he said to his companions in a soft voice. "I don't want to let him out of my sight until we are safely back in Ra'Tahal."

The three humans, the brownie, and the drake joined the old dwarf on the lift just before it began descending back to Parsigar's quarters.

～

Daylight shone through the windows in Parsigar's sitting room. Ian approached a window and peered out across the frozen landscape. Steam continued to rise from the lava flow but there was no sign of the dragon.

Parsigar's old, creaky voice came from behind Ian. "I am ready."

Ian turned to find the dwarf in the doorway. "It is daylight already."

"I told you that time is different here. In addition, it is early summer. The gaps between sunset and sunrise are brief. During the winter months, it is quite the opposite."

"Well, let's depart before any more time passes," Ian said.

Vic and Revita stood from the sofa while Lint hopped off the neighboring chair.

Ian drew in his magic, cast a spell, and a portal opened. Morning light came through the bedroom window on the other side of the portal.

"Oh, my," Parsigar shuffled closer to the portal and stuck his cane through, into a room halfway across the world. "Where does this lead?"

"As I promised, we go to Ra'Tahal."

Vic ducked through. Revita and Lint followed.

Pressure against the gateway rim required Ian to strain to hold it open. His energy was flagging after a long day, affecting his abilities. "Please. Go through. This is difficult to hold open."

Parsigar planted his staff on the other side of the gateway, lifted the hem of his robes, and stepped over the lower edge. He then shuffled into the corridor.

Hurriedly, Ian stepped through and released his magic. The gateway snapped shut with a pop.

"Winnie!" Ian called out as he joined the others in the common space on the fourth floor. "We are back!"

"Ian!" She raced up the stairs with her skirts in her grip. She slowed when she saw a dwarf in their party. "Oh. I didn't know anyone else was here."

"This is Parsigar," Ian explained. "He has come to help."

Winnie passed the dwarf and gripped Ian's hand when reaching the landing. "I am glad you are back. Korrigan stopped by at sunup, looking for you. Something has happened. Something terrible."

Ian groaned. Sleep would have to wait.

CHAPTER 55

TALASTAR

L ate afternoon two days after the pirate ship encounter, Arangoli stood on Sunstreak's deck while staring toward his destination. Although sunset was over an hour away, the land was cast in a gloomy shadow, for a dark, thick storm covered the western sky above the flat marshlands north of Talastar. A flicker of lightning bloomed in the distance, giving a hint of the storm's anger. The front appeared ominous although it was likely still an hour from reaching them.

The ship sped south, toward a bay where the peninsula to the west met the main landmass. The city walls, towering and made of charcoal colored stone, stirred memories. The last time Arangoli had seen those walls, he and the rest of Gahagar's army had come in from the south. The Drow, in a surprise attack, hit the dwarven army's flank. A fierce battle followed, one that helped to earn Arangoli his fame as the most skilled warrior of his generation. The dwarves ultimately won the day, and Talastar would have soon fallen if not for Gahagar's death. After a five-decade campaign, the dwarves packed up and began the long journey home with each clan heading back to their own lands. For Arangoli and his crew, who had trained as warriors for half of their young lives, quitting the field was beyond disappointing. Fame and glory were earned on the battlefield, not in the comforts of home.

"Now, I have returned."

Talastar was known for its stark, dominating presence. This was true when the city was active and thriving. Now, as the ship neared a port bereft of watercraft, workers, or anything else that would indicate signs of life, it felt as if Arangoli were approaching a mausoleum. Until that moment, he had doubted the report shared by Korrigan. The Drow abandoning Talastar was unthinkable. As far as Arangoli knew, it was the only city across all of Drovaria. *Where did they go?* The answer to the question was out there, somewhere. He just hoped to find a clue by searching the city.

The ship crossed the breakwater, the waves calming. Captain Kasgan shouted commands. The crew responded by scaling the rigging and furling the sails. As the ship drifted toward the pier, Arangoli turned from the rail and headed towards the stairwell leading to the cabins.

Descending into darkness, he navigated the narrow corridor and began pounding on the doors he passed. "We have reached port. Get your things and get on deck."

Again, and again, he repeated the message before reaching the last door, which he opened and stepped inside. Rax and Pazacar sat in the middle of the room with a lantern on the table between them.

Gortch lay on a lower bunk with his arms behind his head. "Are we there yet?"

"Docking now."

"Finally." The big dwarf sat up and reached beneath his bunk. He dug out his armor, gauntlets, mace, and pack.

Arangoli, already wearing his armor, buckler, and hammer, scooped up his pack. "Gather your things and meet me on deck. I am going to speak with Kasgan."

He headed back topside as the ship drifted toward the pier. Lines were tossed and secured just before Arangoli reached the quarterdeck stairs.

Kasgan looked over his shoulder, to the northwest, beyond the ship's stern. "She is an angry storm. The sea will soon be roiling." He turned back to Arangoli. "I delivered you here as promised, and while I appreciate your company and what you did with those pirates, I'd prefer to push off as soon as possible."

"My squad will be off the ship straight away." Arangoli gripped the captain's forearm. "You are a dwarf of your word. I am glad we have met."

"Same here. You've given me some tales to tell. The wine on board should yield a handsome profit in Galfhadden, which will likely triple when I return south with silk and other commodities not found in the free cities."

"What of the pirates?"

"I'll make for deeper waters during the return trip. With any luck, I can sneak by without notice. The longer route will cost me a few extra days, but the gain will be worth it."

Arangoli turned to find the Head Thumpers gathered near the port side rail. The crew slid the gangplank out, and dwarves began crossing it. "Time for me to go. Thanks again, Kasgan. I wish you luck."

"You as well, Goli. I hope you find whatever it is you seek."

"Usually, trouble is what I find, whether I seek it or not."

Kasgan laughed. "Well said, my friend."

Arangoli descended to the main deck, waved to the crew as he walked past, and crossed the sloped plank. The moment he joined the other dwarves on the pier, the plank was reeled in and the lines were pulled free from the posts. The ship drifted off, slowly turning as the sails were unfurled. The winds picked up, driven by the oncoming storm. Those winds filled the sails and the ship headed northeast, toward its next port.

"There goes a good dwarf." Pazacar said.

"Aye." Arangoli turned toward his crew. "We are here. Now, it's time to search the city. Perhaps it is not as empty as the harbor."

Nobody replied as he walked past them and led the way toward shore. In silence the dwarves warily eyed their surroundings.

The city walls, dark and dreary, towered above the bay. No gate was visible in the mile wide stretch of wall visible from the pier. The thin strip of land between the bay and the walls was occupied by clusters of warehouses and outbuildings made of dark stone. A wagon with a broken off wheel lay in a gravel yard between a trio of warehouses. What became of the horses or wagon's owner was anyone's guess.

A wrecked ship, likely beached from a storm, lay against the rocky shoreline just to the east. Its hull had been split in two, its masts lying in a crisscross mess of dark wood, broken lines, and tattered fabric. The destroyed craft was another ominous sign amid an unsettling scene.

Upon reaching shore, Arangoli headed west with the intent of circling the city while searching for a way in. Lightning flashed across the western horizon. Distant thunder rumbled, the gap between the flash and boom giving him a sense of the storm's location, still some ten miles away.

The dwarves reached the end of the harbor outbuildings and followed a road that ran below the daunting city wall. Not far from the road, the lands sloped to down pools of water that dotted the landscape. Reeds and muddy bogs rose above the marsh. Willows with drooping branches stood here and there, looking like lonely and forgotten soldiers amid what once might have been a mighty forest.

The road turned south, mirroring the wall. Again, no gate was visible in a stretch of wall that exceeded a mile. Dark mountains lurked on the horizon, beyond open, grass-covered land. It was there that the confrontation between the dwarves and dark elves had taken place six years earlier. In some ways, Arangoli felt as if he had returned to the scene of a crime, the place where he had first proven his skills in live battle. Blood had stained the dirt that day. He wondered if those stains had washed away.

Arangoli and his squad continued in silence. The rush of wind and the occasional rumble of thunder added a haunting melody to the steady beat of crunching footsteps and clanking armor. The wind picked up, marked by gusts that buffeted them as the storm marched on.

When they reached the south end of the city, the wall and road turned. The gate came into view, a half mile away. Made of black, petrified wood the gate had earned fame for its resilience. The city of Talastar had never been breached. With walls a hundred feet tall and a dozen feet thick, invaders had no choice but to target the gate, but even that had proven to be resilient against all attacks. For that alone, Arangoli could not fathom the Drow quitting the city. As they drew near the gate, a chilling sound greeted them.

Arangoli stopped before the entrance and drew his war hammer. The doors, twenty feet tall and ten feet wide, stood open just a crack. Through that gap, the wind howled as if the city were moaning in agony. With the hammer in his grip, Arangoli approached the gate and stepped inside.

Refuse and debris dotted the square inside the city walls. Amidst the already dark setting, shadows lurked in the narrow streets connected to the square. No people, living or dead, were visible.

When everyone was inside, Arangoli set off at a wary pace. He made for the central street, and when the square fell away, shadows rushed in. The buildings he passed appeared abandoned, the shop windows empty. Nothing but gloom waited inside the open doorways.

"What happened here?" Pazacar asked in a hushed tone.

"Something bad." Rax replied.

"Aye." Arangoli agreed. "Try to remain quiet. If something waits for us, I prefer that we don't wake it."

They passed intersections, open plazas, and dark alleys as they continued toward the heart of the city. All along, the wind's howl surrounded them. In an odd way, it provided Arangoli with a sense of comfort. The empty, lifeless city would have been that much more chilling had it been still and silent.

They came to the sprawling city center and stopped.

Castle Umbra, home of Queen Liloth, ruler of the Drow, had collapsed in a twisted pile of charcoal colored rubble. Fallen towers lay bent over while broken walls leaned against each other. Stone blocks the size of bread boxes littered the area.

"What happened here?" The question had echoed in Arangoli's head a dozen times over before he voiced it. When nobody replied, he approached the destroyed castle.

The arch of the main entrance remained intact. Beyond it, shadows lurked below a wall leaning on another. The floor sloped down between the two walls, leaving him curious as to where it led.

Carefully, Arangoli eased down the slope. Loose shards of stone tumbled down ahead of him. After a half dozen tentative strides, darkness surrounded him.

He looked back toward the dim light outside. "Brannigan. Dig out a torch."

With his arm in a sling, his shoulder still healing from the arrow strike, Brannigan had been designated as the torch bearer. As he drew a torch from his pack, Rax produced his flint. Two strokes from the striker later, a spark landed on the kerosene drenched cloth secured to the torch. Flame bloomed, the warm light flickering off the walls leaning above them.

"Hand me the torch." Arangoli held his hand back as Brannigan passed it to him. "Rax, ready your bow and come with me. Everyone else remain here until I call you."

Rax pulled his bow over his shoulder and drew an arrow. Holding both in one hand, he used his other hand to steady himself along one of the walls as he descended. When Rax was right behind him. Arangoli continued downward.

The torchlight ate away at the darkness and revealed a large cavity below. That cavity had carved walls and a stone floor. An open corridor lay straight ahead.

"This must be the castle dungeon." Rax said.

"Aye."

Loose rock beneath Arangoli's feet caused him to slip. He fell onto this backside and slid down the last six feet. Rising, he held the torch high while peering into the corridor.

Rax scurried down and came to a stop beside him. "What are looking for?"

"I don't know. We need to figure out why the Drow left and where they went. I am hoping that the answer lies in this castle...or what is left of it."

"Why did you have the others stay behind?"

Arangoli had hoped Rax would not ask, preferring not to say it aloud. He did so anyway. "If something goes wrong, most of us won't die."

"Wait" Rax stopped cold. "What is going to go wrong?"

"I don't know. A collapse is my first thought. Other than that, we have no idea what lies ahead."

Rax groaned. "Why me, then?"

"Your bow for one. Also, you are the fastest and most agile in the squad, which might be required if we need to run. Even if I don't make it out, you might."

"Sometimes, I envy Gortch."

"Well, there are plenty of times when his size and strength come in handy. Right now, it is your skill I need." Arangoli headed toward the corridor. "Now, be quiet and listen hard."

"How do you listen hard?"

"Just do it."

They entered the corridor, the amber flickering light battling against the shadows. A dozen strides later, they came to an arched opening leading to a small room surrounded by cells with barred doors. The stench of death emanated from the chamber. With his hammer in one hand and the torch in the other, Arangoli could not cover his mouth and nose, so he hurried forward, hoping to get beyond the odor.

The corridor ended at a chamber where the ceiling had collapsed, burying the far end. They took a few strides into the room and stopped. With the torch held high, Arangoli slowly turned.

Someone had painted images on the walls, each depicting strange humanoid monsters with dark green skin, red eyes, and nasty claws on their hands and feet. The creatures were hairless and sharp, pointed teeth filled their mouths.

"What are these things?"

"I don't know, but..." Arangoli frowned. "Do you hear something?"

A scraping noise came from the direction of the collapse. He eased toward it while listening.

"I think it's coming from beneath this section."

"Maybe someone is trapped," Rax posed.

"We could lift it and free them."

Rax appeared doubtful. "I don't think the two of us are strong enough."

"I'll help." Gortch said as he emerged from the corridor.

Arangoli spun toward him. "You were supposed to wait outside."

"Tell that to them, too."

The rest of the Head Thumpers came from the corridor and spread out in a half circle.

Arangoli groaned. "Why does nobody listen to me?"

"We listen. We just don't always agree with you."

"Well, since you are here, help me lift this thing. Brannigan. Come and take this torch."

The two dwarves approached, one taking the torch, the other flexing his gauntlets while eyeing the fallen section of wall.

"I suggest everyone draw your weapons in case we have trouble." Arangoli set his hammer by his feet and squatted. "Ready?"

Gortch nodded. "Now."

Grunts filled the air as the two dwarves strained against the weight. The section of wall, no more than three feet wide and four feet deep, rose up and then tipped over from a hard shove. The underside of the wall was marred by scratches. Its removal revealed a hole, dark and foreboding.

Something burst from the darkness. Arangoli twisted and dodged, causing it to miss. Brannigan was not as quick to react. The creature, its green, leathery skin so dark it was nearly black, struck the dwarf in the chest, driving him backward and slamming him to the floor. The torch flew out of his hand and skittered against the wall. With a flurry of raking strikes, the monster tore at Brannigan's leather armor.

Rax, having an arrow already nocked, was the first to counterattack. He raised his bow and loosed. The monster, only two strides away, lurched, arched its back, and howled when the arrow struck near its spine. The other dwarves darted in, a slash of Fesgar's sword taking the arm off the creature. A spin of Pazacar's staff struck its jaw and sent it flying back toward the hole. Arangoli followed with his hammer, crushing the monster's face. He cast a glance toward Brannigan as the downed dwarf sat up.

"It burns," Brannigan's face was twisted in agony.

A streak of blood seeped through the shredded leather armor.

"Arrgh!" Throwing his head back, Brannigan began to convulse.

Foam bubbled from his mouth and crimson tears seeped from his eyes. He slammed onto his back, jerked three times, and fell still. His bloody eyes stared into oblivion.

"Poison!" Rax hissed.

"Blazes!" Arangoli approached Brannigan, who was clearly dead.

"I know this creature from legend," Pazacar said. "They call it an orc, a creature of evil. The stories claim that long ago, Vandasal banished the orcs into the underworld, far below where the living roam."

"What is this thing doing here?" Gortch asked.

"I do not know."

Arangoli shook his head while staring down at Brannigan. "I am sorry my friend. I pray Vandasal welcomes you into the hall of heroes."

A round of "Ayes" echoed in the chamber.

"Someone grab his pack. Dig another torch out."

Fesgar sheathed his blade, squatted, and slid Brannigan's pack off his arm. As the dwarf dug out another torch, Arangoli picked up the lit one. He turned and touched one torch to the other. Light bloomed as the second torch caught fire. Walking up to the hole with both torches before him, Arangoli peered down into the darkness. He then tossed the first torch down. It spun slowly as it plummeted much farther than anticipated. The torch landed with a bounce, over a hundred feet below. The flames grew brighter, their light revealing the surroundings. It was a massive chamber with stone columns standing in rows, each running from floor to ceiling.

"Why would they build something like that so far underground?" Arangoli muttered.

"It's a long way down," Gortch, who stood beside him, noted.

"Aye."

Something moved in the darkness. Another orc scurried into view. It was not alone.

A wave of black poured into the chamber, surrounding the flames as if they were metal shavings and the torch was a powerful magnet. Orcs by the thousands swept across the floor and then began scrambling up the columns, toward where the dwarves stood watching.

"Run!" Arangoli bellowed as he raced past the others with the torch held high.

Following their torch-bearing leader, the dwarves rushed down the corridor, into the next chamber, and scrambled up the sloped stone. At the top, Arangoli was met by a gale of wind, snuffing the torch. A dark storm cloud loomed overhead. Lightning flashed. Thunder boomed. Rain was imminent.

"Form up!" Arangoli bellowed as other dwarves emerged from the dark opening. "We fight! Beware their talons!"

Discarding the torch, Arangoli rounded the angled wall as his companions drew their weapons and formed a half circle to block the exit. Arangoli readied his hammer and moved to stand beside the leaning wall while waiting for Gortch. The big dwarf stumbled out, fell to one knee, and hurried to his feet. He then turned and took the center position in the wall of dwarves.

With a sweeping backswing, Arangoli brought his hammer high over his head and struck the wall. A thump echoed as the weapon's enchantment released an impulse. The wall cracked. He swung again, targeting the same location. The crack spread as shards sprayed in all directions. Terrible, angry growls drew near. The first few orcs burst out. They moved with terrifying speed, but the Head Thumpers were ready. Arrows pelted the first monster. A mace crushed the face of the second. An axe cleaved into the head of the third. A staff crashed against the neck of a fourth. Orcs piled up before the dwarven warriors, who fought with fury, striking any monster daring to draw near. Then, Arangoli's next hammer strike landed.

The wall split in half. The lower portion crashed down with a mighty boom, crushing the monsters caught beneath it. The upper wall section dropped with the first, balanced upright for a beat, and then toppled toward Arangoli, who scurried to get clear. The wall slammed down and launched a puff of dust and bits of rock that covered Arangoli. The dust cleared. He blinked and wiped his eyes.

An orc pulled itself through a narrow gap, its red eyes filled with hatred. When its body was halfway through, the remaining wall, which had supported the first, began to tip. The orc turned toward it and released a shriek that was cut short when the wall flattened it. A massive puff of dust billowed up and was carried away by the blustering wind.

Then, the rain struck.

The downpour was hard and heavy, the rain so thick it was impossible to see more than a few dozen feet away.

"Follow me!"

Arangoli ran back toward the castle gate, crossed the square outside the crumbling walls, and made for the nearest street. He reached a building with an open doorway and ran inside, slowing as he entered the dark confines.

Empty shelves lined the walls while long, wooden tables ran along the room's interior. It was a shop of some sort...or it had been before it was abandoned. The other dwarves gathered in the room, panting for air, wet and ragged.

"We will hold out here until the rain passes." Arangoli announced.

"Then, what?" Rax asked.

"Then, we leave this city. We now know why the Drow did the same."

Pazacar nodded. "Agreed. Those monsters present a dire threat. When the Drow realized as much, they collapsed their own castle, hoping to seal the orcs below."

"Right. They then abandoned Talastar."

Rax asked, "To go where?"

"That, we don't yet know." It was a problem for another day. "For now, we are going to get as far away as possible before those things dig their way out. I fear what will happen once they are free."

"We could fight," Gortch suggested.

"You all know I would rather kill these things, but their numbers are too great. We need more warriors. If we die here, what happens then? Who will warn the innocents who fall into the orcs' path? Imagine the slaughter that will occur when a horde of these monsters strikes those who are unaware." With conviction, Arangoli gave a firm nod. "In this case, flight is required. We will warn the world, and maybe we can find a way to slow their advance, so the armies of dwarf, elf, and man can prepare."

He just prayed they could outrun the orcs. Worse, he feared what would happen should the monsters from the underworld outnumber the dwarves, elves, and humans hoping to stop them.

**The Dawn of Wizards saga concludes with
The Dark Lord's Design**

Note from the Author

I hope you enjoyed the second book in a series that peers into the distant and legendary past of the world of Wizardoms. You can expect **The Dark Lord's Design**, the third in final book in this series, to release in October 2024.

In the meantime, if you have not yet read my **Fate of Wizardoms, Fall of Wizardoms,** and **Wizardom Legends** (*The Outrageous Exploits of Jerrell Landish* and *Tor the Dungeon Crawler*), those 18 novels are set in the same world, some 2,000 years AFTER the Dawn of Wizards saga concludes. If you enjoy fun and fast-paced epic fantasy adventures, I suggest you check them out.

I am grateful to have you join in my wild adventures.

Best Wishes,
Jeff

Follow me on:
Amazon
Bookbub
Facebook

ALSO BY JEFFREY L. KOHANEK

Dawn of Wizards

The First Wizard

Paragon of Solitude

The Dark Lord's Design

Fate of Wizardoms

Eye of Obscurance

Balance of Magic

Temple of the Oracle

Objects of Power

Rise of a Wizard Queen

A Contest of Gods

* * *

Fate of Wizardoms Boxed Set: Books 1-3

Fate of Wizardoms Box Set: Books 4-6

Fall of Wizardoms

God King Rising

Legend of the Sky Sword

Curse of the Elf Queen

Shadow of a Dragon Priest

Advent of the Drow

A Sundered Realm

Fall of Wizardoms Boxed Set: Books 1-3

Fall of Wizardoms Box Set: Books 4-6

Wizardom Legends

The Outrageous Exploits of Jerrell Landish

Thief for Hire

Trickster for Hire

Charlatan for Hire

Tor the Dungeon Crawler

Temple of the Unknown

Castles of Legend

Shrine of the Undead

Runes of Issalia

The Buried Symbol

The Emblem Throne

An Empire in Runes

* * *

Runes of Issalia Bonus Box

Wardens of Issalia

A Warden's Purpose

The Arcane Ward:

An Imperial Gambit

A Kingdom Under Siege

* * *

Wardens of Issalia Boxed Set

Printed in Dunstable, United Kingdom